BLOOD LAMENT

By

Raven Dane

First edition published in Great Britain in 2007 by Discovered Authors Diamonds

ISBN10 1-90510-816-8

ISBN13 978-1-90510-816-9

Printed in the UK by BookForce

Available from Discovered Authors Online –
All major online retailers and available to order through all UK bookshops

Or contact:

Books
Discovered Authors
50 Albemarle Street, London
W1S 4BD

+(44) 207 529 37 29

books@discoveredauthors.co.uk

BookForce UK's policy is to use papers that are natural, renewable and recyclable products and made from wood grown in sustainable forests where ever possible

BookForce UK Ltd.
50 Albemarle Street
London W1S 4BD
www.bookforce.co.uk
www.discoveredauthors.co.uk

This book is dedicated to my father.
After Blood Tears, you called me a real writer.
That means the world to me. You believe in me, in
 my work.

To Paryan

Thank you for
your friendship

Ram Dass

Sep 2007

Acknowledgements

Once more I am indebted to my ever stalwart supporters. Helen Hollick who somehow finds time away from writing her own novels to patiently edit and sort out Blood Lament. Claira for being my rock, always there for me. Rachel and Anita for their honest and enthusiastic criticism and my family for their continued good natured forbearance and total support. I will get on with the hoovering one day, promise!

I am indebted to Jennie Paterson and Natalie Matthews at DA Diamonds for their hard work and unflagging support on my behalf, Andy Hey for his continued, much valued friendship, eBiz Solutions for my wonderful website.

I am so grateful to the enthusiasm and creative flair of Vicky White and Mik Valentine of SMV Solutions for my beautiful and evocative cover.

As ever I have to thank my musical collaborators, I cannot write for hours without their company! So my gratitude to Muse and Keane and a special, huge, thank you to Editors for lending me a few lines from 'All Sparks' from the wonderful 'The Back Room' album. A great honour.

Blood Lament can be read on its own or as the second part of the Blood Tears series. It continues the story of the last surviving Dark Kind, beautiful, deadly, amoral beings who have preyed on mankind in the darkness of night for countless millennia. Neither supernatural nor the Undead but a living, passionate species of flesh and blood. Blood Lament focuses on the misadventures of one of the most charismatic of the Dark Kind, the vain, hedonistic and beautiful Jazriel, whose courage and loyalty coupled with his recklessness and insecurity lead him once more down a dangerous path. When the twin demons of hope and optimism that have always plagued him are finally defeated, his downward spiral of dissolution threatens not just his life but also the Dark Kind's scattered survivors.

A human woman, Khari saved his life before, could her special gift, her legacy passed down to her granddaughter do the same again?

"The reanimated corpse of a suicidal, junkie, male whore vampire." Jazriel's description of himself. Other opinions about him are far more colourful and explicit! With the world's future hanging in the balance, the unlikely pairing of a dissolute wreck of a blood drinker and a feisty, argumentative, vampire-hating, human woman could be the only hope. With defenders like these does the Earth stand a chance?

Prologue

He prepared himself for the ritual. The obsessive and necessary rite that trapped him, teetering on the edge of insanity. He disconnected the phone line and switched off his mobile and with the everyday world totally shut out, he moved with precision through his beautifully furnished home. He was outwardly relaxed, at ease among his own surroundings. It was illusion. Beneath the serene exterior, he was trembling, fighting his fear and self-loathing.

He ran a scalding hot bath, ready to purge himself after time spent in the room. Then, taking a deep breath to steady his nerves, he fished behind an exquisite 18th century clock on a mantelpiece to retrieve the key to the room, the hellish inner sanctum where she waited for him.

Despite doing this every night, his hand shook as he turned the brass key in a richly polished, dark mahogany door; a solid –looking barrier to keep her corrosive influence from polluting the rest of his home, his life, his mind.

He entered the room with his head down, not yet ready to meet her gaze, that direct golden stare that pierced right through to his soul, scorching away any pretence, any secret. When he found the courage to face her, he kept his back ramrod straight, the stance of a career military man. He strode across the room to address her. Face to face

"So many years have passed and I have not found you," he murmured, forcing his gaze to remain fixed on her beautiful, ethereal face. "But I will. And I will kill you and any of your offspring, for all will carry the cursed taint of your damnation."

Then he removed the fading flowers from the crystal vase and replaced them with fresh blooms. Perfect white roses of glacial purity.

Part One

MIRRORS

O, what may man within him hide,
Though angel on the outward side!

William Shakespeare

Chapter One

Jendar Azrar's Stronghold, Isolann.

'It was never going to be right, was it?' Jazriel sighed to himself as he gingerly pulled a cream, wild silk robe over his shoulders, wincing as the soft, luxurious material touched the raw and bleeding fang marks down his neck and back. He smoked three cigarettes, one after another in quick succession, and then, with difficulty from the effect of jarring on his spine and some internal bruising, moved to a nearby table. He poured his first large measure of cognac of the night. One of countless many.

As he drank the amber liquid Jazriel gave a low growl, the vintage brandy tasted of nothing, there was no fire, no brief moment of welcome numbness from his turmoil. He finished the drink and threw the empty glass goblet to the floor in a gesture of futility and despair. That was it; there was no stronger intoxicant in this snow-bound tomb.

'Mierda!' He needed something to get him through the nights and even longer days! Perhaps the Isolanni nomads had a potent brew, some mountain moonshine with a hearty kick to it? The difficulty, he did not know which human to ask. All who dwelled within the stronghold despised him, for one reason or another. Not openly - none would dare because of the Prince - but he had seen the look of scorn on their faces and the sideways glances. The averted eyes, always filled with contempt.

What did he expect? For him, nothing had changed during the forty-five years since the ending of the war, the cataclysm that had rocked the human world. The conflict had changed everything else, even this remote and backward land. But not Azrar. Nothing could change Jendar Azrar! The Prince of Isolann.

It was Azrar who had brought him back to miraculous life here in the Jendar's stronghold. And in doing so, stranding Jazriel in the last place on earth he would want to be. Jazriel's life with the Prince had drifted back to the same pattern, the same stark inequality as all those centuries before. All the reasons why he had previously left Azrar still existed.

Jazriel cursed his own naivety, for the foolish optimism that always returned to bite his hand like an ungrateful cur. Would he never learn? What the hell was he thinking? The Jendar Azrar could not change what he was - even if he could, he would not. He was created a warlord, a ferocious Dark Kind Prince. In his imperious, unyielding eyes, Jazriel would always be sha'ref, no better in status in the rigid caste system of their Kind than a male whore would be in human society. Which was why the humans in this isolated stronghold shunned him. It had probably little to do with his fangs or his need to survive on human blood; had nothing to do with what he was. Dark Kind. A vampire. Only with what they perceived he *did* with the Lord Azrar. Rather, more accurately, what the Prince did to him. Jazriel shrugged with the irony, their limited human imagination could not envisage what really went on between the Dark Kind!

There was a powerful bond of genuine love between him and Azrar but it was not enough, not for Jazriel. Not anymore. He was sick of hovering in the background, aware in public he was an embarrassment to the Prince. What was he supposed to do? Hide himself away? Remain in the dark of Azrar's private rooms? Never show himself in the presence of the humans that infested the stronghold? He was left for nights on end to drift about in this gloomy mausoleum to a long lost past, waiting for Azrar to notice him. To want him.

Barely literate, he had no interest in browsing through the books of the great library or riding out in a country where the natives were forbidden to his fangs and his instinct to hunt. He had nothing to do except wait and be available to meet Azrar's ferocious and demanding physical need.

Jazriel tried to find comfort in the fact he had known real happiness during his long existence, but that happiness had always been for brief moments, and only when he had lived far away from Isolann, this wolf-ridden, frozen land of secrets and shadows. The brief and heady early years with Azrar, before the burdens of his duties and those endless long wars had created a rift between them. One that had not lessened with time.

Jazriel had only known true freedom when he'd met a handsome young pirate. A human. There had been real respect and unconditional affection between the two mis-matched adventurers. The man had been a predator, one who hunted others and he had treated Jazriel as an equal, with no fear of what he was. Jazriel's heart twisted with pain at his loss. 'Damn it!' He had only survived these past centuries by never thinking of those times. By locking the memories in a forbidden vault in his mind. Where they must remain. Where they *must* remain!

And there was that other, far too brief, time as a covert agent for the British in their desperate war against the Nazi menace. Again he had been valued for his courage, agility and ability, working undercover in the night-clubs of Berlin alongside the delightful and brave human girl, Khari. And that had ended badly for him. Most humans despised what he was, a vampire who preyed on the male of the species to survive, and because of that hatred Jazriel had paid the ultimate price; death and near oblivion in a hellish afterlife.

He forced away the memory of this past terror with a shudder but the bitterness gnawing at him remained. For even those few friends had let him down. Where were they now? Khari lived but she was an old woman in the winter years of her life, and the others? They had existed centuries ago.

Jazriel fetched another glass, poured another drink, saluted the empty room as a toast to his one-time companions and adventurers. They were the exceptions. The rest of humanity could all go to their hell.

Damn them for their spite and their snide glances. Damn them for their sniggering whispers, their treacheries and their lies! The second glass smashed against the wall. The Dark Kind could not weep, but a well of emotion was drowning Jazriel inside. He would never love or trust a human again. May the streets of the entire planet run red with their blood!

He pulled the silk robe closer about his chest, wandered around the room, touching things without seeing them, glanced at the crumpled bed where he and Azrar had lain, a low, panther-like growl of self-scorn escaping his lips. This self-pitying mood was destructive, unworthy. He knew it held him in a vice-like grip, was a monster feeding on his deep well of despair, refusing to let go. A legacy from his distant past.

But what else was there for him? He could stay forever in Isolann, bored out of his mind and unfulfilled, waiting to be used at Azrar's whim. Or dare he risk venturing outside to the deadly modern world of humans again? He wished there was someone he could talk to, someone who could advise him, for as sha'ref he had not been given a high intelligence. He was not stupid, but he was created to charm and seduce, to pleasure, not to reason. Aside, there was no sympathy for his plight among his own Kind. No Dark Kind had ever questioned their allotted place in life. Perhaps that was why there were so few of them left? Doomed by the total rigidity of the Dark Kind caste system. They had all been created with it hot-wired into their genes; they had to be what they were made to be. Jazriel did not envy humans with their short, fragile lives but he wished he had their unlimited choices. Their ability to define their own destiny. To be free.

So, what of Khari? She understood him, loved and respected him as a friend. He knew she was living happily in America with her husband, Joe Devane, and their four sons. Grandchildren too, no doubt by now. Could he find her? Would she help?

He grabbed one of Azrar's black, wolf-pelt cloaks, gasping as the weight of the garment fell on his torn back and shoulders, and left the subterranean confines of the vault.

The sun had only recently set, a greenish light showed through jagged gaps in the Arpalathian mountain tops, giving the snow cover an ethereal glow. He ignored the inevitable disdainful, mocking, stares of the inner keep guards and made his way to the nearest high battlement.

Created by restructuring a mountain, the Keep, despite its vast and haughty grandeur, felt increasingly claustrophobic to Jazriel. It was a prison, not a home. He stood on the open parapet, his hands gripping the frozen stone, oblivious of the intense cold against his fingers; breathed in a deep lung-full of night air. The freshness of the breeze gave a faint illusion of freedom and movement, like an ocean squall billowing through sails, sending the ship dipping and skimming across the wide Atlantic. Ah, those wild days at sea had been true freedom! Jazriel's head dropped into his hands as grief and loss for the past threatened to overwhelm him.

This stronghold was where he was supposed to belong. He was expected to be at Azrar's side - well, behind him in the shadows - expected to be here for the extraordinary being whose love and power had brought Jazriel back to life after the Germans had gunned him down in the filth of a Berlin cellar. Jazriel loved Azrar with every cell of his being, despite all the passive humiliation and emptiness of this life in the Prince's mountain stronghold. But damn it! Could he endure much more of this bleak and baleful land?

Isolann lay prone in the grip of another hard winter, blizzards had raged for many days at a time, often merging into weeks. Huge icicles hung from every parapet and tree like some monstrous creature's fangs. The snow surrounding the stronghold was over ten feet deep in places, even higher in the wind blown drifts. The castle was cut off, virtually all movement impossible, and to add to his woes, Jazriel was hungry. Very hungry.

But what could he do? Nothing but return below and await Azrar's pleasure, and grieve for the past. And the long, long, empty future.

Chapter Two

Cliff tops near St Ives, Cornwall, 2002

"I'm not some sort of Lara Croft you know, hold that bloody rope steady!" the young woman urged through clenched teeth as she launched herself off the side of a cliff.

Far beneath her, high waves, sullen grey and foam-capped, crashed with noisy finality against the jagged rocks. Gabrielle tried hard to resist temptation and not look down, focusing on the crumbling cliff in front of her. Since when had she become a fearless daredevil?

Above, a team of university colleagues watched in admiration as Gabrielle Railton abseiled slowly and tentatively down the steep rock face, bravely enduring a buffeting from a sharp sea wind lashing her with abrasive salt and sand. Time and time again the gusty and strengthening wind threatened Gabrielle, pushing her away, trying to force her from her goal, as if it was the restless ghost of whoever was buried here, furious at the sacrilegious disturbance of its last resting place.

"Sorry, my friend," Gaby muttered to the angry spirit as the rope once again swung alarmingly out from the cliff face, " I don't think you would like to be washed away by the sea. We will learn all we can about you then leave you in peace again, but only if you let us get you to safety."

"Oi up there! Stop ogling and keep that rope taut," she shouted to the rest of the team. As she rightly deducted, most of the young men on the expedition were focused on her slim athletic figure. As her tan Timberland boots briefly touched the cliff, it began to crumble away in a mini avalanche of stones and sand.

"Forget looking at my bum in these tight shorts and check the line, it's getting really hairy down here!"

Hillary Britton, the expedition leader laughed and shouting above the gale, reassured her of their full attention on her safety. But there was no doubt the cumbersome harness her life depended on emphasised her seemingly endless legs and her pert behind! Who thought archaeology was a dry, dusty world full of stuffy old professors? Gabrielle was feisty and beautiful and a damned good field archaeologist. He could think of no other team member better at investigating the high status burial erosion had exposed in these cliffs. Or one so easy on the eye, with her honey-blonde hair and strange, but lovely, green and gold flecked eyes with their exotically eastern almond shape.

Hillary snapped back into focus, this was not the occasion to ponder over his hopeless crush on Gabrielle, not when her life was literally hanging by a thread. "Can you see anything yet, Gaby?"

"Wow! There's something else down here, I've already spotted tiny glints of gold, some bone fragments. Could be human. We will have to move fast to save this, the cliff is going to give way soon and dump the whole burial in the sea."

"Get what you can now, we'll have to rig something more substantial when this infuriating wind drops," Britton announced as excited as Gaby at the discovery of these ancient artefacts. He watched, increasingly nervous for her safety as carefully she teased the soil away from the visible remains. With her bag full and nothing more close to hand, Gabrielle tugged on the rope and was hauled to safety.

She stood on the edge of the cliff as Hillary helped her out of the abseiling harness, holding her bag of finds high in the air, a gesture of relief and triumph. She had beaten the unstable cliff, the unforgiving wind and her own crippling vertigo.

Her legs trembling from the after affects of exhaustion and the adrenaline rush from the abseil, Gabrielle sought out her ancient motor home, parked close by with the other dig team vehicles.

"Gaby, you are such a dreadful slattern," she muttered to herself, fighting her way through the clutter of discarded clothes, mugs and plates and magazines covering every surface of living space in the tiny vehicle. Finding a recyclable mug, one that only needed a brief rinse and not a hard scrub, she made herself a coffee with lots of sugar. Perfect to cure the post abseil jitters. And to make doubly sure, she added a generous measure of cheap brandy from a supermarket-bought miniature. She had bloody well earned it, hanging from a cliff like an inept novice spider all morning!

She retrieved her favourite, rather battered tan leather jacket and reached into a pocket to find the latest letter from her grandmother. She had read it many times already that week but felt the need to look at it again. Her hand caressed the handmade, pale lilac Japanese paper her beloved Gran loved to use; she raised it to her face and breathed in the faint smell of flowers. Then Gabrielle read the letter, written in a secret language that only the pair of them understood; the magic key to their own private world.

Normally, her Gran's letters would be full of gossip and funny anecdotes. This time it contained only a curious warning.

"Gaby my precious girl, you must be careful, so very careful. The world is becoming a far more dangerous place. I am fearful that some of that danger could be heading your way."

Her grandmother's strange advice gave no further details leaving Gabrielle feeling both apprehensive and sad. Gran's mind had been so razor sharp, so full of gentle but incisive wisdom. Was this worrying missive a sign that the cruelties of old age were finally catching up with her? "Please, God, no," Gabrielle pleaded, "don't let that happen to my Gran. She is all I have." But what other explanation could there be?

Carefully, Gabrielle returned the letter to its envelope, then tucked it back into her jacket pocket. The safest place in the chaos of her motor home. She made herself another coffee with far more fortification, tried to forget the oddness of the content of her grandmother's letter. At least the old lady was writing to her, the elegant handwriting as beautiful and precise as ever. That must be a good sign.

Later that afternoon, in the comfort of their camp, Gabrielle watched with rising excitement as her friend Lily Hung slowly and meticulously cleaned the first pieces recovered from the site. Why was she so transfixed by this scrap of ancient gold, Gabrielle wondered to herself? The rest of the expedition were in their trailers, relaxing, warmed by vast quantities of fish and chips from a nearby village, the hard-earned calories washed down by locally brewed scrumpy. Gabrielle was too intrigued by the finds to be distracted by food, as was her close friend, Lily. She could not define why, but there was something different to this find, not just the precarious position of the burial, discovered by a sharp-eyed rambler a few days before. Of course, whoever interred the body all those centuries ago had no concept of coastal erosion, the site would have been situated well inland and safe from disturbance.

"You are right, hon, there is something weird and wonderful about this burial," mused Lily as she minutely scrutinised a gold pin under a microscope. "We know the ancient Cornish traded their tin with the Phoenicians. But how did a piece of jewellery from Southern India get here?"

"Are you sure?" Gabrielle shook her head in disbelief. Just what had they discovered?

Lily carefully replaced the slender and fragile clothes' fastening pin and picked up another object, a garnet encrusted ring. "This is a really beautiful piece but it doesn't belong here either, it is ancient Scythian. We normally associate gold in burials of this period with royalty. But perhaps our body belonged to an incredibly well travelled trader?"

Britton stuck his head into the temporary on-site lab and listened with amazement at Lily's musings. Within minutes the entire tent was filled with the rest of the group, all chattering animatedly, fascinated by the finds.

It became too much for Gabrielle. She wandered outside, feeling claustrophobic with the entire expedition crammed in reeking of greasy chips and raw cider, leaning over Lily and the gold objects, loudly expounding their own theories. All instant experts! She walked to the edge of the cliff and looked up at the gaudy sunset glowing above the white-topped, navy sea. This was a stunningly beautiful coastline. She wondered if the individual interred beneath her feet had ever stood on this same spot and watched the sun go down in such a glory of gold and pink.

By the end of the week the entire burial site had been safely removed and taken to their university base near Bristol. Two days later, heavy storms battered the Cornish coast and the cliff face at the area of the excavation was lost to the sea. Knowing they had saved the site, added to Gabrielle's satisfaction as she worked on unravelling the mystery of the man buried there. So far the team had learnt the well-preserved bones belonged to a well-fed, healthy man in his sixties, such an age was a rarity in ancient times. He had been killed by a single blow from a sword to his neck and buried with an astonishing quantity of fine jewellery, with origins from all over the known world. Who the hell was he? Carbon dating put the native born man living in the region around 500AD. A time when the country was learning to survive without the power of Rome.

Two items intrigued Gabrielle, to the point of a curiosity growing towards obsession. A piece of naturally dense, light, black bone, clearly not human but of no known beast either. It had been set as a brooch with an ornate gold mounting. Placed over his chest, it must have been a thing of great importance to the ancient Cornishman. The other was a pendant found around the skeleton's broken neck. A gold talisman in the form of an abstract dragon, at first it looked like half was missing but closer examination showed the object had been deliberately made in that form, not accidentally broken. The design of the talisman was of no known origin, the workmanship especially fine, beyond the skills of any of the Cornishman's known contemporary society.

And there was something else. Something she could not admit to anyone else, even to her close friend Lily. When she had lifted the dragon piece from the cliff she had felt...what? A jolt? A tingle? An electric shock? Gabrielle was not a fanciful woman, yet she had to know; was the strange sensation caused by an overactive imagination stoked up by adrenaline? She had been dangling off a wind-swept cliff petrified at the time! There was only one way to discover she had to hold the talisman again.

To protect the precious and fragile artefacts no find could be handled with bare hands, but to find out the truth Gabrielle had to hold it again without gloves. Gabrielle decided to wait until late when she knew the lab would be empty. She couldn't face the inevitable questions, the indignation from the rest of the team if they caught her handling the talisman with bare hands. How could she explain this crazy compulsion rationally to a team of dedicated scientists and academics?

She waited until nightfall. No one on the team worked after pub opening hours. Gabrielle felt ridiculous, entering the University grounds, sneakily, like a burglar; she was a member of the archaeological staff, perfectly entitled to work late. Gabrielle, her head down, tried not to be noticed as she approached the main building, jumping with alarm as a clichéd owl hooted from a spinney of trees close by. She nearly gave up following through with this impulsive, ill-thought out plan, muttering to herself. "Could you be any more ridiculous, woman?"

But the strident pull of curiosity was stronger then her dignity. To her relief the night security man in the hallway was too deeply engrossed watching a Bond film on his television to notice her walking swiftly through the corridors. It was a sign, a portent, one that spurred her on to continue her quest. Gabrielle hurriedly entered the deserted laboratory block. No alarms sounded, why should they? She was not a trespasser, she had not broken in and she had a valid security key to the lab. She was not an intruder, just felt like one!

Checking she was indeed alone, her bare hands shook from knowing she had crossed the line, that she was behaving with a shocking lack of professionalism. Unlocking a cabinet, pulling it open, she picked up the dragon talisman and held it lightly in her right palm. At first there was nothing, nothing but the feel of the cold ancient metal in her hand. Gabrielle shook her head, angry with herself for such fanciful notions. What did she expect to happen? This was real life, not an episode of Indiana Jones! She leant forward to put the jewellery back, thankful no one had witnessed tough, no-nonsense Gaby succumb to absurdity. Suddenly her hand snatched back clenching tightly, painfully around the gem. A possessive gesture, one she had no control over. What was happening? A sensation, a slight warmth and vibrancy emanated from the talisman. It lasted for only a few seconds, but it was enough to confirm the weird notion that it was calling to her, that it was telling her it had been lost beneath the earth for a reason and it was hers by ancient right.

Hurriedly Gabrielle returned the subtly gleaming object to the safety of its box, her hands shaking even more. "You are an idiot," she ranted to herself. "A prime nutter." The dragon talisman was beautiful, mysterious and desirable. And valuable. Of course part of her wanted it for herself. Who wouldn't! She forced aside the imaginings, deciding to blame it all on her Gran and the unease caused by her letter. So, the world was getting more dangerous? Only a fool who never read the newspapers or watched the news on telly would think otherwise.

Like most people getting on with their lives, Gabrielle tried to shut out images of the Outrages, the news reports of carnage and horror from terrorist attacks on all the major cities of the world. A small, but fanatic group called the Imadeen originating from a remote and largely unknown country were trying to firebomb unbelievers into embracing their harsh faith. The Outrages. Gabrielle had decided the best approach was to defy them by living her life her own way, by walking with her head high. Getting on with the everyday things that mattered as if the Imadeen didn't exist. Her Gran loved her, she knew her granddaughter worked in and travelled to major European cities. Why wouldn't she want to warn Gaby of danger, why would she not want to protect her?

Chapter Three

Bristol, England

Gabrielle pulled the collar of her denim jacket up and gave the leaden sky a baleful glare. "You were supposed to be a dry, sunny afternoon! Where did all you bloody horrible rain clouds come from?"

She picked up speed, striding down the road that led to her home. With every second the day darkened ominously, an already brisk, irritating wind grew increasingly squally. In the distance, but nearing, deep rolling thunder rumbled with apocalyptical fervour.

"Yeuch! Oh bollocks!" Gabrielle gasped as a sudden cloud-burst of sharp hail followed by rain drenched her through to the skin. She swore colourfully, cursing all weather-men and their fancy but obviously moronic computers. No. Not stupid, she corrected, sadistic, human-hating computers. Waiting, biding their time before taking over the planet. "Softening us up first," she reasoned, "cutting down the population by tricking people into holding picnics in deluges. Or wrapping up warm in heat waves."

"Delightful, Gaby, as always!" laughed a male voice from the entrance to the converted Edwardian hospital where she had a ground floor flat. Gabrielle, feeling like a drowned rat, made out the familiar shambolic form of Hillary Britton waiting for her. Great. Now she had to be polite to her boss looking like something dredged out of a duck pond.

"The golden beauty of an angel with the mouth of a fish-wife!"

"I love you too, Hills. Now, what exactly are you doing lurking in my doorway?" She wanted to add, 'like some mentalist stalker,' but bit back the jest, it would hurt the scruffy bear of a man, whose feelings for her were so obvious. There was no need to be cruel to a friend and respected colleague. And her boss!

"I'm here to bring you good news and bad news," he answered, holding the front door open for Gabrielle as she squelched and dripped into her flat, her entrance made more dramatic as nature's pyrotechnics flared above her.

"Tell me after I've found some dry clothes. You know where the kettle is," she suggested, trying not to flinch at the lightning. She had handled venomous snakes and conquered heights. The prospect of being struck by lightning was the only thing left to be afraid of now.

Britton watched wistfully as she disappeared into the forbidden zone of her bedroom, envying the towel that she would be using to dry herself. Unsuccessfully, he tried to force such lecherous thoughts from his mind, busying himself finding coffee and mugs in the chaos of her tiny kitchen, bracing himself before opening her fridge. Last time, he had discovered a yoghourt that wasn't just alive, but preparing to move in as a flatmate. His plan not to think lustful thoughts fell at the next hurdle as Gabrielle popped her head around the door, her hair loose, falling about her slim, naked shoulders in wet tendrils, the rest of her clad in only a fluffy white towel.

"Forget the coffee," she laughed apologetically, holding up a couple of beer bottles in one hand, the other clutching the towel tightly, "I haven't got any left. Or any fresh milk."

Relieved he didn't have to face the lurking horrors in Gaby's fridge Britton ousted a fat, surly, ginger cat off her sofa and waited till she had dressed. Gabrielle returned clad in an oversized, faded black sweatshirt with a 'History is Bunk' logo and black leggings, normally unflattering garments on most females but her tall, slender figure made them seem chic. She smelt delicious too, of coconut-scented shower gel; Britton decided visiting Gaby's flat was an act of extreme masochism on his part.

"The bad news first," he announced when she sat down beside him. "The archaeological grape vine has been busy with our news.

The 'Ground Beneath Us' team are seething, livid we didn't come to them about the cliff top burial. Let's be honest, it would have made exciting TV."

Gabrielle wasn't worried. She hated that programme, especially the obnoxious, ego-driven and ignorant presenter. And though she didn't have a vain bone in her body, she was a realist and knew it would focus too much on her. That wasn't fair to the others on the team, who were equally dedicated and worked just as hard.

"The good news is that 'World Beyond' wants to do an hour long documentary about our mysterious Cornishman, even offered to pay for a facial reconstruction of our man's scull using Necromans."

That was more like it! Gabrielle's face broke into a wide, excited grin. World Beyond was a popular but respectable documentary series, science made fascinating without any tiresome dumbing down of the facts. Necromans was the latest American technology for recreating human faces from sculls, very fast, accurate and expensive. The results were so realistic; it was almost like bringing the long dead back to life.

"I hope you said yes," she urged, dreading the decision would have to go through endless University bureaucracy.

Hillary Britton decided to tease her a little, an unworthy and petty punishment for being so beautiful and desirable yet beyond his, or it seemed, anyone's reach. He settled back on the sofa and let Monster, the fat cat climb on to his knee, gritting his teeth as the creature dug its claws through the denim jeans. He stroked and fussed, chatting away to the old flea bag, delaying his answer to wind Gabrielle up. It worked.
"Hillary Britton, you hate cats! Tell me what is happening!"

"Someone is cross, Monster," he teased, stroking the cat's off-white chest. "Someone needs to chill out and drink her beer." "Someone is going to tip her beer over your head, cat and all," Gabrielle replied. Britton quickly put the cat down, not wanting to be scratched if Gaby carried out her threat, which was perfectly likely!

"They start filming next Tuesday."

Gabrielle's scream of delight had the same effect as pouring beer. Hillary Britton also yelled as the startled cat whirled, scratched like a demented ball of fur studded with barbed wire and fled, catching his ankle with its claws.

"Now I remember why I hate cats," he muttered darkly.

Chapter Four

Azrar's Stronghold, Isolann

"This is bad, very bad," Jazriel muttered searching frantically through the boxes in his own spacious quarters, the luxurious open prison he dwelt in when Azrar was conducting affairs of state in the Great Hall or in his offices.

"Zaard!" He swore to the empty room, "Where the hell are the rest of my cigarettes?"

Jazriel was certain he had enough to get him through Isolann's seemingly endless winter. But where were they? With the brandy in the cellars nearly gone, the thought of losing yet another support system was intolerable and he began another anxious search. Rifling through his wardrobe brought reminders of more horrors. For the past decades he had worn Isolanni-styled clothing made in the fine fabrics bequeathed the Dark Kind from their unknown benefactors. Lush bariola velvets in jewel colours, silks so fine they seemed made of glimmering gossamer; ghiall leather, incredibly tough but pliant and light. Gorgeous clothing, but none were his own. All were garments he hasd found stored in chests for Dark Kind guests.

Guests? That was a sick joke. Who was left to come to Isolann now? Where was Mahdial, with his strange brown and gold eyes and quiet, studious ways, so at odds with his warrior status? Or quick-witted Jendar Rhagan, the steppe wolf? Both of them long turned to dust, blown away to oblivion. A fate he would have shared but for the intervention of an extraordinary human woman, Khari. Her gift of *Knowing* had stayed Azrar's hand from lighting Jazriel's funeral pyre.

Forgetting his vow to ration his remaining few cigarettes, his hand shaking, he hastily lit another one up. This sorrowful dwelling on the past was another serious symptom of the bad effect of his incarceration here in Azrar Keep. It was a shrine to the Dark Kind's forgotten past.

Every room was full of artefacts, every richly decorated wall hanging, every display of ancient weaponry brought him back to his old life where Dark Kind royalty ruled the entire known world. And his place was to serve them in bed. Or wherever they wanted to use him. Without question, thought or argument.

Jazriel's life had truly started when that old way of life had crumbled and was destroyed by the fires and blades of the all-conquering humans. Despite the occasional near-disaster, like nearly being hung, mutilated and incinerated alive in Prague by a witch-burning mob, Jazriel had proved he could live with humans and their ever-changing turmoil-filled society. He could survive hidden amongst them, preying on them from the shadows. A life lived independent and free. And he so wanted to be free!

What had he to wear in the modern world? Nothing! This was a disaster! A nightmare! The treacherous thoughts of leaving Isolann in spring, once the snows had gone, never left his mind, no matter how hard he tried. But how could he leave without modern clothes? There were no fine tailors, no couture houses, no cloistered novice nuns with skilful needles in this backward, goat-loving dump of a country!

Damn! That's what became of arriving at the Principality as a stone-cold corpse! He had been brought here by his human and Dark Kind friends for two reasons. They had come to ask the impossible, to plead with Azrar to attempt to reunite his body with his spirit. Failing that, to see him properly cremated and given the respectful last rites of the Dark Kind, a ritual denied him by his female lover, Sivaya, who had not accepted his death and abandoned his spirit to the nightmare void of near oblivion.

Jazriel's body had arrived at the stronghold for his final journey thoughtfully laid out in his finest Saville Row suit, clothing wisely chosen by Khari and his Dark Kind commoner friend, Garan. Selected with love and care from Jazriel's considerable collection of beautiful clothes. There was now no sign of the charcoal-coloured suit. The Prince probably had it destroyed to leave no reminder of that awful time. When only a human female's intuition, her *Knowing,* had saved Jazriel's body from being consumed by flames.

But now, Jazriel was so desperate he would even have endured wearing his funeral clothes. The elegant, perfectly fitted suit had been hand made for him in a fine cashmere and silk fabric by the best tailors London had to offer. The subject of clothes brought him inevitably back to more morbid imaginings...His appearance.

One of his first conscious acts after his resurrection was to order the castle's human servants to remove every mirror from the inner keep. He could not face the truth, that he was some kind of monstrous re-animated corpse. That Prince Azrar never flinched from his practised and skilful touch or from his intimate embrace, should have reassured Jazriel, but it did not. He had often been called vain through his lifetime, but his obsession with his looks ran deeper then mere narcissism. Jazriel survived by trading on his stunningly beautiful appearance.

He had been created to be desirable, deliberately made to attract his noble-born clients in India, in those far distant times when he was sha'ref, in human terms a whore, the lowest caste of commoner. He had used his fine-honed skill of beguilement to enthral, to be irresistible, only to be dismissed, usually brusquely, after driving them delirious with pleasure; always leaving their palaces alone, the saddle-bags on his horse laden with payment of gems and gold. It had been enough, then.

In later life, he had used his seductive wiles and disarming beauty to lure human prey, and to win favour and protection from those in power. Without his looks, how could he survive alone in the world beyond Isolann?

Jazriel resigned himself to confronting the truth. He must discover whether anything of his allure, the treasured perfection of his features were intact. He had to find a mirror. And he knew where one existed. In the depths of the keep. In the forbidden rooms.

Chapter Five

The Cornish Coast, England

'I am not going to let those po-faced eco warriors on campus make me feel guilty,' Gabrielle decided, striding across the Cornish cliff tops with the early Spring sun caressing the deepening gold of her skin. 'Today, I am really enjoying global warming!'

Not for the first time, she was grateful for her mixed ethnic ancestry which blessed her with blonde hair, already streaked with platinum from the sun, and flawless skin that tanned quickly to golden brown rather then turning a livid, burned red.

The third day of the 'World Beyond' location shoot was in full swing. Blessed with a Spring heat wave, the peace of the cliff normally only shattered by the raucous squawk of gulls, now also endured the full assault of a film crew. Generators droned, powering up miles of fat, snaking cables servicing a mobile village of trailers and lorries. Purposeful folk clutching clipboards scurried about in all directions. Technicians laughed loudly as they swapped outrageous stories from disastrous shoots. They gathered, relaxed, around the honey wagon, the all important source of bacon butties and hot coffee.

Gabrielle enjoyed the organised chaos. A fact not unconnected to the production team's choice of presenter, Ciaran O'Rourke, six foot two of dark-haired, blue-eyed Celtic eye candy. Inevitably, the focus of much of the filming so far had been Gabrielle's photogenic descent down the cliff face to discover the burial. At least she didn't have to recreate the abseil herself, a trim, professional stuntwoman in a blonde wig was on hand. What had been a terrifying experience for Gabrielle was all in a day's work for her.

To her discomfort, Gabrielle was aware of the hurt in Hillary Britton's eyes as she flirted openly with O'Rourke, but hell, she was young, free and single, why shouldn't she?

"I discovered some of your colleagues call you Lara. After watching that recreated decent of the cliffs you made in those shorts, I can see why," laughed O'Rourke, his voice, rich and dark as a pint of Guinness, with a lilting Southern Irish accent adding to the alarming effect on Gabrielle's normally calm exterior.

They walked slowly together to the honey wagon, already relaxed with each other's company. With a mischievous glow of satisfaction, Gabrielle spotted the look of envy from the other women waiting in line for refreshments. She could imagine what they were thinking; how had that scrawny bitch captured the star of the show? Their envy not helped by the openly appreciative glances from the men gathering around the trailer. Let them ogle! Gabrielle was unashamed of her looks and the effect they caused. She had decided long before to make the most of these gilded, fleeting days of her youth and beauty. She knew they wouldn't last and some time in the future, she would be one of the bitter, envious ones.

"Me? Lara Croft? Only the lads call me that!" She laughed accepting a plastic cup of coffee from him. They strolled to some nearby canvas director's chairs and sat, turning their faces to the warm sun.

"You are wasted on these uni digs, Gaby," suggested O'Rourke. "There are enough earnest academics to do the work. You have the looks and natural charisma to be a huge hit on TV. If you presented a history show, you'd wipe the floor with Ground Beneath Us."

Gabrielle smiled and shook her head in good humoured denial of such a fanciful notion, although the thought of TV work certainly was alluring. Thoughts of pissing-off that little creep of a presenter, Barry Tinson, and paying off her horrendous student loan certainly appealed.

"I am not just a pretty face, you know Ciaran!" she added in her defence, "I am a highly qualified archaeologist with years of experience in the field."

Ciaran's blue eye's had a mischievous gleam, there was one experience in a field he would love to have with this beautiful girl. Time to switch off from flirt mode and be a professional, he decided. Quickly!

"Gabrielle, with this fantastic weather we should be able to wrap up this location shoot today. Can we start filming the finds later this week?"

Gabrielle felt a pang of disappointment, filming on the Cornish coast in the height of a freakish heat wave had more attractions then the dry subterranean archives of the university.

"Will you be there?" she ventured, lowering her eyes in an unconscious flirting gesture.

Ciaran shook his head, all too aware of the signals from this lovely young woman. Could he stay in Cornwall for one more night?

"But the production team will not be on the road till tomorrow," he replied with a conspiratorial smile. "Fancy grabbing supper in Falmouth, tonight?"

Chapter Six

With the Worlds Beyond location shoot finally over, it was back to mundane reality for Gabrielle and the team. They had enjoyed their brief flirtation with show biz, Gabrielle especially. When the filming was over for the day, she still had excitement of a different sort to look forward to by night! Ciaran and the film crew had returned to London, Gabrielle returned to her research on the cliff-side burial finds.

In the carefully monitored atmosphere of the university's labs, the modern lighting and clinical atmosphere did nothing to take away the sense of ancient magic and mystery. Gabrielle made her way down the empty corridors to underground environmentally-controlled vaults where precious objects were stored. Prior to entering the restricted area, she paused, patted her pocket, re-assuring herself her protective gloves were there. She had already taken a foolish, unprofessional risk with the objects. It must not happen again.

Out of the Cornish burial horde, the golden dragon talisman remained her favourite item, its curious hold over her undiminished despite frequent handling with gloves on, all in the name of research, of course! The light but dense and strong, black, bone ornamental brooch also intrigued her. The ebony colour was not from a stain or charring but the natural hue of the object. What creature on the earth had ever had naturally black bones?

She planned to take a small sample of it to be DNA tested at the high tech facilities of a medical research unit off campus. Like all the university team, she was eager to know the origins of the strange item, as did the documentary makers; revealing its origin could be a highlight of the programme although the biggest moment would be the recreated head of the mysterious Cornishman. Gabrielle was excited, she couldn't wait to meet the man face to face. Spiritually shake hands with the enigmatic being whose life and death had sparked this hectic and often frustrating research. Would they ever really know who he was? Why he was buried in Cornwall with treasure from all the corners of the known world?

As Gabrielle walked through the near-empty corridors, a curious sense of foreboding and wrongness made the back of her neck tingle unpleasantly. Without knowing why, she hastened her steps from brisk walk to near run. She hurried into the archaeology labs - there was nothing obviously untoward. She chided herself for her foolishness and entered her section; again nothing was out of place, nothing strange or worrying. She opened the special cabinet and pulled out the tray containing the grave goods. Ran her gaze over them, went cold from realisation. Two items were missing. The dragon talisman and the black bone brooch. She shivered as the implications sank in; losing these precious objects was a disaster, not just for the team but in a crazy, illogical way also for herself. Contrary to all reason, to all common sense, Gabrielle thought of the dragon pendant as hers. What the hell was going on?

Maybe someone else from the team was working on them? Gabrielle forced herself to stay calm, not to jump to wild conclusions. There was no sign of a break in, nothing had been forced or damaged. She sat at her workbench and made a few 'phone calls, leaving the most difficult, the one to Hillary Britton, to last. With each call, her heart grew heavier, nausea welling up in her throat. No one had the items. It seemed they had indeed been stolen.

The next few days passed in a blur of investigation and accusations, conspiracy plots and suspicion. At the end of the police inquiry no firm conclusion could be reached, it was as if the precious objects had vanished into thin air. With no evidence to the contrary, Gabrielle and Hillary as the expedition leaders took the brunt of the storm and even the police publicly clearing them did not stop the whispering campaign. Luckily the excitement and mystery only added to the interest of the Worlds Beyond crew, the documentary would be made, but with an unwelcome new emphasis on the theft. Every night since the loss of the finds, Gabrielle endured anxiety nightmares. Shadows appeared under her eyes and she began to forget to eat. Worse, she was tempted to start smoking for the first time in her life and not necessarily cigarettes.

With only the indifferent company of Monster to stop her, Gabrielle decided to call Ciaran. Another night of wild, uninhibited sex was a better relaxant then nicotine or alcohol. His mobile phone apparently switched off, she called the World Beyond production office but he had already left London for his home. With a lot of strident persuading and some shameless truth-stretching about important production matters to discuss, a nervous office junior gave her Ciaran's home number. Which his wife answered.

Bloody typical; the bastard had conveniently forgotten to mention he was married before they nearly shook the roof off a hotel in Falmouth! Gabrielle sighed, philosophically, with no anger or bitterness. It had been brilliant sex but she had always known it was only a fling; O'Rourke was too in love with himself for anything else. 'Bloody good in bed though,' she mused as she recalled their horizontal activities. Well, horizontal some of the time, Ciaran had been very creative and athletic!

Instead, she decided to drown her sorrows with the ever dependable Hillary, who had taken the brunt of the flak from the theft and was even more down then she was.

They took solace in two pints of real ale at a river-side country pub, as far away from the university as they dared drive in Hillary's battered and wheezing Vauxhall Astra.

"The suspicion won't stop till we track the jewellery down and find the culprit," said Gabrielle after taking a much needed swig of yeasty warm beer. It was comfort food from her student days, like slightly stale doughnuts and weak hot chocolate on wet winter afternoons, studying in her room at the cramped, noisy halls of residence. "And why those two particular pieces? They left virtually everything, including the Scythian ring, the carnelian and Baltic amber brooch. All the gold pins."

Hillary shook his head, his long grey-brindled, brown hair tied back in a pony tail, yet another academic who couldn't let go of his hippy past. He had pondered endlessly on the same question over the past days. "They took the oddities, the strange pieces with no obvious origin. I think we need the help of an expert in inexplicable antiquities."

Gabrielle repressed a shudder of distaste, knowing what was to come next. Hillary Britton was one of the few academics who had any respect for the American maverick Professor Jay Parrish. Hillary had read every book by the man who was discredited by the establishment but who survived as the venerable, though frail old man of archaeology. She had met him once and her flesh crawled at the memory, there was something profoundly disturbing about him. At well over ninety, his brain was sharp though his body was wizened and desiccated as an Egyptian mummy. It was the way he had looked at her, pale grey eyes boring through her with an unsettling mixture of fascination and loathing. As if he knew her; although they had never met before.

Hillary was right, no one else had dedicated so much time to researching the very rare finds that had no explanation to their origin or purpose. No one else had the huge resources of the Nemesis Corporation at his disposal to payroll his esoteric research. Ominously, no one else was more likely to have taken the Cornish finds.

"When are you going?" asked Gabrielle, taking another swig from her beer, thoughts of the odious Parish had made the ale taste bitter in her mouth.

"When are *you* going?" Hillary returned. "I can't leave here, I am head of the department. It would look bad. It would look guilty. But you could slip away to Switzerland for a few days."

"Good old expendable Gaby," she retorted, furious with her boss, though what he said was undeniably true.

"Good old resourceful, knowledgeable and brave Gaby" Britton returned. "If any one could charm an answer from that old bastard, it will be you."

"That's right, send in the blonde tottie," Gabrielle muttered darkly.

"He's over ninety!" Britton laughed, spilling his beer. "Your spotless virtue will be quite safe!"

Chapter Seven

Jendar Azrar's stronghold, Isolann

Jazriel knew he had to be swift, act only when the Prince was at the start of an important campaign in the mountains with his human militia. The danger from the eastern borders was worsening. Jazriel hardly saw Azrar now, he was so occupied with shoring up Isolann's defences, its human army needed fine-tuning, organising. Once more, his people needed Azrar's skills as a warlord and Jazriel had not seen him happier for many decades. It made what he was planning so much easier to bear.

He hurried through the labyrinth of torch illuminated corridors until he arrived at the unlit gloomy area where only Dark Kind could go, confidently navigating the twisting route with his perfect night vision. In his hand, a sliver of crystal mounted on a silver chain, taken from Azrar's discarded garb while he slept in Rest. Jazriel had not wanted to be caught rifling through the Prince's clothes, he made sure exhaustion and satisfaction from a tumultuous union had deepened his sleep.

Finally Jazriel came to an ornate stone door, carved with fanciful black wolves, their fierce eyes studded with gemstones; garnets, emeralds and rubies. Even the fiercest carved wolf would look like a friendly puppy dog compared to Azrar if he caught his companion opening this room. Her room.

Breathing fast in his anxiety, Jazriel paused on the threshold. He could turn back. Why provoke the rage of the notoriously volatile warlord? Why risk alienating the most precious thing left in his life? Azrar's love. Why? Because he needed to know. Was he still Jazriel? Was he truly alive, and as beautiful as before?

Jazriel retrieved the crystal from a hidden pocket within the Isolanni-style tunic he wore, though no nomad would ever wear such a luxurious fabric as wild silk. The crystal lay in his hand, a dull piece of green rock hewn from hell knows where; technology from the Dark Kind's mysterious creators and benefactors, that was all he knew. As he held it close to the locked door the crystal began to vibrate and glow, brighter and brighter, until with a sigh and a low groan from long disuse, the heavy door opened to reveal its forbidden secrets. Yet, he could still turn back, the crime against Azrar's orders, the violation of his trust, was to cross the threshold and enter her room. He could turn back...

"Merde," he whispered, "I was never known for being cautious. Reckless, shallow, vain and not too bright. But never cautious!" Suppressing a low growl of self disgust at his trepidation, Jazriel walked into the sealed chambers of Jendara Zian.

Though he did not need the light, for comfort Jazriel lit a series of sconces laden with many candles beside the door, instantly flooding the room with a warm, flickering, golden light and stepped into a scene frozen in time. The unknown technology was at work again; there was no musty, airless atmosphere, no accumulation of dust and cobwebs. No decay. All the fine bariola velvet and lush silks of the furnishings were jewel bright in rich shades of crimson, gold and scarlet, every gold goblet gleamed as if freshly burnished. Jazriel wandered about the room, so strong was Zian's presence he illogically expected the Jendara to stride in and demand to know why he was there. Or maybe not. Maybe she had arranged for Jazriel to be there, to be sha'ref and serve her voracious needs.

On a huge raised bed covered with embroidered gold and crimson brocade and soft furs, lay the Jendara's wedding dress, an exquisite and delicate robe of pure silver thread woven as light and fine as silk, her unworn crown of platinum set with a universe of glittering diamonds lay beside it. Jazriel tentatively touched the gown, admiring its beauty, the craftsmanship, then snapped his hand back as if burned. Why did he have this bizarre feeling of being watched, judged and condemned? It was not Azrar. Could not be, he had seen the Prince ride out with his elite guard. Jazriel turned, drawn to a heavy gold brocade curtain on the wall, sensing this was the source of his discomfort.

"So, there you are," he muttered, walking to the curtain and pulling it aside in one hard tug to reveal a vivid and powerful portrait of a beautiful Dark Kind female astride a pure white Arab stallion. Zian. The bewitching but insane princess who had ensnared Azrar's heart and nearly dragged him down to her own self-engineered doom. Zian's beautiful navy eyes, arrogant and scornful, seemed to dismiss Jazriel from her high-born presence. Jazriel knew that look all too well. He'd seen it on all the noble born Dark Kind females he'd serviced. Seen it as they paid and dismissed him, no longer wanted, their craving for recreational sexual pleasure sated. The same females that, hours before, he had reduced to dazed and whimpering pleading, begging him for more.... He had pleasured Zian many times, in the era when they had both lived in India. Long before either had encountered Jendar Azrar. How could Jazriel forget her? More then once Zian had nearly killed him with her insatiable and ferocious demands!

She had not been intimate with Azrar, had kept her distance from him. The Prince had been besotted with this creature, yet she had tormented him for decades, promising so much but giving him nothing. A dangerous, pointless, cruel game. But then, she had been dangerous, pointless and cruel.

Jazriel shuddered and backed away from the imposing portrait, the strange sensation of being watched by malevolent eyes refusing to yield to the light of reason. Why was he feeling such intense unease? Azrar would be furious with him if the Prince discovered him in Zian's rooms; and though he might rage and swear and break things, he would never physically harm him. Instead he would curtly and coldly dismiss Jazriel from his bed, from his presence – a psychological punishment that would trigger Jazriel's deep insecurity and neediness. His fear of abandonment by one who loved him.

And what could Zian do? She was dead. Ah, but Jazriel had been dead too, he knew only too well how ineffective and powerless he had been as a lost and lonely spirit.

Though no warrior, Jazriel had never been short of courage. He'd taken on the dangerous world of humans, shared wild adventures with sea-faring rogues, fought hard alongside them with cutlass and fangs.

He'd served bravely with the allies against the Nazis as a covert agent, working undercover right in the heart of Berlin. So what was this creeping sensation here in these long-empty chambers?

He desperately needed a cigarette but that would leave a trace, a sign he had entered these rooms. "Pull yourself together, fool," he snarled to himself; "you are here for one reason. The damned mirror."

He found it within the next chamber, a thin sheet of highly polished silver and ancient glass. A tall, young man stood before him, lean and elegant in frame but undeniably masculine. His glossy layers of below-collar length black hair was shot through with the blue-green iridescence of a magpie's wings. His light golden face had the chiselled beauty of a fallen warrior angel, hurled down from paradise for his vanity. A face lit by expressive, hypnotic, all–turquoise eyes without a trace of white, framed by long silken blue-black lashes. This was no dead-eyed, chalk-white, corruption-ruined zombie. He raised his hand, touched his right eye; saw perfection. No scarring, no sign of damage or blemish. He was Jazriel, the most beautiful of his kind and a deadly predator. He slowly lowered his fangs from their scabbard in his scull, the four inch long silver scimitars glittered in the candlelight. The most striking symbol of his true nature, yet they did not distract the eye from his beauty.

All his anxiety fell away, hope and joy rose in his soul in a surge of forgotten emotions. Now, if he could just get back to being the louche, carefree and effortlessly charming Jazriel and not this depressed, grieving shadow of the being he once was! To possess again the relaxed predatory self-confidence of a sleek black panther, the creature Khari used to say he most reminded her of. That would be harder to do. A hell of a lot harder in this dour place.

Jazriel missed the modern world of humans; he needed his exquisite clothes, his fast cars; his many and varied intoxicants and the headiest fix of all, the pleasure of hunting through the dark streets of Europe's capitals. But he also wanted Azrar. His life was only real, only tangible when in the Prince's formidable presence. And that was the dilemma haunting his every waking moment.

Returning to the portrait of the Jendara, and with his hands on his hips, Jazriel stared boldly up at the image of Zian, directly into her beautiful but wild eyes. "Well, Princess, with your haughty superiority and beauty, where has your scheming and cruelty led you? You could have had it all. Azrar's love, a country to rule at his side. Stupid female, you could still be alive!" Jazriel's taunting was full of scorn. He could not hate but he could feel fury at what she had done in the past.

"It is I, the despised and lowly sha'ref here in your place. I share Azrar's bed, I have his heart. You are nothing, nothing more then a fading memory, a half forgotten nightmare, locked away and alone forever."

And with that, he covered the portrait with the heavy brocade again and prowled out of the room. He would not return to this shrine to an insane ghost. He had no need to.

Chapter Eight

The Monastery Gardens of St Valarin, Tobaar, Amantzk.

Alejandro Reyes wandered slowly through his favourite place of meditation and prayer. He walked down a narrow, well kept gravel path beneath a perfect, cloud-free azure sky, where swifts soared and whirled in a carefree aerial ballet. That morning nature was joyous, celebrating its rebirth with sweet-scented pastel blossom and the song of busily nesting birds. The warmth of the spring sun caressed his back and shoulders like a gentle embrace from a caring friend.

He appreciated and enjoyed the beauty but carried a heavy heart, grieving the loss of an old friend, Father Gerard. The cleric had passed peacefully in his sleep from old age. How had so many years flown past since Reyes had last walked through this garden with Gerry, then an eager young priest, full of optimism and enthusiasm? No one could have asked for a better assistant. Reyes would miss him dreadfully.

It was time to find a replacement, someone with the strength of character, the courage and the intelligence to accept extraordinary truths; to adapt to a far stranger world beyond the one they had known since birth. This person did not have to be a clergyman, the battle to come had nothing to do with Reyes' own chosen belief. Or any other religion. On this world or any other. But it was a matter of faith. Faith that humanity had a chance. The Enemy that would one day threaten this world had never been defeated. World after world had fallen. Planets that once teemed with life had been left as lifeless, dark and sterile cinders drifting, forlorn and forgotten in the uncaring void.

Reyes had faith that the ancient prophesies of his people were true, that this little blue world warmed by a golden star had an opportunity to fight back, using all Mankind's resources of courage and intelligence, inventiveness and co-operation. Hardest of all for Reyes to accept was the *other* prophesy, the one concerning the role of the accursed blood drinkers, the ferocious abominations that plagued this world. But the ancient text was clear and unambiguous; those murderous creatures would be needed. Their presence could be the edge that gave the Earth a fighting chance. His organisation had been founded many centuries ago, appointed to protect the scattered survivors of the vampire race. To Reyes it had been a necessary duty-and a terrible curse.

Reyes paused, a growing tiredness seeping through his body, reminding him of his own frailty and transience. He had lived a long time, but he was mortal, getting older and ever more weary. He found a wooden bench and sat down with a sigh. There was time to rest awhile in this place of peace and serenity. To revive his battered spirit.

Fate would send him an assistant. Someone to shoulder his burden, to allow him to concentrate his intellect, his dedication to Earth's defence against a fearful future. Someone to deal with the noisome distractions from those persistent old men, the founders of Nemesis who jeopardised the future with their obsession to destroy the Dark Kind. Nemesis must be stopped before the danger it posed became insurmountable. It had grown from a minor irritant led by three ageing fanatics, to a multi-billion pound super-corporation.

In its new form Nemesis was an enemy that needed new tactics to defeat it. Stronger, more aggressive measures that his high-minded organisation was morally unable to fulfil. It was time to find a more ruthless ally.

Chapter Nine

Isolann

"Zaard! Enough!" Azrar's hands slammed down onto the table, onto the mound of papers that covered and engulfed the ancient wood. If he had a broadsword in his hands he would have cleaved the table, papers, all this human-created disorder into many pieces in a whirlwind of violence and fury.

His councillors and administrators, all Isolanni-born humans had already scattered, even before the eruption of his wrath, mindful of the danger darkening in the Prince's emerald eyes.

Azrar growled, he was a warlord, a Dark Kind warrior prince by Dezarn's bloodied sword. But the end of the twentieth century had brought the outside world to his principality in the form of demanding treaties from neighbouring governments, approaches from hungry international corporations eager to exploit this remote little land. All had to be fought away but not with the sword. With paper and diplomacy!

Azrar sought his refuge from the increasing pressure of ruling Isolann, to spend time in the one place in the stronghold where he could forget the treacherous ways of humans and their constantly changing governments, all with their own hidden and not so hidden agendas for his domain. His people looked to him for protection and guidance, yet their young wanted change, seduced by the modern world already at Isolann's borders. The centuries-old nomad society, self-sufficient and serene was becoming increasingly fragile, as if on borrowed time. As was he.

Leaving his offices, Azrar prowled through the labyrinth of corridors of his black granite stronghold, scattering his human retinue as he went. So many now, filling the places of his long dead Dark Kind Ha'al administrators and warriors. He walked with difficulty, relying on the metal frame that held his shattered leg together. By rights it should have healed, but the enormous and sustained effort needed to restore Jazriel to life had damaged the Prince's regenerative power. Azrar cared little whether the limb self-repaired. He could hide the pain from his humans, ride a horse and wield a sword, could do everything he had done before sustaining this injury in a Nazi ambush. What he did care about was Isolann and Jazriel.

Where was he? The Prince craved the physical release and emotional support that only the beautiful and skilful sha'ref commoner could give him. With no more long campaigns, no mighty battles to fight with blood-lust surging through every vein, he was cut off from all that made him feel fully alive. To revel in being a ferocious Jendar of the Dark Kind. The time spent deep within Jazriel was so precious to him, where ecstasy lifted his soul free of this unworthy existence, free from the pain of his injury - the sharp reminder of his mortality. Making love to Jazriel he could be fully Dark Kind, fully Azrar again.

From the shadows, Azrar's chief aide watched, a sneer of contempt on his features. Where was the Prince going in such a rage? Hah! Lomak knew, and the thought turned his stomach. There was work to be done, important work. Isolann needed the Prince's full focus and tireless energy, now, but yet again he was turning his back on what should take priority.

The tide of political change was on the turn and Isolann was under threat and not just from the old enemy, Svolenia to the south of the mountain girdled Principality. That country was wallowing in a consumer free-for-all spending money it did not have on all the West could sell it. An invasion of rich foreigners had swamped many coastal and rural villages, destroyed vast tracts of countryside with their hastily built holiday homes. Making a few wily native-born rich, but most others far poorer, unable to afford to live in the villages of their ancestors.

If that mood spilt into Isolann, the country would be lost to the acquisitiveness and greed of the young, heedless of the future. Peace would rot Isolann from within. It would become an exploited province of a bankrupt Svolenia without a shot being fired.

A more immediate danger arose in the East. From Abhajastan, throwing off a corrupt and decadent Western-supported ancient monarchy and embracing an extreme fundamental religion. Unlike Svolenia, it had no territorial claim on the Principality. Instead it desired and pursued the souls of its people, not Europeans, but those descended from the Dholma, an ancient race of Asiatic steppe nomads.

And what was the Prince of Isolann doing? Off to screw his pretty boy!

The distaste threatened to choke Lomak with bile, he loathed Azrar's nature, his inclination. He swallowed the nausea, he must force these views aside, for now. Without Azrar's strength, his total dedication to the people, what use was this vampire lord ruling Isolann? The solution was simple - in theory. Get rid of Azrar's toy.

And if that did not work, get rid of Azrar.

The Prince found the luxurious vault of Rest he shared with Jazriel empty, but four discarded brandy bottles and many broken glasses lay on the floor. Fury overrode his anxiety; Azrar knew only too well how fragile his lover's hold on life was. Why was Jazriel risking losing it again with this ridiculous and escalating alcohol abuse? This was not how it was meant to be! This should be a time of celebration of a life reborn! Azrar grabbed the empty bottles and hurled them into the blazing hearth with a howl of fury. Why was Jazriel behaving like a petulant, spoilt prima-donna, one with a callous disregard for his own life?

Had it been so wrong? Was bringing Jazriel back to life an act of supreme selfishness? Had Azrar made a terrible mistake by his monumental and unprecedented feat in reuniting his lover's spirit with his long dead body? Perfectly preserved by Sivaya, she had hidden Jazriel's corpse in a filthy cellar and kept the body soaking in gallons of fresh human blood for five years. This had regenerated the shattered bones and organs torn apart by humans and their machine guns, but had not, could never have restored him to life. Azrar's high caste power and passion had.

The Prince accepted the early years of Jazriel's new life had been an ordeal for him. Even after the initial shock of awaking in a cold tomb of inert flesh, the horror for Jazriel had continued. Azrar shuddered at the memory of Jazriel's helplessness and anger, the frustration at trying to mesh together his impatient soul with the stubborn, dead flesh. It had been a long, fraught year before he could walk unaided. Or lift his hand to his face to smoke or drink. To add to his torment, Jazriel was terrified of sleeping, as if by closing his eyes he would allow the blackness to reclaim him.

All Azrar had been able to do was to be there for him, patiently guiding his arm, catching him when he stumbled, holding him tight through the long hours of daylight, doing his best to fight away Jazriel's twin demons of fear and despair. The Prince was a warrior, he had fought every minute of Jazriel's troubled resurrection at his side. Out of duty, out of love.

But now, with the demons defeated, with his restoration to life complete and successful, Jazriel was far from content. Azrar neither expected nor demanded gratitude. All he desired was for Jazriel to be happy. He did not regret bringing him back to life but had it been the right thing to do? Was it what Jazriel had really wanted?

Jazriel sat on the furthest edge of the wide stone lintel, one leg dangled precariously over the parapet, with nothing but the long drop to the Keep's snow-covered courtyard beneath. The other leg was bent, close to his body. He sat, leaning against the stone lintel, resting a hand on his knee; inevitably he was holding a lit cigarette from which he took a long, languid draw.

Azrar's hot anger turned to a frozen shiver of anxiety, Jazriel was within a hair's breath of plummeting to his death on the courtyard far below, a fall that nothing could bring him back from. All the stern, commanding tone left the Prince's voice, replaced by a calm, persuasive manner; "It is cold, my friend, come, join me by the hearth. I will send for some fine Armagnac from the cellars."

"It is always bloody cold here…" Jazriel drawled, taking a long drag from his cigarette before dropping it, watching it spiral slowly down to be lost in the late Spring snow that filled the courtyard in large, billowy drifts. "You live in a freezer. Not that you would know what that is. Uses electricity. Far too twenty-first century."

Azrar forced himself to stay calm, ignoring the blatant disrespect; Jazriel was in a strange and unpredictable mood and so vulnerable perilously balanced on the edge of the sill.

"And there is no brandy left," Jazriel stared up at the night sky, at the millions of bright but indifferent stars. "I've had the last of it."

The Prince ignored this, desperate to get him off the parapet. "There is much of this age I do not know, Seymahl." Azrar replied, using a Dark Kind term of deep affection between males, "And you are the one who can teach me. Come down from that ledge."

Jazriel gave a slight, indifferent shrug and in one lithe movement, jumped down. "I wasn't planning to leap to my death, my lord Prince, there was no need to fuss and fret."

He drifted back into the warmth of the keep, descending the wind of stairs, his steps unsteady from the brandy. Returning to Azrar's chamber, his eyes darted around the room for the next source of numbing intoxication. Damn! There really was nothing left here! He began to make for an inner door, to wander down to the wine store in the cellars deep beneath the keep but the Prince barred his way by grabbing his shoulders.

Azrar's eyes blazed with a furious fire. "Jazriel, by Dezarn's blood, you know how I feel about you, do not insult me with such flippancy."

The growing gulf between them appeared to stretch wider, to become an uncrossable chasm. Jazriel met and held the Prince's gaze, the expression in his turquoise eyes for once completely unreadable to Azrar. That was more alarming then seeing Jazriel so close to disaster on the window ledge.

A question stirred in Azrar's mind, one he dared not ask, because he already knew the answer and the consequences it would bring. A question he had asked before, but Zaard! He was a warlord, afraid of nothing, even the brutality of the truth. He would risk questioning his companion of so many centuries. "Jazriel, by all the stars in the universe, what will make you happy?"

Yet more disrespect, Jazriel turned his back on the Prince and loped over to the fireside, watching the flames dance and swirl, reflecting in the shards of warping glass as he gathered the courage to answer. Readying himself for the storm he would provoke, his head down, Jazriel addressed the flames. "To be at your side, helping you govern this land. To be closely involved with your life."

He moved away from the hearth to confront the Prince, his eyes flared briefly with light then darkened to a stormy, troubled navy. "To do something worthwhile with mine!"

This was what Azrar was expecting - and dreading. He pulled back from Jazriel, unable to stifle a growl of weary inevitability. "We have been through all this before. Centuries have passed but nothing has changed. It is impossible."

Azrar saw the intransigence in Jazriel's stance and sighed, the old anger building again. Why couldn't Jazriel take delight in what he was, revel in the exceptional skills he'd been created with? His great beauty, his desirability. His duty. Every Dark Kind was created to be a part of their rigid caste system. Duty was all, duty was the master that controlled their destiny. Azrar was engineered to rule and protect his subjects, only death could release him from this burden of service. Jazriel was made to bring pleasure and solace. That there was such great love between them was wonderful and unexpected. And under threat from Jazriel's mood swings and dramatic gestures which were increasingly bordering on the suicidal.

Jazriel's eyes darkened to a furious black, he paced the room like a caged panther. Should he risk all by showing his anger with the Prince? Hell, yes, what had he got to lose!

"Nothing has changed?" he growled. "I have changed. I have been out in the world, surviving for centuries among humans, not locked away in this frigid museum to lost memories of power and triumph."

He paused from his pacing to fix his gaze directly into Azrar's anger darkening emerald eyes. "But to you I am still just sha'ref. I have no use beyond my services in this bedroom."

Azrar was now seething with the volatile anger that Jazriel knew he should not have provoked, but he was beyond caring for consequences.

"Sha'ref? How dare you throw that insulting term at me! I have never thought of you like that. I despised the decadent ways of the southern Dark Kind nobles. When I took you from the court of Prince Tevan, it was to help you escape that life."

The Prince took Jazriel's face firmly in his strong warrior's hands and kissed him, his whole being electric with powerful, conflicting emotion. "I love you Jaz, but why can't you ever understand? You are a commoner. You have not been created with the complex skills for statecraft and diplomacy as I have. You have…"

"I know too well the skills I was created with," Jazriel interrupted bitterly, pulling away from the Prince and throwing back the wolf pelt cloak and yanking aside his tunic to expose recent fang scars on his neck and shoulders, not fully healed. "But clearly something went badly wrong in my making. I am the aberration, the sha'ref who wants more from my life and if I cannot have it here…then…" Jazriel did not finish his words, let them trail off, a futile waste of his breath. The threat to leave was pointless. A weapon with no edge. Azrar would not try to stop him, the inbuilt war lord arrogance made the Jendar too proud to plead with Jazriel and more importantly, too proud to change anything about their relationship. There was nothing more to be said or done.

Head down and silent Jazriel stood for a moment, as he gathered the tattered remains of his self control, of his dignity. Then he smiled, dazzling, bewitching as ever, his turquoise eyes gleaming with seductive allure. The old ability to switch on the charm was something he would never lose. In this warrior stronghold, cut off from the outside world by the iron fist of another long winter, it was all he had. "We should not fight like this, my Prince," he murmured his voice low, in a silken panther-like purr. "You are right, I am bloody cold from sitting on that parapet. I can think of far better ways to get warm, then this foolish arguing!"

Azrar gave a low groan of desire. He reached out with one hand towards Jazriel, but he had moved just out of reach, in a deliberate and tantalising action. Zaard! Azrar wanted him! Now! When it came to Jazriel, powerful forces controlled the Prince, they overwhelmed him, made him helpless, bound him by the intensity of his desire. He followed Jazriel in silence to the vast raised bed, piled high with luxurious furs and velvet covers.

Hastily, the Prince threw off his wolf pelt cloak. Azrar would never admit, except to himself, that it was Jazriel who really held the reins of power between them.

He always had.

Chapter Ten

Nemesis Foundation Headquarters, Berne, Switzerland.

Gabrielle stood, statue-still and anxious at the foot of the steps of the Nemesis Foundation, Parrish's headquarters. Nemesis? What a pretentious doom-laden name for a company run by bunch of computer geeks. Rich and successful though they may be, that was all this company did. Invent things no-one realised they couldn't live without.

But one of its founders gave her the creeps, made her unaccountably nervous; Professor Jay Parrish, the living skeleton. Gathering her courage, she looked up at the sky. Icy angel's kisses touched her cheeks and eyelashes as the last snowflakes of the retreating winter began to fall from a sky the colour of unburnished pewter. She inclined her head slightly to one side as if she could hear the cheering up in the alpine villages, another lucrative week of skiing was underway.

'Maybe,' she thought with a wistful sigh, 'I should jump on the nearest train and escape to the mountains. Sweet-talk my way into a chalet for the Easter break.' Her mind wandered to imagining hard-muscled, tanned Swiss ski instructors with impossibly white teeth. 'Mm, now, that would be fun.' An appointment to see the deeply unpleasant Professor Parrish was anything but!

Why had she come here alone? She missed Hillary's presence, his quiet strength, his devotion to her and the team. She had no idea what reception she would receive within the impressively tall tower of black glass and white concrete, Parrish was an oddball who held outlandish views, a heretic in archaeological circles. Gabrielle knew she ought to like that, being one who never towed any establishment line, but some strange, visceral instinct made her loathe a man she did not know. They had met briefly only once at a tedious conference on Balkan pre-history that Hills had dragged her along to. During a lunch break, Parrish's wheelchair had bumped into her leg, hard enough to leave a bruise that lingered for months. Instinctively, being British, Gabrielle had apologised. He was a disabled old man after all! Even after three years had passed since that briefest of encounters, she shuddered at the strange, piercing stare Parrish had given her, needlessly hostile, paranoid, questioning.

Her current disquiet had even spread to the building that housed him, she was convinced the tower excluded a baleful menace. "Bloody hell," she cursed her own skittish thoughts, "what is so scary about a building full of secretaries and computer nerds?" She watched a grim-faced young woman stride past her into the building, her hair pulled back in a painfully tight bun, an eighties' power suit with huge shoulder pads clad her gym-toned frame. The woman spoke animatedly and loudly to herself in curt French, courtesy of the mobile phone clipped to her ear. "Now *that* is scary!" laughed Gabrielle. Feeling foolish for her nervousness.

Before Gabrielle could reluctantly ascend the pretentious steps made from over-the-top white marble inlaid with granite, she felt a firm but not aggressive hand on her arm. She whipped her head around to see a small, thin, clergyman of soulful Latino appearance. Middle-aged with dark, silver brindled hair and kind, large brown eyes. A priest was the last person she would expect at this subsidary site of Nemesis' legendary rapacious greed.

"Miss Railton, I implore you. Do not keep your appointment with the Professor." He pleaded with her in a quiet, pleasant tone, his English perfect but with a slight Spanish accent. There was an unsettling flicker of real anxiety in his eyes as he continued, "I can give you more answers then anyone in this soul-less place. And I swear it will be the truth."

Gabrielle's green-gold eyes widened with astonishment, how did this quiet-spoken little priest know her name and her business in Switzerland? It was such a bizarre encounter, for once she was lost for words. She gazed back up the steps, at the foyer of the Nemesis building, knowing there were security guards, a whole building full of people there to help her. Should she brush him off, make a dash for the safety of the foyer?

"I can understand your reluctance, Miss Railton," the man continued, his voice calm and reasonable. "I would feel the same in your place."

"Tell me what you want," Gabrielle demanded, "If it is so urgent, you can talk to me here."

The priest looked up at the building. Again that flicker of anxiety crossed his dark eyes, feeding Gabrielle's own inexplicable concerns, but curiosity began to override her suspicions. And in all honesty, finding out what the man wanted to tell her was a more appealing prospect then an audience with Parrish.

The clergyman smiled, a gentle, compassionate smile bereft of any sign of guile or madness. "Let me make it easier for you, Miss Railton. I have a car waiting. In five minutes we can be at a delightful coffee house in central Berne. Hear me out, then if you wish, I will bring you straight back to these steps."

He indicated an ordinary small car, no hooded gang of kidnappers, no suspicious van with blackened windows. Gabrielle walked up to it, glanced inside. Just a small blue car with discarded sweet wrappers on the seats and floor, a big dent in the back bumper. It looked harmless. Perhaps more harmless then the mysterious priest! She nodded assent. What the hell. Could coffee and cake with a clergyman, even a seriously deluded one, be worse than enduring an interview with Jay Parrish? She opened the door and slipped into the passenger seat. "Let's go."

A short journey lasting under fifteen minutes but with each mile a leaden weight seemed to lift and disappear from her shoulders. By the time she had settled in a coffee house with a steaming, tall glass of hot raspberry juice laced with kirsch and a generous slab of chocolate cake before her, all thoughts of Nemesis and her meeting with Parrish had evaporated.

Though the priest was a complete stranger and had introduced an element of mystery to her life, Gabrielle felt comfortable in his company, there was something gentle and trustworthy about the man. It had nothing to do with his dog-collar, any serial killer could plonk one of those on, it came from within, the goodness of his soul shone out of his dark brown eyes. And he could certainly eat! Their discussion was put on hold for another few tantalising minutes as he tucked into another large slice of rich Sacher torte.

He pushed the empty plate back with a sigh of satisfaction, before becoming serious again, "My name is Cardinal Alejandro Reyes and I represent a highly secretive but totally benign organisation dedicated to protecting the future of this planet."

"Right," Gabrielle said, her heart sinking. A nutter! She had made a serious error of judgement here. She remained calm, she was safe in a public place full of people. Taking a deep breath as her disquiet deepened, she quipped, "Of course you do, what else is there to do but save the earth?"

She rose abruptly to leave, gathering up her rucksack and coat but an element of curiosity remained. How had he known so much about her movements? "Exactly what has this to do with Nemesis? And more important, with me?" she demanded, placing both hands, challengingly, on the table.

"Everything. I have a complex story to relate, one that stretches back in time and will carry on into an uncertain and perilous future."

For once, Gabrielle was unsure what to do. Her whole world spun on an axis of weirdness. Sensible, academic Gaby Railton would walk out without another word to this obviously tragically deranged individual. Adventurous, curious Gaby Railton wanted to hear what he had to say. She sat down again. "You have exactly five minutes, Cardinal, to convince me I'm not wasting my time."

Reyes dropped his head, steadying himself for the difficult conversation to come. As he looked up, the glistening of tears welled in his eyes. "Have you never wondered how your mother's car could crash on a clear night with no other traffic in sight?"

Gabrielle's face drained of colour, her fingers curled into tight fists. An accident. That's what her grieving grandparents insisted on calling her mother's death. She had never believed it. Never!

"Your family has many connections to Prince Azrar of Isolann. Did you know that?"

Gabrielle shook her head, she knew her maternal grandmother, Lhalee, was Isolanni by birth, her grandfather Sir Stephen Railton had been the British ambassador to Isolann before his retirement. "What has this to do with my mother's death?" she persisted. Desperate for answers, for the truth.

"Nemesis is a super-corporation. Its communications business is perfectly legitimate, all above board, it makes a great deal of profit. Its three elderly founders, however, have a secret agenda. Nemesis funds are siphoned off in order to track down and destroy an ancient race of creatures that have shared this planet since before recorded history."

"Creatures?" Gabrielle's brain reeled. She took a deep breath, again wondering how quickly she could get away from Reyes.

"They are known as the Dark Kind. I prefer Blood Drinkers. Your grandfather, Steve Railton, befriended one, saved his life. Your paternal grandmother, Khari Devane was raised by the same creature as his ward. We are talking of the Jendar Azrar, Prince of Isolann. A vampire."

"You *are* insane!" Gabrielle stood up abruptly, sending her glass of hot fruit juice flying across the table, staining the white linen tablecloth a vivid shade of crimson. Logic screamed at her to flee this man and his wild story. Her heart screamed even louder to stay, listen and discoverer the truth, however bizarre, however painful.

"How I wish I was, my dear." Reyes sighed, "Please, sit down, let me get you another drink. You deserve to know everything. The truth."

Uncertain, Gabrielle paused, eyeing up the quickest route to the café entrance as a waiter hurried over to clear up the mess. How much could she believe? This seemed beyond the wildest fantasy. Her first instincts about this man were way off kilter, he was a complete nutter. Right off the seriously deluded scale all his plausibility had evaporated at the first mention of blood drinking immortals. She had enough Swiss currency to get her a cab back to her appointment with Nemesis, hopefully Professor Parrish was forgiving of ill-mannered tardiness in the young.

Reyes could read in her eyes her readiness to flee. With a kindly smile he waved the waiter away, said hurriedly, "Please, Miss Railton, I implore you, give me a few more moments. Then you are free to walk away. This should help you decide." He reached into his pocket and produced the gold-mounted brooch of curious black bone stolen from the university. He placed it into her hand.

"Tell me where this comes from, Miss Railton. What creature on this planet has bone like this?"

Gabrielle's mind reeled; of all the thieves she imagined, the likelihood of a Catholic priest did not make the shortlist. With a shaking hand she put the gold-bound relic on the table. An enigmatic jet mystery, it lay untouched on the once pristine white linen, now stained with vivid red juice.

"I will tell you about the creatures who have black bones and why I had to remove this ancient thing before your scientists could analysis it," Reyes continued in a gentle voice, and for the next half an hour she learned about the Dark Kind and her own ancestors' involvement with the terrifying creatures. She discovered Professor Parrish and some like-minded minions had founded Nemesis to seek out and destroy the blood drinkers. She learnt that paradoxically this was 'A Bad Thing'. That ancient prophesies foretold the future of the planet depended on at least one Dark Kind, maybe many, surviving to help humanity and protect all life against a terrible mutual enemy.

"Let me have it all, your eminence," Gabrielle challenged, "I am sure you are about to add where the unicorns, werewolves and fairies fit in?"

Reyes smiled sadly, how could anyone be expected to believe the truth about the Dark Kind unless they had experienced the vile creatures at first hand? As he had, under protest and with such great reluctance throughout the long years. His duty was to protect and preserve them with the same devotion, the same energy as he loathed them.

"I'm sorry, my dear. There are no unicorns and werewolves. Just the beautiful Arabian Oryx and sad little babies born with too much hair."

"So I can believe in fairies?" Gabrielle quipped without a trace of humour.

Reyes smiled again, this time with a flicker of warmth. "Yes, it might be wise to carry on believing in fairies." He liked this girl, she was feisty and courageous. She would need to be.

"Even if I take all this baloney as truth, what has it got to do with my mother's death?" Gabrielle's anger began to rise again. Her mind already raced with confusion, her legs felt weak as the entire foundation of a lifetime's beliefs had been blown away. She had just been told vampires stalked the earth and her own family had helped them survive.

"It was a botched attempt to force your grandfather's hand, to kidnap his daughter, hold her hostage. They thought he could use his position of trust to get some of their agents close to the Prince. To kill the vampire lord and steal his library."

"She was killed over a lot of old books?" Gabrielle was outraged. "I don't believe it! That is insane! "

"It was probably an accident. Her death destroyed any chance of the plan succeeding. No human life is worth sacrificing, even for a wondrous treasure house of ancient knowledge. But Jay Parrish is a ruthless, corrupted and obsessed individual. He would stop at nothing to acquire the library, in his belief the greatest treasure in the modern world." Reyes paused, placed his hand over Gabrielle's.

"And now Parrish knows about you, Miss Railton. Our fear is that he may try to use you in his ongoing game plan. He will never relinquish his hunger for the library. Your paternal grandmother is still alive, she is the closest any human has ever been to the Prince, she was his beloved ward. We must protect you."

Gabrielle could take no more! Forget damn vampires, Parrish was an evil bastard! She ran from the coffee house, near blind from her tears. Evil, evil bastard. She had always had this instinctive loathing for him, now she knew why. She had never hated anyone in her life but now she hated the founder of Nemesis and his murderous minions with a fury that consumed all sense and reason.

Nemesis had killed her mother. Part of her had always believed the road crash was no accident. What of the mystery of her father's disappearance? And now they were after her as well? As her Gran had warned, her life was in danger. Really in danger! She sank to her knees and voided the entire contents of her coffee house meal onto the pristine, fresh-fallen snow. Felt strong, comforting arms around her shoulders. "It's alright, Gabrielle. You are not alone. Nemesis is a powerful organisation but so is mine. You will be protected."

"Protected? Like my mum?" she managed to say bitterly through her sobs and retching, "Where were you pious bastards when Amela Railton needed your protection?"

Reyes sighed, what answer could offer comfort? "We underestimated one twisted individual. It will not happen again." Cannot happen again, he prayed, the stakes were too high to lose another weapon in the planet's defences.

He helped her to her feet and supporting her with an arm around her shoulders walked her back to his car.

As they drove slowly, in silence, through the slush-thick streets, Gabrielle's head rested on the window, watching the thickening fall of snowflakes, no longer enchanted by their fragile and transient beauty. They were a hindrance, delaying her return to the sanctuary of her hotel room. Keeping her with Reyes, this quiet-spoken Catholic priest - if that was truly what he was. She doubted it. How could a seemingly humane, peace-loving churchman have anything to do with be-fanged creatures that drank human blood?

Taking her rucksack from him, she curtly refused his offer of an escort to her hotel room. His help? She didn't need it. What use had his protection been for her mother? Had they been able to discover the whereabouts of her father, if he still lived? Alone and with the door of her room locked, Gabrielle ran herself a deep bath to wash away the stream of flowing tears from her face. Vampires? A wondrous library full of precious books? She didn't believe any of it. But she did believe Parrish and his cronies did. Believed it enough to kill.

Chapter Eleven

Nemesis Headquarters, Geneva

"So where is she?" The man's voice was tremulous with anger at enduring another long and painful journey made in vain. Dragged off to Switzerland on a fool's errand!

Raker paced the floor, the slight but sharp onset of arthritis the only indication of increasing age and infirmity. He was otherwise fit, stood upright with unbowed military bearing and mentally his mind was as sharp as a gin trap. As was that of Professor Jay Parrish his co-founder of the now powerful Nemesis Corporation, a telecommunications monster that had spread its spider web of influence around the world. Its threads tenuous yet as strong and entrapping as gossamer. And as deadly. Global commerce, the security of entire nations, all depended on Nemesis and its ever-evolving products.

Time had been less bountiful to the American academic. Confined to a wheelchair or bed, permanently attached to oxygen and nutrition tubes, Parrish's wizened, wasted body looked less then alive. Bone-thin, grey-toned and desiccated like a re-animated Egyptian mummy, only his pale grey eyes gleamed with life and fervour. Now they shone with anger to match Raker's. Where indeed was Gabrielle Railton?

"I must assume our guest has been waylaid by our enemies. The same traitorous dogs who stole the Cornish finds." Parrish ventured, incensed at being out-manoeuvred again. He guessed that damn, so called priest, Reyes, was involved. The same little cleric who had visited him at the New England Sanatorium when Parrish had returned from the Upper Balkans ranting about castles filled with treasure, guarded by a Vampire Prince. To the world, it was his madness talking, but it was all true. Parrish was convinced this Reyes was not human nor was he Dark Kind, though what he was remained unknown. It was almost irrelevant, Reyes' low-key organisation was constantly thwarting the ambitions of the powerful corporation. Whenever Nemesis traced the whereabouts of a vampire, Reyes and his dog-collar wearing cronies were one step ahead. This had to end!

"Raker, I am disappointed with you. With all Nemesis's money and the world's finest surveillance equipment, your department cannot keep track of the collaborators and their activities."

The old fossil was right. Nemesis had failed spectacularly again. Raker's anger was directed at himself as much as anything else. That archaeologist, Gabrielle Railton was somehow connected, why else would the enigmatic Reyes be involved? There was a tenuous but important link to the war time Spook Squad through her grandfather Sir Stephen Railton, the British ambassador to Isolann. A link that could possibly lead to the golden-eyed witch, Khari Devane. Elderly though she must be, Khari Devane could probably still read minds, could still endanger every Nemesis operation. She must be found and taken out of the equation - permanently.

Parrish watched his fellow Nemesis founder march out, straight backed and energetic, ever the military man. His mind seethed with envy and regret, the strongest emotions that plagued Parrish now. Raker was younger, he had his health despite the swift-flying years that had left them both wealthy and influential yet unfulfilled. Nothing had been achieved in exposing the Dark Kind to the world, confirming their belief that powerful forces were at work to protect them, shield them from exposure.

What would it take for someone in authority to believe him? Did they have to get as close as he did? To be within a heartbeat of having his throat ripped out by savage scimitar fangs. Did they have to wake up screaming in terror, haunted by memories of that monster, Azrar?

One thing had fuelled this quest, his lifetime's mission. To liberate a treasure house of human knowledge, Azrar's library. A vast and astonishing collection of unknown and precious ancient texts, reaching back to the earliest days of mankind's recorded history. Parrish wanted the library not as an act of greed or self-aggrandisement, it belonged to all humanity. Not locked away in the mountain lair of a cursed vampire!

Parrish had accepted that the collection's survival was due to the indifferent stewardship of the prince. So indifferent to its contents, the warlord could easily destroy a treasure beyond any price purely on a whim, in a fit of his legendary volatile temper. Parrish gripped the side of his wheelchair in impotent rage. The library must be secured for the world! He had been there, held in his hand a lost gospel written in Christ's lifetime; the surrender and plea for clemency penned by Alexander the Great himself to the Vampire King Dezarn; a clay stele from an unknown civilisation pre-dating Ur and Sumer. So many marvels, so much more to discover, all for the benefit of mankind. And all of it inaccessible because of that monster!

The Professor had once been prepared to sell his soul to gain possession of such wonders. The Prince held information that could change all written history. Now Parrish would gladly re-mortgage his soul just to spend one day in that treasure house of lost knowledge. He couldn't die, wouldn't die till all hope of seeing it again had gone. That it was already too late was something he refused to consider. That his life depended on oxygen machines and heart monitors, that he was too old and frail to travel to Isolann was pushed from his thoughts. Completely.

He had even considered pleading for forgiveness from the vampire, to beg Azrar to let him study the ancient books, to hold the precious manuscripts and papyrus scrolls of mind-numbing antiquity, all of them miraculously preserved in pristine condition in the Jendar's remote mountain lair.

Insanity to dwell on this of course. Parrish had gloated as Azrar fell, badly wounded beneath his dying horse, mown down in a hail of Nazi bullets. He had openly taunted the stricken vampire. And worse had happened since then. Over-zealous Nemesis agents had killed Amela, the daughter of Azrar's most trusted human friend, Sir Stephen Railton. The Prince would never forgive Parrish and the Nemesis organisation for that.

It was clear any progress in stripping Azrar of his realm, his library, his life, must fall to the next generation, to Parrish's great nephew, Freddie Hain. A man who had no interest in the past. Less then no interest - open contempt!

Parrish's bony hands gripped the side of the wheelchair that confined him. No! He did not deserve the prize! It was his, Professor Jay Parrish by rights! He was the one who had sacrificed his entire life to pursuing one goal, narrowly escaping death from Azrar's fangs, suffering incarceration in a lunatic asylum and thrown into a British jail under threat of execution as a traitor. He who had to endure the ridicule of his fellow academics. All this hardship and grief to have some snot–faced computer nerd take over Nemesis? Never! Parrish refused to die. Refused to turn his back on his quest. The day he gave up trying was the day he gave his last breath. If willpower alone could keep him alive, he could live forever!

Chapter Twelve

Gabrielle dumped her rucksack on her bed, accidentally sending her sleeping ginger cat off in a tail-flicking feline huff. Home. How strange it felt after her trip to Switzerland. Superficially nothing had changed. Her flat was the same chaotic, over–crowded home she had left four days ago. Her elderly neighbour had collected her mail, fed the cat and watered the plants. But outside the whole world was becoming a stranger to her.

She made herself a mug of tea, old Mrs Jones had thoughtfully left her a fresh carton of milk. Grabbing a whole packet of custard creams, she perched on the pile of comfy old cushions on her wide window seat and looked out at the busy street beyond. Daylight. An aqueous spring sun warmed the brave heads of daffodils and crocus tricked into an early appearance by the recent freak heat wave. Such was an English spring, they could be plummeted back into an arctic blast at any time. That's what she felt like now, a daffodil born of warmth and sunlight suddenly plunged into a domain of ice and snow.

Damn that little priest! Reyes had stolen all certainty from her life, dragging her into a shadowy world of fanged night-dwelling monsters, and sinister organisations. Just what she was going to do with herself from now on was a question she could not answer. To return to her old life on campus and going on digs? Her hand instinctively went to the gold dragon talisman around her neck, the jewellery stolen from the Cornish horde.

Reyes said it belonged to her, that she alone could wear it. She alone should protect it. This made no sense. Why was an ornate scrap of gold so important? The enigmatic Spanish cleric had refused to tell any more secrets. Perhaps that vile Professor Parrish could tell her, but he was a major part of the danger she now faced. Parrish was the founder of Nemesis, a communications corporation secretly dedicated to destroying the Dark Kind, the vampires. And as Reyes was at pains to point out at every opportunity, bizarrely, this was a bad thing.

Gabrielle's fingers trembled as she reached for the clasp, she had not taken the amulet off since leaving Switzerland, the thought of it leaving her neck and being examined by another person felt strangely uncomfortable, as if she was handing over part of her soul. What a fanciful idiot she was becoming! It was only a delicate piece of gold. Jewellery! Yet her strong emotional connection to the amulet was impossible for her to explain. She recalled her conversation with Reyes as he accompanied her home on the flight back to Britain. "Long ago, there were once many thousands of such pieces, though few as beautifully made in pure gold as this one." Reyes had murmured as he had gazed in wonder at the amulet.

"Most were little more then crudely carved wood, the wealthier owners had theirs painted gold. But all had the same symbolism, a sign of the wearer's loyalty to the Vampire King Dezarn, Dark Kind ruler of the Three Kingdoms. At his death most talismans were destroyed, wearing them was a death sentence to any of his foolishly loyal subjects. Those of precious metal were hastily recycled, melted and re-crafted as crucifixes."

"Then, it is extraordinary this one survived." Gabrielle had ventured, her curiosity about the amulet's origin growing, it was far older then she could have imagined. And how had it come to be worn by a Cornishman buried on a cliff in Britain? The ancient legends of the Vampire Kings that Reyes spoke of were believed to have originated from the vast steppes of ancient Eurasia and the Upper Balkans. None from Cornwall, or anywhere in the British Isles.

"Why would any human want to stay loyal to the memory of a dead vampire?" She had then asked, puzzled at such skewed morality.

"Indeed," Reyes had continued, carefully handing it back to the young woman. "But many courageous, if not misguided, citizens of Altar did." Reyes had opened his briefcase and showed her a photo of a scrap of decaying, torn parchment. The barely decipherable words were in Latin. Reyes knew the young woman was comfortable and familiar with most classic ancient languages but still he read out the poem's English translation;

> *Think you wise, People of Altar*
> *When you gave up your King to his death?*
> *Wise to lose centuries of peace for your children*
> *Sheltered beneath the golden dragon's wings?*

'The Heretic's Lament,' Reyes had murmured as he passed the image of the carefully preserved scrap of ancient parchment to Gabrielle. She had read the words for herself, struggling with the ancient tongue. Reyes explaining they were written by an unknown, incredibly brave but suicidal or foolish person in the turbulent and bloody years following the fall of King Dezarn. The Dark Kind ruler of the Three Kingdoms. Reyes spoke of a legend, of one unseen man nailing the poem to the doors of Bishop Alaric's Cathedral, built on the site of Dezarn's marble palace which had been razed to the ground.

The poem was torn down and destroyed but reappeared the next night and every night for a month. Despite a heavy presence of Alaric's troops, so the story went, no one ever saw who posted the protests. It was a miracle, a dark miracle attributed to the cursed followers of the Vampire King. But accursed as it's highly educated, mystery writer was, his words were prophetic. Svolenia's history was a sorry catalogue of its people's suffering from many conquests and endless draining wars worsened by a succession of weak leaders. A fate that continued into this century.

"Why do you say I have been entrusted with the pendant?" Gabrielle had questioned. "What is so special about me?"

"Maybe another legend, another prophesy, my dear child," Reyes had replied, his eyes gentle and concerned for her distress. "A mystery, but one we will solve together, you have my word."

An infuriatingly enigmatic reply, but it was all she had coaxed out of the priest. Reyes had left her at the airport, lightly kissing her hand in an old fashioned gesture and melting away like a ghost into the crowds.

The whole visit to Switzerland felt unreal and dreamlike now she was back in her familiar and pleasingly mundane surroundings. One thing was certain, she could not return to her old life wearing the stolen talisman. A complex mixture of guilt, apprehension and curiosity had plagued her since Reyes had carefully and reverentially fastened it on her neck as if bestowing an honour. Some honour! It was one that could get her a criminal record and a ruined career! Gabrielle's initial sensation, that the talisman had called to her across oceans of time had changed. Now there was something deeply unsettling about the amulet; it gave out a curious aura, a deepening awareness of foreboding and dread. With a sigh of relief, she removed it from her neck and hid it in a small trinket box sent as her 18th birthday gift from her Gran. The box was of a curious grey precious metal, set with uncut rubies and Baltic amber. The lid was adorned with a fierce, snarling dragon's head, an appropriate container for the talisman. As if it was always meant to be. Maybe by hiding it away, she could also hide all this strangeness, return to her old carefree life as if she had never encountered the Spanish priest, or whatever the hell he was.

Who was she kidding? Not herself. She had scanned every crowd looking for hostile faces since leaving Europe. Tonight, when the sun had gone, she would be nervously looking out for strange-eyed, beautiful young people in the shadows. Vampires! But she was not to be afraid of these deadly creatures, for according to Reyes the Dark Kind would never harm her. They killed only male prey. It was goons from Nemesis, all very human, who might endanger her. Great! In a matter of a few days, her life had become a mad zone, detached from reality. Up till now, her only brush with life's darker side had been buying a dodgy M.O.T at great expense for her old Ford Crappie car. Purchasing the forged document needed to run her old banger on the road legally left her wracked with guilt. It was almost a relief when the Capri had seized up completely and permanently the next day. Crime didn't pay!

Gabrielle realised, too, that she would have to lie to Hillary. The truth was just too fantastic.

Chapter Thirteen

Jendar Azrar's Stronghold, Isolann

At last, the feeble and nervous season that was spring in Isolann prevailed over the stubborn and determined winter. Every attempt at warmth and thaw had been foiled by another onslaught of bitter high winds and heavy snow. Now the white landscape was finally gone, a brief, brilliant riot of sweet scented flowers carpeted the open plains to the south. Streams and rivers burst their banks, tumbling full of crystal-clear melted snow water heading to top up the icy depths of Lake Beral, the eerie, inland sea to the south of the Principality.

The thaw also brought an increasing threat of unwelcome visitors to Isolann. Intrepid and earnest adventurers from all over the outside world, eager to explore this secretive and unique land were arriving with increasing numbers every spring. They provided plentiful and fine hunting for the two resident Dark Kind, and though some visitors did not return home after unfortunate 'climbing accidents', most were allowed to live and go back to their homes with tales of a largely uninhabited, bleak landscape of little interest.

That none wanted to return to Isolann was due to an elaborate plan devised by the Prince. With the willing and amused co-operation of his plain land dwelling nomads, the Jendar had created a charade to deter any travellers. He had instructed his people to intercept any knapsack-wearing intruder and offer them nothing but grudging hospitality. All the richness and colour of Isolanni nomadic life was to be well hidden. The nomads pretended to be dull–witted, wore drab, filthy clothing and made out they lived in damp, draughty tents stinking of badly tanned hides. They apparently had no music, no fascinating oral history or interesting customs. They worshiped no bizarre gods. But the greatest deterrent was to be their appalling food. The nomads made it clear from the start that to refuse their hospitality was a terrible insult; a starter of raw sheep's eyes, followed by a bowl of cold, rancid and greasy stew of very undercooked sheep's offal soon sent the most intrepid explorer rushing back to the comfort of the nearest outpost of civilisation - Svolenia. Those with a stronger stomach eventually left through boredom.

Infiltrators sent from the rabid clerics of Abhajastan on Isolann's eastern border were given a different reception. They came to preach and foment unrest amongst the Isolanni. Azrar was determined none of these poisonous enemies would return home alive. If that led to war, so be it. He would not allow Isolann to be destroyed from within. Cruel memories of what happened in King Dezarn's city, Altar, haunted Azrar. While the noble Vampire King and his army were fighting barbarian hordes for the very survival of his human subjects, an early Christian bishop, Alaric, was polluting the minds of the Altari. Dezarn had been brutally killed by his own people. Azrar was not afraid to die in battle against any enemy, but to lose his life to the humans he'd dedicated his entire existence to protecting, was beyond bearing.

Azrar found his companion at his own favourite place in the Keep, the highest point on the towering battlements. Like him, Jazriel also loved to feel the sharp winds sting against his face and ripping through his iridescent, blue-black hair.

"The captain of one my border patrols has brought us gifts. Four infiltrators from our new eastern enemies. Fine, healthy young males, full of hate and spite. We will hunt well tomorrow night."

Jazriel turned sharply at the sound of his high-born lover's voice and bowed his head low in welcome. He adored the sound of the Prince's harsh, wolf growl, stripped of the disguising velvet tone he used to address humans. This was welcome news; humans to hunt at last! Jazriel had never endured such a long period without feeding, hunger had gnawed at him throughout the cruel and unrelenting winter. Spring was finally here, and with it, the welcome excitement of killing strong, healthy prey to renew his life force. Perhaps fresh blood coursing through his being would drive away this weakening and pathetic despair that had tormented him through the long winter months. Jazriel was desperate, hoped the blood would cure him, he so hated what he had become. Bitter, petulant, needy and demanding. Not the ideal attributes of a Dark Kind lover to a warlord Prince, and appalling behaviour for one created as sha'ref, one who must be charming, willing and compliant at all times.

Azrar joined him at the battlements and together they gazed across a slumbering landscape, the light from the stars in an unpolluted and clear sky faintly illuminating the dark tangled forests, already burnished and heavy with spring foliage. A lone wolf called. Azrar threw back his head and howled across the valley in answer, the eerie, deep and resonating cry of the Dark Kind. Above the stronghold and surrounding valley, the hulking presence of the snow-topped, black granite Arpalathians glowered, a scene unchanged for countless millennia.

Yet changes were there for the two Dark Kind to see. Above them, flying silently through the diamond-studded panorama, the clever little apes that had overrun their world had sent up satellites to orbit high above the ancient land of secrets and shadows. The very air above Isolann buzzed with humanity's noisy barrage of radio waves. This land cherished being remote and self-contained, but it was increasingly hard to shut out the strident clamour of progress that tried to intrude from the rest of the world.

But it was a world Jazriel missed, one he had learnt how to function and survive in, if only he could curb his reckless nature and his love of adventures with humans. He reached into his pocket to retrieve a slim platinum case, brought out and lit another cigarette. He took a long drag then turned to look at the Prince. There was one thing that hadn't changed; the sight of Azrar made his heart hammer with desire, as it had the first time they had met in India, when Azrar had arrived in Prince Tevan's white and gold, marble courtyard, riding a proud black stallion.

The Prince had looked magnificent in his matte black armour and long wolf skin cloak, the barbaric splendour of his broadsword in its ornate scabbard slung across his back. There was nothing to compare among the decadent and indolent Dark Kind nobility of India, believing they were safe from danger, protected by the Himalayas. When humanity's uprising against their vampire rulers gathered momentum, they had been the first to be wiped out.

Jazriel's heart grew heavy with sorrow and love. There could be no place for the Prince beyond Isolann. Azrar needed a sword in his hand, needed to ride to battle on his high stepping war horse. The modern world would always encroach, closer and closer and with it, Azrar's doom. To survive, the Prince of Isolann needed time to turn backwards.

Jazriel shivered as if some baleful dark wings had brushed past his soul. As a commoner he was forbidden to initiate touching Azrar, all moves towards intimacy had to come from the Prince. Jazriel yearned to defy the Dark Kind's rigid caste system, to take the sepulchral pale face of the being he loved in his hands, to let him know all the dammed-up emotion welling to breaking point within Jazriel's heart, but he could not. Dared not.

So he lit another cigarette and turned his head to watch the night hawks hunting on silent wings through the forest canopy. Deep within him, his heart prepared to mourn. Again.

On his throne as the prisoners were led before him, Azrar sat with the statue-like stillness of his kind, suppressing a low growl of hunger and anticipation. As they neared the Prince of Isolann, the men's dark eyes flashed with defiance and hatred, turning to disbelief and shock as they realised their despised enemy was not human. They had been raised on childhood horror stories of the Demon of Isolann, as were all living in the dark shadow of the Arpalathians. That these ludicrous folk tales believed only fit for feeble–minded old women were based on reality was the stuff of nightmares, enough to turn a man's mind to insanity.

Yet here was the creature before them, not myth but a flesh and blood, black-clad monster, his youthful sharp-planed yet handsome face lit by shimmering green opalescent eyes. In-human eyes without pity or remorse but a creature with an incisive, predatory intelligence.

"Demon! Your bloody rule is over, death to the Unbeliever tyrant!" screamed one of the braver prisoners stepping forward, somehow finding the courage to flaunt his defiance of the Prince. He finished his tirade by spitting towards the Prince's face. Azrar's stern features broke into a slow smile, predatory and cold. He wanted this one! In the glorious past, before his Keep was infested with humans serving him, Azrar would have torn open and drank this human, there and then, before releasing the others for his warriors to hunt and kill. Nothing like knowing their fate to make the remaining survivors run fast and fight back hard in a futile attempt to live! In a stronghold teeming with his human retinue, discretion must now rule.

Azrar's whole being was vibrant with anticipation. Tonight he and Jazriel would hunt well and afterwards, their bodies electric with renewed energy, they would make love with the passion, fire and ferocity of their Kind, an extreme and protracted onslaught engaging all their sharp senses; until they collapsed in each others arms, exhausted and sated.

But this time it had to be different. Azrar had seen the future in his lover's eyes. The Prince knew he soon faced a life alone once more. Next time they made love it must not be for the pursuit of physical pleasure alone. Nor would it be the rare and beautiful time when in the tumultuous merging of bodies, their disparate souls only briefly touched. No, Azrar wanted, needed, so much more. Their spirits must soar and merge as one, so that when they separated they would be transformed, would be a part of each other, the one spirit forever dwelling in the other. Azrar had felt an icy shadow sweep across his heart, a cold that owed nothing to the departing winter, but seemed instead to be a chilling prophesy of his impending death. With Jazriel living on unnatural, stolen time, Azrar needed to give him some extra inner strength. Just in case.

His attention snapped back to the prisoners, the rich source of energy that he would need for this wild and dangerous idea to work.

"I am no tyrant, and I have no idea what an Unbeliever is in the context of Isolann." The alien timbre of his voice added to the prisoners' rising terror. So much so, they did not take in that he spoke their own language fluently.

"I have no interest in the beliefs of my people, that is their own business, but I do cherish their loyalty. This precious thing you have tried to undermine and destroy. And for this crime you will be released into my forests."

The prisoners were mentally prepared for martyrdom from the moment they had crossed from their sacred homeland into this infidel hinterland, the despised and accursed land of secrets and shadows. They were to be freed, made to run for home like cowards? Like women?

"No!" one cried, outraged. "This is not the honourable fate that awaits us! We are Imadeen! The living flames of the one god, Tahjr–the Cleansing Fire. We, his disciples, his children will incinerate all the filth polluting his creation, burn away all Western decadence and corruption. Scorch away all devil worship from the people of Isolann.

Azrar had heard enough from these invading fanatics. The people of Isolann had enjoyed many centuries without fear of hostility from Abhajastan. These fools were spoiling for a war, for bloodshed. That was something he could oblige them with. Whether his once loyal and valiant people had the same resolve was another matter.

Lomak, his face impassive, unreadable, watched as the struggling and cursing prisoners were led away. Who were these dark skinned men from the east? What was the source of so much courage? Knowing what they faced, they had willingly walked hundreds of miles deep into a strange, hostile land, armed only with their conviction. Surely they must have known once they were brought before the ruler of Isolann that they were doomed? Yet none had begged for mercy for their lives, one had openly spat at the Prince. Lomak was fascinated by the prisoners, they had a deep-held faith, one that gave them strength. He wanted to know more about these men and their beliefs, before it was too late, before Azrar and his Blood Drinker plaything ripped out their throats.

Chapter Fourteen

London

Freddie Hain sat back hard against his chair, unable to stop his hands from shaking. He swivelled the high backed white leather chair around and gazed bleakly across the London landscape, the eclectic mixture of old and new buildings soaked by an equal amount of squally rain. But no amount of bad weather could compare to the chill Hain felt in his heart. He stood up, on unsteady legs, and moved away from the data banks accumulating on his desk, unable to look at them any more. The facts had poisoned his life, threatened his sanity.

Could it be? Could the crazy obsession of those demented old men, the collective madness they had harboured since the Second World War, truly be based in reality? The police reports of strange deaths throughout Europe, Russia and Asia seemed to confirm it. By collating the data of young human males found with throat wounds and drained of blood, he believed he could track the movements of a least three separate murderers operating in Europe and Eurasia over a long period. Maniacal humans? A cult perhaps? That was the answer he wanted to believe in. Needed to believe in. But there was not one scrap of forensic evidence on any victim; no fingerprints, nothing to link a human aggressor to these horrible murders. No human DNA traces. No DNA from any unknown source. The only conclusion was that Parrish, Raker and Banks had indeed encountered the Dark Kind. Vampires.

No one had brought all the information together and found a pattern before, it had been impossible until the highly evolved computers he'd had designed for the Nemesis corporation were set to the task. Suddenly the trappings of his success, the big bank balance, the lavish lifestyle, all felt fragile, threatened by this startling and unsettling new reality. One he desperately wanted to be false. How could he accept that somewhere, lurking in dark shadows, were ferocious creatures that had survived for countless centuries by tearing out human throats?

Hain's head leant on the cold glass of his vast, luxury office on the 30th floor of Nemesis London headquarters and the obsession that drove his uncle began to take its poisonous root in his own soul. Hain turned and looked across the pristine chrome and white, orderly perfection of his office. Brightly lit, spotlessly clean and state of the art modern. This was the centre of his world, where he was the master of his own fate, his own fortune. He did not want to live in an uncertain and strange world where dark and deadly creatures from ancient myth and legend lurked. The old men wanted these beings, these vampires to be destroyed. Wiped off the face of the earth. Humans were the superior race on Earth, there must be nothing higher in the food chain!

Hain spent the entire day trying to get his head around the mind-blowing facts. To come to terms with a new world order where the ground beneath his feet could no longer be trusted to be solid or the sullen sky to be a leaden shade of grey. Nothing was certain anymore. He finally came to the conclusion the old men were right, these Dark Kind murderers must be destroyed.

But not straight away. His uncle had told him the creatures, though mortal, never aged beyond some fixed point in their youth. Think of the possibilities! Hain had never believed the silly old fool, but what if they could regenerate after serious injury? Were stronger and faster then humans? His mind reeled. How could those old men not see the prize within their grasp? The founders of Nemesis were redundant relics of an age long gone, overdue for extinction themselves. How could they not know the power, the priceless treasure lying in vampire genes?

Exploiting what made the creatures live so long, recover from terrible injuries, never age beyond a youthful perfection? That was beyond price; controlling that knowledge would make Hain a god among men! To hold the power of curing all humanities illness? To stop people growing old? He would be invincible, ruler of the world!

Hain's excitement was building. He needed more time to plan what to do with this truly world-shattering data. Nothing would ever be the same again if this information got out. History, science, even religion, all that humanity now accepted as fact would need serious revising. Knowledge was power and power was wealth. If anyone held this control it must be him and not the crazy old coots who funded his research and development department within the Nemesis super-corporation. It was too late for them, desperately hanging on to the last strands of life as the fabric of their existence frayed away to nothing. Surviving on hatred and fear and thwarted ambition. Hain was young. He had time. And a greater, more worthwhile vision to surpass the petty vindictive and failed war waged on the vampires by those old fools.

As the hours passed, he began to fantasise wildly, his initial fear totally gone. What if he could extract more then the creatures' longevity and regenerative ability? What if he could affect the way he looked too? All Dark Kind were reputed to be stunningly beautiful. Hain braced himself before looking at his reflection in the shiny chrome of a lamp on his desk. He could not bear mirrors in his presence. He had inherited none of the Parrish genes, was not blessed with the family's height, blond hair, aquiline patrician characteristics. He had drawn the losing ticket in the gene lottery. He was short, overweight, with porcine features and mousy, lank hair. Expensive clothes and top range designer glasses did not enhance his appearance, if anything drew more attention to his failings.

Because he was rich he could buy beautiful women to sleep with, high class courtesans and greedy little cows trying to trap him into a loveless but potentially profitable marriage. But no money could buy their respect, not one looked at him with anything less then scorn and contempt. Bitches! How he hated that look! How he would like to wipe their smirking disdain from their painted faces.

To be forever young and handsome. That was a prize worth diverting Nemesis' funds and resources to his personal use. He would form a crack squad of skilled operatives and find these fanged bastards.

The vampires could no longer hide in the modern world, a world of surveillance, of computers, of tracking satellites. The Dark Kind days, or should it be nights, were coming to an end. And he, Freddie Hain would be the author of their doom! Perhaps that old fart, Uncle Jay could stay alive a little longer, just to see his nephew succeed where he had failed, to watch in decrepit impotence as Hain reaped the rewards of the old man's lifetime of endeavours.

He liked the sound of that. Hain pushed away the offending image of himself in the chrome lamp and returned to the window. It was late afternoon, but the cloud-hidden autumn sun had already begun to set, the low clouds and endless driving rain adding to the premature gloom.

"Enjoy the night, vampires," he murmured "enjoy stealing human lives and drinking our blood while you can. There soon won't be a dark corner of the world where you can hide from me."

Chapter Fifteen

Jendar Azrar's stronghold, Isolann

"Ride with me tonight," Azrar murmured, in a deep, sensuous growl, tracing the elegant curve of Jazriel's spine with the edge of one fang. A careful caress with a fearsome natural weapon, applied too carefully along the golden skin to draw blood. Jazriel turned to face the Prince, blue-green eyes glittering with anticipation.

"Are we hunting? It seems an age since we took down those spirited Abhajastani fanatics." Jazriel's memories of the excitement of the hunt and the delicious reward at its inevitable conclusion triggered renewed hunger. The brief summer had drawn to a close. Despite his confused and ill-thought out plans to leave in spring, Jazriel was still in Isolann, haunted by other memories. Of how discontented, miserable and hungry he'd been during the last snow-bound winter. Trapped again by that interminable season of blizzards and ice. Yet he did not leave. Could not leave. Forget the endless cigarettes, the alcohol and bribing the locals to secretly smuggle in cocaine, all the human vices he relished. He could stop using whenever he wanted. Azrar was his real addiction and nothing could get that powerful narcotic from his veins.

Azrar lay back against the generous pile of velvet and brocade cushions, one eyebrow raised in amusement by the predictability of his companion's ways. Jazriel was always in a hurry, rushing from one sensation to the next. Keeping him in cigarettes, imported at some difficulty from Svolenia was hard but it did not stop Jazriel getting through them at an alarming rate. He also rode the Prince's horses too hard and fast. When he dwelled in the modern world it was speeding about in hard-pressed motor cars. If the Prince had to hear one more time about Jazriel's beloved dark blue Bugatti Atlantic - with its cream, leather upholstery; how Jazriel had reluctantly abandoned it in Nazi occupied Holland when he joined the British secret service during the last world war!

Azrar shrugged in apology. "No hunting tonight, but I have something I want to show you. Get dressed for riding and meet me in the courtyard."

The Prince got up from the bed and leant across to take Jazriel's face firmly in one hand to address him in a stern tone, a severity not reflected in the amused gleam in his emerald eyes. "We have a long ride ahead. For the first time in your life, just grab the nearest thing to wear, or the sun will be over the horizon before we reach our destination!"

Behind the Prince, the captain of his guard swore under his breath and gritted his teeth as a fast-pressed horse cantered up to the Prince's side. It was ridden by the indolent young male who had become their leader's constant companion. Another blood drinker. The captain flinched as the young man leant over and the Prince kissed him on the mouth in greeting. An affront! The Isolanni had not lost his respect for the Prince as a warrior and leader but the companion's continued presence was becoming intolerable to many of the elite inner Keep guard.

As Azrar greeted his lover, he was aware of the captain's open contempt. The Prince considered a punishment for such blatant disrespect but held back. The cause of the human's distaste was not going to be around much longer. Azrar's heart was heavy and sorrowful with awareness that this precious time with Jazriel was nearing an end. Jazriel did not belong here. This harsh land lost in time held little to amuse such a pleasure-loving creature. They loved each other, nothing would ever change that, but Azrar could not leave, he had no choice, he was as much a part of Isolann as the towering Arpalathians themselves. Destiny had welded him to this land, only death would part him from it.

But Jazriel was a free agent, a commoner, a sha'ref with no living clients, so therefore one whose only duty now was to himself to seek out all the pleasures life could offer. Apart from their relationship, there was precious little to keep Jazriel here.

The warlord rode towards Cadera on the pretence of a meeting with one of his nomad tribes. In truth it was a ploy, a gift waited for Jazriel in the settlement that served as Isolann's capital, another expensive trinket to keep him amused. There was a special irony in this latest plaything, however, for it was something that could speed his exit from Isolann and from Azrar's side.

Azrar looked at the sweat soaked sides of Jazriel's horse and shook his head in disapproval. "If you left at the same time as the rest of us, Ferius would not be in such a state."

Jazriel had thrown the reins down onto the tired horse's neck, steering the iron-grey stallion with his heels as he lit up a cigarette. "I couldn't decide what to wear," he replied with a disarming smile of mock apology. "You don't want your loyal subjects to think your companion is unkempt."

The subjects will be thinking the same as the disapproving captain, mused Azrar. They didn't want to share their Prince with anyone, but would have tolerated a beautiful Dark Kind Jendara. They would more readily accept an evil, crazy but female beauty like Zian over the loyal, devoted and very male Jazriel. That Dark Kind relationships were different to human made no difference to their lack of understanding and acceptance. It mattered little. He had lived through worse problems.

As impatient for action as his plunging horse, Jazriel spurred his star-dappled grey stallion to ride in front of the Prince. A competent enough horseman, he did not have Azrar's complete oneness with the horse, the lightness of touch that controlled the animal as if by telepathy. Jazriel's stallion grabbed at its foam flecked bit, pawing the ground with first one shod hoof then the other in its impatience for action. Azrar noted with exasperation that its silver neck and chest were already sodden and black with sweat overlain with white foam. He could also see that Jazriel had held it in by the long curb bit at the same time as lightly spurring it on to produce an animal almost ready to explode in its tormented desire to run and run. In contrast, Azrar's horse, though just as eager, was dry and calm and stood like a statue when its rider dropped the reins onto the arched, taut-muscled neck.

"Come on, My Lord, you can see how desperate they are to gallop. I'll race you to the main gate of Cadera," Jazriel challenged.

With an imperceptible gentle nudge from the Prince's heel, the black horse sprung forward into a flat out gallop, it's rider in perfect balance despite the sudden explosion of momentum and speed. Jazriel's horse already tense and agitated spun and whirled with confusion in a mini dust storm of thrashing hooves, forcing him to cling precariously to the soaking wet mane for balance. Then he was away, flying across the thick, lush grassland in pursuit.

By the time Jazriel and the rest of the party clattered into the settlement, the Prince was already relaxing, one leg casually cocked over the high pommel of his saddle to emphasise the gap between them

"You wound that poor horse up so much, it's nerves had already tired it out. You could never have beaten me. Well, my friend, that is the last time my horses have to suffer from your impatience. I have arranged a new mount for you."

The Prince leapt lightly from the saddle and handed the horse to one of his men, signalled for Jazriel to do the same. Azrar led him into the centre of a collection of stone dwellings and felt and hide lemecs that constituted the only permanent encampment in Isolann. The settled life was unbearable to the majority of the nomads. It was practically deserted as was to be expected at such a late hour, only dimly lit by the few households with inhabitants still awake. The passers-by they encountered where all Isolanni and kept a polite and reverential distance from their Dark Lord and his equally dangerous partner. They reached the one mechanic operating in the town who gave them effusive but respectful greetings. The Prince indicated that the gift be produced and the young man proudly wheeled out a huge red enamel and silver chrome Ducati. The powerful bike had been polished to a dazzling shine, that glistened even in the gloom.

Jazriel's eyes sparkled incandescent with pleasure as he leapt aboard the powerful motorbike. He reached down and kissed the curving chrome engine, caressing the cold, gleaming metal with both hands, it was so beautiful! He was in love! Jazriel had ridden fast motorbikes in Europe before his death but nothing so powerful and sophisticated in design. With some basic instruction from the understandably nervous mechanic, within seconds Jazriel had the engine thundering like an angry, shackled dragon, destroying the silent peace of the settlement's sleeping citizens. As he revved the Ducati, candlelight streamed out of openings as the disturbed townsfolk investigated the monstrous sound. Many came out to see the new marvel for themselves, and once they overcame their nervousness at being in close proximity to Azrar, pay their respects to their beloved Prince.

An old woman broke free from the crowd and dropped to the ground to kiss Azrar's hand. He gently lifted her to her feet and spoke in the reverential and formal tone used by the Isolanni to address their elderly; *"Gentle mother, you should not be down on knees on this cold ground, but warm and safe in your bed.*

The woman smiled, her eyes stinging with tears, *"My family have slept deeply in peace and safety for more generations then I can recall, and it is all due to the protection and courage of our Dark Lord."*

To the utter astonishment of the crowds, their proud and stern ruler dropped down on one knee to kiss her hand. *"It is I who must thank you and all your steadfast ancestors. You have kept me safe while so many of my people have perished to the blades and fires of human hatred. I will serve you, my loyal people, until my last breath, this is my sacred duty as Dark Kind Jendar of Isolann."*

"I am your Prince forever, I will never leave you."

As Azrar rose to his feet, his eyes met Jazriel's and was saddened by the depth of sorrow clouding their turquoise splendour. He addressed him in the vampire language. "I am the Jendar Azrar, I am and will be forever High Prince of these lands. You have always known this."

Jazriel dropped his head. All his naïve hope of some change in his role at the stronghold, however small was finally abandoned. "I have always loved you my Lord Prince and this will never change. I will stay here forever by your side if that is your command, your desire." His words hung in the night air, heavy with resignation, with defeat. How could he, a lowly commoner, worse then that, a sha'ref, compete with a whole nation? How could he demand a change in his status from a being who had lived by the rigid code, the inbred honour and duty of the Dark Kind's Princes and Kings for countless centuries? It was hopeless, utterly hopeless.

They stood in silence, the chasm between them opening yet wider. Jazriel could see that soon it would become impossible to bridge, their history together was repeating itself with sad inevitability but Azrar's austere face showed no emotion. "Try the bike out, I can see how impatient you are to ride it."

Casting aside the pointless melancholy, Jazriel's face broke into a borrowed smile of delight, a human gesture that had become part of his nature now. A survival tactic he had learnt centuries ago. He gave the big bike another thunderous rev and released the power to send it roaring out of the town, speeding down the rough dirt road that served as a main highway.

"One night, he will keep riding, out of Isolann and out of my life." Azrar growled sorrowfully to himself. He saw it in Jazriel's expression, first that dejected resignation and then the sheer joy of freedom that the motor bike expressed. With the undercurrents of deadly change within Isolann and the increasing threat from his neighbour states, maybe it would be for the best. His role was as warlord protector to his subjects, yet ironically the outside world may prove a safer place for Jazriel. An outrage to his pride, but the brutal truth.

One of the stronghold's most influential human administrators, Lomak, was content, he'd found a lever to undermine the Prince, using his one obvious weakness, his devotion to his male bed mate. Lomak watched the creature hurtle around the plains on the powerful machine, destroying the serenity of a star-filled summer night with its roar, polluting the scented air with its noxious fumes. A monstrous blight on the purity of Isolann – like the creature itself. Like Azrar.

Lomak felt for the wolf talisman around his neck, worn since birth for his protection. A symbol of the Pact between the people and their Jendar, their un-ageing protector. The courageous men from the east told him to tear it off and throw it far from him. The black wolf talisman was the yoke of a slave, they said, burdened with damnation. A symbol of a pact with satanic forces. A human who vowed to protect such an evil creature, a cold blooded killer of his fellow humans was forever damned

A frightened Lomak did not want to be damned. He wanted to live with the same valour and fervour as those martyrs, who had been brutally slain by that demon Azrar and his male whore's fangs.

He watched as Azrar's depraved creature sped back into Cadera, pushing the machine to its limit with an ear-punishing roar, the vampire's in-human eyes glittering with pleasure, indifferent to the clouds of dust thrown up at the spectators or the distress the machine wrought on the horses. He rode the machine without any headlights, wore dark clothing. The blood drinker could not be seen well, speeding in the darkness. If something should run in front of those powerful metal wheels......

Chapter Sixteen

Argente Del Diablo, New Mexico

An unlikely setting for such an important meeting, a gathering of minds, men and women who worked together to alter the fate of an entire planet and the billions of human souls dwelling upon it. A deserted mining town, deep into the Mojave Desert, the thin seams of silver long stripped out, the town abandoned to tumble-weed traffic passing along the dusty main street. Overhead circled optimistic, but luckless buzzards.

As a hot, mean-eyed wind agitated the town's only inhabitants, the rubbish accumulated in its brief period of prosperity in the 1960's, the first car arrived to park behind a disused and rusting trailer diner. The whirling garbage gathered in greeting around the tyres, but at least it was pristine rubbish, long picked clean by rats and scoured by the desert winds. Even the rats had left, leaving the wind to moan alone. Until today. At last there was an audience for its gripes.

Over a period of two hours the visitors arrived, one by one, driving themselves in a tatty collection of rent-a-wrecks and hastily purchased inconspicuous small cars with state plates. People used to being driven in luxury limousines, their every move shadowed by gimlet–eyed, craggy-jawed, heavily armed security. Today they arrived alone. They wore down-to-earth local clothing too, everyday folk passing through, going about their business. Until they reached the diner.

Only Cardinal Reyes looked at home in work-worn jeans, sun-faded plaid shirt, and a battered straw Stetson, just another Hispanic local, as opposed to the bull–necked and sweating Russian diplomat sitting opposite him.

The big man was the first to talk. "I take it there have been developments."

The tension around the table tightened, no one wanted to hear of any changes, quiet boring times were better. Best of all, would be an untroubled future, spreading on and on to eternity. Reyes offered around cans of cola from a cool box, the best refreshment he could muster in a hurry so far from any large town.

"I've met the girl, she really is quite something. Beautiful, brave, resourceful and intelligent. As it should be, after all, it's in her genes!"

"But," interrupted a Japanese representative, the one most conspicuously out of place in the gathering," has she any traits, any abilities?"

Reyes dreading this inevitable and inescapable question, sighed and shook his head.

"Another disaster then, just like the father," grumbled the Russian in disgust, an anger bred from fear. And the terrible burden of knowing too much.

"You didn't bring us all the way to this appalling, dead town in the middle of a desert just for that." Demanded the British representative, her clipped, upper class tone more at home hunting across the Shires on the back of a tall thoroughbred then nursing a warming cola in a ruined New Mexico diner.

"I wish I had," agreed Reyes. His sad, dark brown eyes misted over. The bad time had not arrived but they had to face the truth. As brutal as a kick to the head. It would come.

"My own people have done their best, we have looked after the special one for centuries, kept it safe, ready for the time…" Reyes voice trailed off, no one, including him wanted to articulate their worst nightmares of a possible future.

"But we do not know if any of the others will be needed. All the survivors must be given more protection. The Isolanni Prince, in particular. He has never been so vulnerable, so under threat. What can your governments do to assist the creature?"

The uneasy, embarrassed silence that followed spoke volumes to a distressed Reyes. Though normally gentle and mild natured by demeanour, his dark eyes flashed with fury as he rounded on the representatives of the world's most powerful and influential nations.

"If you let Azrar go to the wall, you could be sealing the fate of humanity. You are cursing your children, or your grandchildren to certain doom. We hate having to protect these vile things as much as you, but it must be done."

The American representative, a Texan by birth and the most at home in the desert setting tried to calm the little cardinal. He did not know exactly what Reyes was, certainly not a slight middle-aged Latino priest. But like all the others here at the diner, he accepted Reyes was benign and sincere and had the best interests of mankind in his heart.

"You must understand our view point, Cardinal. This has gone on for so long, this waiting, preparing for a terrifying future based on scraps of ancient legends, of fragmented and vague prophesies," The tall Texan spread his palms open in a consolatory gesture, "Maybe, that's all they are."

"One of the medallions has been found - by Gabrielle Railton." Reyes replied quietly, looking down, unable to face the shock in their eyes. In one simple sentence he had extinguished their hope.

Even if they stepped out into the heat of the surrounding desert, these solemn people, gathered from all around the world would now have ice in their veins. Just one medallion, but so far, still only one. Even now, there was time. But how much before the cataclysmic nightmare descended? Till this moment, they could get on with their lives, pretend to themselves that all this talk of ancient legend and prophesy was nonsense. That other life forms, such as the gentle and kindly Reyes and the monstrous Dark Kind did not exist. But proof of all this strangeness came in the small form of a trinket, a slender ancient bauble. A sliver of broken gold in the form of a dragon.

"Do I have your permission to approach the Lady Eshan for help, to join forces with her considerable organisation?" Reyes asked, his voice quiet but firm. This had to be done. They must understand.

Reyes bowed his head with a sigh of relief as one by one they agreed.

Chapter Seventeen

Bristol, England

Gabrielle's valiant attempt at picking up the fraying threads of her comfortable and safe old life was coming apart. Unravelling faster than her favourite, old wool jumper when it had snagged on barbed wire on a dig.

The Worlds Beyond documentary had recently aired on the television and was a success. Ciaran O'Rourke may have been a handsome, self-obsessed shit but he had made the world of field archaeology fascinating and understandable to the general public. Gabrielle had finally come face to face with her ancient Cornishman, a disappointingly plain man, anonymous, mundane, no different to any ageing human in a crowd. But that under whelmed response might have just been a reflection of her own negative mood.

She enjoyed a few fleeting weeks of fame; there had been national newspaper interviews and one toe-curlingly embarrassing slot on breakfast TV where her golden looks but not her work was the focus. A tabloid newspaper added to the brief flurry of excitement by speculating whether the Cornishman could have been King Arthur Pendragon himself. If only, Gabrielle had sighed, such a discovery would have been beyond an archaeologist's wildest dream! But all evidence pointed to one fact, the burial was that of a well-travelled merchant. Not a warrior king. The public soon forgot both her programme and her face and all talk of King Arthur. Her return to near-anonymity was a great relief.

Wanting to sink into the background, Gabrielle had become increasingly paranoid since her unsettling visit to Switzerland. She had taken to wearing a grungy old wool hat pulled down over her glossy blonde hair, never wore any make up and dressed down at all times. Any approaching stranger became an object of fear and suspicion. Damn it! She did not want to live her life like this! She lost count how many times she had cursed Reyes for changing her life then disappearing. She accepted she was probably being watched and protected by his shadowy organisation, but that was not a source of comfort, it only added to her sense of mistrust.

Her Gran's letter, with its mystifying veiled warnings of danger did not help her state of mind. Gabrielle accepted she was not writing a generalised warning of her fear of the Imadeen, of the danger from their incendiary bombs. The danger she feared was something else. Maybe they were not the ramblings of a confused elderly lady but an acute awareness of a real threat to her granddaughter. Gabrielle wanted to be with her, to ask her directly what the hell was going on.

Doing her best to bury her fears and insecurity, Gabrielle immersed herself beneath a punishing schedule of work. There was plenty of research on the Cornish burial to keep her occupied. The aftermath of the TV documentary had brought many requests for lectures, at first she shunned them as being too open, too public, but in a determined attempt to reclaim her old life, she finally agreed to give a talk about on-site forensic archaeology to a newly created university in the North.

What peril could there be in addressing an audience of ardent students? Some would be genuine, eager to learn, others oblivious to her lecture, snoozing off the previous night down the student bar, a few would be ogling her cleavage and endless legs. The usual mix.

Although it was the first time at this university, everything about the lecture assignment was familiar, the embarrassing glowing introduction from the head of the history faculty, the anticipation on the sea of young faces, the big screen behind her which would inevitably show her slides upside down to great hilarity. So why were her hands shaking as she prepared to speak?

Furious with herself for being so skittish, Gabrielle concentrated on delivering an interesting and informative lecture, but unwittingly, her eyes wandered up to the packed galleries. What the hell was she looking for? Stupid girl! Sinister men in dark glasses and trench coats? Beautiful fanged beings with sparkling eyes, or a lurking gang of mysterious priests? This was a wet afternoon in Wigan for goodness sake!

She struggled through to the end of her lecture, feeling her legs go weak with relief when the final slide was shown. There were a few desultory questions from the students, mainly from smitten girls about Ciaran O'Rourke. Most were too impatient to head for the student union bar to delay by asking unnecessary questions. The head of faculty gave an equally gushing and embarrassing thank you speech. And finally she was free to bolt for the safety of her car and head for home.

As if the long drive down the crowded motorway was not arduous and dangerous enough, Gabrielle became convinced she was being followed. A dark blue Volvo estate had pulled out of the University car park at the same time as her, ten junctions later and it remained close, trailing behind her. Abruptly, Gabrielle pulled off the motorway at the last moment without giving any indication, taking a slip road into a service station. She parked close to the collection of shops and fast food outlets, an area always crowded. She waited and watched every vehicle arriving but there was no sign of the Volvo.

Utter madness again, just what havoc had that little priest spread to her life? Gabrielle wished her boss had never sent her to Switzerland, maybe she would have never encountered Alejandro Reyes. He had filled her head with fear and suspicion, drained her of all joy, all serenity. Was it a sin to swear and call a priest rude names? Hell, she belonged to no religion, she could be as rude as she liked! Yet it felt strangely uncomfortable, somehow defiantly wrong to mutter obscenities at Reyes, even though the man was probably thousands of miles away. Another sign of his influence on her life. A few months ago, she would have happily turned the air a vivid shade of blue!

Gabrielle reached Bristol by the late evening. Exhausted and furious she could not find an empty space in the road close to her home, forcing her to park several streets away. The long walk back to her flat had never bothered her in the past. She never walked like a victim, her long stride and self-confident expression was her protection against any would-be muggers and rapists – that and a black belt in karate. It only existed in her mind, but it gave her a sense of power that might deter any creeps. Tonight, Gabrielle forgot her imaginary martial art skills and scurried home as fast as she could, shying away from shadows like a racehorse filly. Even once in the sanctuary of her flat she had to check every room, every cupboard for intruders before she could attempt to recover from a long day.

This could not go on! She wanted her old life back. The old certainties. A world where vampires could be defeated by a shaft of sunlight or a well-placed stake. She fell into her bed, exhausted and depressed. But sleep would not come, her mind was on a frantic rollercoaster, refusing to slow down. By 3 a.m, Gabrielle accepted her determination to carry on her life as before was futile. Constant paranoia was draining her, who needed vampires when her own fears were destroying her life? She decided to take a long, overdue holiday. Why not trace her Gran in America and get some answers? Real answers, not the enigmatic, half truths that Reyes had left her with.

She spent the next morning maxing out her already over-laden credit cards, booking flights to Montana. Though they had met when Gabrielle was a little girl, contact with her grandmother over the past ten years had been through their regular letters. Now she was determined to meet her for the first time since becoming a young adult. The thought sent a shiver of excitement down her spine, the first happy shiver since returning from the Alps. She was going to see her Gran! But first she had to find her!

Gabrielle's hand went to her neck, this time with no feeling of dread or guilt. The dragon amulet was safe in its box. Instead, her heart swelled with love as she held her mother's gold locket. She gently prised it open and ran her finger over the faded photo inside, Amela Railton. An exotically beautiful young woman, half English, half Isolanni. "What's happening, Mum?" Gabrielle murmured, kissing the photo. "Why has the world gone mad?"

With her fingernail, Gabrielle eased open a secret compartment at the back of the locket where a slip of paper had been hidden. It contained three phone numbers to be used only in emergencies. She had never understood this need for cloak and dagger secrecy in her past. Since her encounter with Reyes in Switzerland, Gabrielle accepted this subterfuge as part of a complex plan to keep her and her grandmother safe. And now she knew who from.

Chapter Eighteen

Isolann.

As if aware of the vulnerability of its rider, the black stallion stood completely still, an ebony statue with no sign of equine impatience, no stamping, swishing tail, or tossing head. Exhausted from a long tour of his eastern borders, Azrar paused before dismounting, taking a deep breath and gathering himself to alight gently with all the weight carried onto his left leg. It was the briefest respite from pain, once he began to walk the white-hot knives would be back to torment him, raking up and down his metal-clad, shattered limb. Only time spent in bed with Jazriel gave him more moments of respite, brief snatches of pleasure that flooded the senses and temporarily lifted his burden of pain.

Though greatly fatigued, Azrar was pleased he had made the long journey across Isolann's mountain passes. At least the rumours of enemy troop movements along the eastern boundary of his realm had proved illusory. His presence gave the anxious nomads reassurance; though living some distance from the Prince's stronghold, they had not been forgotten.

Azrar made his way across the inner keep, handing the reins of his patient warhorse to a waiting groom. There was a time the Prince would have spurned such an even tempered horse, now Azrar was grateful for its rhythmic paces and quiet spirit.

Thinking of quiet spirits, Azrar was delighted his gamble of buying the motorbike for his companion had paid off; the restless, discontent look had left Jazriel's eyes to be replaced by an animated sparkle. He appeared relaxed, the old languid charm had returned. He had even cut back on his alcohol intake, though not those damn endless cigarettes!

Azrar found him already waiting in the vault of Rest, in a carefully prepared welcome. The room was lit by the warm light of hundreds of honey-scented candles, gleaming off the gold woven into the bed brocades and silk tapestry wall hangings. Bare-footed, Jazriel wore a loose white silk shirt, open to the waist, and dark trousers, informal garb, ready to relax and sleep through the long hours of daylight. He remained seated on the bed at first, letting Azrar feast his journey-tired eyes on his companion's golden-hued beauty.

Jazriel held the Prince's gaze for a few seconds, his eyes mesmerising, promising so much before lowering them and climbing off the bed to drop to the ground in correct and respectful obeisance. All well-planned sha'ref tricks, designed to inflame desire, of which Jazriel was the supreme master. Azrar knew he was being skilfully manipulated but did not care.

He helped the Prince undress, slowly, trying not to wince in sympathy as he gently eased Azrar's leather boot from his devastated right leg. What a mess. Why wouldn't it heal? Azrar had drunk plenty of blood! A being brighter then Jazriel would have realised that the extraordinary effort needed to bring him back to life had drained Azrar badly, the Prince's regenerative power was compromised. But Jazriel was not that bright being. He had been created to satisfy sexual desire not as an intellectual thinker. He poured the Prince a goblet of warm, spiced wine and waited for the Prince's command. Azrar fell back on the bed, propped up by a plentiful collection of richly embroidered, cushions, raised his goblet in a toast.

"Here's to Isolann, thankfully safe from the eastern menace."

Jazriel's beautiful face broke into a seductive smile, he raised his own glass but before he could speak in reply, spilt a trickle of warm plum-red wine onto Azrar's marble-white chest.

"I am so sorry. With your permission, my Lord?" he whispered in a soft growl of mock apology, turquoise eyes glowing, pulling the Prince's soul down into their azure depths. Azrar's reply was a low groan of assent as Jazriel began to slowly lap the wine from his icy skin, each sensuous movement of his tongue growing in intensity. He moved slowly down to Azrar's shattered leg, more metal then flesh, and lightly kissed each sliver of exposed skin, focusing on the reluctant limb, cajoling it to heal.

"Take away my pain, Jaz. It's been a long hard ride."
Azrar's voice was a deep, growling whisper, curiously vulnerable and weary in tone.

Jazriel's heart swelled with his love for this austere warlord, created to be imperious, unyielding. Hiding his agony from the world because it was impossible for Azrar to show weakness in front of any being - human or Dark Kind. Except here, with him.

Moving up the bed and holding the Prince's face firmly with his hands, Jazriel began to kiss him, deeply, languorously, flooding Azrar's senses with luxurious warmth, the melting taste of hot honey and cinnamon mixed with spiced wine. Azrar groaned again, this time in relief as the pain became temporarily a memory. Jazriel pressed on, the kiss taking Azrar's mind and body away from the reality of duty, of broken bones and tired muscles, away from the leaden restrictions of time and place, captivating him, taking him on a sensuous journey of rising desire and excitement. A deepening whirlpool of growing exhilaration, every cell in Azrar's body becoming vibrant and alive, electric with desire. A journey that must be resolved later by Azrar entering him, hard and fast, Jazriel's skills prolonging the Prince's pleasure to almost unbearable tension, finally bringing him to a shuddering ecstatic, soul merging climax.

But not yet, not while he, Jazriel was in control. Now was the time to play the Prince like an instrument, manipulate his emotions and sensations using all his fine-honed sha'ref skills. That's what the Prince wanted, needed. That's what he would get.

What Jazriel needed, wanted, was of no importance.

Chapter Nineteen

Montana, USA, 2002

The melting snows of winter past could not compete with the chill in the old woman's heart. She shivered and pulled the collar of her sheepskin coat tighter. Her gaze took in the rolling beauty of her white valley with its patchwork of emerging fresh, vivid green and the snow-bound mountains surrounding it, holding her home, the Whitethorn Ranch, in their stone embrace. The fear that gripped her heart began that morning with a phone call, a warning. Gabrielle was trying to find her.

Guilt added to her torment, the child should have been raised here at Whitethorn, safe from the world, safe from the evil old bastards at Nemesis. But Steve and Lhalee Railton had lost their daughter, how could she deny them their beautiful grandchild as well? At least her own son was alive, she had to believe that. No word, no news for over twenty years yet she had no sense of his passing. Her youngest son Cameron, though missing, must still be alive - somewhere.

There was nothing more she could do to ease her heartache and distress over Cameron's disappearance. Her friends in international intelligence had spent so many years in futile searching. Now she must concentrate on the result of Cameron's fleeting union with Amela, Steve Railton's daughter. The enchanting Gabrielle. How could she get the young woman to Montana, to the safety of her remote cattle ranch without unleashing the jackals of Nemesis who would trail her from England, endangering her remaining three sons and their families? She was a grandmother now, she had lived a long life and was unafraid for herself. But the innocents must be protected. Including Gabrielle.

She needed advice, so great was her dilemma that she could not collect her thoughts. "I'm like a wasp trapped in a bottle," she murmured to herself, "a foolish old wasp hitting my head against the sides but unable to do anything." She was aware that standing on the porch of her ranch house, wringing her hands with anxiety was not a way out of her predicament. She called one of the ranch hands over and asked for her old Appaloosa mare to be saddled. Concern in the man's eyes turned to distress when she insisted on riding alone.

Damn it! Ok, so she was 85. But thin, healthy and fit as a greyhound. She had ridden since a small child, and not on quiet ponies but spirited, well-bred stallions! She refused all offers of an escort, grateful her other sons, Clay, Brad and Joe Jnr, were far away, checking stock in the mountains. It would be harder to mollify their concerns.

She let the rotund, spotted Indian pony have a long rein and ambled across the icy meadows, how beautiful the melting snow looked in the mid-morning sun, glittering rainbow light from a myriad of tiny diamonds. There was so much stunning beauty here in Montana, less harsh then her homeland yet it was an epic landscape that demanded respect and provoked a fierce, protective love. This morning the sky was a cloudless deep azure, the sun held little heat but prompted a sense of longing for summer's warmth. But this benign weather could change in a heart-beat, even now blizzards could sweep down from the mountains, throwing the spring back to mid winter. That was what sparked the anxiety in the ranch hand. Understandable, but misplaced. She had lived in the shadows of high mountains long enough to read their fickle and frequently deadly moods.

Her journey brought her to a silver birch grove, fenced off from cattle and deer by a high wrought-iron fence. She tied the pony to a wooden hitching post and pulling a nose bag from the saddle, attached it to the Appaloosa's bridle, leaving it enjoying a feed of oats. She then walked into the family's own, private cemetery, placed high, with the best sweeping views of the ranch and surrounding dramatic landscape.

There were three well-tended graves. She had no fresh flowers to place on them, nothing grew yet. Instead she lightly caressed each carved headstone above the resting place of her adopted mother and big brother and knelt beside the third one, and sighed. "Joe, my beloved. What am I to do? I love this child with all my heart, I must do all I can to protect her, but not at the cost of the rest of my family. I am in an impossible dilemma. I need your guidance."

Of course there would be no answer, her husband was at peace in a distant place beyond her reach. Her enemies were relentless and single-minded. They would follow Gabrielle to find her. Her granddaughter was of no consequence to them, as expendable as ... her thoughts trailed off, too painful to continue. It was as it had always been, she was the one Nemesis wanted. Would giving up her life put an end to this? Would the evil that stalked her and her family then finally leave them alone?

She felt an unexpected warm breeze on her face, gentle as a lover's caress, it touched her cheek and rippled through her silver hair. She gave a slight, sad smile and nodded her head. "OK, my darling. You are right, as always. I must not wimp out now and give into despair. And I will not do this alone. I know I have friends out there, who will stand by me and protect me. And our lovely Gabrielle.

Chapter Twenty

London

Raker watched the information on the screen before him, comfortable with the cutting edge technology despite his advancing years. Not teach an old dog new tricks? Hah! He could run rings around these arrogant whelps. Especially that odious squat pup arrogantly thinking he could best an old hand like Raker! All the information Hain had gathered about vampire movements had also found their way straight to Raker's own files.

His so–called special covert operatives were all in Raker's pay and the laboratory Hain had funded to do DNA research on Dark Kind genes was also secretly under his control. Eternal youth? Let Hain waste his life pursuing a foolish dream. The Dark Kind were like smoke, like wild storms, impossible to trap. Raker had been the closest when he had betrayed the vamp agent Jazriel to the Germans. But the fanged bastards had removed the creature's body before anyone could make use of the precious scientific data.

Chase the vamps around Europe, idiot boy, it will keep you occupied, out of the way, while the professionals get on with engineering a more sophisticated trap. One baited with a compelling lure. Raker was certain that drawing Khari Devanc out of hiding was the key. She was Jendar Azrar's ward, beloved friend to all the Dark Kind, who were honour and duty bound to protect her. And Raker now knew exactly what would make the woman break cover.

Chapter Twenty-One

Soho, London

"Look at her, Eshan. Isn't she beautiful!" The old woman's eyes misted over, a lump in her throat threatened to choke her. The resemblance to her long lost son, Cameron, was so striking, so poignant.

She sat in the shadows of a dark old Soho pub, the Victorian building bustling with people. On the surface it seemed a safe place with so many potential witnesses, but the woman's Dark Kind companion knew otherwise. Eshan's hidden, all-lavender eyes scanned the busy bar, she growled quietly under her breath, recognising several known Nemesis operatives. They leant on bars alone or sat in groups at tables, chatting, drinking, laughing at jokes but their eyes were sharp, hard and always on Gabrielle. More lurked outside. She doubted Gabrielle had been left unshadowed for many days. Getting her out and away from these malevolent parasites was going to be dangerous and difficult.

"I'm sorry. This will not be easy, the place is crawling with Nemesis hyenas."

The woman nodded in agreement and sighed, only too aware of the danger. She was grateful to have a ferocious Dark Kind friend with her, but also aware that the female vampire would be a prime target for Nemesis too. Eshan was, as ever, a consummate chameleon, the long centuries of survival in the shadows had taught her the optimum use of disguise. An expert in hiding in plain sight, Eshan constantly changed her clothes, her hair, even her status amongst humans. But her greatest asset to staying alive undetected was her great wealth, the fortune accumulated over millennia. Money to buy the best security, the most loyal human body-guards, and now, the latest surveillance equipment.

"I just want to hold her in my arms, Eshan. I have been apart from my granddaughter for far too long and all because of those vile, vindictive old men and their minions."

Behind their protective intensely black glass, Eshan's eyes darkened. "You cannot make any move towards her. That is what they are waiting for."

The woman groaned. The vampires could not reproduce, how could an inhuman creature like Eshan know the agony of seeing your own flesh and blood in danger, and not be able to even give the girl a hug of love and support?

"I am deadly serious about this," the beautiful vampire female insisted, fixing the elderly woman with the full power of her hidden gaze. "I will not lose you or the girl to this vermin. Let my people get her to safety. You know I only employ the best."

It was difficult not to trust Eshan, they had worked together for so long, and in the most perilous circumstances. But seeing her vulnerable granddaughter just yards away from her, surrounded by human jackals, was unbearable. Gabrielle was uneasy, she could see her hands shaking as she raised her wine glass, her green-gold eyes flashing around the room, looking out for her grandmother. The image in her mind would be from their last meeting, when Gabrielle was just a little girl.

But the elderly woman was well disguised. A bandanna hid every tell-tale strand of her silver-blonde hair though far more silver then blonde now! Dark blue lenses hid her unusual golden eyes. Her clothing was nondescript, charity shop chic. She would have painted herself bright blue if it could keep Gabrielle safe. Instead she had to trust a creature of the night, a vampire, to arrange the girl's escape from danger, to get her across to America, to the ranch in Montana without any Nemesis agents following, discovering the safe haven from a hostile world.

She felt a firm grip on her arm, the unnatural cold of a Dark Kind hand. "Do not be afraid," Eshan whispered in her harsh, wolf-growl language. "Everything that is about to happen is under my full control."

The bar suddenly erupted into pandemonium. A woman screamed as a large, beer-bellied, tattooed and clearly drunken man began a violent brawl with another, a young sharp suited business man with a foul temper and matching language. Both smashed beer bottles and waved them menacingly as weapons. A blousy, bottle-blonde female became involved, screaming obscenities at both men. Soon others joined in the fracas, taking sides or trying to separate the combatants. Eshan's people moved swiftly and skilfully, targeting the known Nemesis operatives, tipping over their tables and dragging them into the affray.

Distracted by the raucous brawl, Khari didn't notice Gabrielle being escorted away by Eshan and her operatives, leaving an empty chair and a half finished glass of red wine. Gabrielle was gone; as if she had never sat waiting in vain for her reunion with her grandmother whose relief was mixed with the pain of searing loss. She so wanted to hold her granddaughter close that night. Now she had to get herself to safety, unhindered and not followed, to eventually arrive back to Montana. Maybe then they could have their overdue reunion.

She felt a firm but unaggressive hand on her arm, guiding her through the madness, a whispered password in the vampire tongue that she alone among humans could speak. But she knew already to trust him, that the young man who swiftly escorted her out of the chaotic bar descending now into a well-orchestrated riot was a new member of the Spook squad. Founded during the Second World War, it was a covert agency that she had belonged to. She was Khari Devane, the woman who could enter human minds. The instant he had touched her she had dipped into this man's mind and found the truth.

Fleeing towards the safety of an unassuming, anonymous grey car, she was aware of a nearby, baleful presence. Her escort put a protective arm around her shoulders but in the rush and confusion, Khari brushed up against a man standing on the pavement, he seemed unaware of the encounter, his entire focus on the uproar coming from the pub. But Khari's whole being shuddered with horror at the brief touch, her mind flooded with painful images. Raker! The intensity of his hatred as potent as ever. As the car drove away she looked back and watched him, standing ramrod straight, staring at the bar, seemingly unaware that she had already fled the scene. An old man living on bile and bitterness.

Why did he hate her so much? Enough to threaten her son and kill his lover, Amela Railton. Gabrielle's mother.

Was accepting the existence of the Dark Kind such a crime in his eyes that her family must also pay the price with their lives? Or was there more? A hidden twisted motive he had held from her all those years ago, when they both worked as covert agents for the allies against the Nazis. Perhaps festering guilt in his important role in helping Banks to commit an act of treachery, by luring a loyal fellow agent, the Dark Kind Jazriel to a bloody death in a filthy cellar? Khari Devane did not want to get close enough to know. She had entered poisonous, evil and debauched minds enough times during the war to last a lifetime. She just wanted to live out the remainder of her life in peace, surrounded by her family at Whitethorn, a family that included Gabrielle Railton. But Raker had answers, maybe to the whereabouts of her son, Cam.

"Turn back," she pleaded with the driver already speeding away through the night. "Please, I must go back."

"No way, darlin,' " rasped the young driver, risking pushing the car to an even greater speed, skilfully weaving through the narrow, congested London streets. " The Lady said I must keep you safe."

"Stop the car!" Khari demanded, she had to confront Raker! Had to find out what happened to Cam!

The driver ignored her distress, locked the doors and sped on through the night. His devotion to the Lady was absolute. Her orders overrode anything else.

Chapter Twenty-Two

Gabrielle had no choice but to trust the two insistent but polite young men who firmly escorted her from the pub brawl to a nearby car. She trusted them because they reassured her in the private language she shared with her Gran. Their familiarity with something secret from her childhood astonished her. How could they know these words unless they wanted to help her and her grandmother? Though which side was good and bad was open to debate. Her Gran's enemies and therefore her enemies wanted to destroy the vampires. In films that would make them the good guys. But this was real life and a lot more complicated, Gabrielle's world grew weirder by the minute.

The young men said little and beyond being reassuring and courteous to her, drove through the city swiftly, making many sudden turns and detours to shake off any pursuers. They took her out of the city and beyond the suburbs, after a long stretch of crowded motorway, drove through seemingly endless narrow country lanes to finally reach the Chiltern Hills. Their destination lay at the end of a long, winding, gravel drive as the car pulled up outside a fine, neat Georgian country house, set in many acres of gently undulating pasture and old woodland. It was built in the distinctive local style of red and blue brick with insets of pale blue and white knapped flint.

Her rescuers ushered Gabrielle through a large oak-panelled hall and up an imposing wooden stair way, then through meandering corridors to a substantial and beautifully appointed bedroom. A welcoming fire crackled and danced in the hearth, an old fashioned English tea with sandwiches and cakes was already set on a low table. Left alone to explore the room it was clear her arrival had been well planned. Gabrielle was unnerved to find new clothes in her size and style in the wardrobe, her brand of cosmetics and toiletries waited for her in the en-suite bathroom, including a large and expensive bottle in her choice of perfume. A generous vase of her favourite flowers, yellow roses and white gypsophilia sat on a table by the window.

If this was meant to reassure her, it failed. It was as if they did not want her to leave, that everything she needed was provided for here. Gabrielle half expected to see her fat old cat waddle in. Thank goodness for her elderly neighbour Mrs Jones, at least the Monster would be well cared for in her absence. How long an absence was worrying Gabrielle. She wanted answers and she wanted them now! Gabrielle looked at the tempting tray of cakes and sighed. She was tired and hungry, would it harm to have a shower, a change of clothes and something to eat before discovering just what the hell was going on?

She woke up on the sofa, still fully dressed, had no idea how she had ended up sleeping right through to nearly midday. She remembered having a shower, sitting on a comfortable sofa in front of the fire and tucking into the delicious high tea... then it was the next day.

She washed and changed into fresh clothes and wandered through the old house to find someone. There were many questions filling her mind, someone in this place must have the answers. At first it appeared empty, but following delicious cooking smells she found the kitchens where three young women were preparing lunch. They were friendly and welcoming but non-committal.

"All the trainees are out on exercises, Miss," one announced, "They'll be back by two for lunch."

"What trainees, what is this place?" Gabrielle insisted but the women just smiled. The only forthcoming one repeated, "They will all be back at two, they will be able to answer your queries, I'm sure, Miss."

Gabrielle walked through the manor house looking for clues, for any other people, but finding it empty of both, decided to take a stroll in the sunlit gardens. She crossed the neat, well tended lawns, where clumps of the last daffodils waved defiantly, unwilling to fade and give way to the emerging early summer flowers. At the end of the lawns she heard the gurgle and swirl of fast running water tumbling over stones. She headed for the sound to find a delightful small river.

Walking slowly down a narrow path, Gabrielle followed its meandering route, pausing only to duck low beneath the old willows that crowded the banks. Sunlight glinted like liquid gold across the surface, catching fire on the scales of darting fish. She saw a flash of shimmering turquoise, a kingfisher. How magical! Found a little glade by the river where someone had thoughtfully placed a log seat.

"This was always my favourite spot at Chess Manor."

Gabrielle spun around to see her grandmother approach from another direction, a large bunch of wild yellow gorse blooms in a straw basket hooked over her arm, scenting the air with their sweet, delicate, coconut-like fragrance. Gabrielle gave a delighted squeal! Her Gran! At last! They embraced and kissed, both women beaming with the delight and wonder of their re-union.

"Look at you, all grown up!" sobbed Khari, her pleasure at holding Gabrielle in her arms tainted with the leaden burden of guilt. It had been so long since she had last seen her, held her. Far too long. How had she let her fears get so strong that she had practically abandoned this girl to live alone in Europe?

"All grown up and so beautiful," she repeated, unable to hold back the tears. Gabrielle knew the cause of her Gran's distress. Even if she had any residual anger or bitterness, it was not in her heart now.

As they sat together on the seat, Khari explained that Chess Manor was the headquarters of the war-time covert agency she had once served with and was still in operation.

"I fell in love with my commander here at the Manor, Joe Devane. Your granddad!" Khari sighed sadly, "You would have loved him, you share the same fearless and indomitable nature."

"I bet you sat here with him," murmured Gabrielle giving her Gran's hand a loving squeeze.

"He made the seat for me, while I was on an assignment." Khari answered with a sad smile, running her hand over the smooth wood, imagining Joe's strong, steady hands crafting it. How she missed him!

Khari reached into the straw basket and rummaged beneath the gorse to produce a maroon and gold leather-bound book fastened with a silver lock. She leant over and lightly kissed her granddaughter's forehead. "This is for you, my precious girl. It's my journal, started when I left Isolann with Lady Eshan. Early stuff, embarrassingly mawkish, I apologise in advance! I was very young, naïve and thought I was in love with Prince Azrar. A Dark Kind warlord. Madness! I will always love him but not in that impossible, romantic way."

Gabrielle gently and reverently unlocked the journal with shaking hands, were all the answers she sought captured in this book? Her grandmother loved a vampire Prince, how could that be?

"It's written in our secret language, Gaby. Only you must now know it is more then that. It is the ancient language of the Dark Kind."

Gabrielle nodded, too full of wonder at the journal to speak. It could reveal all the details she craved; her Gran's extraordinary life lay in her hands, all the wonders and adventures written in a simple, inconspicuous book , bound in plain red leather.

"Nemesis would kill to get this book," Gabrielle murmured out loud, suddenly putting her hand to her mouth in shock, realising what she had just said. Her mother!

"Indeed," replied Khari, her eyes filling with tears. "Those relentless bastards would kill. And already have." She paused, swallowed her tears.

"Read it here, at the Manor where you are safe. Then I will give it to Cardinal Reyes. I should have done so, long ago. He has the means to protect it."

"He didn't have the means to protect my mother," snapped Gabrielle bitterly.

There was little Khari could say to comfort the young woman, in many ways she was right. But the move against Amela Railton, an innocent young mother had been unexpected and shocking. Everyone had been so focused on Nemesis targets being either Khari herself or the Dark Kind.

"I learnt a bitter lesson by underestimating the enemy. One paid for with my daughter-in-law's life and the loss of my son, missing since her death. The guilt has haunted me for half my lifetime. And beyond. But they must not prevail! I will not have you put at risk, my precious child or any of my family."

Khari stood up. "Walk back to the Manor with me, I am famished and lunch is always good here. Let us rest and relax and get to know cach other again. This evening there is an important person I want you to meet. A lady from my past, who may be as important to your future."

The lunch was indeed good but Gabrielle was more intrigued by the other diners then the food. Twenty young people sat down to eat in a bright hall, the walls hung with gracefully fading tapestries of Victorian hunting scenes. 'So', thought an intrigued Gabrielle,' these are the mysterious trainees.'

They were a roughly equal mix of male and female, apparently from a wide selection of backgrounds. They sat and enjoyed their meal and appeared animated and good-natured. Gabrielle was soon aware they treated her grandmother with great deference, as if she was someone famous, someone revered.

Persistently Gabrielle found her eyes wandering over to one particular trainee, the only one tense and unspeaking, hostile. A whip-thin, sharp-boned young man about her age, with troubled dark eyes that met hers and made an instant connection, electric in its intensity. Enver Thorne. How the hell did she know his name?

"So, what are you?" Thorne's tone was abrupt, defensive. Gabrielle took in the once black, now faded to grey, demon's scull biker t-shirt, the bitten nails, the leave-me-alone attitude. "Another bloody mind-reader?"

Gabrielle shook her head. "Just a guest, passing through." The young man shook his head with derision. "If you are here, you must be another freak. No normals allowed. Bad for our karma, or some other airy-fairy New Age crap."

Gabrielle laughed; to her astonishment, she was drawn to this difficult young man. He was most definitely not her usual type! As far from the handsome and suave Ciaran O'Rourke as a man could possibly be! But there was a spark of attraction, one Thorne was feeling too. How did she know that? Not in his words or body language. There was no give away gleam of interest his eyes, so why did she think there was a mutual attraction? Intuition? Wishful thinking? Insanity?

"I'm off for a cig break, you coming?" Enver asked, his voice sounding bored, indifferent, as if he didn't care what her answer was.

Gabrielle knew with her new clarity of perception that he cared very much. "Yep, why not."

They walked out of the dining room, ignoring the in-take of breath, the disapproval rippling through the others. The meal was only half way through! They sat on the stone steps of the manor's courtyard where Thorne fished out a cigarette, lit it and let it dangle, untouched in his fingers.

"I take it you do not want to be here," Gabrielle ventured. The young man smiled for the first time, and her heart jumped a beat at the poignant mixture of shy awkwardness and cynicism. His accent was from somewhere up in the north of Britain, Manchester? Newcastle? Gabrielle was hopeless at recognising regional dialects.

"I refused, at first. They said it would keep my sanity, give me a purpose. Help mankind and all that shite. Didn't want to be a lackey of some pseudo-fascist government."

The cigarette burned on, untouched. "Then my mam took my kid brother Christmas shopping down in London, a big treat. His first time away from Doncaster. Both burned to death."

"Imadeen?"

Thorne nodded. "So, I joined up with the Spook Squad after all...thought I could help fight the mad fuckers. Hit them hard, make them pay."

He got up abruptly, he'd said more then he'd planned to this woman, dropped the cigarette and ground it beneath his heel.

"You didn't touch that..." Gabrielle queried, climbing to her feet.

"Hate them. Never smoked one in my life. It gives me an excuse to get away from the Dudleys."

"The what?" Gabrielle laughed.

"The rest of the whackos, the other trainees. Dudley Do-Rights."

I like you, Enver Thorne, Gabrielle thought as they walked back across the courtyard to the dining room. As if reading her thoughts, he gave her a quick, warm smile, no awkwardness, no cynicism, merely recognition of a soul mate.

Khari saw the brief transaction and sighed, relieved she would be taking Gaby away to Montana. She had enough trouble in her life from the jackals of Nemesis, she did not need to get mired down salvaging such a disturbed soul. It was tragic, but the boy was in safe hands at Chess Manor; a bright future awaited him, if he seized the opportunity, the powerful gift of telekinesis that at the moment haunted him would be nurtured and controlled here. As had her gift of *Knowing*.

But the encounter gave Khari some vital and important insight. Reyes had been wrong. Her beloved granddaughter also had the *Knowing*. Dormant but awakening. Even more reason to get her safely away to the ranch.

After lunch, not wanting to miss a moment of her time with Gabrielle, Khari reluctantly retired for a nap. The young woman had so many questions, she looked ready to burst from anticipation, but Khari's body told a different story. It was hard, sometimes, to ignore the many passing years, occasionally, she had to give in to her age.

Gabrielle retired to her room as well, not to rest, but to read the journal, impatient to learn about her grandmother's intriguing past. She sat on the sofa, someone had thoughtfully re-built and lit the fire, left her a tray of steaming hot tea and yet more cakes. As if she could be hungry after the generous lunch! The afternoon stretched on to evening, unnoticed by Gabrielle, totally lost in an unbelievable world of allied secret agents with unusual powers, of covert and highly perilous missions to Nazi Germany; of the vampires that had served with them. She learnt that Khari had an ancient power called the *Knowing* - both a gift and a curse. She discovered how brave and resourceful this remarkable woman had been and still was. How she had fallen in love with Joe Devane; her difficulty in leaving him to go on a dangerous mission with a handsome, charming vampire called Jazriel who had been betrayed and killed by one of their own agents. A human. Gabrielle found tears rolling down her cheeks at her grandmother's moving account of her shock and grief at losing him, a very dear friend.

There was so much more to read, but darkness had crept up on the manor and Gabrielle's eyes stung, strained and tired from the intense reading session. The rest of the journal must keep until her eyes let her continue! But it already had served its purpose, Gabrielle had a greater knowledge about her grandmother's extraordinary life, and the people and Dark Kind that shared it.

A gentle tapping on Gabrielle's door awoke her, she glanced at her watch, 2 a.m! Instantly nervous and alert, fearing something wrong with Khari or another run from Nemesis, she pulled on a jumper and jeans and ran to the door. Her grandmother, standing apologetic but relaxed, quickly reassured Gabrielle there was no emergency. She welcomed the old lady into her room, making her comfortable on the sofa and raking up the last embers to bring a pleasing and comforting glow to the hearth. "Have you read in my journal about Lady Eshan yet?" Khari asked, taking hold of her granddaughter's hand.

Gabrielle nodded.

Are you ready to meet her? There is no pressure, Gaby. You may chose never to deal with the Dark Kind and I would understand. My choice doesn't have to be yours."

Gabrielle's eyes widened, she hated the idea that murderous vampires really existed but curiosity about them burned fiercely within her. How could she refuse the chance to meet one? And the journal had affirmed her passion for the past, she had always loved history, a devotion nurtured by her grandfather Sir Stephen Railton. She had became an archaeologist because of him.

Her mind raced with the possibilities. The vampires had lived for thousands of years, what wonders had they seen? What battles? What famous people had they encountered? They held the answers to so many questions of human history, questions she suddenly, excitedly, wanted to ask. Gabrielle fully understood the obsession that drove Parrish now, how torturous to briefly hold priceless books of great antiquity, to know you would never have access again in your lifetime. Understood but she could not forgive. No book was worth a human life.

So Gabrielle overcame her nervousness and prepared to meet a real, living vampire. One that had looked after and protected Khari. Though Gabrielle had been reassured the Dark Kind would not harm her, both as a female and as part of a family they respected, a shiver of nervous anticipation bordering on outright fear chilled her as Khari went to the door and brought in a tall, slender woman.

The woman sat in a chair, poised and elegant, studying Gabrielle with coldly beautiful lavender eyes, alien eyes devoid of any white. This was not a woman, Gabrielle realised, a whimper of fear rising in her throat. It was a female vampire, a deadly predator that ripped out human throats and drank blood to survive. Hell's Bells! What more craziness could happen in her life! Would there be a convention of Egyptian mummies downstairs, were the students taking the local werewolves out for walkies? The boundaries of reality were being shattered. Anything was possible now.

Gabrielle tried to keep calm, this creature would not hurt her, it was just the shock of encountering an alien species here in the Chilterns; but her heart refused to stop hammering wildly, a primeval instinct was screaming at her to run away, very fast!

Khari could see and feel her granddaughter's considerable unease but there was little she could do to help her. Each human encountering a vampire had to make their own mind up about the Dark Kind. If Gabrielle wanted nothing to do with Eshan, so be it. Meeting in London this week was the first time Khari had seen Eshan since the end of the war, when they had taken Jazriel's body back to the Prince. Eshan had not aged a minute since that encounter. Her glossy dark red hair was different, worn in a contemporary long bob that framed the hard-edged beauty of her features. Her clothing was up to date too, a very expensive, very classy top designer suit in flattering shades of soft lilac and grey. A simple but exquisite single row of large, perfect pearls adorned her elegant neck.

"I am here to help you find safety, Miss Railton," the female vampire spoke in perfect, unaccented English, her voice melodious but with an underlying huskiness.

"Why am I under threat from these creeps?" demanded Gabrielle, surprising herself at the firmness in her voice as she addressed the vampire. She was so nervous, she expected it to come out as a wavery squeak!

The creature, motionless, with her statue like poise, gave a little sigh of exasperation. "You should not be, but the founders of Nemesis are vindictive and determined old men. They fear Khari's gift of

Knowing - an ability they believe can thwart their attempts at hunting down and destroying my kind."

Khari took her granddaughter's hand, "You were used as bait to draw me out of hiding. But things are worse now, they have seen your eyes. Nemesis now know they are almost as golden as mine." Her hand went up to caress Gabrielle's face, to tenderly stroke her hair.

"They will think you have the *Knowing* too, and for once, those evil old men may be right."

Gabrielle did not argue that it was all nonsense, that she had no special gift. Not now she had touched another mind, not since she had reached out and made contact with the troubled but intriguing soul of Enver Thorne.

"You must be kept safe from these fiends, Gaby" continued her grandmother. "I will not have you put at risk, this family has lost too much already. I want you to come home with me, to Montana. Live at Whitethorn with the rest of your family."

Gabrielle let her grandmother's words sink in for a moment, then her natural rebelliousness took over. Damn it! No! She had a life, why should she hide away in a remote foreign land, with a load of Stetson-wearing red-necks with only elk and cattle for company?

"No way!" Gabrielle turned to her grandmother, her eyes wide, tearful. How quickly the joy of their reunion had turned to more anxiety. As if being pursued by Nemesis wasn't enough. "Of course I will go with you to Montana for a holiday, to meet the rest of my family. But I am not staying, however gorgeous the scenery, however lovely my relatives."

"You have no choice, sweetheart," urged Khari, alarmed, taking her granddaughter's hand, hating Nemesis, hating herself for this escalating situation.

"Actually I have," Gabrielle declared, raising her chin in a defiant gesture, her eyes flaring with a new fire. "Your answer to these nutters is to change your name and hide away for a lifetime in some remote mountain range. Mine is to be bold and brave, stick two fingers up to them and live out my life how I want to."

"That was your father's choice," Khari replied softy, tears flowing freely. She put her head into her hands and continued, her voice barely above a whisper, "Amela Railton paid for that folly with her life. I can't risk losing you, Gabrielle."

"I have a life, a job I enjoy and many good friends. I even love my grotty little flat and flea-bag old cat. And there may be a new man in my life!"

Gabrielle saw the wince of unease in her grandmother's eyes, did she know about her interest in Enver Thorne? Of course, she did, Khari could walk into her mind. The feeling of intrusion added fuel to her rising anger, "Why should I give it all up? If the mentalists at Nemesis want a fight with me, bring it on, I say."

"And you will lose." Khari stated simply, her voice now iron hard. Surely this young woman could see how much danger she was in? Until now, she had thought Gabrielle was no fool. Brave and feisty, yes, but a silly young girl?

Eshan broke the tense impasse and silence that followed.

"There is another way," the female vampire stated evenly, "Gabrielle would not be the first young human woman I have taken under my protection."

Khari shook her head emphatically, with Nemesis well funded and becoming increasingly organised, no Dark Kind could claim to be immune from danger.

"That was a whole different world ago, Eshan," she replied sadly, "And I had advantages to help keep me safe that Gaby may not have inherited."

"Excuse me," Gabrielle announced, standing up, shamelessly using her height to bring home her point, "Don't I have any say in my own future? Being rude to you is not the wisest move I have ever made, but what the hell. My life can't be more crazy or dangerous then it is already!"

Gabrielle turned to meet Eshan's cold lavender eyes, "I have no intention of teaming up with the Dark Kind, Lady. I am not like my Gran. You are a fascinating species, I could learn so much from you about my own people's past. That's my head talking. My heart screams you are cold-blooded murderers, stealing innocent lives. My male friends, my colleagues, men I love and respect are all mere prey to you. I can have no part in that."

Eshan's composure did not change, nor her eyes darken. This girl was fearless. Good! She listened with interest as Gabrielle continued to make her defiant stand.

"My Gran was raised by a vampire," Gabrielle ignored Eshan's wince of distaste at her deliberate use of an insulting term. "She knew no different. I do. I will have nothing to do with you."

Gabrielle sat down next to her grandmother, taking her hand, continued, "I am a professional archaeologist, a damn good field operative. Reyes and his odd little group have already offered me protection. I turned it down, but now I'm changing my mind. I will join their archaeological team, travelling the world discovering more ancient artefacts. And getting paid for it. "

"The great British compromise," she added with a triumphal grin.

Chapter Twenty-Three

Near Holm, Northern Norway,
Summer 2002

Uber-geeks, sociopaths, shifty- eyed weirdoes. Some massively pierced like human pincushions and, or, heavily tattooed. Or insignificant-looking wearing drab, mismatched, ill-fitting clothing. Misfits all, but they were his. These eager recruits hanging on his every word, willing, raw material for Hain to mould into his living weapons.

Over the past three days they had arrived at a purpose built complex in Northern Norway, away from the scrutiny of the rest of Nemesis. A significant, symbolic choice of venue, it was mid summer in the Arctic Circle, later tonight the sun would not set. Midnight would be as bright as day. A land and time all vampires would shun!

Today, Hain's team met together for the first time in person, though most had corresponded with each other for some months on the Internet. As they settled at a modern pine-clad meeting hall, drinking wine and beer, enjoying a lavish buffet, Hain moved around them, smiling, shaking hands with magnanimous good grace. They made him feel important, powerful, a twenty-first century messiah.

Hain had used the Internet to recruit this unlikely vanguard. Of course, he had full access to Nemesis personnel, tough security teams formed with ex-soldiers, intelligence agents, exiles from a police force demoralised by the constant threat of Outrages and world governments' inability to stop them. But these were professionals, though many were hardened cynics, they were men who could harbour a conscience, the shackles of morality. Hain wanted hollow men, living, moral vacuums he could fill to the brim with hate and poison to use as weapons against the vampires.

Hain addressed his team - fifty carefully vetted recruits, all men, aged between 20 and fifty from widely varied backgrounds. They had one thing in common. They shared Hain's belief with unswerving conviction, all were utterly convinced in the existence of vampires. Hain refused to dignify the creatures with their preferred name - Dark Kind.

Their leader mounted a podium to enthusiastic applause, he let the sound roll on and on, bathing in their fervour, their adulation. When he held up his hand, instant silence.

"Gentlemen," he paused, savouring the moment, drinking in their eagerness, their need for a strong leader, for a purpose. "I warmly welcome you on this historic morning. From this day forward, Project Doom is in full operation. Our just war against evil can begin!" Hain fought the impulse to laugh at such melodrama, the ridiculous project title, such nonsensical play acting but it had the desired effect on his recruits, the hall echoed with their loud cheers, clapping and stamping their approval. He had picked well.

These men would be his front line. The ones he would pitch in to attack the vampires directly. Many, if not all, would perish; it did not matter. The protection of Mankind was the highest cause of all. They would not die in vain. They need never know the true motive for Hain's quest for a vampire body, to harvest it for DNA to follow his own agenda. These people wanted adventure, to be fearless vampire hunters. He would give them their dream

"We have the biggest documented history of these evil creatures in existence. We have evidence of a dozen living examples and their movements tracked as much as possible. It makes chilling reading." Hain paused again in his address, watching their eyes for any signs of scepticism and doubt, he saw none.

"They have spread from their heartland in central Eurasia to all of Europe. Thankfully, they have not yet crossed the Atlantic to the Americas."

He continued, "We have evidence they are being protected by forces supported by many national governments. We must not let this sway our resolve and courage. We can - and we will - defy these traitors to the human race!"

Hain banged his fist down heavily to add to the drama. "Today begins our sacred calling. To capture and destroy all vampires!"

Again the hall resounded with enthusiastic cheering, the months of preparing these men, to make them believe they were not fantasists and obsessives, chained to their computers, but a secret, dynamic elite force, was at last coming together. Hain hoped that in six months these recruits would be able to handle weapons, to work undercover, to be obedient to his will without question. It would be tough, transforming this unlikely raw material but Hain was determined to succeed. Under the pale arctic sky it was a beginning, his team dedicated to exterminating all vampires was finally born.

A smiling Hain walked slowly among his acolytes, not engaging them in conversation but listening to their chatter, their enthusiasm, learning more about them then any Internet contact could ever give.

"Can't wait to start staking me some bloodsuckers..." one sniggered, thoughts of extreme violence and glory filled his head. He was convinced his years of role-playing games had prepared him for the ultimate challenge. "How about you?"

His new companion in arms just gave a crooked toothed sly smile. A rotund, pale faced youth covered in cheap, lurid tattoos - he nodded with enthusiasm. Could this get any better? Being paid a fortune to search out and destroy those vampire bastards. For real!

Hain's attention was drawn many times to one individual. A silent, morose-looking man, neatly and plainly dressed, self-contained and self confident to the point of arrogance. His eyes focused, intelligent and devoid of humanity. Predator's eyes. His name tag identified him as Phil Geddoe. Hain's new right hand man.

Chapter Twenty-Four

Isolann

The summer was in mourning for its greenery, now turned to loss and decay, weeping as each leaf died and fell to the cooling earth. The breath of coming winter manifested in silent cold mists, intertwining through the lamenting trees. The full significance was lost to Jazriel as the vampire opened up the Ducati's throttle and roared through a drift of frost-crisp autumn leaves, sending them whirling in flustered protest up into the clear night sky above the low lying , sinuously sinister mists.

When he rode, time lost all meaning; relentlessly forcing the bike to give him all she had, all the power, all the speed and danger he craved. To Jazriel, the motorbike just had to be a curvaceous beautiful female, the bike equivalent of a Dark Kind noblewoman with her sharp-planed beauty, rounded sensuous styling and fiery temperament. The Ducati hadn't wanted to start that night, grumbling at first then refusing to co-operate at all. Jazriel hadn't a clue how the machine worked, he never did with any of his past toys; the Hispano-Suiza he had given to Garan and the adored Bugatti Atlantic. Damn those bastard Nazis!

Forcing aside the pointless old resentment, he had persisted, gently caressing the machine, seducing the throttle until the Ducati had yielded to his demands and came to life in his hands, the bike vibrated and growled, pliant and responsive to his touch. Moving and responding to every subtle shift of his body weight. Like all his high born conquests!

In a celebratory spinning flourish, Jazriel whirled the bike around in a high-revving tight curve before releasing its power to take him out of the inner cobbled courtyard of the keep, through the stronghold's outer compound and into the lush valley beyond.

He wore his latest import from the wider world beyond Isolann, another gift from Azrar. A black leather biker's outfit, hand made for him by Gucci of course, an expensively cut short jacket and tight jeans with matching boots, worn with no helmet. That would look cumbersome and mess up his hair. It was strange wearing total black for the first time; no Dark Kind ever did, it was Azrar's colour, but the Prince had ordered and paid for the outfit himself, so Jazriel felt comfortable to wear it, knowing black suited his dark, dramatic looks.

Jazriel and his freedom machine sped out away from the forests and onto the open plains. He rode hard and fast, leaning forward over the engine, enjoying its roaring vibration coursing through his body. With no headlights he could see perfectly in the darkness, every startled pheasant rising up in terror from the monster roaring through the night, every fleeing herd of deer. The Ducati, however, was built for tarmac roads and not rough grassland, Jazriel had to struggle to maintain control many times, wrestling with the bike with his Dark Kind strength yet never slackening the breakneck speed which would have made controlling the powerful machine so much easier. He did not want to make things easier; he wanted the challenge of pushing the bike and himself to the limit

He found a level stretch of grass, scythed low by nomads making hay for the winter, a warning sign that humans were close, a sign Jazriel ignored, too lost in his reckless ride. Opening up the throttle to its fullest extent Jazriel murmured endearments to the machine

"Come now, My princess. Show me what you can really do for me, give me everything, come on sahma'a, everything you've got…."

Jazriel's eyes stung with the night air lashing his face as he pushed the bike to its highest speed, trying to go beyond any limits, this was pure joy, this was flying, this was better then…. this was so…

The bike juddered and swerved as something caught the edge of his front tyre, nearly pitching Jazriel over the handlebars, the vampire fought hard as the bike careered wildly across the grass, the Ducati's engine screaming in loud, outraged protest. It pitched and yawed at a crazy angle until Jazriel eventually regained control. He paused, breathing hard, shaking with adrenaline, exhilarated and triumphant. The margin between disaster and control had turned into a knife edge struggle. He had won the battle.

What the hell hit his bike? Jazriel braked hard and turned to glance back into the darkness. A deer? At a slower speed, he retraced his route but there was nothing. No stricken beast, no blood. Jazriel shrugged, unconcerned, an injured animal would soon be put out of its misery by the wolves. Revving the engine again, he took off into the night to continue his wild ride.

'Look at that bastard, roaring about as if he owned this land! Isolann is just a playground to the creature!' Lomak thought as he watched from the outskirts of his own tribe's encampment, drawn to the edge of darkness by the sound of the big machine with it's monstrous dragon's roar and foul stench. Lomak knew it should have headlights on, but the abomination riding the machine spurned them in his arrogance. How he hated the beautiful but deadly living sex toy kept by the Prince. Jazriel was a being who embodied all that was evil and decadent and Lomak prayed that Tahjr himself would punish the blood drinker with a particularly cruel and agonising fate.

He reached down, almost trance like in his anger, his hand curled around a large rock, held it tightly as the engine grew louder and louder in the darkness. Heading towards him. Hatred sped the rock hurtling through the darkness, towards the loathsome machine and the creature riding it. Lomak heard a scream. High pitched then silence. No! No! That was not a Dark Kind voice, it was human and so very young…

Dawn's accursed approach was threatening, so with reluctance, Jazriel wheeled the Ducati around in a tight circle, forcing the engine to roar in protest. "Enough, princess," he murmured, reaching down and caressing the hot engine beneath him. "We will ride again tomorrow night."

He cruised at a slower pace towards Azrar's stronghold in the base of the mighty Arpalathians, allowing the sharp night air to touch his face, to rifle through his blue-black hair like an unseen lover. He threw back his head, closed his eyes and smiled, as if seducing the wind in return…

Angry shouting from many humans caused him to brake harshly as he neared the outer compound of the stronghold. What the hell was going on? Jazriel became aware of a large number of humans, bearing lit torches, their anger rising in a noisy tumult. Zaard! Jazriel's heart turned to ice, with chilling echoes of the murderous rebellion against King Dezarn surging into his mind, a long lost ancient time to humans, but horribly fresh in Dark Kind memory. Was Azrar in danger from his own people? What could he do?

Jazriel cut the engine and wheeling the bike, edged as close as he could, sharp senses on full alert, ready to mow down any human daring to threaten the Prince. He left the bike by a tree, crept silently close to the mob, trying to discover their intentions towards their Prince. He had the advantage of his Dark Kind vision, keeping low and silent in the darkness, avoiding the flaring torches, becoming one with the night as if hunting.

What he over-heard sickened him to the core of his being. He, Jazriel was the source of their anger, for something he had done, some terrible crime. And they were baying for justice, for blood - for his blood! He ran back to the bike and remounted, his head spinning with confusion and indecision.

Leaning forward on the Ducati, Jazriel throttled back hard, brutally over-revving the engine, whirling the powerful machine into a tornado of dust and exhaust fumes. What should he do? Must he make a life-changing decision, one forced on him by this torch-wielding mob of murderous humans? Damn them, no! Why should he flee into the night without a word, a gesture of farewell? In truth, for all his plans, his craving for escape, Jazriel wasn't ready to leave Azrar.

Zaard! It was so damned unfair! He had done nothing wrong! He revved the big bike again, poised on the edge of indecision, clouded by a heart-rending despair. Survival instincts urged him to escape but there was also a reckless urge to mow down these ignorant peasants who stood between Jazriel and his life with Azrar. To drive straight through them at high speed into the safety of the keep, where Azrar could protect him behind the black granite walls, not caring how many broken, bloodied and shattered bodies he'd leave in his wake. Damn them all to their human Hell, that's where he was now, unable to reach his lover, the Prince.

The quiet but insistent voice of reason within Jazriel's heart broke through the painful confusion. How could he remain in Isolann as a burden to Azrar? How could he risk endangering the Prince's life? The Jendar could not rule a rebellious Isolann, nor could he command his human army to turn on its own people. But bloody hellfire, Jazriel growled, he wanted to know what terrible offence he had committed! Despite the boredom and the hunger he had kept his fangs out of the natives' throats.

Sharing Azrar's bed wasn't a crime in Isolann? Or was it? Some human societies executed males who were physically intimate with others of the same sex. He recalled how careful he'd had to be in Nazi Germany. Were the Isolann nomads becoming equally cruel and prejudiced? Merde! He and Azrar were not human. And what damn business was it of this furious mob anyway?

Jazriel had faced a painful choice once before, to leave someone he loved in a deliberate sacrifice to save their life from the wrath of humans. Leaving Azrar now would mean his vampire's heart would be broken again. How much more damage could it take?

His thoughts were abruptly interrupted as the baying mob fell silent. The gates to the outer compound flew open. Azrar's elite bodyguard rode out with the Prince at its head. In an important gesture to the people, they were unarmed, firmly parting the hushed crowd by nudging them over with their calm horses. The voice of reason lost the battle for Jazriel's mind, as always his heart, the desires of his body ruled his choice. Azrar was coming to rescue him, bring him home safely. How could he run from the Prince now?

But relief was short lived; Jazriel's unfolding nightmare suddenly intensified; there was no joyous reunion, no protective embrace. Azrar was furious with him. Jazriel lowered his head to escape the accusing ice-fire blazing from the Prince's eyes, was shocked as he watched the Prince order guards to wheel away the bike, taking his precious Ducati from him, leaving him to humiliatingly follow on foot behind Azrar's horse. That short walk back into the stronghold was infinitely worse then the insults and threats from the baying mob, for the first time in their long affair Azrar had turned away from him.

Within the inner keep, dismounting his horse with a snarl of agony from his shattered leg, Azrar stormed from the humans; rage had made him highly dangerous. He had learned long ago to distance himself from them when his fury became beyond bearing, a blind directionless fury needing assuaging in torn human flesh and spilled hot, red blood. But this time his anger was directed at one of his own Kind, the reason his heart kept beating. Jazriel. The reckless, selfish, stupid, spoiled idiot!

How could Azrar balance his duty to enforce his people's right for justice with his obligation to protect a Dark Kind? More than just any Dark Kind. Jazriel. By Dezarn's blood, what could he do?

Outside he could hear the nomad's baying for revenge, they wanted to execute Jazriel themselves with wild talk of beheading or by fire. Azrar grabbed a broadsword off the wall and whirled it in a powerful swinging arc. Never! No human would harm Jazriel. Not while he remained under Azrar's care.

But how could he punish his lover with enough severity to placate the wronged nomads? Would banishment from Isolann be sufficient for them? Hardly. They wanted blood, purple, Dark Kind blood. Nothing less would silence their anger. Azrar would not shed one drop of Dark Kind blood, even if it meant the loss of his realm or his life. Which was in truth, the same thing. Without Isolann to rule and protect, he could not exist. Azrar sighed, unable to see a way through this impossible dilemma but he could not delay the confrontation any longer and summoning a guard, demanded Jazriel be brought to his presence.

With a vicious snarl of contempt Jazriel strode in, brushing aside his human escort, his glorious blue-green eyes darkening to a confused and stormy black. He dropped to the ground in respect and submission but immediately jumped up to his feet and began to pace the floor in agitation, growling his despair.

"My Lord Prince, I have done nothing wrong, I have not attacked any of your people, why are they calling for my blood?"

Azrar took his face in his strong warrior's hands and kissed him; Jazriel could sense the great sorrow, the anger and resignation in the gesture and pulled back, greatly alarmed.

Azrar's voice was all command, a fierce, wolf-snarl demanding full obedience. "Come with me, there is something you need to see in the Great Hall."

Jazriel was faced with a distraught nomad family keening pitifully, a child's broken body at their feet covered with a blanket, one that seeped with red blood at the head. He was appalled - he had not done this! He had checked, there had been nothing along that track... had there?

Azrar's eyes blazing with fury, emerald fire lighting up his sepulchral face "Jazriel," the Prince demanded, knowing Dark Kind do not lie, "did you knock down this human child?"

The commoner shook his head vehemently, pleading in the vampire tongue, *"My lord Prince, you know I speak the truth. I did not."*

Azrar growled in disapproval, "These people deserve to know the truth in their own language."

"They won't believe me!" Jazriel muttered bitterly, ignoring the Prince's command. *"I know humans. They lie, they expect us to lie too."*

Jazriel turned to the grieving family, "Believe me, I would never harm a human child, even by accident. I did not do this."

It was too much for the grieving mother, she ran forward and began to pummel Jazriel's chest with her blood-stained fists, striking him over and over again, screaming curses. He dropped his arms to his side and took her attack passively, he could not harm a human woman. Her misplaced fury was understandable, she had just lost her daughter.

Lomak stepped forward and gently guided away his hysterical kinswoman, handing her over to the rest of the tribe. He ostentatiously wiped tears for his fallen kin from his reddened eyes before fixing Jazriel with an accusing glare. "I saw your machine strike the child in the darkness, Lord Jazriel. It was being ridden at a dangerous, furious speed with no lights. Little Oolie didn't stand a chance."

Shaking his head, Jazriel growled, doing his best to ignore the human, he had always distrusted the man, with his unctuous manner and cold, calculating, mean eyes. Like an ambitious, rabid ferret. How he wanted to break the wretched creature's neck!

Jazriel turned back to the Prince, arms outstretched in a pleading gesture, *"I didn't do this, Prince Azrar, by the great and abiding love you have for me, you must believe me."*

A jagged blade tore Azrar's heart in two. Maybe Jazriel truly believed he had not killed the human girl child, but how could he be sure? Riding that infernal motorbike like a lunatic through the night, anything could have happened. His subjects believed it. They demanded justice, revenge. Lomak vociferously called for Jazriel's blood by the ancient laws of retribution, the fierce and uncompromising tribal laws of Isolann. They had served the humans well over the centuries, now they were being evoked for the first time in this land's long history to take the life of a Dark Kind.

It was an unsolvable dilemma, the Prince could not harm any Dark Kind, let alone his beloved companion, but as Jendar of Isolann, he must also rule his human subjects with impartiality and integrity. This was a disaster, a nightmare. What was he going to do?

Growing angrier, Jazriel rounded on the Prince, again in his own harsh language. *"My Lord, how can you take the word of this poisonous little ape over mine? Humans all lie and cheat and betray. Treachery is bred into their blood, their bones. I have always been your most loyal and loving subject, I swear on Dezarn's noble memory, I did not kill this child.*

"It does not matter, Seymahl. The humans believe it. Without proof to the contrary, they will continue to believe it." Azrar sighed, *"What would you have me do? Destroy the peace and security of this land by ignoring their grievance, their loss?"*

Jazriel snarled, it was so wrong, so unjust. Azrar should defend him! Why shouldn't the Prince defy these creatures, he'd protected the wretches from deadly enemies for centuries.

What gratitude did they show? None! Time would pass, events become forgotten as generation after generation of these quick breeding, short-lived humans came and died. Jazriel looked at the Prince, his austere face tortured by what was happening.

"By Dezarn's blood, Azrar, protect me from these filthy lying apes, I am your...your...." Words escaped Jazriel; what exactly was he to the Prince?

Azrar's fury arose in a fire storm of violence, the mindless actions of this reckless fool could destroy them both, wreck the peace and security of an entire nation. He swung the broadsword at Jazriel, it sang through the air in a swift arc, pausing to hover by his throat, close enough for Jazriel to feel the cold metal but not enough to shed one drop of his purple blood. Azrar kept the blade poised and threatening at his lover's throat, fixing him with his black-eyed fury

"What would you have me do, Jazriel?" he growled in bitterness and despair. *"You have brought this disaster on your own head. You have destroyed the ancient Pact, the age-old trust between Dark Kind and human in Isolann. What am I supposed to do? I am the Prince of Isolann."*

Using every scrap of courage he could gather, Jazriel raised his hand and firmly pushed away the threatening blade. He did not drop to his knees and offer Azrar his throat in the Dark Kind gesture of apology, he had done nothing wrong! *"I love you and I will never stop loving you, my Prince. I am not a warrior but I was ready to ride into battle tonight, to give up my life defending you from the mob. I gave my word I did not harm that human child. That should be enough."*

Azrar's wolf growl voice softened as he tried one more time to make Jazriel see the impossibility of his dilemma.

"Seymahl, I hold the lives of these people in a sacred trust, their lives are in peril once more from forces beyond Isolann's borders. I cannot abandon them now. I will find a way for this difficulty to pass, there will be a time in the future, a time for us…"

Jazriel waved a hand in a petulant, dismissive gesture of disinterest. The nomads of Isolann could go screw themselves. Make a change from goats. *"It has to be now, my Prince. Choose between your stinking human peasants, these ungrateful apes or me."*

Outraged, Azrar's eyes grew angry again, the lustrous emerald darkening to pitch black. How dare Jazriel make such demands! A commoner, no, less then that, a sha'ref! How dare he challenge a High Prince!

Jazriel read the instinctive thought in Azrar's eyes. He had his answer. He stormed out of the great hall, pushing roughly past the now openly smirking Lomak, sending the man toppling to the floor. Let the Prince stop him! Jazriel heart raced, he expected some move to prevent him leaving, some call to the guards but Azrar had dropped the broad sword to his side and made no attempt to stop him. Jazriel took his chance and ran through the keep, the pain of rejection and separation was already too much to bear but he would not stay, not answer to these false accusations. Not be punished for something he had not done! Would not accept that brief but telling flash of contempt in Azrar's eyes.

Leaping on to the bike Jazriel kicked it into life, roared off into the dying last hour of the night, challenged too late by the guards, caught unaware by the dramatic swiftness of his flight and lack of orders from their Prince. He knew this escape would be bad for Azrar's reputation among his human subjects. Zaard! Let the mighty Jendar deal with the consequences!

Jazriel rode straight to the Cadera settlement and sought out the one mechanic. With the terrified man cowering against a wall, huddled with his family, the vampire ransacked the stone cottage and adjoining garage, filling every petrol can and lashing it to the back of the Ducati.

He helped himself to a wallet of Svolenian currency and two bottles of imported French brandy, this man clearly did well with his trading across the border.

With only roughly thirty minutes of darkness left to him, he revved the Ducati and without a backward glance, rode at breakneck speed south towards the Svolenian border. He knew he couldn't travel far before daybreak and would have to shelter, dug down into a rough earth and tree-branch hide in the forest. Cowering, like a hunted animal gone to ground. He crouched low over the machine, concentrating on the rough grassland, focusing on the stand of trees silhouetted on the ever-lightening sky line. He couldn't risk an accident, a fall from the bike. Not with hordes of vengeful nomads chasing him, eager to spill his blood. Not with the blinding inferno of the sun looming below the horizon, the blazing orb swiftly, relentlessly climbing.

Jazriel's hurt grew with every difficult mile. This was the second time he had deliberately left someone he loved. How cruel was that sadistic bitch, Fate, to let this happen to him again? It was unbearable. Azrar! He howled out his name to the swift rushing wind. Part of Jazriel's soul screamed for him to stop, to spin the bike round, to go back to the Prince he loved so much. But Azrar's great pride, his determination to fulfil his duty meant putting Isolann before his love for Jazriel - again. Another brutal rejection. The pain shattered Jazriel's heart beyond all repair. Something must pay for this grief. The whole of Europe and its seething mass of humans awaited his razor-sharp fangs in the darkness, an ocean of red blood waiting to be spilt. If he survived the forthcoming, long, daylight hours.

Chapter Twenty-Five

A shocking affront to all propriety, to Isolanni justice! No one walked away from the Prince's presence without being formally dismissed, yet his bed mate had stormed out, unchallenged. Azrar's court was incensed, the disbelief, the anger rippling in a wave through the crowded Great Hall.

Still lying on the floor where Jazriel had pushed him, Lomak was appalled, for his plan to succeed, there had to be summary and swift justice, the creature must be executed, so there could be no more speculation over who killed the child. If Jazriel was proven innocent, then who was the last person seen near the victim? Lomak shuddered as the reality of his position struck home. He had openly admitted seeing the blood drinker's machine hitting the child. All eyes would turn towards him.

Increasingly anxious, Lomak had watched the Prince closely; had seen the distress and indecision flit briefly across his austere features before they returned to their familiar cold stone. Lomak's plan could have worked, should have worked.

He had to reinforce the guilt of the blood drinker, if not in the eyes of the Prince, in the Isolanni people. He rose slowly and painfully to his feet, his difficulty feigned but effective. Many rushed forward to help him get up from the floor. Lomak waved them aside and made a show of regaining his dignity by brushing imaginary dust from his clothes, attempting to suppress a wince of imaginary pain. He held his hands out in a gesture of hopeless resignation, "You see how it is My Lord…" He was interrupted by the sound of the bike being revved outside in the courtyard below.

Alarmed, Lomak ran to the entrance of the Great Hall, looked out into the courtyard, rage consuming him. The guards were running to intercept the fleeing Jazriel but were too late, the bastard was already clear of the outer compound and speeding away into the forest, heading towards the open plains and freedom. Lomak looked round sharply to the Prince, waiting for the command to his guards to follow the fugitive. But there no orders, just silence.

"My Lord, he is getting away!" Lomak blurted out, too aware of his own precarious position for discretion.

Azrar's emerald eyes darkened and flared with anger but he held it in check. It took all his considerable willpower. Jazriel was gone, he wanted to be alone to grieve his loss, not deal with this impudent human.

"I will send my best troops out to track him down." Azrar growled, "I will have the truth on this matter. This family has endured the greatest tragedy, the loss of a child. They deserve answers."

Lomak's exasperation was unabated, there was no way troopers on horseback would catch up with that infernal machine and the Prince knew it. He was letting his lover escape! He could say little more, stoking up the Blood Drinker's wrath could have fatal consequences.

The captain of Azrar's guard stepped forward, he had no time for Lomak, had distrusted him since the man had showed such interest in the Abhajastani prisoners, spent so many hours alone in deep conversation with them.

"Tell me one thing, Lomak," the captain challenged. "I examined the machine after we wheeled it away. I saw no sign of damage, no blood stains. How do you explain this, if you so clearly saw him hit the child?"

Lomak's face blanched, he stuttered incoherently, "I... I only know what I saw. A child is dead. Her murderer must be brought to justice!"

Azrar's ferocious gaze fixed and held the man; had Jazriel been falsely accused? Was he to be bereft for nothing?

"I swear, my Lord Prince, by all the tribal gods, I saw your companion strike the child. He did kill her!"

The human was lying, Azrar was convinced. He wished his ward Khari was here, with the gift of the *Knowing*, she would discover the truth for certain. But her destiny was to live on the other side of the world, he had not forced her to stay in Isolann. The Prince was a stern, autocratic ruler but no tyrant. He ruled solely with the consent of his subjects. That was what made this nightmare scenario with Jazriel so dangerous, undermining his ancient and unbroken authority with these humans.

"This family must be allowed to mourn in peace. But the cause of their distress is yet unproven. I am not convinced my companion hit the child with the motorbike, there is not one scrap of evidence."

With his own life in the balance, Lomak's fear made him bold, reckless, he stepped forward to remonstrate, "In all respect, My Lord Prince, I know what I saw!"

"The darkness plays tricks on human eyes. But not on Dark Kind vision. Jazriel swore he did not hit the girl, there was no sign of damage or blood on the machine. I believe him. That is the end of the matter."

"But my people deserve an answer!"

Azrar's eyes darkened and he found his hand tightening around the hilt of his broadsword. How easily he could silence this worm! His eyes blazing into Lomak's, Azrar answered, his voice pitched low but laden with menace, "And they will get one, I assure you. They will get one."

The prince terminated the audience by striding from the room in a sudden and violent wave of power, cold and strong like a blizzard roaring down from the mountains. He knew the humans would be cowering, struggling to keep their feet from the onslaught. Good! It was time for them to remember who he was, to rediscover the lost respect, eroded by the creeping influences slithering on fetid bellies across the borders into his land. Damn humans, damn them all, both treachery and these apes had the same stench!

Azrar approached his vault of Rest with a heavy heart, for he faced a desolate future, of long hours of cursed sunlight spent alone and in pain. Again. He paused outside the oak and iron door, his hand gripping the ornate handle. No! He could not face the empty bed, the indentation in the sheets where Jazriel had lain with him but hours before. Maybe a fading scent of honey and cinnamon, of Jazriel.

A surly dawn was already lightening behind the eastern mountains. Azrar was beyond caring. He strode to his favourite place on the highest battlement where the ice-laden wind from the surrounding mountains was at its strongest. With a howl of fury, he brought down his fist, hammering the unforgiving black granite until he felt flesh tear and bones break, his blood spilling to drench the old stones. Out of sight of any living thing, Azrar dropped onto one knee with a low keening of anguish, his head bowed, resting on the bloodied stones. He did not feel the pain from his shattered leg or broken hand for that in his heart overrode all else.

Chapter Twenty-Six

In a shatter of small stones, Jazriel braked suddenly, the back wheel swerving in a tight half circle. Above him, silhouetted against the relentlessly lightning sky, towered tall poles topped with wolf sculls and long, tattered banners. The wind passing through the sculls created an eerie wail marking the border, the invisible line that separated Isolann from Svolenia. He could turn around. Return to Azrar and the Land of Secrets and Shadows, fall to his knees and plead with the Prince for protection. A deep snarl of anger rumbled in his throat. Could he hell!

At first Jazriel fought against the rising grief and hurt then exhausted and overwhelmed, gave in to it, throwing back his head, he released a piercing howl of Dark Kind sorrow that rose and joined the cry of the long dead wolves. It echoed across the dying nightscape, a melancholy lament that rode high on the air. Azrar had made his choice, his stubborn allegiance to his damned humans. To his insufferable pride and honour.

Now Jazriel would make his. He turned the bike away from Isolann, kicked it back into life and howling again above the Ducati's throaty roar, crossed the border into Svolenia. Desperation joined his sorrow, dawn was breaking across the horizon. He pushed the bike hard, seeking shelter from the sunlight, seeking anything, a barn, a graveyard crypt, a burrow beneath the earth like an animal. It had come to that. Jazriel, the most beautiful, most desired sha'ref to the nobility, who had once dwelt in the finest palaces in creation, reduced to cowering beneath mud and twigs.

The pain of loss, betrayal and injustice would turn him into a burning comet of destruction that was to scorch across the Svolenian and Amantzki countryside spreading mayhem and death in his wake. Through the next week, Jazriel rode like a demon, as fast as possible, every night pushing the bike to its limit. Stopping wherever he could to hide from daylight in hotels, isolated private houses, farmyard barns.

Killing often as he helped himself to whatever he needed to survive, cash and petrol, fresh blood. To the vampire, it wasn't murder and theft, these primates had stolen the Dark Kind's entire world, it was token pay back.

The journey was a nightmare, a blur of grief, missing Azrar with every minute passed, every mile of dusty rural road ridden away from Isolann and its accursed humans and their lies. Jazriel had planned this escape from Isolann so many times, but on his own terms, in his own time. He now had his freedom but it left a bitter taste. Worse, then that, it was like poison.

East Germany

A burning cigarette bounced across the tarmac, flaring briefly in a mini meteor shower of tiny sparks. Jazriel paused at the edge of an unknown world. Modern Europe, an alien land. He had been incarcerated in Isolann for more then sixty years.

He sat back on the Ducati, his face and clothing filthy from travelling across the back roads of the Upper Balkans, a world little changed since the Second World War and therefore familiar. The unknown lay before him in the darkness, as dangerous as the edge of a bottomless abyss.

The vampire gazed on in fearful wonder as vast ground-shaking machines and cars as swift as arrows roared past him on a massive route of many lanes, a confusion of engine-thunder, stinking exhaust fumes and flashing bright lights. The huge lorries battered him with the earthquake power of their passing, he felt insignificant, lost, abandoned. A piece of roadside rubbish, an unwanted dog, left to the mercy of the traffic.

A whole new world. So much to learn. Perhaps too much! He growled, fangs bared. There was no choice, he could hardly turn back. Jazriel started up the bike again, took in a deep breath and throttled back hard to roar away, quickly matching the speed of the furious headlong rush. Soon a manic exhilaration took control of him, dicing with death at high speed on the autobahn pushed his reflexes, his concentration to the extreme edge of his skill. One mistake, one misjudgement and he would be beneath the wheels of the vast but fast-moving behemoths. Not the worst fate, it would be a quick death. Unlike his first.

With dawn threatening, the vampire followed a stream of lorries and cars pulling off the main road. He was exhausted in mind and body, despite frequent kills on his headlong flight from Isolann. The Ducati was filthy and hard pushed, too. Even in his distressed state Jazriel knew he needed time to recover, to think about his future, learn how to survive in this new era and to give the machine some desperately needed attention.

He stopped at a depressed and rundown industrial city in what was once East Germany, big enough to be anonymous, poor enough to welcome his cash. With the valiant Ducati now resting at a nearby garage, getting a full service, Jazriel booked into a hotel, shabby and decrepit but the best in town. He had used his looks and easy charm to convince the buxom manageress that he was a harmless traveller seeking nothing except a chance to rest without any fuss or attention. The small fortune in stolen euros he paid in advance, with the promise of much more if he was left undisturbed, had ensured some measure of security.

Jazriel brusquely pushed away his third empty bottle of local schnapps. The fiery liquor briefly burned the back of his throat but left him alarmingly sober with no desperately needed numbing of his emotions. He sat in the shadows of a small tavern, eyes hidden behind purloined dark glasses, motionless and silent with only the occasional glow from a cigarette raised to his lips

The bar was busy, some televised football match had attracted a crowd of intent and hard drinking males, bellowing their disapproval at each missed attempt at a goal or heavy, bone-crunching tackle.

The vampire glanced up at the huddle of excited humans gathered around the little box of light, of coloured moving images. It was set high above the bar, attracting the humans, hovering like moths around a flame. The box was more new technology to Jazriel, a marvel that illustrated just how ill prepared he had been for the modern world. So much had changed since his death in 1944. He had no identity papers and none of those new rectangles of plastic humans used instead of currency. Fortunately, here, hard cash was welcomed. Jazriel wore the same black biker leathers, now grimy from the long nights of travel, any humans around him were fortunate the Dark Kind did not sweat or have rank body odours after he given the clothing many days continuous use. He was loathe to help himself to any other clothes on his killing raids, the thought of putting on anything a human had worn was appalling. With one exception; one victim had a new full length coat, bitter chocolate leather lined with sable. It was beautiful, Jazriel had made an exception with that particular item!

So what now? Where could he go? Who would he go to?

He took a deep drag on the cigarette and waving his hand, ordered more schnapps. Maybe the fourth bottle would work. Something had to. He would not go near that self-righteous and dismissive bitch, Eshan, though she had the means and power to set him up in a new life. Especially as she may have Sivaya with her. He suppressed a shudder at the sound of his past lover's name. Sivaya. She was supposed to have adored him, so why had she not done the right thing once he'd been killed? Was it cowardice or an insane distortion of the intensity of Dark Kind love? She had wanted to possess him completely, even after his death, her obsession to preserve his body had thrown his fettered spirit into a realm of torture, to become nearly nothing, a formless, terrified and fading thought. His spirit lost in oblivion, calling without a voice for help, forgetting what he was, who he was, as he drifted in the nothingness of non- being. He could not bear the thought of ever meeting her again.

So, with the whereabouts of the few other scattered Dark Kind survivors unknown, that left Garan. The maverick commoner was good if somewhat unreliable company. Jazriel knew the teenage-looking vampire loved Paris. At least now Jazriel had a destination to aim for, though no purpose beyond surviving the desolate wasteland that was anywhere in the world where Azrar was not.

Chapter Twenty-Seven

'I've got you!' Hain gasped, trying but failing to contain his excitement, as he watched the stream of data scroll onto his computer screen. He bit into his clenched fist-hard, almost to the point of drawing blood as he struggled to control his outburst. This exuberance was foolish. He mustn't alert the spies of the malevolent Raker. The old man's baleful influence infiltrated every part of Nemesis. The prize was within *his* grasp, not that of the grim, obsessed old man.

"What a very busy and very bad boy you have been!" murmured Hain, as he meticulously followed a trail of violent death across Europe starting from the Svolenian borders of Isolann. A horrifying list of healthy young men found with a traumatic neck wound, always a deep, precise, clean cut into the jugular vein, their bodies almost totally desanguinated. The forensic departments, whose data Hain had hacked into, were all puzzled by the cleanness of the killer; there were no signs of gore splattered around the unfortunate victims. No sign of a struggle. And where was the victims' blood? The police scientists were perplexed. Hain was not. All were the classic signs of a Dark Kind attack.

So the literally blood-thirsty bastard was crossing Europe on a killing spree, leaving a trail of devastation so obvious, it was as if he wanted to be caught. Witnesses spoke of seeing a powerful motorbike ridden by a dark-clad rider close to the scene of many of the murders. There was even CCTV footage from a petrol station! Hain had looked at it many times, now knew the prowling, arrogant gait of the Ducati's young male rider, every inch of his sharp-planed features. Even caught a glimpse of the strange in-human eyes, when the vampire had briefly removed his dark glasses. A stunningly handsome, ruthless and remorseless killing machine. A prime subject to be the genetic blue-print for a new species of human.

But first Hain's minions led by the fanatically loyal Geddoe had to capture the creature, get the body to his own secret laboratories. He doubted whether it would be possible to take the vampire alive. All without the Nemesis organisation discovering what Hain had achieved.

Hain knew that without doubt if he did capture a vampire, his discovery would be taken off him. He knew what the old men thought of him, a useless idiot, a fool with a flair for modern information technology. A paid geek. And this situation would never change unless that vile old monster Parrish finally stopped hanging onto his miserable over long, artificially sustained life and died. Then Raker would be 'retired.' Only then could Nemesis truly belong to him. To the despised computer nerd nephew. Hain. And the secrets of the Dark Kind, along with the future evolution of humanity would be his to control without opposition or interference.

Life was good, no wonder those old bastards hung onto to it with such infuriating and successful tenacity. Perhaps it was time to loosen their grip.

Chapter Twenty-Eight

"That isn't doing the job, is it?" The manageress of the hotel sidled up to Jazriel and pushed away the pile of several empty bottles of vodka and schnapps. She shook her head in amazement that the glorious looking young man was upright and appeared stone cold sober despite the night-long binge of neat alcohol. "She must have been some woman!"

Jazriel groaned inside, the last thing he wanted now was undue attention from this human female but he was unsafe with dawn approaching, he needed her to protect him through the long, vulnerable daylight hours. The vampire shrugged and gave a dazzling yet heart-rending smile calculated to melt the hardest human heart. "What makes you think it was a woman? There are many other reasons to want to forget," he replied in faultless German.

"No man tries to drink himself to death over anything else," she laughed. A pleasantly rich sound, betraying warmth beneath a hard, cynical veneer. She was a buxom redhead in her late thirties, world-wise, and intelligent. She was not a fool to have her head turned by the young stranger's exquisite looks. She knew there was nothing innocent about this handsome traveller, but he was rolling in money, enough to buy her silence, enough to get her out of this dead-end town. And yes, it helped that he was so easy on the eye!

Jazriel was aware of the desperation behind the smile, behind the sparkle in her hazel eyes. Needy and greed - the ideal type of human to manipulate.

"If you really want to get out of it for a while, I have something in my private rooms, something far better then this rubbish," she murmured with what she thought was a seductive smile.

Jazriel switched on his own far superior version, a megawatt smile that could reduce an angry lion into playful submission. "That is the best offer I have had for what seems like an eternity. Lead the way, my princess."

He found himself in a basement apartment beneath the hotel, claustrophobic but mercifully free from natural light. It was perfect. The woman, Marta, sat on her bed, signalling with her hand for her guest to join her. She had made the best of her living space, everything was spotlessly clean and tastefully decorated, clearly someone with aspirations to a better life. Or one who had known a better life but has fallen on hard times.

"Have you been on the road long?" she asked, trying to put this unsettlingly beautiful but mysterious young man at ease. Jazriel did not answer, but stood, poised on the edge of flight, his shielded eyes scanning the rooms for any hidden danger, any sign of a trap.

"Please, you have nothing to worry about," she tried to reassure him switching on a machine that emitted music, music so strange, so different to what he had known in the 1940's but he liked it. A lot.

"I don't care who you are or what you have done," Marta continued, "but I have watched you all evening. Someone in that amount of pain could do with a few hours of oblivion." She rummaged in her bedside cabinet and produced a mirror, a razor and a bag of white powder. "This will wipe away the bad memories, take away the heart-break...."

The woman was wrong. Jazriel knew that, but he was beyond caring. Taking the razor blade and the mirror, he helped himself to enough cocaine to stun an elephant. Marta cut herself a generous amount but a night spent taking drinks from her customers began to catch up with her body. She had to move faster then she wanted to become intimate with the traveller, to make him desire her, to make him want to help her. The woman tried to snuggle close to Jazriel oblivious to his instinctive shudder of distaste, to the unnatural coldness of his skin, before she passed out on the bed.

The vampire sighed with relief, one awkward situation he didn't have to charm his way out of! His metabolism was jittery with the drug and unable to Rest, he paced like a caged panther for hours, trapped in Marta's basement apartment till the sun dropped down behind the monolithic slabs of concrete block skyscrapers. He made the best of the time, looking at all the strange new things in the woman's apartment that the clever apes had invented since World War Two, many had a purpose beyond his comprehension. He had so much to learn. Too much, he needed a Dark Kind guide to ease him into human society. Garan was the perfect choice.

As the woman slept on, oblivious to the passing hours of daylight, Jazriel sat on the floor surrounded by the woman's many glossy, life-style magazines. His lustrous turquoise eyes glowed with wonder at the elegance and understated style of the men's clothes, the sliver-thin stylish watches. This was clearly a perfect time for a creature of Jazriel's exacting sensibilities. As he carefully studied the latest fashions for men he took in as much as he could about contemporary culture. As always, reading came difficult for him but the magazines were filled with glorious images. Despite his sorrow, there was much to enjoy. Jazriel's mind reeled, a dizzying blur of so much change. People were more affluent, well fed and dressed. Sophisticated and better informed. But still just humans, their blood would taste the same! At least he knew who he wanted to design his clothes from now on, who were first on his list once he hit Paris. Jazriel was miserable, lonely and lost but he could still look good!

When at last he was able to leave the sanctuary of the apartment, he took the woman's little portable box of music with its tiny headphones and retrieved the Ducati to disappear into the night.

Marta was out cold, unaware an envelope containing five thousand euros had been left in her hand.

Chapter Twenty-Nine

Paris, France

Throttling back on the Ducati, Jazriel idled cautiously through the outskirts of a Paris that had changed beyond recognition. He had only known the confident cosmopolitan Paris of the late nineteenth century. This post Outrage city was wounded, paranoid and nervous. A succession of massive road blocks, bristling with armed police and the military hampered his route into the centre of the city. He was in no position to take them on, but somehow found a slow, tortuous route through the suburbs, along alleyways and Seine-side walks barred to motorised traffic.

Yes, to his disappointment, Paris had changed. But he had not. That was part of the problem, if he didn't get some new clothes soon, he'd go crazy! The ones he'd worn since fleeing Isolann were well beyond rank.

Jazriel paused outside a wide avenue in the centre of the city; he recognised some of the names of the top hotels but there was a problem, a major problem, one he had already encountered on route to France. Since the Outrages, proving identity was of great importance to humans living in the world's great cities, all had suffered from the huge incendiary devices of the Imadeen, their terrifying and destructive 'cleansing' fires. His stolen cash got him through the countryside, but he would need more then money to survive in Paris. He had enough stolen cash to book into a top hotel but he wouldn't get through the security barriers without a provable identity! Zaard, so much for his wonderful plan to seek a temporary base, to acquire a new wardrobe and seek out Garan - if he was in Paris! In his normal act first, maybe think later manner Jazriel had not planned beyond reaching the French capital.

It would be so easy to tap into Eshan's well-established network to help all the surviving Dark Kind in Europe, she had access to his bank accounts, could set him up with accommodation, a new identity, protection. But Jazriel wanted nothing to do with her. The Lady, as she was known by her human employees, would preach her tedious diatribes, try to change him, he could not endure her tiresome lectures about the need for discretion, to live alongside humans in peace, respecting them. Safeguard their lives. Yeah, right! And worse of all, drinking that awful concoction of artificial blood she just about survived on. Gross! He was Dark Kind, a vampire. He gloried in his dark heritage, his killer instinct. His pleasure in the taste of human blood.

And he'd had enough of nobles commanding his fate. He had been free to command his own destiny once before, briefly, but it had been wonderful. That's what he craved now. Garan would understand, he was created a maverick, with no respect for the Dark Kind's rigid caste system. There was no better vampire companion for his new, independent future.

Except his future was going nowhere but a windy street with daylight not more than three hours away. Damn humans, especially those fire-obsessed fanatics! In the past, he could have sauntered into any hotel in Europe, an exquisitely attired, handsome young man with a particularly charming smile and the promise of great wealth, to be instantly given the best suite in the house. Now it was all bits of plastic, computer identity checks and retina scans, whatever that was. What the hell was a retina? Humans had so many disgusting bodily functions, was it something to do with those? With a sinking heart, he realised he had two choices. One was to seek a rough, lawless area of the city, they always had them on the site of the Outrages, the smouldering legacy of their destructive infernos. An area where his fangs and ferocity could engender cash and buy some tenuous security. Or swallow his pride and find Eshan's network.

He gazed longingly at the nearest hotel. Inside would be luxurious suites, showers of scalding hot, clean water and soft white towels. There would be fine wines and brandies on call. He would be left alone by the super-discreet staff during the hours of sunlight in luxury and comfort. Maybe he would have access to one of those boxes of images and sound and use it to learn more about this dawning new century. Newspapers were too difficult, too many words.

Jazriel growled his disappointment. Independence Night would have to wait a little longer! He sought a phone booth, searching the directories, struggling with his poor reading skills for something with golden dragon in the name. All he had to do was say the password and within the hour he would be safely in that hotel, in that shower, in that bed.

Two choices? A bomb ravaged ghetto or a luxury hotel? For Jazriel, there had only ever been one.

As he paused on the bike, a sleek, immaculate limousine purred past, braked and reversed back. A young man emerged from the back seat to stroll casually over to Jazriel. Good looking, with long, dark blond hair-a film star or top model perhaps? Or someone from a rock band? Jazriel had discovered at Marta's apartment that these were idolised and important people in this early twenty-first century society. The young man smiled, enthusiastically admiring the bike. He ran his hand over the gleaming chrome, crouched down to knowledgeably study the massive engine. "1500cc? I thought so," he muttered with an attractive smile of appreciation.

Busy admiring the young man's floor sweeping black leather coat, Jazriel wasn't listening. He wanted him. He wanted that coat.

The man looked up and sighed. "Beautiful. A work of art."

Jazriel's voice was low and beguiling. "I can see you are a man who appreciates the best that life has to offer." He reached down to sensuously caress the bike, observing with triumph the man's gaze drift down to his hand as it strayed slowly off the chrome petrol tank and moved up his inner thigh. "It is indeed very beautiful." Jazriel purred. "We both are."

The man's fate was sealed with that smile. Captivating and deadly.

Eshan's help and her tedious diatribes could wait until another night.

Chapter Thirty

Haunt Night club, Latin Quarter, Paris

"Hey, Chief, we've got a live one out there tonight. That guy is either brain-fried crazy on devil dust or has cojones of steel!"

Garan, lounging in an observation room above his night-club dance floor, glanced up at the screen to see who had caught the eye of Toulon, his burly body guard and second in command. Outside there was the usual noisy, edgy throng trying to catch the attention of heavily armed bouncers. The crowd were all hyped up and restless, eager to get into the most notorious and desirable night club in Paris. They had to queue up, possibly for hours and virtually beg for admission. Not everyone made it inside the Haunt. They didn't have to be rich or famous, but they did have to match the ambience. Paradoxically the outrageous difficulty to gain entrance added to the attraction. There was always a huge queue desperate to get in.

Garan watched as a tall, slim, jet-haired young man, wearing a floor-sweeping black leather coat, rode slowly up on a powerful motorbike, casually riding straight through the crowds, oblivious to their shouts of anger. Many tried to stop him but those who risked physical contact were casually nudged out of the way by the bike, without the dark clad figure losing balance or disturbing his enjoyment of a lit cigarette. Garan did not have to see the finely chiselled, perfect features, or the blazing turquoise eyes behind the impenetrable shades to know who it was.

"Zaard! Fantastic!" Garan declared with delight. "It's the Jazzman! Let him through and find a safe place for his bike. Bring him straight up to me."

Jazriel in Paris! Garan could hardly believe the evidence of his own eyes. And the beautiful sha'ref was in a rebellious mood, what else could explain the dramatic, long black coat, no Dark Kind would ever dare openly wear Azrar's colour. Garan's spirits soared, Jaz was saying 'up yours' to rules and conventions, both human and vampire. The vain and hedonistic commoner was a kindred spirit after all!

Everything about his appearance, the cigarettes, the refusal to wear a helmet on that big bastard of a bike, the extravagantly black coat, was a living, breathing statement of insurrection against vampire and human mores. Well, maybe not technically a *living* statement. How could Garan forget? It was seared into his memory, the traumatic time when he had taken the long dead body of his friend back to Isolann. And was he alive or the walking dead? The jury was still out on what Jazriel actually was now!

Toulon deduced that this pretty boy in the street must be another strange being like 'The Chief'. For want of a better term, a vampire, and with a great show of deference he cleared the boisterous partying crowds from the newcomer's path. The chief was the fiercest and most ruthless bastard in the city even if he did look like a skinny white boy of sixteen. Garan had not changed since the night twelve years ago when he'd saved Toulon from dying in a gutter.

Garan's thin, vulpine features had not aged a day, only his hair style altered, frequently! Currently, his fox-red hair was cut in short, spiky layers, his eyes. usually hidden behind dark shades, were all dark violet. So, he wasn't human. Toulon did not care. Once the big man has been the meanest king of the streets but had fallen on hard times through a bad Bliss habit. The chief had dried him out and given him the prime job at the club. Now he had one of the best luxury apartments uptown, his own security team, a king's ransom of a salary and the respect of his peers. He would willingly lay down his life for his eerie employer without a second's hesitation.

Now he discovered other creatures like the chief existed! Toulon was curious, wary but unafraid, he showed the stranger up to the observatory and waited discreetly outside.

Garan could not contain his delight at seeing Jazriel, he had escaped the brooding Balkan at last! They kissed on the lips in the passionate greeting of all Dark Kind, the intimate exchange of emotion.

"I cannot believe my eyes. Jazriel! The coolest dead guy in the world. Welcome to Paris and my night club, a blood drinker's playground!"

Garan and Jazriel fell into other another fierce embrace. "Hell, it's good to see you, man." Garan continued, overjoyed. "We are going to turn this town blood red. We are going to have the wildest nights."

Taking a long drag to finish his cigarette, Jazriel gave Garan a wicked, fang-bared smile, "That's what's I am counting on." He threw off the leather coat. "But first I need access to my own money and not a charity handout from bloody Eshan."

Jazriel had got some funds from somewhere, Garan mused wryly, taking in the immaculate couturier clothing, the fabulous yet discreet platinum watch, at least twenty thousand pounds worth of designer timepiece. For the first time in his life Garan decided to let discretion rule his outspoken mouth.

Jazriel did not elaborate but must have left Isolann after a bad break up with his noble caste lover. Garan was not sorry. Azrar's loss was his gain. The two vampires sat down to relax in each other's company, toasting the future with some vintage Krug. There was no talk of any of the other surviving Dark Kind, not yet. This was a celebration not a time for mourning.

Jazriel ran his fingers through his shoulder length blue-black hair, looking ill at ease. "Garan, old friend. I have a request, it feels awkward to ask this. In Isolann I lived on tediously strict rations, far too little blood and some god awful wine and brandy. Azrar's cellars were a disgrace."

"My friend, I am so delighted to see you restored to life and here with me. Ask for anything you want, it shall be yours."

With a shiver of unease, Garan noticed for the first time the jittery flickering light in his friend's eyes, not the shimmer of fire from a recent kill but something else, something very wrong. With a sinking heart, he knew where this conversation would lead.

"The Haunt is obviously a notorious den of human iniquity and disrepute, have you any...?" Jazriel continued, first dropping his head, then looking up, with the full power of his lustrous eyes, switching on a beguiling, apologetic smile. Garan raised his hand to silence his friend with a sigh of futile exasperation. Reaching into his desk, he produced a locked brief case. He did not give a damn if humans wanted to kill themselves with their idiotic poisons but Jazriel was Dark Kind and therefore, his life was precious. And more importantly, as he had died already, his hold on life could be as fragile as a butterfly. Why the hell did the idiot want to risk his second chance by messing about with narcotics? A healthy vamp, of course, was in no danger, all Dark Kind metabolism would self- repair even after a big over dose. The Jazzman was different to any other living being, however, unique in his miraculous resurrected state. How his body would react to this abuse was unknown.

Garan could really do without this! But he wanted Jazriel to stay in Paris the years of loneliness were already forgotten as he revelled in the sight of the stunningly handsome vampire. How could he deny his friend anything? He watched with a heavy heart as Jazriel opened the case, his blue-green eyes sparkling with anticipation at the sight of a bag of 100% unadulterated Bliss, the gold-coloured fine powder so pure it would kill any human foolish enough to use it.

In Vienna in the 1820's, in London during the war - many times before, Garan had witnessed this obsessive substance abuse by Jazriel. Where had this need to misuse his beautiful body with dangerous human poisons come from? The Jazzman raised an eyebrow in apology before snorting up a copious amount of the killer drug; straight away, his nose bled with a trickle of thin purple which he wiped with an ivory silk kerchief. Jazriel's body shuddered, his eyes darkened to complete black then back to turquoise with an even more pronounced eerie, glittering glaze. Garan looked away in horror, how could he do this to himself?

"Azrar will rip out my throat if he ever finds I helped you mutilate and poison yourself. Isn't dying once enough for you?"

Jazriel gave a lazily disarming smile. "I'm fine old friend, I can handle this." But the age-old manipulating wasn't working on Garan, he was furious and anxious. Yes, Jaz had been through a harder life then he had. There were reasons for Jazriel's mental turmoil. Garan was a commoner but unlike Jazriel, he was not sha'ref, so could hold his head high, with no past indignities to dwell on. Garan had also skilfully escaped the dangers during the centuries of progressive extinction of his kind, the torture of human witch fires and purges. He'd had an easy ride all the way into the 21st century. It was just getting easier and more fun to be a vampire!

How different his friend's life had been. Jazriel's easy-going manner and hedonistic pleasure-seeking masked a lifetime of rejection and betrayal, of physical abuse and, ultimately, a painful death and terrifying afterlife. He had suffered by the hand of both humans and Dark Kind alike. No wonder he had such an addictive personality. Now he had the searing pain of being apart from Azrar, his most powerful and enduring addiction. Garan understood but could not condone it. Shoving this crap up his nose might take the edge of his anguish for a few minutes, but what would Jazriel do when this didn't work?

Garan pushed aside these negative and frankly frightening thoughts as Jazriel entered a state of artificial euphoria. With the Jazzman mellowed out, he decided to risk asking about his relationship with the Prince. "I take it you are arrived in France alone, my friend."

Jazriel sighed and leant unsteadily against a console, inevitably lighting up another cigarette. He watched the thin grey plume of smoke rise before answering. "I love Azrar. He is my life. But that country of his drives me crazy."

He looked down with hunger and fascination at the seething mass of young human bodies lost in dance, becoming one with the hard pounding rhythm, the wild, orgiastic music before continuing. "I want to experience all this human madness and to live in the twenty-first century." He took another long drag. "If he was here with me, my life would be perfect. But he is a Dark Kind High Prince and warlord from creation to death. He will never leave Isolann unless he can openly be acknowledged and respected as a Dark Lord."

There was a moment of uncomfortable silence, for they both knew this would never happen. Just staying alive was all they could demand from fate now. Jazriel swiftly changed the subject, what more was there to say? "This is quite some set up you've got here."

Bowing low in mock humility, Garan walked across to the panoramic one way window looking right across the packed night club.

"I can't believe how easy vampire living is in this crazy time." Garan shook his head, "In fact my friend, perhaps it's too damn easy."

He leant his head against the glass and turned to Jazriel with a mischievous smile, " I am tempted to go down to the dance floor one night with no dark shades and my fangs fully down just to see what would happen."

Jazriel's eyes darkened but not from the narcotic coursing through his veins. Surely he didn't plan to do something as reckless as that! Garan's mischief was legendary among the Dark Kind. It was hard to know when he was being serious. "They'd tear you apart. Don't even think about it."

Giving a foxy grin, Garan bared his fangs for emphasis, "Surely only with adoration? I am what they desperately want to believe in. I am a figure from their darkest fantasies. I am the embodiment of the amoral, glamorous but evil side of their own pathetic human psyche."

"Forget it, Garan, humans may have their dark fantasies but the reality will bring out all their deep instincts of self preservation. They will destroy you. Has anyone got close to knowing the truth?"

"The life blood of this place is a cocktail of hard-driving non-stop music, drugs, rumours and the sharp edge of real danger. I give them all that in abundance. My main man, Toulon knows I am not human but he is my creature. My motto with human cohorts has always been to find them needy and keep them greedy, and then they will stand by you to the death. Usually."

Jazriel did not bother to answer. He had experienced in the most extreme way the consequences of human treachery. The fickleness of human loyalty had cost him his life and he would never let himself be compromised again. Garan suddenly realising he had been tactless, did not pursue it.

He observed the Jazzman as he stood looking across the crowded dance floor. Zaard, he was so beautiful, so desirable! Garan's thoughts grew tortured with thwarted need, aware that his feelings were only natural. Jazriel was made to be wanted. Even if he tried to put his sha'ref past behind him, the instinct to seduce and beguile was always there.

Last time the two friends had been together Jazriel was in a serious relationship with another commoner, that tempestuous tigress, Sivaya. That had made him strictly out of bounds. But now Jazriel was on his own again, yet there was little Garan could do about it. They were just friends and would only ever be that.

Though Jazriel had pleasured hundreds of both male and female Dark Kind in his early years, Garan as a commoner could not insist on using him for his own satisfaction. The use of a purpose-made sha'ref like Jazriel was a convention solely practised by the long gone India-based Dark Kind nobles. Though the northern vampires did not agree with the custom, Garan was livid with the thought that any one of them could just waltz in, snap their fingers and Jaz would have to oblige them in bed. Without question.

"Merde," muttered Garan bitterly to himself, "there is no justice in the Dark Kind world."

Garan dismissed the fact Jazriel had lived an independent life for centuries, had turned his back on the old ways. There were wild rumours he had once sailed across the world's oceans in the early eighteenth century. Something no other Dark Kind had achieved. Jazriel had most definitely been an agent for the Allied forces during the Second World War. In Garan's mind, Jazriel was being monstrously unfair to the last scattered survivors of their species by not embracing his destiny, to be what he was created. A sexual plaything. Something beautiful to be shared. As if reading his mind, Jazriel turned and gave one of his smouldering-eyed, seductive smiles, promising so much but delivering nothing. Zaard! It was not fair!

"There is a whole city out there waiting for me Garan," he murmured with his silken panther purr, "I want you to show me every delight it has to offer."

Chapter Thirty-One

"You didn't get him, did you?" Raker enjoyed watching the shock and consternation blanch out the colour from Hain's florid face.

"Get who?" Replied the younger man in a fluster, now colouring up like a teenager, his burning cheeks adding to his embarrassment. How he hated the coldly reptilian Raker, why was this old fossil still alive to vex him?

"The vampire that your useless team have been tracking from Isolann, the one leaving a trail of dead bodies even a blind bloodhound could follow." Raker continued, highly amused by Hain's discomfort at being caught out running his own operations separately from Nemesis.

"And you could do so much better, old man?" snapped back Hain, "Exactly how many blood drinkers have you caught?"

He reached for an envelope and spilled the contents onto his desk, images of his target, photographs of the CCTV footage caught during the motorbike riding vampire's journey of carnage. "Just the one, I believe. And that was killed by the Nazi's. Not by you."

Raker picked up one of the grainy black and white photos and his heart threatened to explode with shock. It could not be! The vampire with the film star good looks was dead. Mowed down by a hail of bullets in a filthy Berlin cellar, not striding across a garage forecourt in the South of France decades later! Dark Kind were not supernatural beings, they were vulnerable flesh and blood. They only lived so long because their cells could constantly regenerate, it was complex biology not hocus pocus. Jazriel was dead. Yet there was no mistaking the strikingly handsome devil in the photos.

To rub acid into Raker's open wounds, Hain produced another file. "You are washed up old man, time to check into a good care home, to spend your days in some old chair with a rug across your lap, dozing in front of a silent television!"

Raker's hand shook as he read the reports and studied the images, surveillance photos he recognised instantly, the botched attempt at capturing Khari Devane at the Jolly Sailor pub in Soho.

"She was within a few yards of you, Raker! She walked straight past you. Did you know she was also in the pub with a Dark Kind female? Dark red hair, very tall and beautiful by all accounts."

Eshan too! Raker grabbed the side of the table for support as the implications of his failure struck home.

"I'll call for some help to get you home, old man. You have gone as white as a sheet." Hain's face was wreaked in a smirk of satisfaction and triumph. He watched Raker crumple and visibly age and wither before him, like the moment Count Dracula is exposed to daylight in an old Hammer film. One miserable old bastard down with the oldest and feeblest to go.

Chapter Thirty-Two

So that was it. Khari Devane, the golden-eyed beauty who had haunted his dreams and turned them into nightmares had been within his grasp, just yards away. And she was gone, melted away into the night with the same ease as the vampires. Smoke and mirrors! The other female had to have been Eshan, the little bitch must have had Dark Kind help to avoid his team. The vampire survivors, the ones that escaped the great purges of the Dark and Middle Ages were all experts at eluding capture.

For the first time Raker felt like a feeble old man, his failure to capture any Dark Kind, alive or dead, or the mind-reading, vampire-loving witch Khari Devane had stripped away his strength, his military composure, his reason to live. The erosion triggered by the discovery that Jazriel, the vampire he and Banks had betrayed during the war was still alive. Raker could take no more.

He returned home in a stumbling, distracted daze, unaware of anything but the need to be with her. He unlocked the room, not bothering with the usual ritual and strode in to confront the portrait of Khari Devane, the painting he'd stolen from one of the homes of Dassler, her Nazi protector. Khari's husband Joe Devane thought he had burnt it, a portrait of Khari in a lilac silk dress, her hair up in an elegant chignon, but that had been a copy. He, Raker possessed the original.

As always, her beautiful golden eyes fixed him with their powerful unflinching gaze, a woman who could see into the inner soul, know all a man's hidden desires. Except his! What the Spook Squad had never known was that he had been planted by their superiors as a control mechanism, that Raker's gift was the ability to block out the probing of mind readers and empaths at will.

Raker had wanted her from the moment he'd first seen her, a slender, petite and seemingly fragile young woman. Her elfin beauty combined with an inner steel had captivated his heart like no other. Once he'd fallen in love with her, the possibilities of being with any other woman in the future ceased to exist. It was Khari or nobody.

That she had feelings for Joe Devane was a serious set back, but one that he thought he could overcome. Raker was taller, better looking and better educated then the American, beyond his leadership of the Spook Squad, Devane was a nobody. Raker was from an upper class, landed, British family with old money and a large ancestral pile in Northumberland. He could win her heart away from that Yank! It was a challenge but one he would not lose.

But then came the arrival of the accursed vampires and Khari's ease with the monsters had been unsettling. An ease that became more then wrong in Raker's eyes, it was abhorrent, deviant behaviour. There was something perverse about her relaxed and openly warm friendship with the one called Jazriel. For all his louche, easy charm and stunning looks, he was a murdering monster, Khari should have been repelled and revolted by him! Not kissing and hugging him; giving him an affectionate nickname. Worse was had come, he had overheard Devane lamenting in despair that Khari openly loved Prince Azrar of Isolann. Not just another of the damned blood drinkers, but the evil heart and soul of the hell-spawned legion, the fearsome leader that gave the others inspiration to carry on.

Khari, who looked so angelic, so pure of heart was tainted, cursed by her liaisons with the vampires. She had damned her immortal soul to hell, these vile things were demons, cold-hearted killing machines. How Raker hated her. How he desired her.

"You've won," he sighed addressing the serene and youthful beauty in the portrait, the glistening ruby necklace around her slender neck, the encircling Blood Tears, an obscene symbol of all the innocent life lost to the fangs of the vampires. All the tears of heartbreak from the bereaved the Dark Kind left grieving with such callous disregard.

Raker's voice cracked with emotion, "You and your demon friends have prevailed over good. Since my crusade has begun, not one blood drinker has been killed and you are still out there, Khari, invading the sacred sanctity of human minds."

He dropped his head, the burden of guilt, of defeat, was crushing, unbearable. "I have failed humanity, utterly and shamefully." Raker reached into a drawer of a large mahogany bureau to pull out his service revolver. He did not pause or waver, his hand now rock steady as the colours in the portrait and the tribute of glacial roses beneath, the soft shades of lilac, silver and purest white were hidden by a new patina, clashing and brutal in its horror. The congealing spatter of blood, bone and brain tissue.

Chapter Thirty-Three

Hain took the news of Raker's suicide to his Nemesis co-founder himself. How he relished giving dear old Uncle Jay the full gory details, lingering over a detailed description of the ruined portrait of a youthful Khari Devane.

Parrish dropped his wizened head at the news, he was not fond of Raker, the man had been impossible to like, too driven, self-contained and arrogant. But his commitment to their mutual cause had been admirable and along with Banks, lost to cancer five years ago, the three men had been partners for decades. That the man had an obsession with the mind-reading witch was no surprise, nothing had escaped Parrish's scrutiny over the years. He had discreetly encouraged it, hoping it would sharpen Raker's resolve to track her down. Now that obsession had killed him and only he, Parrish, the eldest and most frail remained.

Surrounded by life support equipment, the portable oxygen and heart monitor that sometimes made him feel more like a machine then a human, Parrish glanced up from his wheelchair. He studied the gloating expression on his great nephew's florid face. The squat little creep was greedy and impatient, desperate for Parrish to die so he could inherit the massive and wealthy corporation. Hellfire! He was still alive! Hain was not having Nemesis while one brain cell in his mind sparked, while the worn out old pump of a heart still beat, even with the help of a machine.

A moment of intuition made Parrish glance up at the security monitor - the subtle hum; the dim light was missing. It had been switched off. Dawning realisation and horror spurred his frail frame into action, his arm as thin and shrivelled as an unwrapped mummy reached down to fumble for the alarm at the side of his wheelchair.

"Don't bother, old man, we are completely alone. The joy of running the communications department means all Nemesis security comes under my control too."

Hain suppressed a shudder of distaste as he kissed the top of the old man's head, a graveyard scull with the thinnest veneer of pale, crêpey flesh. "You have been on this earth far too long, Uncle. Your destiny with the afterlife is long overdue. Time to make room for the youthful, the energetic. Time to hand over to me."

Parrish struggled but was too weak to prevent his nephew pulling out wires and unplugging all the equipment that kept him alive. He tried to shout for help, but Hain put a broad, sweaty palm tightly over his mouth.

"Hush now, don't let your last moments be unpleasant. Relax and savour your achievements, this fine, rich and powerful organisation that you created from nothing. It will be in safe hands. I will continue your crusade. I will achieve what you could not."

Hain tightened his grip on the old man's mouth, not from necessity but from spite, punishment for making him touch the parchment dry, thin, mottled skin.

"So obsessed with those damn books you missed the real treasure, the real prize. Vampire DNA, the magic code to eternal youth, to a life without ageing, without disease."

Bending low, Hain whispered into the old man's ear, "I will not grow old, feeble and disgusting. Peeing into a bottle! I will become immortal! Using Dark Kind genes, I will never age."

As the light faded from Parrish's weak and pale eyes, the younger man continued his sneering, "But in a mark of respect and tribute to my beloved and much mourned uncle, when I acquire that Balkan vampire's library, I will name it after you. The Jay Parrish Collection."

Hain patted the dead man's back. "Won't that be nice."

Chapter Thirty-Four

Under the ever-watchful eyes of both Eshan and Reyes' security operatives, Khari and her granddaughter spent three meandering months visiting any European city or region that took their fancy. The backdrop to their holiday was almost irrelevant, getting to know each other better was the true motive for their travelling. Staying constantly on the move was also a security measure; they would not make life easy for Nemesis jackals.

Khari could not believe how swiftly the weeks with Gabrielle had flown past. The constant threat of discovery by Nemesis meant they never spent much time in any city and the travelling and anxiety was beginning to take a toll on her health. She had rarely felt her age in the wide, open, empty spaces of Montana. In the peace and comfort of family life on the ranch.

The thought of yet another hotel, another airport on route to somewhere else was hard to face and though she would miss her terribly, part of Khari was relieved her granddaughter was soon due to start work in Rome with the finds team.

The last city on their itinerary was Budapest, gracious, bustling, a mixture of eastern and western Europe with a long and fascinating history. Neither women had ever visited Hungary though it's proximity to the Upper Balkans gave Khari many sleepless hours, it was her first time back in Europe since the end of the war. She doubted she would be here again. Should she go back to Isolann, visit Prince Azrar and Jazriel, the two Dark Kind she loved?

The two women walked slowly along the river bank watching the Danube's timeless meander in companionable silence. Their presence by the great river just a tiny flicker in time, little more then a mayfly's brief dance across its surface. The muddy brown-green waters had flowed in the same stately progress through Europe for countless millennia. And should for millennia more.

Khari's heart was torn with anxiety for her granddaughter. Her own life was nearly over, her dangers faced, her battles fought and won. Only her grieving for those she had loved and lost would remain with her till the end. But Gabrielle was at the start of her life, and it would not be an easy one. By her own choice the young woman had turned her back on any chance of living in peace and security. Walking away from Gabrielle and returning to Montana was the hardest thing, Khari had ever done. There was so little she could do to prepare Gabrielle, nothing more she could do to protect her.

"So, my precious Gaby. It seems we must part and follow different destinies today."

Gabrielle put her arm around the older woman's slender shoulders and gave her a tight hug. "I wish we could have more time together. These past weeks have flown by like minutes."

Khari smiled, "It doesn't have to be this way. I would get down on my knees, here on the embankment in front of all these tourists, anything, if it would change your mind."

Gabrielle kissed her grandmother's head, breathing in the sweet scent of wild spring flowers that always surrounded her.

"I cannot be a fugitive, running from my life, Gran. I have made a big compromise agreeing to join Cardinal Reyes, but I promise, I will visit you and the family in Montana, soon." Gabrielle shrugged sadly as the reality of the limits imposed from worrying about wretched Nemesis sunk in. "OK. Maybe not that soon. When a visit can be safely arranged."

Khari nodded her head sadly, Gabrielle's determination was remarkable, she was an extraordinary young woman. But would her bravery be an asset or a danger?

"Promise me one thing, Gaby dear. I know you want nothing to do with the Dark Kind. I can accept and understand that, but if you need a friend, someone to trust with your life, then take their help. They have an unbreakable code of honour, an oath of friendship that once made cannot be taken back. Even at a cost to their own lives. No human on this planet is so trustworthy."

To please her Gran, Gabrielle nodded her head in assent. She had no intention of getting anywhere near one of the fanged nightmares. Let alone befriend one.

Chapter Thirty-Five

The Latin Quarter, Paris, France

Garan walked out of the Haunt, sniffing the night air with a shiver of unease. A breeze wafted in from the north, carrying the stench of charred brickwork and an underlying taint of burnt flesh. The last Outrage to hit Paris was over a year ago. Yet nothing seemed to dispel the miasma of the disaster which hung across the city like a putrid shroud.

Garan growled his displeasure, they were certainly methodical and even-handed, those damned Imadeen. The most recent attack, for instance, left three mosques, three synagogues and three Christian churches destroyed in one day by their incendiary devices. And three banks and large department stores just to show they were not fixated on places of worship. All targets inevitably had human casualties, those in the bustling stores the most horrendous. Garan knew that nightclubs could well be their next targets following the pattern of systematically escalating Outrages in other blighted cities. Hot spots of wild debauchery were ripe for their 'cleansing fires'. How ironic, Garan mused, he had avoided the great purges of his Kind in the Middle Ages, the witch fires that had claimed so many Dark Kind lives, only to be at risk of immolation for owning a club seething with human vice!

Jazriel had also noticed the tainted air, a smell he was more familiar with, having had many narrow escapes from the infernos of human hatred in his life. Since fleeing Isolann, he had encountered it several times on his journey to France, it was a stench hanging over many great cities across the world.

The two vampires pushed such unpleasant thoughts aside as they walked in companionable silence across the Pont-Neuf, the gracious sixteenth century bridge over the Seine. A comfortingly familiar landmark to the un-ageing beings, where warm, glowing light from the lamps along it's route danced on the wind-choppy water below. Only the tap of Garan's sword stick marked their silent passage through crowds of bustling sightseers and locals taking an evening romantic stroll over the river. Paris was, as ever, a stoic, enduring city; its inhabitants nervous but not beaten or cowed by the new enemy.

"So my friend," ventured Garan, pausing to watch a party boat full of noisy revellers pass beneath the bridge. Maybe that was the answer? The terrorists would find it harder to bomb a moving target. "Have you become less picky, do you still insist on only hunting good-looking prey?"

"What do you think?" Jazriel replied with one eyebrow raised in wry amusement. "Do you persist in going after the most risky, the highest profile quarry?

Garan nodded, "No point in a hunt without a challenge! So. What was the best kill you've made lately? I assume you have been busy since arriving in Paris."

Jazriel traced the side of one fang with his finger as he recalled his adventure in the first weeks in Paris, spent in the company of the young man with the limo, a successful record producer.

"He thought himself quite the ladies' man and had never dreamt of being intimate with a male before…"

"Until he met you."

Jazriel bowed his head with a grin of mock humility, acknowledging his success, his prowess. He'd had the same effect on many straight human men in the past, on one in particular. That had been a spectacular success! Garan was not surprised, his friend's method of trapping prey was completely alien to him. For all his declaration of change Jaz was ever the sha'ref using allure and charm instead of stealth and speed. Garan was convinced Jazriel would seduce a rabid rottweiller if he thought he'd gain some advantage.

"I had a wonderful three weeks with that human! It was easy to lead him on. He was so confused by his reaction to me, I was able to keep him at arms length." Jazriel gave a feral smile of triumph. "I had my own rooms in a superb luxury mansion off the Rue St Honore. We spent many great nights out partying and most importantly, he bought me a new collection of fantastic clothes."

To his surprise Garan found himself appalled. He was a natural breaker of rules yet Jazriel had surpassed even himself by killing a human who had offered him hospitality and kindness. Outrageous! Those acts of friendship should have made the man safe from a Dark Kind's fangs. Honour dictated that Jazriel should have spared that human's life.

"Don't look so shocked, Garan. At least I didn't take him down at his home. I lured him deep into the Bois de Boulogne for an unforgettable night!"

Garan knew exactly what had happened to the unfortunate benefactor. Jazriel would have taken the man's face in his slender, strong, fingers and kissed him, enveloping him in a deepening whirlpool of pleasure, intense and intoxicating. Then he would have struck hard and fast. The man may have never known what happened, had been killed while enraptured. A small mercy!

"But you were the first vampire boy scout, helping save the war for the allies, what about honour?"

"Honour can go fuck itself." Jazriel replied evenly, a trace of raw-edged bitterness seeping from beneath the flippant reply. He'd had it up to here with honour.

Chapter Thirty-Six

Ferihegy Airport, Budapest

Khari's heart leapt as an angry commotion broke out at the arrivals lounge. Instantly nervous, her bodyguards leapt to their feet, ready to protect her, to rush her to safety. She glanced across to the source of the disturbance as sprinting, heavily armed airport security guards and police rushed towards enraged male voices. A party of exotically robed, dark skinned young men gesticulating wildly with the airport officials. Abhajastanis. Khari recognised the clothing but not the meaning of their language.

One of her escorting party walked over to investigate and returned with bad news. "There may be a long delay. They are a group of Abhajastan religious leaders and have been barred from entering the country. Bloody Imadeen! They're ranting on about burning us all away and there's talk of angry demonstrations outside the airport between their waiting supporters and those opposed to them." The man shook his head, impatient to get his charge safely home to America, "This could turn nasty. It's a blue touch-paper waiting for a flame."

Khari groaned, equally annoyed at the thought of a delay. What had these firebrands and their intolerant religion got to do with the Hungarian people? She was weary, had done enough travelling and yearned for home. She missed her boys and her other grandchildren, the peace and beauty of Whitethorn.

With time suddenly on her hands, she decided to stretch her legs before the flight and look for some local treats to take home. With her bodyguard in close attendance, Khari walked towards the shops. Renewed and even angrier shouting made her turn her head back towards the furore, some of the other passengers had been allowed through. One caught her eye, a neatly-dressed middle aged man with a briefcase, superficially a businessman, one whose facial appearance was distinctively Isolanni. The western clothing looked incongruous but there was no mistaking the broad Asiatic features of a Dholma nomad. Astonishment and curiosity spurred her to change her plan for last minute shopping. What was a man from Isolann doing in Hungary?

Breaking an old vow to herself not to enter any more minds, Khari made sure she passed close to the traveller. She entered his thoughts, instantly confirming he was indeed Isolanni. It was no good, she had to speak to him. She dismissed the concerns of her guardians and strode up to him boldly, holding out her hand, greeted him in her perfect, fluent Isolanni.

"You are far from home my friend, can I assist you in any way?"

Lomak's eyes widened, startled at the sight of an elderly American woman addressing him in his obscure language. This was never part of his plan! He and the other martyrs were determined to slip into Hungary unnoticed while the decoys in their group created a diversion. Lomak pretended not to understand her and brushed past with an apologetic shrug but the old bitch was determined to talk to him. What was she? A tourist perhaps who had fallen for the Isolanni culture? Hah! Culture, that was a joke. Did she know Isolanni life centred around blind obedience to a blood drinker, a creature from the lowest depths of Hell?

Lomak reached out and firmly pushed the woman out of his way. For the first time he noticed the curious golden colour of her eyes, stirring up a forgotten memory….

As he touched her arm, Khari's hand flew to her mouth in horror. What a roiling pit of hatred! Her brief journey through the man's mind told her so much. He was here as a vanguard, the first of a new breed of non-Abhajastani Imadeen. Seemingly innocuous travellers who were secretly fanatic, committed terrorists, catching the World off-guard. His mission, to go to the busiest shopping centre in Budapest and commit an atrocity designed to claim as many Western lives as possible. One of the wave of Outrages designed to terrify the world into embracing the belief in Tahjr. Paris, New York, Jerusalem, Washington, many more and now Budapest!

Lomak had escaped from Isolann, hunted there for that last few months by his own people for his open devotion to a foreign religion, evangelising a faith embracing bloodshed and terror. To protect her sanity, Khari had kept her mind unpolluted from human evil for many decades. Now it reeled with the anger and cold, calculating cruelty in this man's warped mind. How she yearned to flee but she could not. She must know more, for the sake of innocent people throughout Europe, in Isolann. Could there be others in her homeland who thought the same way as this man? Was Jendar Azrar safe?

Khari insisted on talking to the man, her minders surreptitiously but firmly preventing him from bolting away from her questioning. All the time she walked deeper and deeper through the dank corridors of his thoughts, an unnerving but necessary journey. One image kept re-appearing, a motorbike of all things, a big powerful machine with a throaty engine roar and gleaming chrome fittings. Khari probed further and gave a startled cry…Jaz! Oh no, Jaz!

She fought the desire to run from Lomak, thankful she was being accompanied today by Eshan's men, ruthless and dedicated, trained in military and security skills to the highest level. Reyes' people were all well meaning idealists, who vowed to do no harm to their fellow humans.

"There has been a change of plan, Mr Lomak will come with us." Khari commanded. "Unless he wants to be handed over right now to the Hungarian authorities."

Lomak's eyes widened as he suddenly remembered about the golden eyes. This was the demon Azrar's tame human witch, the mind reader, Khari! She knew everything! His Outrage must begin here… in the airport... Now...

"He's got a bomb!" shouted Khari in Hungarian and pulling her men away from the Isolanni fanatic, ran towards the entrance, "Everybody run," she screamed. "Run!"

The pandemonium confused Lomak, he wanted to shout the martyr's death chant in Abhajastani but panicked, it was a foreign tongue to him, he couldn't remember the right words! His hand reached down to his brief case, for the detonator that would send him straight to his reward in Paradise but a security sharp-shooter felled him in a clean head shot before he could even move his hand.

Khari left the airport hurriedly with her minders, before the shock subsided and the whole place erupted into panic. She felt no shred of remorse for the dead man, she had seen what the Isolanni had planned, had wanted. An Outrage. One with no limit, the more Unbeliever deaths, the greater the tribute to Tahjr. Her mind was also made up. She must make one more journey, must go to Isolann, to Prince Azrar. He deserved to know that Jazriel was innocent, framed for the death of a nomad child. Lomak himself had killed her in a freak accident and used the tragedy to foment unrest against Isolann's Prince, to destroy his beloved companion. To kick-start an Imadeen revolution in the Land of Secrets and Shadows.

And Lomak had not been alone. There were others in Isolann who shared his extreme views.

Chapter Thirty-Seven

Paris, France

After spending the hours of darkness night-club crawling and killing, the two vampires returned to one of Garan's many apartments, this one close to the centre of Paris. It had once belonged to a favourite courtier of Marie-Antoinette and retained the over-the-top gilded elegance of pre-Revolutionary France. On a whim, Garan had paid a fortune to have the building restored and the contents sourced as close to the original. An emperor's ransom's worth of precious antiques now jostled for space with his ephemeral collection from each proceeding century. Now bored with the lot of it, he treated the priceless objects with callous disregard, unbothered if a beautiful, priceless vase was broken or a painting torn.

The Jazriel he once knew would have been appalled to see such damage to beautiful things, he appreciated and treasured the fine things humans made. This new version was indifferent; Garan was certain he was probably too stoned to notice. At least it saved getting an ear-bashing from the luxury-loving vampire!

Jazriel threw himself onto a raw silk chinoiserie chaise longue, scuffing the 18th century fabric with his Gucci loafers and reaching into his Versace suit, brought out the inevitable platinum cigarette case. Garan watched as ever fascinated by the studied elegance of his every move, the carefully lowered eyes, the calculated smiles. Jazriel couldn't help it, Garan knew that. But it made being in close proximity so difficult.

Being in Jazriel's company again made Garan realise in a rare unguarded and honest moment just how lonely he was and how much he missed physical contact with his own kind. He remembered jeering at Eshan for not suggesting to Azrar that they should forget all the tedious Northern Dark Kind obsession with true love and passion, and just get on with a purely physical coupling. The southern nobles had no hang ups indulging themselves with their sha'ref sex toys! The humans did it all the time. Why not simply have sex because it would feel good?

It was insane, in Garan's reasoning Jazriel should be willing to go to bed with him out of friendship, out of a sense of duty, to honour what he was created for. Merde, Jazriel was sha'ref made for one purpose - to provide pleasure! With Jazriel's legendary erotic skills it would be incredible, mind blowing! But the last vestige of Garan's own pride and deference to Jazriel's feelings made him hold back. It seemed crazy in this modern world of knife-edge survival to worry about respecting ongoing relationships but both he and Jazriel were Dark Kind commoners, nearly equals and definitely friends. No vampire would make a move on another whose heart was so clearly and foolishly still enthralled. Damn Azrar! In fact damn all the nobles! Dame the whole bloody ridiculous Dark Kind caste system; as a commoner Garan had no right to demand sexual favours from a sha'ref. It was so damn unfair!

Garan made an effort to push such tortuous thoughts from his mind but the temptation created by Jazriel's stunning looks encouraged him to try a hint, one made in jest but serious in intent. He sat on the floor beside Jazriel, leaning back to rest on the side of the chaise longue and Jaz's hand strayed down to lightly ruffle through Garan's fox-red hair. A sign of affection that meant nothing more then friendship. But it was torture for Garan whose body betrayed him by responding to the skilled and deliberate touch with a shiver of need. He leapt to his feet, aware that Jazriel was smiling, triumphant, amused by his discomfort. The bastard was driven by the compulsion to make everything that breathed desire him. Why couldn't Jazriel have been created an ordinary commoner or a warrior? Sadists, that's what the Dark Kind's creators must have been! 'Sod it.' Garan decided to press his luck with a heavy hint.

"Jazzman, I have tried to work out when I last had sex and I've got as far back as the twelfth century. Then a deep depression set in and I had to stop trying to figure it out."

"In that case I suggest we go straight out on the town again and take your mind off it with some old fashioned, cold hearted vampire killing. There's still some hours of darkness left."

A disappointed Garan nodded, resigned to failure. Well, nothing ventured anything gained! He put his arm firmly around Jazriel's leather-clad shoulder and walked him towards the door.

"When you arrived here I had never seen you in such low spirits, it did not suit you. Let's shake off all that damn Balkan doom and gloom once and for all. In fact, I have something special to share with you tonight," Garan continued, "I have recently bought another club in New York. Come with me, Jaz. Let's be the first vamps to take a bite of the Big Apple!"

Chapter Thirty-Eight

Isolann

Was it possible that nothing had changed? Khari wondered wistfully as she set foot on Isolanni soil for the first time in sixty years, could the Land of Secrets and Shadows resist the determined encroach of the modern world?

Eshan had arranged for one of her private jets to take Khari to Isolann, the pilot landing it on the wide plains above Lake Beral. As Khari descended from the plane, she took in a deep breath and felt reassured. The sharp clean air smelt of the mountain snow and pine trees, the scent blown down from the encircling black granite monoliths of the Arpalathians that held this ancient land in their unyielding and protective embrace. To Khari's relief, no roads scarred the landscape of open grassland, no concrete leisure developments crowded the eerie stillness of the vast lake fed by the melting snow of Isolann's long winters. It looked the same, unchanged from the day she left her home for a new and happy life in America. It was a harsh landscape, full of danger and hardship for its nomad inhabitants, yet, Khari could not bear the thought of it being tamed, it's deep, tangled forests cleared, sprawling towns of tacky holiday homes for rich Europeans spawning around the silent inland sea of Lake Beral. Isolann looked as mysterious and deceptively tranquil as ever, a land lost in time.

She looked up to the mountains again to beyond the dark, wolf-ridden forest, to where she knew Azrar waited in his towering stronghold and her heart beat faster. After all these years, a long happy marriage, a growing family, the thought of Azrar turned back time, leaving her a giddy teenager again, one with a hopeless crush on the utterly unobtainable. She was such a silly old fool!

Khari's attention was caught by a lone circling eagle, unchallenged master of the azure, cloudless sky and she wished the jet had not invaded its airspace, the eagle belonged here, the aircraft with its brash loud engines and pollution did not.

A group of nomad horsemen approached from the north, her escort to Azrar's stronghold. Her home. She waited until the riders were at close hand and walked through their minds, seeking the most steadfast, the most loyal to their Prince. With a slight, sad smile on her face, she walked up to one young man and pressed a letter into his hand.

"Make sure Jendar Azrar receives this. It is vital you ensure he and only he reads it."

Then she turned around and re-boarded the jet. Call it the folly of old age or misplaced vanity but when the Dark Kind Prince she loved last saw her, she was a slender, beautiful young woman. Let his memory of her be forever that image. Khari wanted to go back to the people she loved in Montana, her human family. She had not many more days left on this earth before joining Joe in the next world, that precious time belonged to her family. Her long adventure with the Dark Kind was over.

Chapter Thirty-Nine

Rome

Gabrielle looked up from her papers and suppressed a smile. She was meant to be in a furious mood. Her new boss, Cardinal Alejandro Reyes approached her desk with a huge carton of freshly brewed, aromatic cappuccino in one hand, a golden cardboard box in the other. He placed the peace offerings before her and backed away, his hands raised in apology.

"My dear girl, before you bite my head off, please taste one of these delightful cakes; they are carefully hand made by an order of nuns from a convent in Seville but they must have got the recipe from angels. They are divine, straight from paradise."

Reyes had just arrived back from an assignment in Southern Spain, one Gabrielle had badly wanted to be involved with. The discovery of an exquisite casket of unknown origin, buried under the foundations of a cathedral. Gabrielle feigned a frown and pushed aside the golden box.

"I can't be bought off with cake, your Eminence" she replied evenly. "Chocolate maybe, but not cake."

Reyes sighed and sat on the edge of the desk, undoing the thin golden ribbon and slowly opening the box, allowing the sweet sugar and almond scent of the delicate cakes to waft out. "There was no point you going, Gaby. It was not archaeology, it was a snatch and grab exercise. Your talents are better utilised elsewhere."

He did not reveal the true reason why Gabrielle had not been sent to the excavation of Santa Maria de las Flores. Reyes had been tipped off that Nemesis had dispatched their most ruthless and dangerous squad to the site, a team led by Phil Geddoe, a vicious, borderline psychopath, there was no way Reyes was going to risk his most precious asset and now good friend Gabrielle over a mere box. Well, a platinum casket. But it was just a box.

"Getting the find out of Spain was tedious, a routine pick up any one could do. Learning its secrets is another matter, it will be all down to you. The casket is waiting for you in the lab."

Gabrielle shrieked with delight and punched the air. Reyes snatched the coffee out of harm's way and smiled warmly at her exuberance. Having this delightful young woman as part of the team was so right on many fronts. Gabrielle being close to hand meant his people could protect her better and she was a hard working, talented scientist and archaeologist, was therefore an asset on discovery and research projects. And all agreed, she was a breath of fresh air, fun to have around. Someone who boosted morale.

Reyes fought back an unbidden tear, her youthful enthusiasm and vibrant spirit reminded him of one of his own kind, lost to the enemy. His youngest daughter Ma'eem. Another time, another world, and so long ago. He had dedicated his life trying to prevent this world suffering the same appalling fate. His given assignment - working to protect the Dark Kind seemed an unjust punishment. At least being with Gabrielle felt like a reward. "And wear a hard hat. That is a direct order, no arguments!" he called after her, aware his sensible advice would be ignored.

Stuffing a cake into her mouth, Gabrielle grabbed the coffee and hurried down the narrow old corridors, then down the secret lift to the basement labs. In truth, she was enjoying her new life and though not going to Spain had annoyed her, there would be other assignments, other opportunities to shine. The worse part of the change to her life was over, it was not just the awkwardness of handing in her notice to a distraught Hillary Britton, but being unable to tell him where she was going and why she had quit her job at the university. Perhaps one day in the future she could reveal the truth to a good man and a good friend. But with the baleful shadow of Nemesis constantly behind her, for now, it was best and safer for Britton to not know.

Gabrielle was part of a small and tight-knit team of scientists, security experts and of course, the inevitable priests, all based in a stunningly beautiful 16th century palazzo in Rome, close to Vatican City. Beneath the historical exterior lay an underground network of offices and state of the art laboratories. No one looking at the building's gracious old exterior would believe such an array of high powered computers, satellite links and other paraphernalia of the 21st century existed beneath their feet. All with one purpose; to seek and obtain any potentially Dark Kind artefact, to study it and keep it safe from a hostile world and to protect the last surviving vampires. The archaeology was easy, keeping watch over the scattered and secretive Dark Kind was almost impossible, even with help from Ha'ali Eshan's far older, better funded and superior intelligence network.

Gabrielle followed the guiding lights down to the crypt beneath the building, shored up with modern scaffolding. It needed to be. The structure was considered possibly dangerous, damaged by a recent nearby Outrage bomb which had shaken the old building to its foundations. As was the surrounding ancient city and its teeming population. She pushed aside her own murderous views on the damned Imadeen and edged her way down to the laboratory, thankfully untouched by the bomb's shock waves.

She refastened the strap of her safety helmet, knowing it made her look like a dork but what the hell, it would only take one loosened brick, one broken beam to take her out of the picture permanently. And she wanted to be around for many more years to come, to plague and ultimately bring down Nemesis.

The casket sat on a steel work bench, wrapped in the protective shrouds of fragile, greying linen that had swathed it for an unknown number of centuries. Several members of the team who had rescued the antiquity stood by, happily allowing Gabrielle the privilege of unwrapping the object - it had already been meticulously X rayed and scanned, but only the highly decorated outside of the box was revealed, exquisitely crafted, depicting herds of galloping wild horses and antelope. The bizarre alien technology that characterised all Dark Kind artefacts were, as ever, unwilling to give up their secrets.

Gabrielle was surprised by the size of the object, more like a platinum trunk then the trinket box she had been expecting. She stepped forward, scalpel in hand, ready to gently cut away at the shrouding but hesitated, a strange foreboding sensation spreading through her body. She remembered the strong feeling she had when first holding the dragon talisman, but this was on a whole different scale. The dragon had called to her, this casket screamed for her to keep away. She stepped forward, towards the table but her legs became weak as if all her energy was being drained to nothing. She felt her hand reach out to grab something solid, her head span, darkness overcame her as she passed out, falling heavily to the floor.

She came to on a sofa in an ante-room in the main building, an anxious Reyes pacing the floor; he saw her rouse and ran to be beside her.

"Are you all right? Do you need a doctor? Gabrielle, you scared us down there."

Gabrielle tried to smile, but felt like she'd taken on a ten ton lorry and lost. Whatever was in the casket was powerful, too powerful to be released.

"I'm OK, Cardinal. At least I think I am."

She tried to sit up, but the woozy feeling overcame her and she sank back onto the couch. Her whole head thumped with throbbing pain. Like the mother of all hangovers, which would have been bearable, it meant she'd had a good time earning it. There had been no wild orgiastic party, just an old box.

"Lock it away, Cardinal. Seal it up again, whoever interred it knew exactly what they were doing. I have no idea what is in there, but it will do mankind no good to find out. As you know. I am the most curious, determined cussed female on the planet.

"I can't disagree with that," answered Reyes with a wan attempt at a smile.

"So, it stands to reason, if I don't want to know what's inside that box, it must be something really bad."

Alejandro Reyes let go of her hand and stood up. Mysteries were also a bad thing. All knowledge was power, and they needed as much power as possible in the battle that would one day come. But Gabrielle was not a fanciful young woman, never hysterical or exaggerating. She had an archaeologist's burning curiosity and her own brand of courage, sometimes bordering on the reckless. What else could he do but heed her advice?

"It has lain undisturbed for many centuries, not harming anyone," he replied with a soft sigh. "Nor has the world suffered for not knowing of its existence. We have another storage facility, a highly secure and secret vault. It can remain there. For now."

Gabrielle sighed with relief, she had expected a tougher battle over the box and its unknown contents. There was something of great importance in the casket, something powerful; she did not know why, but it would be a part of their future. Whether its influence was malign or beneficial was a mystery, one, though she burned with curiosity was not in a hurry to find out about. This was not through ignorant fear but a deep instinct, a visceral sense of understanding born of her legacy of *Knowing*.

Chapter Forty

Montana, USA, 2008

The last warmth of the fading Fall sun caressed their faces with a loving touch as Gabrielle linked arms with her cousins and watched as her uncles stood silently by the graveside. As one, a generation held back to allow the two older men some quiet and serenity to say goodbye to their mother, their grief at this moment beyond the comfort of words.

Yet there was some solace for the bereft family. Khari had a peaceful, pain–free passage to the adventure beyond, slipping away surrounded by all her family. Save two; Gabrielle who flew to Montana as soon as she heard. and Khari's youngest son Cameron, Gabrielle's father. Khari was a mother who carried the heartbreak of not knowing where he was, what had happened to him to her grave. A tragic postscript to a long, extraordinary life.

Khari had reached ninety-one with her mind sharp, her body spry till a heavy fall finally weakened her constitution. She had been serene, accepting, during her last days, that it was her time for her to move on.

Gabrielle shivered as scudding matte-pewter clouds racing down from the mountains, briefly hid the sun, bringing with them a scattering of early snowflakes which danced skittishly in the breeze before landing on the freshly turned rich earth and on the last flowers of the summer, the prairie blooms Khari so loved in her adopted Montana home. Gabrielle had brought a tribute on behalf of Prince Azrar, pure white roses, glacial in their perfection. There was no accompanying note. Perhaps Khari and the Prince had said their farewells on her last visit to Isolann.

The snow briefly thickened, a flurry that foretold more was to come in the months ahead. "Ma would have loved this, she was always a sucker for snow!" murmured Clay Devane, turning back to the rest of Khari's friends and family, brushing tears from his rough-hewn, weather-tanned features. Stepping forward Gabrielle gave her uncle's hand a firm, comforting squeeze. She knew the reason why her grandmother had always loved the first snow of winter. It had reminded her of her other home, the towering black granite stronghold set in the harsh snow-bound landscape of Isolann. Where her first love lived, her guardian, Prince Azrar of the Dark Kind.

But these hard-working ranchers knew little of their mother's past. It was for the best, let them remember her as the beautiful golden-eyed woman who had raised and nurtured them with her limitless love and understanding, carrying over her wisdom and great devotion to their own children. A legacy of love founded in the strong and enduring marriage with their father Joe Devane. Now Khari lay beside her Joe, but Gabrielle knew she was not here, not in this beautiful wooded glade. Nor was Joe. Both were reunited, carrying on their love affair in another dimension, another plane of existence. Gabrielle had the full *Knowing* now. The moment Khari died it passed onto her, an event that saddened and scared her at first. Now it gave her great comfort, for she knew with certainty that Khari was at peace, and happy.

Isolann

Prince Azrar waited for a clear night and a full moon. A silvered night, with only the creatures of the darkness as mute witness. Not humans. They did not belong here, not tonight.

How better to remember Khari then to walk alone in her garden, her gentle little world snugly growing within the outer compound of the warlord's harsh stronghold? The garden nestled against the sheer granite walls of the keep, drawing on its strength to endure and shelter from the harsh winters. As Khari used to snuggle up to him as a child. She had never feared him. She had loved him and now she was gone.

Azrar walked through the carefully tended rows of fragrant flowers, it had been his strict order to the household staff to keep the garden perfect for her return. But she had never come back. Until now.

Carefully, Azrar carried a dark grey metal casket, held it reverently in his strong warrior's hands, a box decorated in amber and ruby gems. Once they had carried the Blood Tears, now as he knelt beside her favourite bush of purest white roses, it carried her heart.

Paris

Jazriel stepped out onto the balcony of his apartment overlooking a gracious 16 th century square. In one hand was a battered old crocodile skin case, in the other a glass of finest cognac. A well-filled glass. It was not the first he'd drunk that night and wouldn't be the last. He drained it down in one, before opening the case, trying to ignore the dark stains ingrained into the pale green leather. His own blood. Reverently, he removed an elderly, well-burnished saxophone. He had last played it on the night he was killed.

His hands trembled as he removed the instrument, 'Ruthie', named after a Holocaust victim, the beloved wife of Lenny Dawn, one of Jazriel's spook squad colleagues. Lenny had taught him how to play saxophone and had lent the instrument to Jazriel as a good-luck charm when the vampire and Khari had been sent to Nazi Germany to work undercover as entertainers in a Berlin night club. Garan had somehow acquired it and in his unique, unpredictable way, had looked after the instrument, returning it to Jazriel soon after his arrival in Paris.

The night held its breath as Jazriel played the beautiful, haunting folk melodies that Khari had heard and learnt in Isolann. He refused to play the maudlin, sentimental songs that had moved Nazi monsters to mawkish tears. Instead, ancient Dholma music floated and soared above the Parisian street in an emotional lament, his farewell tribute to a true and loving friend.

Then he put the instrument away, never to play it again.

Part Two

COKE AND MIRRORS

Well, be careful, Angel,
This life is just too long,
All sparks will burn out in the end.

Chapter One

Rome, Italy, 2009

A morning of such azure grandeur that the moon lingered, faint in the cloudless perfection, reluctant to return to it's realm of darkness. Gabrielle paused briefly to marvel at the wan moon, brazenly sharing the sky with the sun. Night and day together, almost as strange as her own life had become.

Faced with negotiating a narrow back street in Rome, Gabrielle and Cardinal Reyes abandoned their armoured car with its driver and walked. The lane was busy with local people going about their business, yet Gabrielle warily watched every face, always on her guard. The old man walking with difficulty over the cobbles, the overweight housewife struggling home with her shopping, the handsome young man, whistling, perhaps on his way to meet a new conquest. All harmless. Or any one a potential Nemesis assassin. Such was her life now.

Gabrielle and Reyes were not alone. Discreetly, wandering down the street blending as tourists and locals were Eshan's eagle-eyed, well-armed agents assigned to protect both of them.

She carefully studied the face of her mentor, her protector, Alejandro Reyes. Normally his narrow, solemn features were frequently lit by warm smiles as befit a man in love with life, with the world. Over the past six months, Gabrielle had noticed the smiles had become rarer and appeared more forced. Was he keeping something from her?

Reyes paused, glanced anxiously around him then firmly taking Gabrielle's arm, steered her into an ordinary looking shop. She barely had time to take in the cluttered collection of antiques and curios within, so quickly was she ushered through the building. Reyes slipped through a nondescript inner door and urgently beckoned her to follow, his eyes anxiously alert for danger. Gabrielle found herself in a dusty back room, packed to the ceiling with boxes and surplus stock. To her astonishment,

Reyes opened a tall cupboard with double doors and stepped in. "Hurry, Gaby, follow me."

She hesitated, this was crazy! Then thought to herself, 'I look after the welfare of vampires, I can do crazy. What's a bit more insanity?' Stepping through, she half expected to crunch into the thick snow of Narnia on the other side. The reality was more prosaic, not a magical land peopled by talking animals but the entrance to a lift, taking them down to a labyrinth of modern catacombs beneath the streets of Rome.

"Nobody beyond the highest level of our organisation has ever seen this place." Reyes announced, his demeanour more confident and relaxed away from the street with its constant threat of danger from Nemesis.

"I am honoured, I think!" replied Gabrielle Railton, intrigued and not a little nervous.

Reyes led her down the winding featureless corridors to a steel door. It was equipped with a retina scan and opened with a soft, mechanical sigh to reveal a large, startlingly modern vault, brightly lit and clad in pristine softly matte steel. Temporarily, Reyes disabled the most sophisticated and highest grade security she had ever seen. No one without the correct protocol would ever get into this vault.

"Eat your heart out Nemesis," the Cardinal gave a humourless laugh. "There are objects in here they have spent decades searching in vain for."

Reyes took Gabrielle's hand and looked intently into her eyes. Was she ready? The calm enjoyment of her young life had been turned into one of danger and turmoil, she had to accept so much strangeness now. Was she ready to take in yet more? Gabrielle returned his intense scrutiny with courage and candour, her grip on his hand was steady and firm. She was ready.

The priest stood before a cabinet set within the wall. At his touch, it opened with silent ease and Reyes removed a black velvet pouch from the security alcove. He gave it to Gabrielle who opened it with trembling fingers. Within was an extravagant waterfall of pigeon-blood rubies but the weight of the necklace was nothing to the weight of history that it represented.

"The Blood Tears," she gasped, her eyes filling with salt tears of her own. Reyes reached into his pocket and handed her an envelope. Instantly, Gabrielle recognised the lilac Japanese paper, a letter written by her grandmother.

"My precious girl, these stones belong to you and have done from the moment you were born. Keep them safe and when the time is right, pass them on to a golden-eyed female descendant of your own. Hold them in your hands and they will tell you their history. I love you. Khari."

Gabrielle caressed the rubies, their cold hard-edged beauty reflecting that of the being, the Vampire King who had them made. She closed her eyes and saw the image of her most distant ancestor, the Dholma princess who had become wife and Queen to a vampire sovereign. The first Khari. The Blood Tears were a gift created with love and respect for her, a remarkable woman. They had been passed to Jendar Azrar for safekeeping when Queen Khari had known her life was in danger from her own brethren. In turn, the warlord had given them to Ha'ali Zian as proof of his obsessive adoration, only to have them thrown back in his face. Locked away unseen for centuries, he then gave them to her grandmother, their rightful owner. Indeed, the stones told her their story.

"Khari Devane gave them to us to protect. By rights they are yours," murmured Reyes quietly, aware of the emotional impact the gems were having on the young woman. Gabrielle held them tightly, as more vibrant, living images of the past flooded her soul. The memories of her distant ancestors, their shared blood sang across the centuries through the stones.

She could feel the winds whipping through the lightly scented steppe grasses caress her face as a fearful young woman rode bravely to her destiny, felt the same young woman's heart near to bursting with love for her vampire husband as he fastened the gems around her slender neck.

She shuddered as she briefly touched the cruel, insane mind of the next wearer of the Blood Tears. A female Dark Kind mind. The gems, too, cried out against the wrongness, they were never meant to adorn that insane creature's neck.

But her tears flowed uncontrollably as she made spiritual contact with her grandmother, her gentle touch, her love enduring and undiminished. Gently Gabrielle kissed the gems and returned them to the cardinal, her whole being overwhelmed by their spiritual power over her.

"Keep them here," she managed to say as her legs grew weak and her body swayed. "My grandmother was right to leave them in your care, they must be kept safe."

Reyes caught the woman as she almost fainted. The gift of *Knowing* was so strong in Gabrielle, the culmination of centuries of genetic manipulation. His instincts about her had been right from the start, she was another important weapon in the battle to come. But to Reyes, it was a tragedy she had to be thought of as a weapon. Gabrielle should live out her life in peace and happiness, find love, raise a family. All the things the Enemy had denied his own daughter.

Regaining her senses Gabrielle let the priest guide her to a chair, recovering quickly by the time he pressed a glass of water into her hand

"I'm fine. Honestly, I'm OK. I had a jolt of intense, undiluted *Knowing*. It was awesome. I felt at one with my ancestors, as if I had physically gone back in time and met them in person."

There was comfort, knowing she had only to hold the Blood Tears again and that wonderful emotional connection would return. She would have to find a way to shut out that vampire bitch though!

"I have more to show you, Gabrielle," the priest said as he filled her glass with more water, "but only if you are up to it. There is always another day."

'Is there?' Gabrielle mused darkly to herself, Reyes' distracted, sombre mood over the past months had not been reassuring. She stood up, folded her arms, head slightly tilted, eager to hear more.

Assessing her, Reyes decided it was time. Gabrielle was definitely ready; her power of *Knowing* had been strengthened by contact with the Blood Tears. He paused before continuing his tour of the vault and taking a deep breath, prepared to reveal his true identity. His superiors had given him a free rein to tell Gabrielle. Now was the right moment.

"Gaby, you have met Lady Eshan and have no doubts in your mind over the existence of the Dark Kind."

Gabrielle nodded, uncertain where this conversation was leading, aware something important was about to happen. "I haven't seen her fangs, thank goodness, but other then that, of course I believe in the Dark Kind."

There was a pause, awkward, seemingly endless. Reyes took in a deep breath, preparing himself. "They are not the only non-human, sentient life-form sharing the planet with humanity."

He waited till Gabrielle's puzzlement turned to curiosity. "You cannot leave it there! What are you talking about?"

"Many centuries ago, the last traumatised survivors of an alien race fled to Earth seeking sanctuary when their own beautiful, peaceful world was destroyed, all their people slain."

Reyes gestured for Gabrielle to sit down, she would need to. He closed his eyes, a golden light seemed to shine from him, and an astonished Gabrielle could swear she smelt a light, floral fragrance, like a summer meadow. Reyes appeared to grow more youthful, all the grey in his hair had disappeared. When he opened his eyes, they shone with a greater gentility, and an even more benign compassion.

"My real name is Mal'ore. I am of the K'elphin race."

"Wow," Gabrielle somehow managed to utter, her whole body shaking in fearful wonder. A real life alien being! Not some bug-eyed monstrosity but a slight, ethereal and gentle soul. Not so much different from his human guise. Her heart raced, her blood felt colder from shock. But this was not a frightening, ugly monster, it was the same Reyes, just a little more fragile, more unearthly, in appearance. Not threatening at all. Though too astonished to leave her seat, she began to calm down as Reyes continued to talk.

"At first we lived quietly and in secret on your world among our unknowing hosts. As deeply spiritual beings, we too gravitated to this world's great faiths. To the healing and teaching professions. We were content to live out our lives in anonymous peace and serenity. A life of contemplation and meditation, doing our best to help the human race, for we soon grew to love mankind as much as our own lost species."

He paused, the sorrow and despair obvious. "Then came the Great Warning from our most revered mystics. It broke our hearts; the Enemy that had almost destroyed us would target the Earth. We had no choice but to come out of the shadows, make our presence known and work with Earth's leaders, both spiritual and secular. At first they thought we were angels, some even suspected us as devils, luckily not enough to endanger us."

Again he paused, gathering his thoughts. This was the hardest thing to admit to. To speak openly of his duty, his shame, his betrayal of his deeply held principles.

"The worst part of the Great Warning was the abhorrent part my people have had to play in saving the blood drinkers, the unnatural abominations plaguing humanity. No human organisation or leader wanted to take on this role. Though we hated doing it, we have worked tirelessly to preserve the last Dark Kind survivors as best we can."

He looked at Gabrielle intently, "The prophesies are so damn vague! We don't know why we have to preserve these monstrosities, these insulting mockeries of creation. It can be unbearable, letting them slaughter the innocent and doing nothing to prevent it."

Gabrielle could see how tortuous it must be for a gentle, compassionate being as Reyes, his sworn duty to protect the Dark Kind went against everything he believed in, went against his love for humanity, the race who had provided a home, a sanctuary for him and his people.

Maybe prompted by the stress of talking about vampires, Reyes returned to his human appearance, the golden light and sweet floral fragrance gradually dissipated. Feeling relieved that he was back to the form so familiar to her, Gabrielle smiled to herself, remembering her first meeting with the slight, little Cardinal when he had said she could believe in fairies! Were the ethereal K'elphin a source for that legend, as the Dark Kind were the source for the Undead vampires of popular fiction?

Reyes spoke further, telling her more about the K'elphin and their beautiful lost world. "Ah, Gaby, what wonders, what beauty was lost." His eyes filled with tears. Concerned, Gabrielle got to her feet, offered him her chair. Grateful, he sank into it. His normally confident demeanour diminished. Gabrielle was shocked, he had never looked so old, so frail.

"Twin white suns once shone gently on crystalline cities rising proudly from valleys lush with wild flowers, a riot of vibrant colours and dizzying scents."

He continued with a soft sigh, recalling such cherished memories was impossible without the twisting, sharp cruelty of heartache. "Our lands were lapped by vast sapphire seas, the waves topped with silver foam. Oh, to sail those seas again!"

His shoulders slumped, rubbing his eyes with one hand. "But worse was the loss of our people, our parents, our children, our friends." Reyes face paled, his throat constricting, "My own wife and three children."

Gabrielle forgot he was an alien , forgot he was a Cardinal, she saw only a living being in pain, grieving for his slain family. She went to him, held him tightly in her arms, not speaking, there was nothing to say. Her shoulder felt damp and she realised he was weeping, perhaps for the first time in years. She had known grief, for the loss of her mother and more recently for Khari. She knew there were no words that could comfort, just to be there for Reyes was all she could do, all she could offer. Understanding dawned in her, he had always treated her like a daughter despite being a celibate priest. Now she knew he once had a family, once had children of his own and her heart wept for his loss.

Reyes sighed again, composed himself, wiped his eyes. "It is going to happen here, Gaby. The Enemy *will* target Earth and somehow, I do not know how, we must stop them."

Chapter Two

Time passed, how much was irrelevant. Gabrielle and Reyes were in no hurry to recover from the emotional impact of his revelations. There seemed no point in leaving, nothing had changed, so they continued to wander through the labyrinth of underground corridors, all with state of the art environmental controls and security. Gabrielle marvelled at so much money spent - to preserve what? She could not bear the suspense, firing a barrage of questions at him was more her style but after his poignant revelations, knew better then to badger the cardinal. She could tell from his expression part of his mind was dwelling on his family, on the danger to come for his adopted people. Her association with Reyes had taught her patience was always rewarded with intriguing revelations told with an ease born from their mutual trust and honesty.

"It's all here," he announced suddenly, regaining some of his poise, "Centuries of collection and storage. Before our order was created, Pope Flavian founded another in the early days of the Holy Roman Empire. Its mission was to collect and destroy all evidence of the existence of the Dark Kind. No written records were allowed to survive, no artefacts, no treasures. It was a well-orchestrated attempt to obliterate the Dark Kind completely, not just to take their lives, but eradicate their culture, everything that challenged humanity's status as supreme masters of the world.

With one notable exception, Azrar's stronghold, all the palaces of the Dark Kings and their Jendar's fortresses were mysteriously destroyed before falling into human hands. Now we know they were built with a powerful self-destruct mechanism."

Gabrielle nodded, she had come to the same conclusion herself some time before, the same compulsion that drove the Dark Kind to destroy the bodies of their fallen by fire.

"When, in later years, our more enlightened order was founded, we saved what we could of the evidence of the Dark Kind and what we gathered is safe in these vaults. As I said, what would our friends in Nemesis give to gain access to this treasure house?"

Gabrielle shuddered with the thought of what far-reaching damage Hain's army of fanatics of Nemesis could do to the world's future. The tools of that harm could be here, underneath the Eternal City.

"Do not fret, my child, they will not prevail. They cannot be allowed to."

Reyes pondered on what else he could show Gabrielle. There was so much choice! Within the vaults were stored exquisite jewellery, gem studded gold goblets, treasure boxes inlaid with scenes of Dark Kind life, even scraps of the beautiful fabrics in indestructible jewel-bright colours that never faded. Ancient tomes describing life under the Vampire Kings were stored here as were accounts of the long centuries of war against the blood drinkers. More macabre artefacts included souvenirs made from Dark Kind bone from the days of the witch fires and purges. There was an old superstition that the naturally black bone of the vampires had magic healing power. Total rubbish of course, or was it? Gabrielle mused, what else was the information stored in Dark Kind genes but magic of a different nature. Could Dark Kind DNA hold secrets that could alter humanity's future? She instinctively understood that Reyes and his organisation were right, Mankind was not ready, this material must stay locked away, maybe forever.

Gabrielle shuddered as a familiar sensation emanated from a deep alcove. She knew what lay there, sealed within its own vault. The casket. Even encased by concrete and metal, it continued to send out it's warning to keep away, to leave it sealed. She had thought long and hard about the box's unknown power. A mystery, perhaps something every government leader, every big corporation director, every scientist in the world would sell their soul for. At least Reyes and his organisation had agreed with her, that the casket perhaps carried its own pathway of danger to humanity.

Reyes saw her reaction to the alcove and its baleful contents, and steered her tactfully away. The poor girl had suffered enough from exposure to the casket. There were plenty more wonderful artefacts to gladden her archaeologist's heart instead.

Gabrielle paused, "Er, that trick you did earlier, with the golden light and the scent of flowers?"

Reyes smiled, the first warm, meaningful smile for many months. "Nothing magical my dear. We employ a similar biology to certain types of squid and chameleons, manipulating pigment in our cells as a disguise." He shrugged, "Sorry to disappoint you."

Gabrielle was not disappointed, there was something reassuring in that neither of the species she knew shared her world were supernatural, that everything about them could be explained by science. That, like humans, they were vulnerable. At heart she was still a rational scientist, wanting a logical and believable reason for every phenomenon. It was self-delusion. Her gift of *Knowing* would always defy the laws of rationality.

Chapter Three

New York, 2009

Jazriel yawned and stretched in a movement as lithe and sensuous as a waking panther as he rose from Rest. He stepped onto the balcony of his penthouse apartment to gaze out over the sprawling city below with his fierce but indisputably beautiful eyes. He lived in a modern society that echoed an earlier barbaric time. This soaring block of luxurious high-tech security apartments could easily replicate the Dark Kind's massive stone fortresses. Private security teams and surveillance equipment replacing paid armies of fighting men.

Down on the lawless streets beyond the brutally massive security barriers that protected the wealthy were lawless gangs. Heavily armed, vicious and feral, they had become the new barbarian tribes. This city was in turmoil, reeling from the last devastating Imadeen Outrage, but though human society was fragmented, paranoid and frightened, Jazriel had not been so secure for centuries or lived in such comfort. His wealth accumulated in the distant past when servicing Dark Kind nobles as sha'ref, now cushioned his life. It had been worth being in such high demand; being screwed senseless for centuries had finally paid off.

It had not always been such a cosseted life for the vampire. There was the wretched time, after the fall of the Vampire Kings, when the remaining scattered Dark Kind had found they had to fend for themselves, survive in any way they could.

He recalled with a shudder those past horrors, seeking protection from the sun in dank foul smelling cellars, crouching in low caves like an animal, or hiding in draughty castle vaults. Worse of all, once he had to endure the daylight hours in the filthy crypt of a human graveyard. The dirt! The stench! Truly a nightmare for such a fastidious and luxury loving being as Jazriel.

Now, he had comfort and his own, hard-earned wealth to support him. He was surrounded by beautiful things, his art collection, wardrobes of fabulous top designer clothes and his diversions, gadgets using the most expensive, state of the art technology. Down in the subterranean garages, he had the latest, most exclusive vehicles, all built to his exacting specifications, silent and swift to cut through the mayhem of the streets like the thrust of a rapier.

But pride of place was his most treasured vehicle, his beloved high powered Ducati motorbike. High tec toys for an ageless being whose race first domesticated the horse while mankind grovelled naked in the dirt looking for grubs to eat.

Jazriel stood up abruptly, the hours of darkness were too fleeting to waste brooding over the past. It was time to continue his quest, to seek relief from his painful yearning for Azrar. And the far more painful longing that he kept tightly locked in the deepest, most hidden vault in his heart, a vault that must never be unlocked. There must be something out there, some new powerful narcotic; humans were ingenious at inventing new ways to seek temporary - and not so temporary oblivion. What was the point in dwelling on what could not be? It achieved nothing.

Azrar had chosen his duty to a bunch of ungrateful, lying, scabrous goat-shagging human peasants over his lover. Who wanted to live in that frigid backwater anyway? Jazriel was disinterested in politics, unaware and indifferent that Prince Azrar was caught up again in the complex power games of nations. Jazriel could not think past his own hurt, his sense of rejection by the Dark Kind noble he loved to distraction.

He did not know or care that in a time of growing world-wide chaos, anarchy and violence, Azrar's people once again sought his power and protection. The Prince successfully ruled his lands unchallenged, fighting off the threats from the corrupt south and the religious fanatic east. Flushing out and destroying the traitors, the lurking vipers hiding among his own people. No doubt other world leaders looked on Isolann in envy. The ancient and mysterious Land of Secrets and Shadows was once more peaceful, law abiding and safe - at least for its citizens. And again it was a barrier to unwanted influences invading Eastern Europe, holding back the Imadeen as it once held back the Nazis. The world looked to Azrar to defeat the Imadeen, taking the fight to their homeland. The Prince was a revered and respected warlord again.

All that mattered to Jazriel was that there was no place there for him. Mierda, it was Azrar's loss, his own fault his bed stayed empty and cold.

Jazriel had tried hard to make the best of his new life. Garan had helped him find the apartment and buy vehicles and had organised the best security in the United States. Garan had also dealt on his behalf with Lady Eshan for Jazriel to access his money. He even had a new identity. He was now the enigmatic Isolanni playboy, Jaz Oberon. A young man of mystery and obscenely vast wealth from a distant land few had heard of. With his devastating good looks, money and effortless charm, the Jazzman was a hit with New York's high society crowd. The city's night life claimed him as one of its own, its lights dazzled around him like the multi coloured glittering sequins of a vast theatrical backdrop, the stage ready for adventure and amusement.

Only he found no pleasures in this New World, no matter how hard he tried. No human-fashioned toys such as his fast, beautiful cars, or any quantity of clever new technology truly amused him. No narcotic or intoxicant blurred his emotional pain. No amount of killing revived his senses beyond keeping him alive. Though his apartment always echoed to loud music, the hardest pounding, thrilling rock music or achingly beautiful operatic aria did not touch his emotions. No music could lift his spirits. Nothing drove out this soul-deep loneliness, this acid-etched despair. This centuries-old mourning.

Standing high on his fortieth floor balcony, Jazriel felt a sudden impulse to leap from it. To soar above the city like a black-winged nighthawk, feel the sharp night air rush swiftly past his body in a brief moment of freedom and exhilaration before plummeting to the ground. It would be so easy, easier then what passed for living. He sighed and stepped back from the ledge. What was he? Nothing more then a Dark Kind whore cursed with the twin demons of hope and optimism. Life had been good for him once, when the blustery night winds had billowed into high, canvas sails, when he had sailed across oceans, free from all laws, human or Dark Kind, respected as an equal and hopelessly and unrepentantly in love with a human. It had ended badly, how could it not have? Without realising it, his right hand flexed, reached up and touched his one side of his face, passed briefly in front of his right eye. It was not the first time he had made this unconscious gesture and it would not be the last.

Jazriel re-entered his spacious, high luxury apartment and sat on an oversized silver chrome leather sofa, reaching down to a low glass table for a platinum box. The latest attempt from his tame illicit pharmacist, his mission to create something that could affect Jazriel's metabolism, had so far ended in dismal failure. Maybe this time? The vampire opened the box and studied the fine golden powder within. He dropped some in a glass with a small helping of champagne and watched as the two fused together into the potentially intoxicating alchemy he craved. Once the Bliss was mixed, he pulled some up into a syringe and rolling up the sleeve of his dove-grey silk and pashmina shirt, searched for a vein. Zaard! It was getting harder, he never gave his abused body enough time to recover. What was the point? He was not going to wait before damaging it again.

Giving up trying for a surface vein, Jazriel unleashing his fangs, with the edge of one, ripped deep into his arm. His head snapped back sharply with a howl of pain, then shuddering, forcing back some control, he poured the Bliss mixture straight into his blood stream. He sank back onto the sofa and waited for the hoped for hit, the journey to artificial euphoria or pain-free oblivion. Somewhere his phone rang and rang. Somewhere an animal whimpered in pain and distress. Somewhere in his confused brain was the awareness that the injured animal was himself. Jazriel's head slumped forward, he saw the ruinous mess of his shirt, soaked in purple blood mixed with the sickly green-gold Bliss residue. He closed his eyes, sank back, waiting for something, anything, to happen.

In another part of the city, at his latest nightclub, Hell, Garan's foxy features tightened with fury. He had tried to reach Jazriel but there was no reply. They had made arrangements to see an exciting new band, one of the vanguard of a new wave of zybar punk bands. Garan wanted to branch out beyond the night clubs he owned, sign up a few bands. Be part of the roller-coaster of madness of post Outrage life in New York. And he wanted Jazriel on board, to snap him out of his dangerous decline into a nightmare of abuse, wallowing in the mire of human-made degradation. Damn the apes, damn their cleverness, their science warped into creating a narcotic hell for his friend.

If only he could drag Jazriel out of this ruinous self pity, Garan was convinced he would soon forget living in a draughty old Keep in a remote and backward Upper Balkan country. Leave the region to the wolves and peasants. Leave it to that brooding warlord endlessly re-living past glories, drowning in memories of a world that would never return. This sprawling, overcrowded, wounded city was where real vampire living could begin. Where possibilities were as endless as the number of humans dwelling here. A tantalising smorgasbord of prey.

Garan prepared to leave, there was no time to swing by Jazriel's apartment he would go to the gig alone. Jazriel knew how important this night was to his friend. So where the hell was he? With a sinking heart, Garan knew. Stoned. Od'ed in his high rise apartment. Garan's nightmare continued to worsen.

Chapter Four

Chess Manor, The Chilterns England 2009

Ancient oak and beech, their gnarled limbs heavy with summer green stood silent witness to Gabrielle's rebirth. She strode along a forest path, the sunlight filtering through the canopy glinting off gold highlights in her hair. A powerful handgun in her clenched fist.

She paused, raised it and fired. Shattering the serenity of the forest with an ear-numbing explosion, a brief shocked silence before the woodland echoed with the screech and squawk of panicking wildlife.

"Miles off! Support you wrist with your left hand and fire again."

Gabrielle turned sharply as her instructor from the Spook Squad caught up with her. Enver Thorne. The troubled, skinny youth she'd briefly encountered all those years ago now ran the Manor's operations. He had grown into a lanky, troubled and almost good-looking man. Gabrielle had slept with him from the first night of her training at the Manor.

She had put away her archaeologist's trowel, her ancient tomes, her peace of mind. One phone call and her life had taken a different direction. A quiet night in her apartment in Rome had shattered into shards of painful nightmare. Just one call. Nemesis had found the Montana refuge of the Devane family.

Gabrielle would not squander any more of her life digging up old bones and ancient decaying trinkets. Let them stay buried. She had other things to do now; she had to learn to fight, to drive like the devil. To kill.

Taking her mentor's advice, Gabrielle supported her grip on the deceptively light handgun. She had changed. Every ounce of rounded feminine softness on her already slim frame had been honed and pared away. She was taut-muscled, lithe and agile as a cat. A light had gone from her eyes replaced by a humourless steel determination. Someone must pay.

Whitethorn had been burnt to nothing, charred cinders blown away by the first mountain gale. Joe Jnr, Clay's son Toby and two ranch hands were dead, shot down defending the ranch from unknown assailants. Masked, heavily armed men who had arrived by helicopter, hurt the family grievously and disappeared. A random act of malice, no doubt ordered by Hain himself to flex his power. As the supreme head of an organisation, he was as fanatical in his way as any Imadeen terrorist. The attack on the ranch was a warning shot of his determination to destroy anyone who harboured and aided the Dark Kind. That no one living at Whitethorn had ever heard of vampires was apparently deemed irrelevant.

"That's enough for today, Gaby." Enver's hand covered hers, slowly and firmly lowering the gun. "You will learn nothing if you strain a tendon from overdoing it."

"Sod that," Gabrielle muttered and roughly shrugged him off. "Just bugger off and leave me alone, Enver." She would know when she was finished. When she could shoot with perfect accuracy. When she could place a bullet straight between Hain's eyes.

Chapter Five

Phoenix City, New York

Jazriel loped unsteadily down to the high security underground garage of his apartment block. He glanced across at the gleaming Ducati, it was as if the red and silver, hand-built, high-powered motorcycle called out, plaintively, to his soul. It did not belong, motionless, poised on its stand in this tedious long rest. Like its Dark Kind owner, it craved the unlimited freedom of high speed and the far horizon. But it was not to be, not that night.

Though he had many vehicles, nothing was so treasured as this last gift from Jendar Azrar. The powerful and swift machine that had helped him escape the stifling, backward realm of Isolann, flee a lynch mob after his blood for a crime he had not committed. Time had not softened his hurt, on the contrary, the injustice made him burn with fury. Jazriel realised the gift of the big motorbike had been a desperate gesture from his lover, opening the cage door in the hope that he would remain. Well, if it hadn't been for those lying human bastards and Azrar's refusal to defy them, he would still be there. Hating his life, but loving Azrar.

Halting, Jazriel raised a hand to stop the progress of his body guards through the labyrinthine garage complex to the fleet of armoured Hummers that would flank his latest vehicle, a one-off Maserati. Built to his exacting demands and needs it had gadgets like totally sun-proof windows that could protect him if caught out in daylight. If only the idiotic humans knew the extraordinary wonders of their modern technology had actually made vampire life so much safer!

Leaving the body guards, muttering anxiously about not guaranteeing his safety, Jazriel changed his mind about the bike and wove an uncertain route over to his Ducati. He swung astride the powerful machine and leant forward to grasp the handlebars, closing his eyes to better remember the first time he had ridden the machine.

Zaard! Why did love have to tear at his heart with so much pain? He was in modern America. His life should be one of excitement, re-discovering his freedom, his independence as he sped through a night-shrouded city. But it was an empty life, living a lie, his playboy lifestyle a pretence to hide his turmoil from Garan, the last vamp in the world to understand what he was enduring.

No. He would not drive out, protected by bullet-proof glass, armoured steel and the armament of his security team. His soul craved freedom, the exhilaration of life-threatening speed. What freedom did he have with these muttering, restrictive minders? He pushed the bike off its stand and started up the distinctive roaring engine, nothing else could sound like a Ducati, its engine note was unique. He revved the bike loudly, to drown out the yells of protest from his startled security team running towards him. As well they might, if anything happened to Jazriel they would lose the highest-paying employer of their lives!

Ignoring their pleas, Jazriel let the big bike rumble up out of the garage complex and into the night, as always, spurning a helmet. The cold night air stung his face, the wind sent icy fingers tugging through his hair, gently at first then with greater spite as he picked up speed. Jazriel's extraordinarily handsome face broke into a fang-bared grin of hunger and anticipation as New York City and all it's vibrant human life lay exposed before him, a banquet of almost infinite variety. And not just blood; all the narcotics and intoxicants with new dangerous substances coming onto the street every day. All there for him to take in his restless search for pleasure and sensation. For something, anything, to block out the emptiness consuming his soul.

Revving the engine noisily he pulled up outside Garan's night club, the bouncers and club minions rushing forward in an unruly scrum, elbowing each other viciously, eager to be the one to take care of the Ducati. Their boss's junkie boyfriend was a favoured guest - he always tipped lavishly!

Jazriel strode inside, his head clearing from the ride through New York's streets. Zaard! He needed something potent. Now! How else could he get through another night? And far worse to come, another long, long day of sleepless, haunted Rest.

Garan would be furious with him for not turning up at the Girl, Decayed gig. He shrugged it off, one of his famously disarming apologetic smiles and a long and lingering, smouldering kiss promising more then he would ever offer and his transgression would be instantly forgiven.

His progress through the dancing throng of sweat-soaked humans was slow. One girl moved towards him, eyes glittering with desire. She worked for the Boss and was intrigued by his friend, not wanting to believe the rumours that they were more intimate. Anyway, it didn't matter, this gorgeous creature hadn't met her yet.

"Jazriel? A name for an angel! You certainly look heavenly to me." She intertwined her arm with his, gave a lascivious grin, "I know you could take me straight to Heaven tonight!"

"Sadly, you are looking in the wrong direction, princess." Jazriel replied with a rueful smile before moving away from the scantily clad girl, too drunk to notice any discomfort from his cold skin as he passed through the mayhem of Garan's club. Dancing bodies filled every inch of floor space, wildly gyrating to the relentless hard rhythm, a harsh, discordant yet thrilling sound .The distinctive driving heartbeat of the club packed as always beyond its official capacity. The girl did not want to lose such a handsome catch. She caught up with him and stroked his arm through the soft fabric of his exquisitely tailored casual clothes, Armani? Duroubon? Wondering what lay behind the intensely black shades.

"You know, Lucifer was once the most beautiful heavenly spirit in Paradise. You could easily be another fallen angel."

"One big difference, princess. Lucifer means Bringer of Light. I only bring darkness."

Firmly Jazriel removed the girl's hand and kissed it, giving one of his dazzling smiles, a calculated mixture of sincere apology and naughty little boy, one that always worked well with human females, then disappeared deeper into the hot, vibrant mayhem. He found Garan up in his office high above the club observing his friend's passage through the dancers. They greeted each other with the intimate kiss and embrace of their Kind.

"I know, I know," Jazriel said, dropping his head in mock contrition, his hands raised in apology. "I fucked up yet again." He took Garan's face in his hands and began the long, seductive kiss he knew would disarm his friend's indignation, drawing him down into a whirlpool of pleasure. Garan's senses began to drown in the intense sensuality before he snapped back, pulling away abruptly. A damn sha'ref ploy! It was cruel, Jazriel was manipulating him again. It would be different if the kiss led to something else, but of course it never had, never would.

Jazriel smiled, "That gig was important to you, I am sorry." He lowered his turquoise eyes, deliberately hiding their power beneath long silken lashes, his manner seductive, "After all you have done for me, I am such an unreliable, selfish bastard." He looked up, hitting Garan with the full impact of his beguiling eyes. "Am I forgiven?"

Moving away, Garan growled, turning his back. "Of course you are, but stop being such a whore. We are friends; I don't want or need this sha'ref crap."

Indifferent to his friend's bad mood, Jazriel shrugged, he would soon change it to something more affable. "Again, sorry to offend, but that *is* what I am."

Garan sighed. He was right, Jazriel could not stop behaving in that way, it was how he was created. Once again, he was grateful to have been made an ordinary commoner, no battles to fight, no lands to rule, no complete, unquestioning submission to nobles' demands. "It is my turn to apologise, my friend. That was harsh and totally uncalled for."

Relieved the brief tension between them was over, Jazriel lit a cigarette. "I'm bored - it's all too easy around here. I fancy meals on wheels tonight- expensive wheels."

Garan gave a hesitant shrug of assent. With the low boredom threshold of a gnat, his companion was in a thrill seeking mood yet again; since his resurrection, Jazriel's adventures always meant danger, pushing the risk of discovery to ever-closer limits. Sometimes, during these exciting years in New York, Garan enjoyed the wild roller-coaster ride, but more often it caused him great anxiety. Their roles had become perversely switched somehow. Garan, the Dark Kind maverick now had to watch over the once rock steady Jazriel. To add emphasis to Garan's dilemma, it was clear the other vampire was, as usual, high as a kite, his eyes glittered with something unrelated to a recent kill.

Jazriel gave a rueful apologetic grin as a trickle of purple blood ran from one nostril. He wiped it with an ivory silk handkerchief which he tossed into a bin. Garan was horrified, the reckless, stupid idiot! Would he never bloody learn about this modern age? Growling with fury, he retrieved the bloodstained object and borrowing Jazriel's lighter, incinerated it to ash.

"How many times have I told you? This is a whole new century, human science is advancing at a frightening pace. Their latest toy is genetics...our DNA would revolutionise their society, change their world forever. Leave nothing for them to find and use, Jaz. Not one drop of your blood, not one glossy hair from your beautiful head."

Jazriel waved a languid hand in assent. His companion was becoming increasingly anxious and uptight; he had become a different Garan to the one who had prowled the dark streets of the Old World with him.

"Lighten up, my friend," Jazriel urged, holding Garan's thin, vulpine face in his hands and kissing him again. "We came to New York to live to the fullest limit. We have no idea how long we have left on this wild ride, so let's make every precious second fun."

There was no arguing with that, mused Garan, this century gave the illusion of greater freedom for the vampires, but that's what it was, just an illusion. The humans were watching them, he was convinced, watching and waiting for them to make a rash, careless move. An appointment with a steel laboratory slab and sharp scalpels awaited both Dark Kind friends. But, then these humans had to catch them first!

"I've bought you a new toy, Jaz", announced Garan later as they arrived at his apartment block's underground garage. "I know how much you loved that Atlantic."

Knowing Jazriel's fascination for cars and speed, Garan threw him the keys to a classic Bugatti Veyron, a sleek silver-lilac monster pumped up to the max with racing car specs and the very latest state of the art technology. With a mind-boggling price to match.

"She is absolutely beautiful," sighed Jazriel passing a caressing hand slowly over the elegant, silken metal curves. His turquoise eyes gleamed with pleasure. The car was like himself, a thing of beauty and desire, a manufactured creation.

'Not as beautiful as you, Jazzman,' thought Garan, his body tense with thwarted desire. Having Jazriel here in New York was proving an ordeal, on many levels, yet he would not have him leave. He sat back in the soft, grey leather seat and let Jazriel get a feel for the car. Nothing had changed in these few years of hunting together. He could not have the pleasure of the Jazzman's body and that made him feel bad. Tonight would take many ripped-out human throats to make him feel better.

The Bugatti sped through the rain slick streets of New York, Jazriel's fast vampire reflexes handling the powerful car with consummate ease. Though it was 2a.m., it was strangely quiet and traffic free in the city that never sleeps. Just a few desultory yellow cabs prowled for late night revellers.

"No cops about, must be big trouble somewhere. Shame," mused Jazriel aloud.

Garan was relieved. Deliberately provoking and killing policemen was just another game to Jazriel, but one that risked dangerous exposure in this time of swift information gathering and CCTV cameras.

Another high-powered sports car drove up beside them weaving between furiously hooting cabs. Two good-looking and expensively dressed young men waved and taunted, jostling for a race.

"That's more like it," Jazriel murmured, hunger and blood lust tightening in a painful knot inside him. "Time to play." He gave chase after the lurid red MacClaren, staying provocatively close to the bumper of another ridiculously expensive and rare super car. The driver was forced to keep his speed high, any braking and the Bugatti would hit its bumper. As the red car negotiated a twisting course through parked cabs and traffic, Jazriel eased alongside the MacClaren, leant over and blew its driver an even more provocative kiss, before pulling back. The outraged driver lost control, giving a parked car a heavy, glancing blow.

"Ouch!" Jazriel exclaimed with a wide, predatory grin, his fangs already down in anticipation of the kill. Garan growled, he did not like the direction the red car was heading, too close into the exclusive wealthy area of this divided city. Garan never killed on home ground. Neither was Jazriel supposed to.

Accelerating hard, Jazriel pushed the Bugatti to overtake within a hairsbreadth of the other car in a grit-blasting burst of speed.

"There goes more of his pristine paint work! Those humans are good and mad now. Delicious!" Despite his concerns, Garan began to relax, enjoying the chase.

Jazriel nodded agreement with a fierce grin as he powered away, doing an impressive high-speed turn in the road and leading the MacClaren to a more run-down area of the city. Their prey were by now incandescent with rage; soon terror would add more flavour to their blood. Cutting his lights, Jazriel pulled into a deserted alleyway, stopped, the MacClaren in hot pursuit.

Garan and Jazriel got out of their car and waited, leaning insolently against the Bugatti. With a screech of burning tyres, the MacClaren pulled right up to its bumper, the two furious young men darting out, one wielding a gun. Jazriel recognised the other - the son of a rich and famous industrialist. Urgently, he wanted to kill, the intoxicating scent of adrenaline charged blood so maddeningly close. He decided to make it quick, not so pleasurable but also lessening the danger from any passing police patrols. Not that he was concerned, but Garan's generous gift of the Bugatti deserved one in return. A night of slightly less anxiety!

"Stupid faggot bastard – this is a new MacClaren! Worth a bloody fortune, far more then that pile of outdated Italian shit. You're going to pay for the damage with your face, pretty boy!"

"*I want that one,*" Jazriel snarled in the Dark Kind language. Garan shrugged, unbothered, blood was blood and both men were equally young and strong. Moving fast, Jazriel grabbed the rich youth by the throat and lifted him high, fangs bared. In a windpipe-crushing grip, he was held too hard too scream but he thrashed about violently in terror. His companion shook off his initial shock and raised his gun but before he could fire, Garan leapt with tiger like speed and strength, pinning him to the ground. The vampire forced the gun from his victim's hand with a bone-crunching grip. Like his companion, the victim was little more then a boy. He gave a high scream of pain, terror and fury.

"Schrauben sie. Let the cops come. More fun for us." Jazriel changed his mind, this chase had only whetted his new appetite for risk taking.

"I'm not ready to make the prime time news yet," Garan growled, surprised at his own response. Risk taking! That was his favourite pastime, what was going wrong here?   But with his prey's throat so tantalisingly close, Garan was in no mood to argue further. His fangs slashed down, cutting through to the vein in one powerful tearing motion.   Jazriel smiled at his prey, his voice deceptively silken, "You really shouldn't have dissed my new car, man - big mistake." He tore open the young man's throat with a low groan of pleasure, drinking deeply, as every cell of his being pulsed with vibrant new life.

"Ok, Dead Man," announced a sated Garan, "you seem to be calling the shots tonight. What now?

Jazriel, his senses electric with renewed power, turquoise eyes aflame with energy did not answer. He threw both bodies back in their car and urged Garan to move the precious Bugatti to safety. Opening the petrol cap of the MacClaren, he lit a cigarette, after a few deep drags tossed it into the tank. Garan watched as Jazriel prowled back towards him, behind him the inferno of the exploding car, a dramatic movie-like backdrop. It was no good; the excitement of the chase and kill had only heightened his maddening and futile desire for Jazriel. This was going to be a long, difficult night.

Chapter Six

Rome, Italy

"Our two scoundrels have overstepped the mark again. They are dangerously out of control."

Cardinal Reyes' voice was deceptively calm, but his poise masked the depth of his anger and disgust. He was a being devoted to the pursuit of spiritual enlightenment with an altruistic concern for all life. Yet here he was, assigned against his will to protecting the vilest life form on the planet. An unnatural one that should not exist at all.

Reyes was a man of honour, he would not shirk from his onerous and distasteful duty but he didn't have to like it! He threw the latest police reports from New York down onto his desk with some force, the loud bang shocking all in the Rome office. As they wandered over to see what was upsetting their normally gentle mannered leader, many gasped in horror. One ran from the room to be violently sick. Reyes was prepared for this reaction. He'd experienced the same response only an hour before. On the desk lay shocking, brutal images. The police photos of young men with their throats savagely torn out, almost every drop of blood drained from their bodies was seared into his mind. Polluting his soul with the horror of the Dark Kind and their cruel, murderous ways.

"What has that poor blighted city done to deserve those murdering bastards," Reyes murmured, "both are drunk on innocent human blood and one is high on anything else it can get hold off!"

Gabrielle Railton had joined them and nodded in agreement. Centuries of planning and preparation were under threat from two idiotic Dark Kind wild cards. One a notorious and uncontrollable maverick, the other, she thought with a shiver of distaste, was a creature with a serious substance abuse problem, the undead sexual plaything of a Dark Kind warlord. What a charming pair!

"We have to get Eshan involved, this is not a situation any human can deal with." Gabrielle said with conviction.

Reyes nodded in terse agreement, not convinced that the Dark Kind noble woman could influence the renegades wreaking havoc in New York. Destroying them would be the only sane option, but when was anything about this situation anything but sheer insanity? Every Dark Kind, without exception, had to be protected, kept safe from all discovery and from the clutches of the determined fanatics of Nemesis. In the future, the Dark Kind would be needed. A day he prayed would never happen.

"Where is the Lady now?" Reyes asked in resignation. Ha'ali Eshan was the easiest Dark Kind to deal with, one that did not kill for blood but the fact remained she was still an accursed vampire. Nothing would change that.

"She is in Riga, searching for the special one," answered Gabrielle. "Those two idiots haven't got much time left. I can feel the Nemesis cohorts are busy setting a trap for them."

Reyes' thin, aesthetic face lit up, was this another aspect of Gabrielle's gift of the *Knowing?* Descended from Dezarn's human Queen, she was the second Khari's granddaughter and more ancient steppe blood coursed through her veins from her Isolanni grandmother Lhalee.

Gabrielle saw the hope and expectation on the Cardinal's thin face and shook her head sadly. "Nothing supernatural there, your Eminence, just a hunch based on experience. Those Fearless Vampire Hunter wannabes won't miss an opportunity. I think Jazriel must be our greatest immediate concern. He is so out of his head all the time, he's rapidly becoming an easy target."

Reyes agreed. It was good to have Gabrielle back with him but she was no longer on the archaeological team. The tragedy in Montana had galvanised and altered the young woman he thought of as a daughter. Her stormy affair with Enver Thorne has ended badly. Inevitably. With two strong, driven and argumentative individuals, it was always a question of waiting for the storm to break! Reyes was saddened at how life, no, how Nemesis had changed his protégée. The coltish enthusiasm, the sparkle, had gone. What would it take to make Gaby smile again?

Chapter Seven

Nemesis Headquarters, Berne, Switzerland

Unbelievable! Did the creature want to be captured? A triumphant Hain threw down the emailed copy of a recent New York newspaper onto his desk. At last! One of the fanged bastards was within his grasp. His faith in Geddoe had been vindicated. The two creatures Geddoe's team had been tracking had disappeared from the radar for over a year, there had been no more reported sightings in Paris. The beautiful young monsters suddenly and successfully completely disappeared from the Nemesis radar. Until now.

His number one vampire hunter had at last caught up with the two males from Paris. Hain looked again at the newspaper in amazement and disbelief. Were the creatures now getting complacent perhaps? Careless in their arrogance? Believing themselves safe across the Pond?

The evidence that they were indeed flaunting their predatory ways was there in full colour in the gossip section of the Phoenix Times. Hain's preferred target vampire, the physically perfect specimen known now as playboy Jaz Oberon. Intensely dark glasses, his team of burly minders trying to shield him from the encircling, frenzied paparazzi - none of these were foolproof. Oberon was already captured, trapped in world–wide data bases, his image accessible to anyone, including the international police, Hain knew he had to move swiftly. No one was going to steal his prize. Not when it was within his grasp.

Shaking, Hain's fingers reached up to touch his weak, recessive chin, his fleshy, florid cheeks, his own much-loathed features. With a sigh of envy and yearning, Hain recognised the vampire's finely sculptured masculine face, the dazzling looks. A sublime beauty he so craved for his own face. With the vampire so blatantly flaunting his existence in the newspaper photo, Hain felt closer to stealing that eternally youthful splendour for himself. It was a craving that tormented him. The irony was not lost on Hain, he remembered his scornful derision at his uncle's obsession with acquiring Prince Azrar's library. A forlorn dream that died with Parrish.

Hain would not fail. His fingers went down from his face to trace the exquisite fallen angel features in the photograph. "Not long now, creature," Hain muttered. The vampire Jazriel was openly living the high life in New York, unwittingly hastening his final destiny. His inevitable fate - lying on a laboratory slab moved ever closer. And with it, Hain's chance for immortal life, for transformation.

He called up Geddoe, scorning the time difference. "Alive or dead, I don't care. It's time to bring down that vamp."

Chapter Eight

Phoenix City, New York

Jazriel slumped awkwardly in the back of a white armoured luxury limo, his idea of vehicle hell. An ostentatious, vulgar machine for humans with wealth but no taste. He tried to endure the bilious-cream leather interior, the gilded fittings, with ill disguised bad grace, helped himself to the entire contents of the discreetly hidden bar, using the shiny surface to cut one line of coke after another. With some Bliss for good measure.

Why was he here? Had he finally gone insane? Was it because his nightly hunts through New York's post Outrage wastelands with Garan bored him senseless? Everything he did, everything he tried to blank out reality was not working. When a high profile socialite invited him to the opening of an art exhibition with a chauffeur driven limo to the event thrown in, he had accepted. He must have been particularly wasted at the time.

The media-created illusion of a person that was Jaz Oberon was considered a catch guaranteeing column inches in the press for any party host. He vicariously enjoyed the notoriety, the curiosity, at first, finally understanding Garan and his impulse to take off the inescapable dark glasses and reveal his true identity to humans. The centuries living hidden in the shadows in fear of discovery had become unbearable. Shameful for a being from a proud, predatory, species that had once held this world as it's own. Maybe spending a few last hours of life, proudly and defiantly as Dark Kind was worthwhile. Zaard! He muttered, inhaling some brutal unrefined Bliss. Of course it wasn't!

Being chauffeured in this ugly, vulgar limo was no longer such a great idea. He still had standards! But it was too late to switch cars as the limo drew up outside a large gallery in the regenerated, wealthy district of Outrage-damaged New York, named with a stunning lack of originality- Phoenix City. The exhibition was called a 'Celebration of Light.' Wealthy socialites, A list celebrities and their hangers-on were out in force, drawn by the buzz of excitement about the latest works by artist, Stan Ling, his exhibition the current talk of the intelligentsia in New York. Jazriel had the wealth to buy the entire collection, a reputation for extravagant impulse buying of artwork; he knew why he was being feted.

As the limo pulled up his team of bodyguards leapt out of a convoy of other vehicles, ready to escort him into the gallery. Jazriel dropped his head low, to escape the flash, flash, flash from a febrile, jostling hyena-pack of paparazzi. Even the darkest shades could not block out the painful sting of the cameras. He turned to his minders, ordering them to remain outside and not to park the cars, he may need to escape from here in a hurry. Highly paid professionals, they were reluctant to leave their young boss unattended, even if he was just an effete but carelessly generous foreign playboy with endless wealth. But Jazriel insisted and prowled with silent, confident, though unsteady, steps into the spacious gleaming chrome and starkly white gallery.

The milling guests stopped at his arrival, the atmosphere electric, pausing in their socialising to watch him with hungry eyes, hypnotised, intrigued. Jaz Oberon was a mysterious and enigmatic figure in the wealthiest inner circle of city life. Effortlessly glamorous, he had a potent allure none could define. It drew them, moths before an unnerving, unearthly flame. He lived amongst them but defiantly apart, behaving as badly as he wanted, oblivious to their mores and manners. And they adored him for it. Their token desirable but unobtainable bad boy. Who openly broke the rules with his indolent, drug-skewed charm.

Immediately, he was mobbed. Single, achingly handsome, his sexuality an additional intriguing mystery, Jaz Oberon was a magnet for every gold digger, social climber and obsessive, male and female alike, in the gallery. Aghast, believing he needed rescuing, the hostess, a skeletal –thin young woman married to very old money and a seemingly equally old husband intercepted him. Risking over-familiarity by taking Jazriel's arm, she flinched at the coldness permeating from his skin through his dark grey cashmere and silk suit. With a fixed rictus grin that did not meet her pale eyes, she briskly steered him away from the circle of admirers.

"Jaz, darling, I am so glad you accepted my invitation. Now my evening is perfect! Let me introduce you to the artist."

Hidden behind the darkest shades, Jazriel's eyes flashed around the room. Zaard! Nothing worth bothering with, no good looking prey! Not one attractive male in the gallery. Just a boring collection of rich and ugly nobodies. Prowling the wastelands suddenly became a better option, some of those lawless gang members were quite decorative as well as deliciously aggressive. Jazriel firmly disengaged the woman from his arm, kissed her hand with an apologetic, naughty boy grin and despite this society's strident censure against smoking, he removed a cigarette from a slim platinum case. The hostess paled with shock, tried ineffectively to smile wanly, her lips too tight with disapproval to soften but such was Jazriel's allure, she said nothing. Nobody ever did. As always, his dark charisma, his aura of confidence and charm let him do what he wanted, unopposed.

"It would be a heinous crime for me to hoard your company, Mrs Pilsen; your other guests look quite crest-fallen, pining for the charm and beauty of your presence." Jazriel inclined his head in an elegant, yet slightly impudent gesture, "I would not be so cruel to deny them such a blessing." He kissed her hand again, prowling away into the thronged gallery, leaving her feeling curiously bereft, as if she had briefly held something of remarkable but tainted beauty in her hands, only to have it snatched away. Jazriel took a proffered crystal flute of champagne from a waiter and wandered alone around the exhibits, soon becoming more bored and disappointed. Not one human worth toying with. He drained the glass, dumped it upside down in a flower arrangement and headed for the exit.

"There's clearly nothing to interest you here, Mr Oberon." He glanced across at the speaker, a tall Eurasian man, his almond eyes a startling shade of almost colourless pale blue. He had dyed his hair a vivid shade of navy. His looks were unusual but compelling. Many others thought so too, he was surrounded by adoring acolytes hanging on his every word. Beyond that inner circle, more people waited, eyes hungry, desperate to be included into Ling's influential elite.

"What makes you say that?" Jazriel replied with an effortless entrancing smile. The artist's unusual looks and evident power over other humans had triggered his interest, enough to consider an evening of entertaining dalliance before the kill.

"This exhibition is all about a celebration of sunlight and you haven't taken your glasses off once to truly appreciate my work."

"I suspect sunlight is much over-rated, but I do appreciate your work Mr Ling." Jazriel dropped his head in a gesture of apology, speaking in a low silken purr, "I have a condition that makes these shades a necessity not an affectation."

The man feigned embarrassment. "I am so sorry. I had no idea. That was unforgivably crass of me."

"There is no need to apologise," Jazriel replied, slowly raising his face, tantalisingly revealing the deadly beauty of a fallen angel. "Why don't you show me around the exhibition, point out your favourite pieces, convince me of the wonders of sunlight."

Jazriel's outrageously dazzling smile disarmed Ling completely and the artist brushed aside his entourage curtly before enthusiastically leading him across the gallery. The vampire knew why he was drawn to Ling. Watching him interact with his people, observing their faces, their demeanour , he could see the man was a predator, a serial collector of worshipers, a cold manipulator of emotion. Ling destroyed not by killing but by breaking spirits, crushing hearts, trampling ambition and self esteem. This might be a fun evening after all!

Ling paused at a slender, abstract column of silver crystal, infused with prism-like qualities. It rotated slowly sending out a rainbow of light flashed from the sculpture in all directions. "It is called 'Light's Great Conquest.' My greatest work to date," he announced proudly.

"Conquest of what?" Jazriel queried, genuinely puzzled, momentarily forgetting his prey while he studied the scintillating structure.

"Of all the horrors of the night, of hidden evil, of the devil himself perhaps. The darkness that lies in all human hearts."

Unbidden, Jazriel's hand reached out towards the sculpture, letting the light caress it. He snatched it back, the warmth was not painful but uncomfortable. He did not belong in such light. Unnatural and strident.

"Never underestimate the dark, Mr Ling." Jazriel remembered something Prince Azrar had once said. "It's been around a hell of a lot longer then light. And will still be here when every sun in the universe has burnt itself out."

The sculpture no longer held any interest to him, even the company of its creator was palling. Time to play.

"Can you see no beauty in darkness?" Jazriel added, his voice pitched low, entrancing. To his pleasure, Ling looked increasingly uncomfortable as the vampire's voice began to weave its lethal magic.

"A diamond is just a muddy rock from the dark depths of the earth," Ling retorted. "Its beauty can only live when it is cut, when light flashes off its facets. The moon delights us because it shines, but it is from reflected sunlight. So, no, there is no beauty in darkness."

"Would you permit me to prove you are wrong?"

Ling stepped back, alarmed and intrigued in equal measure. Babs Pilsen had scored a massive coup by getting this obscenely wealthy young foreigner to attend his exhibition, a playboy already known to buy works of art on impulsive whims regardless of price. He wanted to keep him interested in the art but there was no doubt in his mind that Jaz Oberon was coming onto him, and Ling was one hundred percent straight! No, make that a thousand percent.

"And how can you do that, Mr Oberon?" The artist challenged, his voice sounding belligerent, infected by nervousness, unsure why he felt so uneasy, so restless at close proximity to this undeniably exceptionally handsome young man.

"Find us somewhere private, somewhere we can be alone and I will convert you to the splendour of darkness, a beauty that will make sunlight seem the gaudy and brash usurper."

Ling groaned, hesitated, his mouth dry. Taller and heavier then Oberon, he was confident he could push him away, should events turn awkward. He nodded and gestured towards a lift. No starving artist but a successful businessman, his work adorning many corporate foyers, Ling had a suite of private offices on the twentieth floor.

All thoughts of winning Oberon's lucrative patronage had gone, replaced by an overwhelming curiosity. Desire rising from some forbidden depth in his soul, not sexual by nature but just as powerful. Jaz Oberon intrigued him. Disturbed him. And he didn't know why. That meant a loss of control and nobody was allowed to have that sort of power over him. He wanted to find out more about Oberon, giving him the knowledge to destroy him.

Ling showed him into his own office and offered him a drink. Jazriel declined graciously, instead his eyes scanned the room. Bloody security cameras everywhere, some hidden and some obvious. This was a paranoid society. Ok, so the humans had good reason, with the threat from lunatics with their firebombs; and of course from creatures like himself. Made life fiendishly harder though!

"So, you have triggered my curiosity, Mr Oberon, what is the beauty in darkness?"

Jazriel leant with languid grace against a desk, lit a cigarette, enjoying the shiver of disapproval in his victim, another twenty-first century puritan! "Turn off the lights and it will be revealed."

The artist could not contain his anger, "I am straight, Oberon. One hundred percent hetero. Forget this, I made a big mistake."

"A mistake? Maybe. You won't know till you have turned off the light, will you?" Jazriel paused to take a drag on the cigarette, watched the smoke's lazy spiral rise above him. "Believe me, Stan, I have absolutely no sexual interest in your body." Jazriel purred, hypnotic, "none whatsoever." He stubbed the cigarette out on the desk's expensive exotic wood surface, enjoying Ling's blood-sweetening outrage. "How brave are you, Stan? Have you the courage to seek the unknown? Can you take a risk in the search for truth, for beauty?"

Jazriel's beautiful, honeyed voice held him captive, unable to move or talk. "What is the matter, Stan? Are you afraid of the dark?"

Ling was angry and confused, terrible childhood memories tried to force themselves to the surface of his mind but he refused to countenance their intrusion. He was the one in control, this was his office, his life but as if being manipulated by an unseen force he reached across and turned out the lights. At first there was nothing, then as Jazriel removed his dark glasses, two points of iridescent light appeared, swirling shades of blue and green, flashing with pulses of silver fire. Truly beautiful, like living opals. Ling was transfixed, astonished, unable to move, wondering...

He had time to register a soft click of bone against bone, as two long, curving, silvered scimitars dropped into view. Then time ceased as darkness did indeed conquer light.

Jazriel hauled the blood-drained body into a private bathroom. Such an unfortunate accident on the night of Stan Ling's artistic triumph. A tragedy. Despite having his body vibrant with renewed energy from the kill, Jazriel wanted more sensation. More anaesthetic from reality. Sitting back on the desk, he cut open a vein with a fang edge and shot up some raw, untreated Devil Dust. Instant death to a human, a short-lasting hit to him. Cursing the drug's weak effect he decided to find something more potent, there must be something out there he hadn't tried in his endless quest to get through another night of life.

Jazriel looked down at his scarred arm, searching his platinum wrist computer for any other interesting activities in the city that night, then prowled unsteadily towards the door, pausing to throw a lit cigarette into a waste basket. By the time the fire took hold he would be long gone. If the security cameras in Ling's office had night vision, he would be totally screwed, of course, but Jazriel was beyond caring. He summoned a lift, "sorry, Stan," he mused, "it wasn't your big night after all."

Entering the gallery, he took out his phone ready to summon his bodyguards. A flash of light caught his eye, he glanced over towards 'Conquest of Light', the sculpture beaming away oblivious to the fate of its creator. Pretentious rubbish! He paused, perhaps he should buy it and insist it was displayed in a down town public toilet? He changed his mind, another impetuous whim evaporating.

Near the exit Jazriel halted, senses flooded by the distinctive scent of wind blown steppe flowers. Ha'ali Eshan. Jazriel's despondent spirit sunk even lower. She stepped up to greet him politely yet strangely distant without the customary fierce embrace and intimate kiss of Dark Kind greeting.

Eshan was New York chic personified in a crisply tailored dark amethyst suit, her luxurious dark red hair worn short in a gamin bob that accentuated her high, fine cheekbones. Like Jazriel, she wore the inevitable dark glasses that kept them undetected among humans. She glared at the vampire in contempt, it was as bad as Reyes thought, the idiot was high as a kite on something. And there was a trace scent of fresh blood about him, had the bastard killed here? Tonight? Insanity! They were both in danger if a body was found. She steered him towards the gallery exit, talking as they walked.

"You have become foolishly careless, Jazriel. I found you down easily. It must be the bad company you've been keeping lately."

"It's wonderful to see you too, Lady Eshan." Jazriel replied, unbothered by her scorn. He knew Eshan always would have her own issues with him. Though she would never admit to such a non-Dark Kind emotion, he suspected she was envious of his millennia–long and passionate love affair with Jendar Azrar. What he didn't know was her discomfort in his company had another, more serious, cause. In Eshan's eyes, although she fought hard against harbouring such unpleasant feelings, the real Jazriel no longer existed. Instead there was this addled dead thing, something re-animated and unnatural despite it's superficial and now flawed beauty. It was wrong of her, but the feeling would not go away.

"You have always been so careful in the past. What is wrong with you? You left a trail of torn throats across Europe and now your careless kills are littering New York. I can't believe you are feting discovery. Getting yourself into the gossip columns as the 'mysterious and devilishly gorgeous Prince of Darkness.' This is lunacy. What is wrong with you?"

"It's called living. You should try it sometime." Jazriel's eyes darkened briefly and he turned to walk away, but Eshan would not be brushed aside, and overcoming an open shudder of revulsion she grabbed his arm.

"You must be more careful. Forget carousing with that malign fool Garan, stop all this suicidal substance abuse and take a lower profile. If not for yourself, for Jendar Azrar. He shouldn't have to lose you again. It would be too cruel."

"I wondered how soon into the conversation you'd bring his name up. It eats away at you doesn't it Ha'ali? Century after century, night after night. It drives you crazy that I could share his bed any time I want and you never have, never will."

Eshan snarled, raised her hand to strike the once-beautiful golden face of Azrar's lover but regained her self-control in time.

"Don't hold back, Eshan. You looked like a real vampire just then. A few brief, wonderful seconds of fire and passion. I live every moment of my life burning with Dark Kind flame. I regret nothing."

This time he succeeded in shaking her off and stalked away in search of his body guards. He could not understand why her censure rattled him so much that night. He was well used to her self-righteous ways. He'd heard many similar lectures from her in the past- and had always ignored them!

There was a time, so long ago, when he lived in the shadow of the Himalayas when any bad moods could be soothed away by beautiful music or a midnight walk in a fine garden on the shores of a mirror-glass Indian lake. His moods now increasingly called out for blood and anything he could score. Anything to blunt the pain and obliterate the nightmares.

Eshan watched as the sha'ref prowled away with a low growl in his throat. She was sickened by her own ineptitude. Jazriel's mood was highly dangerous; no doubt some poor hapless human victim would pay with his life. And it was all her fault.

"I've blown it! I am such a fool."

"Don't worry - you will get another chance, unless our friends from Nemesis get to him first."

Eshan turned as her companion joined her in the foyer, a sleek, neatly attired human in his early forties. He was a good-looking individual with short black hair streaked with becoming silver highlights and large intelligent and gentle brown eyes. Small of stature, slender as a reed, the man wore a discreet silver cross on his black lapel as a badge of his high office in the Vatican.

"I've prejudiced the success of our mission with my problems dealing with him. I know it's wrong, but to me, Jazriel died in Nazi Germany in the last century - what has returned is something else; something unnatural."

"As usual you are too hard on yourself, Eshan, my dear. But I do agree you must put aside this foolish notion. The spirit form of Jazriel was reunited whole and sound with his body. He is truly Jazriel, not some reanimated corpse."

Eshan nodded, her unlikely partner in the protection of her people was right. He always was.

"But he is haunted by powerful demons" Reyes continued. "Some of his own making, but most are created by what life has thrown at him."

Even he, a being who loathed the Dark Kind, felt his heart twist with compassion for Jazriel, but it was a fleeting feeling. Not when so many innocents had to pay for the vampire's despair with their lives.

Reyes and Eshan walked briskly away from the exhibition, blending in with the crowds. This night had hardened their resolve to get Jazriel away from Garan. There were more important and productive ways for a surviving Dark Kind to spend his time on this earth other then wreaking death and mayhem. Another destiny that could ultimately benefit humanity.

"I will try to reason with Garan," she announced. "It won't be the first time and to his credit, he has co-operated with me in the past."

"You don't have much time Lady Eshan," replied the Cardinal, "I am returning to Germany tonight. I wish you were on the flight with me."

"This won't take long," Eshan replied, knowing how urgently she was needed in Europe. "But we cannot take any more risks, Nemesis are determined, organised and able. They want Dark Kind DNA. Jazriel is the easiest target. I must do all I can."

As they left, strident alarm bells screeched throughout the gallery. Screams announced the sprinkler systems were activating, ruining precious artwork, drenching the designer-clad party goers. Eshan's heart stopped. Imadeen? Another blazing Outrage? In her heart she knew the real answer, she grabbed Reyes's arm to encourage him to greater speed, to get away from the gallery before panic and pandemonium claimed the surrounding streets. It was not foreign fanatics that triggered the alarms, it was something connected to that damned Jazriel!

Geddoe's fingers tightened on the limo's soft suede-covered steering wheel, waiting, watching the main entrance of the art gallery. Scrutinizing each rich, pretentious idiot after another as they arrived or left in their luxury cars. What pointless lives! Gawping and adulating paint-daubed canvas or twisted abstract forms of wood or metal. The vampire was welcome to their necks!

Hain's top henchman had followed Oberon's heavily armoured motorcade from his apartment block, watched from across the road as he'd disembarked and entered the gallery. Geddoe preferred to work alone, with so much at stake, he didn't trust his men on this audacious attempt, they would be in the way. The vampire's minders were focused on their employer, not on the now passenger-free limo. Geddoe had pounced as the driver slowly and carefully manoeuvred the over-sized vehicle through a narrow, nearby street. Killing the hapless chauffeur, stripping him of his livery, he bundled the body into the boot. Putting on the driver's uniform and taking the man's place at the wheel, he waited.

The vampire's apartment block was too heavily guarded, bristling with hi-tech alarms and cameras, an army of highly professional armed guards. It housed some of the richest citizens of Phoenix City, they could afford to be expensively protected, it cost mega-bucks to be safe. And Hain had made it abundantly clear that any snatch and grab had to be quick and clean with no possibility of anything being traced back to Nemesis. Geddoe was on his own if he screwed up. His fingers curled around the steering wheel again. Tight enough to hurt. He would not screw up.

Geddoe's attention snapped back to the foyer. The unmistakable elegantly wasted form of Jaz Oberon weaved erratically out of the door. Geddoe gunned the limo forward, ready to pick the vampire up. Oberon would literally fall into the limo, into the plush, upholstered trap. Close by Geddoe's hand was a spray canister full of knock-out gas. How much would it take to knock out a vampire? Geddoe was about to find out.

Chapter Nine

"Ouch! That has got to smart," Garan noted with a fox-like grin, as he watched his two heaviest doormen be grabbed by the throat and lifted from their feet by a slender young woman. With a low growl of disdain, she threw the burly men out of her way before striding into the seething mayhem of the Haunt, full to the brim with revellers, the music at full blast.

It was not one of Eshan's normal, discreet entrances and therefore more entertaining then usual. It was almost worth the ear-bashing Garan was inevitably going to receive - well, almost.

He met her in the middle of the dance floor and after the kiss of greeting escorted her to his rooms above the club. She declined his offer of a glass of Crystal with an abrupt hand gesture and immediately went on the attack.

"You must know why I am here, Garan, the situation with Jazriel is beyond acceptability. You must stop taking him on nightly kill-fests across the city, you must stop supplying him with drugs."

The heavy irony of their encounter was not lost on Garan. So, she thought he was the bad influence? Yeah, right! He fixed Eshan with the full force of his indifference.

"Believe what you want, Lady," he drawled, "You always do."

"You don't have to help the idiot kill himself!" Eshan snarled, "You don't have to supply him with that noxious human-made poison."

"Yes, Ha'ali, I pin an unwilling Jazriel down and force it up his nose!"

Garan had been at the receiving end of noble scorn and admonishment for centuries. He'd had enough. "You have no right to storm into my club, assault my staff and make wild and inaccurate accusations. Leave. Now!"

Eshan's lavender eyes opened wide and darkened with fury, she was a Ha'ali, a high born Dark Kind Lady. How dare this commoner address her with so little respect!

"In fact, if you can do any better, take Jaz with you. I'll be delighted. I have never encouraged his habits. He is completely out of control and frankly, it is terrifying me. So, my high and mighty Lady Eshan, feel free to take my nightmare away."

Garan drank a glass of champagne in one draft, "You will be doing me a favour," he added, a bitter taste in his mouth that no amount of vintage Krug could sweeten.

Eshan felt defeated. Garan was a maverick with no respect for Dark Kind mores but he was not a liar. His show of bravado and indifference masked a very real despair. She could see it in his eyes. If his friend and fellow commoner could not help Jazriel, then perhaps he was truly lost to them, on a ruinous road to self-destruction taking out as many human throats as he could on the way. And the only being –no – the only *living* being - with any power over Jazriel, the Prince, was thousands of miles away, locked forever within the stone embrace of his mountain realm.

"You are worried about the fate of that junkie hustler? Well, welcome to my world!" muttered Garan. "I'm going to find him flat out on some filthy pavement, stone cold dead one night. If the bastards of Nemesis haven't reached his body first. Then they'll have access to all the vampire DNA they need and we can finally kiss our Dark Kind race goodbye." Ignoring vampire protocol, Garan looked directly into the noblewoman's eyes, his voice strained, weary. "Take him away, please, Eshan. As you are all too happy to remind me at every opportunity - I don't do responsibility."

Eshan returned to her hotel in low spirits, feeling helpless in the face of Garan's inability to control his friend. There seemed nothing she could do to save Jazriel and by turn all the Dark Kind survivors beyond bodily kidnapping him and restraining him somewhere. Perhaps that was the answer.

He should have stayed in Isolann, only Prince Azrar had any influence over the once handsome commoner now. Jazriel was losing his precious looks. Eshan had been shocked by his appearance at the art gallery. He had lost weight, creating hollows beneath the sharp cheek bones, his glorious eyes were dull and dark shadowed. The magpie-wing iridescent gloss had gone from his jet hair. Only his impeccable dress sense remained, but for how long?

Eshan was torn. Hain's minions were closing in on a totally unknown vampire that had emerged in a remote region of Eastern Europe. Could this male actually be the one she and Reyes sought? The 'special one'; the long lost Dark Kind who was so important to the future? It was vital she took no chances with this vampire's life. She had to return to Europe to help Alejandro Reyes find and put him under close protection. Eshan had dedicated her life to do her best for all her Kind, now she faced sacrificing one to protect another and potentially worthier vampire. Jazriel had been a brave and resourceful hero once, now he was a disaster waiting to happen. Yet it pained her to walk away from him. Was it time to trust Gabrielle? Could she leave her to supervise Jazriel, to get him off the streets and dried out? Eshan had no time to weigh up the pros and cons. Gabrielle had the *Knowing*, she was intelligent, feisty and brave. It didn't matter she had no liking for the Dark Kind; she didn't have to!

Geddoe never drank, never did anything to lose his much prized self-control. But that night, he demolished a bottle of whisky. No, it was more, he rubbed his eyes, noting the two empty bottles on the floor. His solo attempt at capturing the vampire had been laughable, a farce!

Oberon had not noticed the change of driver, he had not even approached the limo, spurning it in favour of another, far less glamorous vehicle. As the vampire's motorcade had moved swiftly away from the gallery, all hell had been let loose. Fire alarms, sprinklers, an Outrage-sensitive crowd had panicked, fleeing the gallery in a terrified stampede. They had surrounded the vehicle, some pounding on the blackened windows pleading for a ride away from the blazing gallery. He had ignored them, accelerating away fast, brutally pushing aside the fearful crowd gathering in the road like a flock of shocked, bejewelled sheep. He had tried to follow Oberon but the bastard had gone. Geddoe caught a glimpse of himself in the rear-view mirror, a grey-clad prat in a peaked chauffeur's cap. The so-called easy capture had been a joke, a joke played on him. And nobody took the piss out of Phil Geddoe.

Chapter Ten

Garan swept past his friend's ever-present army of security guards and used the high-speed lift to his luxury apartment and let himself in. He had endured a stressful fortnight since Jazriel's exploits at the art gallery, waiting anxiously for the fallout from the mayhem, a possible investigation by the police, questioning, suspicion, danger. Extraordinarily, all the CCTV surveillance tapes from the ex-art gallery, now a fire and water damaged ruin, were destroyed. Nothing remained of that night's footage. Lady Eshan was a right royal pain in the backside but her tightly-run, well-oiled and professional organisation had its uses!

The fire and the loss of Stan Ling was old news. No other lives were lost, the art work insured to the hilt, the gallery would be re-built. New Yorkers were accomplished, swift and determined restorers of their world, they'd had to be. Garan could breathe again, the crazy bastard had got away with it. This time.

Once inside the foyer of his friend's apartment, Garan paused, uneasy. The silence in the suite was unusual, Jazriel always had very loud music blaring from his eclectic collection. It could be anything; soaring tragic opera arias or discordant death-metal thrash; lilting Irish pipes to dramatic Japanese drums; this deathly hush was unsettling.

Alarmed, Garan called out, running from room to room past the exquisite designer furniture, priceless artworks and carelessly strewn heaps of high tec gadgets, mostly used once and discarded.

He found Jazriel, thankfully alive, but sitting precariously on the railings surrounding the apartment's wide balcony. Jazriel showed no sign of awareness of the approach of another Dark Kind, but sat in silence, a half-empty vodka bottle in one hand, a cigarette in the other. He looked out over the glittering night panorama of the towering buildings, the bustle of vibrant and assertive Phoenix City, sprung from the fire-bombed ruins of Manhattan.

"Are you Ok, my friend?" Garan murmured, his voice betraying his anxiety. He doubted even the amazing regeneration abilities of vampire metabolism could survive a fall of forty storeys.

"Look at all the lights, see how terrified the humans are of the darkness," Jazriel's speech was slurred, making Garan's anxiety level rise even higher, the idiot was out of his head again while sitting on the edge of a sheer drop! "So many lights, so many humans. They cover the earth like an infestation of locusts. They will eat up our planet like bugs too, munch, munch, munch. How did they get to be so many?"

"Not enough hungry vamps to keep the numbers in check," replied Garan desperate to get his companion away from the balcony. "Let's go and do our bit to save the Earth. Let's have a competition night, I'll beat you, kill for kill."

Jazriel's balance wavered alarmingly as he took a long swig from the vodka bottle. "I've got a better idea. There's a new wannabe club opened off Lower Phoenix Square. I want to put the frighteners on some hilarious pseudo-vamps. They'll taste as good as the wild wasteland boys."

"No way! They have no fight in them, they're such feeble prey." Garan replied, nothing tonight was going to ease his alarm. The new night club was right in the heart of Phoenix City, the wealthy area of New York. Jazriel was in no state to make a discreet kill. Far better to crash about preying on the lawless gangs, no-one gave a damn about them. All the would-be vamps in the club were the spoilt offspring of New York's wealthy and powerful, all hell would break out if anything bad happened to them.

To Garan's relief, Jazriel leapt off the balcony with a pale shadow of his usual panther-like grace. The relief was short lived. Jazriel poured a liberal line of white powder on a glass table. "One for the road," he muttered, "then sod you, Garan, I'm off to Wolfsbane for the night."

"Zaard, listen to myself," muttered Garan, "since when did I become the voice of reason and restraint?" He knew the answer. Since Jazriel's arrival, the start of Garan's nightmare. And where was bloody Eshan? Nowhere to be seen! He'd pleaded for her help with Jazriel.

Sanctimonious cow, full of self-righteous lectures. But it was practical help he needed with Jaz and he needed it now.

Garan dismissed his own retinue of armed bodyguards for a few hours. This was a safe neighbourhood, for law abiding humans. High tech cameras continuously watched the streets. An unsettling thought. He preferred the lawless darkness of post-Outrage downtown to the pristine, brightly lit streets of Phoenix City risen from the ashes of Manhattan. Who knew what eyes followed the progress of his claret red Lamborghini, the agents of Nemesis? American police? The rising death toll from torn-out throats and total desanguination must be ringing someone's alarm bells by now. Very loudly. It was time to move on!

Wolfsbane was elitist and expensive but anyone with the right look could get in regardless of the depth of their pocket. The club would already be packed with the black-clad youth of the city who would party hard till dawn, before spilling out onto the pale dawn-lit streets, ill at ease with the intrusion of light and the harsh reality of life. Back to the real world, where they were called Tommy and Simone with overdue college assignments to finish, no longer Lord Deathfang and Countess Vladmira, blood-drinking High Priests of the Underworld. There were two levels to the club, one light-hearted, for young people out for a night of escapist fantasy and fun, but in the private, lower rooms the hard-line members met in the gloom, their minds lost to any reality beyond their dream-world, to indulge in fetishist acts and the exchange of blood. These were Jazriel and Garan's target prey. The human wannabees who believed they were the real thing.

Garan with his sword stick cane swinging and an immaculately-clad Jazriel, inevitable cigarette in hand, sauntered up to the club's metal-studded, black-painted door. They ignored the angry curses and threats from the understandably disgruntled queue stoically waiting for their chance to be allowed into the club. Membership and a great look were no guarantee to get in, but the uncertainty only added to the allure. Bouncers eyed the arrogant newcomers trying to jump the long queue. With considerable suspicion. The two good-looking young men in dark shades were not wearing black. They had no piercings or tattoos. Or heavy black eyeliner. In their expensive designer clothes, they did not belong.

"You can't come in, boys. This is a private club."

"No such thing," replied Jazriel evenly with his trademark disarming smile, flashing a diamond credit card, his instant passport to all New York life.

"Our most sincere apologies, Mr Oberon," the chief bouncer grovelled, this effete young playboy could buy the whole club many times over with his loose change. "We didn't recognise you so out of context. Why do you want to go into this bizarro dump? With so many crazies, it can get heavy in there."

"Nothing I can't handle, but thank you for your concern," Jazriel replied with another smile, discreetly handing all the doormen a thousand dollar bill each. As always, money smoothed all pathways in this city. The two Dark Kind walked down the dimly lit stairs into the basement, their sensitive hearing assaulted by Cradle of Filth at full blast. Jazriel braced himself for the onslaught on his fine-tuned senses, the seemingly solid wall of scent, a cocktail, a mix created with unpleasant human body fluids, mixing with clashing perfumes, alcohol and drugs. And the base line of the mix was hot blood, blended by the pounding beat of many hearts. The tightly packed crowds at Garan's club's had the same affect on Jazriel but this one was different, there was an extra edge at Wolfsbane, an additional ingredient to the blend. Fear.

Garan sensed it too, the anxiety of young humans out of their comfort zone, fascinated yet fearful of their surroundings, of the people they would meet lurking in the darkness. He grinned across to Jazriel, "I can taste them already, delicious!"

"Isn't this great?" Jazriel mused in reply, taking in the packed crowd some gyrating to the wall to wall onslaught of hard-driving sound.

Most preferring to stand, morose and silent, desperately wanting to be seen.

Garan, the rival night-club owner sneered in open contempt, "So last century! Nineties Goth retro chic, completely passé." But in truth, apart from the choice of music, the crowd of excited young people was little different to his own clubs, Haunt and Hell. The costumes of the dancers were certainly more extravagant and creative here for Wolfsbane was a vibrant celebration of every vampire and Goth myth, ancient and modern. Look alikes – and many not so alikes of characters from Anne Rice stories, Blade and Underworld, jostled with Buffy and Angel addicts. Marilyn Manson clones were well represented, as were imitators of more recent bands, the new wave of ShockHorror!, Bloodklaw and Girl, Decayed.

Jazriel's attention was caught as a dark-haired young man sauntered past, his face pale, eyes dark-shadowed, dissolute, elegantly attired in casual seventeenth century costume. 'The Libertine' chic personified. The image of dissolution was artificial, a disguise masking a healthy young male, brimming full of life. Jazriel wanted him.

He was jarred out of his predatory concentration by a man's grip on his arm. "Let me guess, you're here to win a bet," a voice bellowed in Jazriel's ear above the loud music, and the vampire's focus on the good-looking prey was abruptly interrupted. He spun in fury, jostled by a tall, thin, young man whose artificially whitened face was covered in sharply barbed piercings. His voice was mocking, arrogant.

"Actually, I'm here to have a drink," Jazriel replied evenly with a humourless smile, with his selected prey moved out of sight, he glanced around the club for any sign of his whereabouts. He was far too delicious to let slip away.

"We only serve blood here. Care to make a donation?" answered the young man in what he assumed was a menacing tone. Certainly blood sharing went on downstairs in the shadows but the bar served mostly warm red wine and neat Jack Daniels. The young man smiled, showing the small pointed fangs fashioned from his own filed down incisors. Jazriel smiled in return before removing his dark glasses and allowing his four-inch long, sharp scimitar blades to slowly descend. "I only do withdrawals."

"Shit! Shit! God almighty!" The terrified youth fell back, shocked into real paleness as Jazriel replaced his glasses, drew back his fangs and disappeared into the crowds, followed by a furious Garan.

"What mad game are you playing, Jazzman? Didn't you lecture me when I fantasised about showing off to these creatures? 'They will tear you limb from limb' were they not your own words to me?"

Was this another sign of suicidal tendencies in Jazriel? The escalating substance abuse, the disregard for his own safety on the balcony and now this recklessness. Humans loved playing at vampires, some were even convinced they actually were the Undead. The once sane and rational Jazriel had been right, reality would kick-start these people's primeval survival instincts, they would never get out of here alive! Garan struggled to stick close to Jazriel, to head off any more wild behaviour. The irony of the night was not lost on him, Garan, the source of so much angst among the surviving Dark Kind for his reckless, irresponsible behaviour was now a nursemaid to the once cool-headed and discreet Jazriel.

Jazriel had got hold of a full bottle of Jack Daniels, he'd taken something else stronger too, his gait was unsteady, speech slurring. Time to go. Garan tried to manoeuvre him from the club but the same pierced creature, now accompanied by similar clones blocked the way. Jazriel smiled, hunger rising, they were all young males.

"*Entrees,*" growled Jazriel to Garan in their own language, "*a couple look worth draining. Time to play.* " Before Garan could stop him, Jazriel sauntered over to the group who were noticeably edgy with a cocktail of curiosity and nervousness.

"Are your fangs some sort of special effects gadget from that new film opening in the autumn?" demanded the boldest of the group.

"Brilliant lenses, where did you get them from?" asked another, gaining courage from his companion.

"Let's go somewhere more private and I'll show you how they work" ventured Jazriel, "My good friend here has the same fangs."

"I have access to a private blood sharing suite," replied one enthusiastic but doomed young man waving an ornate old-fashioned key.

"Just how private?" Garan asked uneasily. If they killed these club goers, and he wanted to, badly, was a safe escape possible? It had been centuries since he'd had to fight his way through a mob of furious, vengeful humans. It was not how he wanted the evening's entertainment to end here in New York.

"No one will disturb us once the door is closed, that's how it works here in Wolfsbane. There's no hidden cameras, just a panic button if someone teams up with a real whacko."

The group of four young club members led the Dark Kind through some narrow, dimly-lit corridors to a cave-like, black-painted room, luxuriously decorated with plush red and purple velvets and gleaming gilt candelabras. Interview with a Vampire chic. Compared to the beautiful palaces of the Dark Kind it was tasteless human fantasy. Jazriel curbed his amusement at the décor, he had planned to have fun with these wannabes, but hunger was over-riding his thoughts. With the door locked he struck fast, killing the two youths whose disease-toxic blood made them unsuitable for drinking. Garan caught both the remaining humans, silencing their screams with a vice-like hold on their windpipes. He handed one over to Jazriel.

"So, you think you are vampires, little man," growled Garan, letting his victim see the slow descent of his fangs. The young man's eyes widened, driven to near insanity at the awareness of his impending death from a very real monster. "This is what real fangs look like." He brushed them lightly against the man's throat. "And this is what they feel like." Very slowly, Garan tore deeply into the human's throat, instantly rewarded with the taste of hot lifeblood.

Jazriel let his victim watch the demise of his friend to allow the terror to sweeten up the blood more. He felt the man go limp, the posturing fool had fainted. Zaard!

"Break his neck and let's get out of here. Come on, there's no shortage of prey."

"No," snarled Jazriel, "I want this one. He robbed me of a magnificent trophy prey tonight!" Opening a side door, he found a hidden washroom and dragging the unconscious man, dowsed him with cold water, reviving him, noting with pleasure, his victim had not soiled himself for that would warrant discarding him with a broken neck and the annoyance of wasting untainted blood.

The man saw the prone form of his friend and with a mixture of horror and morbid fascination, somehow managed to address the assailants as rising terror started again. "Fucking hell, you bastards *are* the real thing aren't you!" he whimpered, frantically clawing his way across the floor to find the panic button and escape but also driven by a fatal curiosity. "What will happen now? Will Joey come back as one of the Undead?"

Garan raised one eyebrow in amusement. "Joey will have a funeral and his friends and family will weep. He's dead. He's not coming back."

"Make me like you. I want be like you, please. I want to live forever."

Jazriel picked the young man up by the neck, high enough for his feet to dangle in the air and kick out in protest. "You are nourishment for us, nothing more." He struck down into his victim's neck but the drugs had blurred his reflexes, it took two more clumsy attempts to subdue the man's violent thrashing, fighting, screaming for his life, before Jazriel finally tore through to the jugular. The resulting mess infuriated Garan, his best clothes spattered with gore; the plush walls of the private suite now resembled a slaughterhouse.

"This has got to stop," he fumed, cleaning himself as best he could in the washroom as Jazriel finally drained his prey. "Since when did the Jazzman make a clumsy kill? This drug and booze thing. It has got to stop before it gets us both killed or captured."

"Don't lecture me, Garan," the vampire glowered, eyes stormy, dropping the human corpse heavily to the floor. "Since when did you become a disciple of Lady Eshan? I'm having fun. Let's get some more."

"I'm out of here," returned Garan, making for the door. He glanced back, Jazriel had no intention of moving, Zaard! He could be a stubborn son of a bitch sometimes. "Ok, I'll lure a few more down," Garan conceded. If it wasn't for the danger he too would enjoy going over the top... if only to piss off the nobles! Eshan's people would have their hands full cleaning up this carnage. Where were the damned

Imadeen when you needed them? It would take one of their firebombs to make this evidence disappear.

But to Garan's horror their visit continued to spiral out of control. Jazriel's predation turned into an outright massacre. Using the club's strict privacy policy down in its lower depths, he killed and killed in an orgy of uncontrolled bloodlust that appalled even the vicious and unprincipled Garan. Terrified of discovery, he managed to barricade the door to the private suite, a sickening charnel house, and physically manhandled the blood-soaked Jazriel back up the stairs. "Faster, you insane fool. That was madness! A bloodbath! These humans will rip us apart, alive, if those bodies are discovered before we can get away."

Jazriel prowled out of the club, unbothered by the fresh bloodstains drenching his clothes. They found the Bugatti and before Garan could stop him, Jazriel, totally unfit to drive, leapt into the driver's seat and roared swiftly away. "Faster, put your foot down," Garan snarled. Surely, it could be mere seconds before the pile of blood-drained bodies were found and all hell let loose? Common sense said go home, but Garan was starkly aware that Jazriel had lost his mind completely as he headed for the elegant theatres and clubs area. Sober and in control, he was a familiar face in this region of town. Stoned, drunk on blood and out of control, he was a truly terrifying liability.

Screaming sirens echoed around them, rushing towards the club. "Ditch the car!" Garan ordered, could there be a less discreet get away vehicle?

"Bugger off," Jazriel slurred, "The bloody Nazi's had my last Bugatti. I'm not losing this one."

"You've lost your fucking mind!" stormed Garan, grabbing the steering wheel, wrestling control of the high powered car, it careered across the road, crashing into a shop window. Jazriel leapt out, standing amid the shards of broken glass, smashed televisions, howling above the shop's screeching alarm in disbelief, "You little shit!" Jazriel was beside himself, "Look what you've done to my car!"

"It's the car or your life, you moron!" Garan was on his phone, frantically buying them time, getting his security team to report the car had been missing, presumed stolen from a car park, the day before. A preposterous move, born of desperation

"We'll have to get home on foot," Garan announced, pulling Jaz away from the Bugatti. "I'll treat you to another one, a better one, but fucking move it! Now!"

The sounds of sirens became more strident, louder, closer, as the two vampires kept to the shadows, using alleyways and side roads. The walk was sobering Jazriel up. A bad sign, he had no intention of spending one second that night with a clear head, lucid thoughts and stark reality. Sod reality. He hated it.

He paused in their flight, to rummage through his clothing, found some pills and swallowed them all. They would do till he found something more interesting, more potent. Ahead lay a rebuilt square, the central gardens surrounded by expensive restaurants and nightclubs. Jazriel began to stride towards the main street. "Come on, Garan. Time to play."

"Oh no, not more," Garan pleaded, his mind in turmoil, why had he let things go so crazy at Wolfsbane, why did he always give in to Jazriel? He knew the doormen at the club had recognised Jaz Oberon, addressed him by name. And there was the ever-present threat of Nemesis. This was not a night to be out killing. It was time to disappear! Garan tried to restrain him, standing in front of him, holding his shoulders. "Enough my friend. More then enough. Getting home will be a miracle."

But Jazriel was completely out of control, pushing him away with a threatening, fang-bared snarl. "Never enough," he slurred. "If I killed every bastard human on the planet, it would not be enough."

Frantically Garan reached into his pocket for his phone, to re-confirm his own security team were ready to pick them up in the square. The whoop of a police car siren announced the arrival of more trouble. Nobody walked at night in Phoenix City, anyone found in dark back streets was up to no good.

"Oh wonderful," groaned a despondent Garan as their way was blocked by a patrol car. "That's all we need."

"Oh, delicious," Jazriel replied, "Uniformed dessert."

Garan pinned him against a wall, ignoring the two patrol men approaching. "Leave it you crazy bastard, you have done enough damage tonight. Our life in New York is over! Over! Thanks to you…"

Jazriel pushed him off with a shrug of indifference. He didn't give a damn. All cities looked the same, all humans tasted the same. Boring. He walked slowly towards the cops, hands in the air, armed only with a dazzling apologetic smile. Damn, Garan muttered, one of the cops was a woman! Jaz wouldn't kill her? Surely he wasn't so far gone? Garan heard the crack of breaking necks. He was.

Jazriel sauntered back to Garan, continuing his journey towards the square. "The male cop was ugly, overweight and pocked-marked. I want another hunt." He brushed his shocked and despairing companion aside.

Jaz Oberon was a familiar sight in the nightclubs surrounding Phoenix Square. The vampire walked boldly into the nearest club and sought out trophy prey, a farewell to New York gift to himself. Finding one in the form of a wealthy and high profile young film director.

One of the demi-gods of Hollywood, worshiped and adored by Phoenix City society. Sleekly good looking, arrogant, self assured, surrounded by beautiful A list women, top models, film stars. Jazriel wanted him, badly enough to take outrageous risks. The man was followed by photographers, approaching him, blood smeared and dishevelled in this busy club was sheer insanity. Garan caught up with Jazriel, already working his seductive magic on the man. The vampire, even drunk and stoned, could charm birds from trees. Or lure humans to their deaths.

"We are leaving, now, Jaz. This is no longer fun, this is no longer thrill-seeking. None of it makes sense anymore. This is suicide!"

Smiling, his eyes unfocused, Jazriel pulled Garan towards him and kissed him on the lips, "You don't have to stay, old friend."

'But I do,' Garan groaned inside. Isolann was thousands of miles away, on the other side of the planet but a warlord so powerful that he could bring his dead lover to life, could find ways of tracking Garan should anything happen to Jazriel. He reached into his pocket for his phone and arranged for his team to pick them up outside the nightclub.

Jazriel's prey was getting angry, aggressive, being photographed in a compromising position with this stoned out-of-his brains, playboy hustler was career suicide! He shoved Jazriel away with a curse and beckoned for his minders. Jazriel backed away, with his alluring smile of naughty small boy apology and regret. The film director, dazzled, doomed, called off his security team. Bought Jazriel a drink.

Jazriel left the club and waited. Lighting up a cigarette, confident he had done enough, he knew the man would step out for 'some air', curious and tempted by the vampire's deadly charm. Jazriel pulled him into the shadows, kissed him, gave him a brief taste of ecstasy before striking. Oblivious to the proximity of the club, of the busy street, Jazriel was too drug-addled to strike swiftly and cleanly, the mortally wounded man's horrendous dying screams alerted every human for many blocks. Outraged, Garan pulled the vampire aside and finished off the tortured victim by breaking his neck. Not as an act if mercy, but desperation, he had to get Jazriel out of the area, fast. How many people had seen Jazriel talking in the club to his last victim? How long before the police would be hammering down the door? If Nemesis did not get there first!

Garan's team arrived, swinging into the square in a fleet of armoured cars, within seconds they were being whisked away in the back of a limo. Garan ordered his men to take them to Jazriel's apartment, not ideal but with the night nearly over, it was the closest secure sanctuary. Only, exactly how secure was anything now? Jazriel's behaviour had jeopardised their charmed life in this city, jeopardised their lives.

Chapter Eleven

The night continued to reek of wrongness, Garan's nerves were stretched to breaking point. The sense of a closing noose around his neck refused to leave him. The flight from the carnage at Wolfsbane had been hellish, the night strident from a cacophony of sirens as the human world discovered the horror wreaked by Jazriel on a bunch of harmless young people. A society shocked to the core by the rising death toll from the Outrages would not tolerate this latest manifestation of nightmare. Jazriel was traceable, his familiar face would have been caught by the nightclub's cameras. He had gone too far. No, well beyond too far!

As they left the temporary security of his car, Garan could swear his sharp night vision had detected the flash of a high powered rifle, the bullet whistling harmlessly over his head. The point of origin unknown. Overactive imagination? Possibly, but the sensation of being stalked, threatened, exposed, was too real. His survivor's instinct had protected him well before, during so many centuries living and hunting amongst humans, yet Garan had never been caught or harmed. Unlike his reckless and less bright friend, Jazriel. Though his body had physically healed, Jazriel's mind kept the memory of centuries of past near-fatal injuries, of torture and eventually his death from the hands of vengeful humans. Garan decided his own instinct was far more accurate and to be trusted. Something very bad was going down and they were the targets.

By some miracle the two vampires reached Jazriel's apartment in one piece although with his mind racing, retracing the night's events. Garan was convinced they had been followed from Phoenix Square by at least one vehicle. He had enough! It was time to leave New York. Now. He revelled in living his life on the edge but not beyond, and this edge he was teetering on was an abyss, created by Jazriel's suicidal madness. He could step back. Walk away and leave Jazriel to the fate he so openly courted. Would any of the Dark Kind blame him? Even Azrar?

Garan watched with horrified fascination as Jazriel sat on the edge of his bed and rolled up the sleeve of his hand-sewn wild silk shirt. Before Garan could stop him, he bared his fangs and tore open a vein above his wrist to pour pure Bliss straight into the purple bloodstream. Already out of his head with too much blood, Bliss, cocaine and alcohol, this further onslaught of narcotic poison sent the Jazzman over the top and he collapsed back onto the bed, unconscious.

"Zaard," Garan groaned, "stupid, stupid bastard!" Unable to take in what he had just seen, realising with shock the full extent of other self-mutilation on Jazriel's scarred arms. This madness had to end. He could not help Jazriel, but he could help himself.

What a bloody mess. How had it come to this? Just a few years ago, Jazriel's companionship would have been the answer to Garan's dreams, a gorgeous Dark Kind to share the nights, hunting and clubbing, instead the dream had turned into a lurid and ever worsening nightmare, Jazriel's downfall from a cool and self-controlled hedonist to suicidally inept vampire junkie.

What could he do? Stand back and let him die again? It could easily come to it as Jazriel did not give his body time to repair between each self-inflicted attack from substance abuse. And there was the increasing threat from Hain's minions and the inevitable tightening net of the police. He had nearly lost Jazriel to the cops, how long could he go on protecting him? Would it be a breach of honour to abandon Jazriel to his own dissolute fate?

It was bullshit, really. The whole Dark Kind obsession with duty, honour and caste. All the strangling, shackling vampire mores, like respect for the nobility, for other vamp's relationships. No Dark Kind must harm another - bullshit! What about psychological damage? Jazriel's presence had done plenty of that to him!

Garan sat in a leather chair, softly silver, luxurious, helped himself to the last of Jazriel's favourite vintage brandy. He wouldn't notice.

Jazriel lay motionless, spread-eagled and comatose on his bed. To Garan's discomfort, his friend's eyes were open but the iridescent turquoise had gone, in its place a death-like opaque glaze. the artificial darkness of Jazriel's apartment Dawn was an hour away. Outside, the sun would soon be rising flooding New York's streets with its blazing torment but the two Dark Kind would be safe here in the artificial darkness. Safe from the sun. Not from humans.

It was no good, he could not take his own Rest without checking Jazriel was still alive. He could not control the Jazzman's seemingly suicidal drug abuse, but his own life would be forfeit if anything happened to the fool while in his company. The anger and grief of the Jendar was not to be risked. He doubted the world would be big enough to get away from Azrar's wrath.

Garan reached down to pull open Jaz's shirt, the dark blue material ruined, the silk ripped and stained with human and vampire blood and sticky Bliss residue. He put his hand on Jazriel's chest and gave a sigh of relief; the heart was beating in a steady though unusually slow rhythm.

The feel of Jaz's cold golden skin sent shivers of intense desire through him. Garan turned him over onto his front, determined to hide those open, dulled yet alluring eyes lost in a drug induced stupor and he felt the anger from years of thwarted desire return. The injustice of being denied what should have been freely available! Jazriel's very existence was a callous joke, a torment. His blind devotion to that grim Prince, his unreasonable faithfulness when as sha'ref, he could be alleviating the lonely lives of so many surviving Dark Kind. It was selfish, cruel!

Garan ripped away the filthy clothes, exposing the taut muscled perfection, still beautiful despite the toll of abuse. His hand reached out, trembling, wanting to touch, to … He moved away, groaned. Angry with himself for pausing. This hesitation was so pointless, why should he be refused? This was a body purposefully designed to give pleasure, to be taken, to be used. How easy it would be to have him now, while he lay helpless and unaware? So damn easy. Too damn easy

Chapter Twelve

"We've got em!" Phil 'Van Helsing' Geddoe, Nemesis's chief vampire hunter used the on board computer and triangulated the police reports of horrific mass murder in Wolfsbane with reports of a man's terrified and agonised screams near Phoenix Square. He turned to his waiting team, eager for some action. The vampires had run rings around them for too long.

"The sadistic little shits have played right into our hands, let's go bag us some bastard blood suckers."

This time, he refused to be further humiliated. Failure was not an option.

Gabrielle sat alone in a tough 4x4 sports car, sipping from an oversized carton of hot black coffee. At least she was dry inside the car, the rain hadn't stopped all day and now it went on all night, the streets of New York resembled rivers. Rain forest rivers at that! It might as well as be the Amazon jungle, Gabrielle lamented, the humidity was so oppressive. Brief pauses in the curtain of rain brought dense steam rising up from the road.

The two vampires had arrived at the apartment forty minutes ago and with daylight not far away, she doubted they would be seen again until the following sunset. Piet, her partner for the night's surveillance, had gone for a leak and looking at the size of the coffee carton he had brought her, it would be her turn next. She glanced gloomily out at the night, at the torrential downpour and lectured her bladder not to let her down. She had no intention of rushing to find some filthy, tramp-infested alleyway in an emergency!

It was her bad luck to be on duty on such a filthy night. Eshan's organisation were watching the two exceptionally bad boy vampires in a tightly run surveillance operation. Gabrielle took more then her share of turns, following them, watching them, as they caroused and killed their way through New York's innocent human population. Not because she had any interest in protecting the blood thirsty bastards, her motivation was stronger then that; she didn't want Nemesis to have them.

Rubbing her tired eyes, Gabrielle was grateful as the strong dose of caffeine began to kick in; she desperately needed the coffee as she kept vigil outside Jazriel's luxury apartment block. Why did the bloody vamps have to be nocturnal? Keeping watch was playing havoc with her sleep patterns, let alone her private life! The last month in New York had become very intense, her whole life centred on watching out for the two vampires.

It seemed so wrong; she felt corrupted by this collusion with murder. She was torn like Reyes, tormented by guilt. Even knowing she served a greater good, a higher purpose. That was no comfort to the families of Garan and Jazriel's many victims. By doing nothing to prevent their activities, she felt like an accessory, as guilty and blood stained as the vampires themselves. Of course, the creatures had no sense of guilt, pity or remorse, they had no moral compulsion, no conscience to trouble them. They were wild animals, predators doing what came naturally to their deadly species. What was unnatural was a human woman standing back and letting them get away with it.

Chapter Thirteen

Jazriel came too, dazed and confused. He was on his bed, naked and hurt, pain seeping through the tangled chaos of his muddled awareness. The remnants of a bad dream lingered. Memories, disjointed and vague, of being held down and entered, brutally taken. Did he fight back? He thought he had tried but was too weak. The fragile threads of recollection dissolved like a dream. It must have been a dream or a drug-induced hallucination.

He tried to rise from the bed but winced from very real injuries. Maybe not a dream then. But what manner of nightmarish reality? Slowly, with difficulty he made his way to a mirror, whimpering with horror at the gouges in his neck and back. Long, thin and deep. Knife wounds? A livid bruise throbbed above his left eye. Jazriel dropped to the floor, rocking, his head grasped in his hands. Trying to recall the night… His clothing, scattered everywhere was torn and bloodied, from what he could see mostly human blood. He remembered vaguely making a clumsy kill, too spaced out to make a clean deep tear in the victim's throat. The man had died badly, slow and messy. Azrar would have been disgusted with him. Jazriel's bruised head throbbed from his night's drug over-indulgence. He couldn't think clearly. Good. He didn't want to. Ever again.

Relentlessly though, his treacherous memory clawed its way back; he became aware with growing alarm that the gouges in his back were not from a knife attack, they were from fangs. Full consciousness slammed into him like a hammer blow. There were other injuries too. Internal damage. No! No! That could not be!

His body had been violated against his will. He had been brutally used and there was only one other Dark Kind male in New York. Jazriel buried his head in his hands, shaking in humiliation and anger. Such cruel betrayal from a friend!

He heard voices from the living room, a vampire's mocking tone, a human's scornful guffaw in reply. This was intolerable! Somehow, Jazriel pulled himself to his feet, anger driving him to dress quickly, ignoring the shock of pain as the clothing touched his scarred and bleeding back. He entered the outer room, eyes deepest black, blazing with bitterness.

Aware of his approach, the bodyguard tapped Garan on the shoulder. The vampire slowly turned to face Jazriel with a surprised expression. Somehow much worse, the smirk on the human's face was beyond bearing, beyond humiliation, the bastard ape knew what had happened and thought it amusing.

"Jaz, my beautiful Undead friend," muttered Garan with a humourless, uneasy smile, clearly not expecting him to wake up so soon. "Don't look so angry with me, you are not exactly a dishonoured virgin!"

Jazriel could find no words, a low animal growl of hurt from this most heinous of betrayals began in his throat and lingered, building in ferocity.

"You have only yourself to blame, Jazzman. All the come-ons, those smouldering looks. The accidentally straying hands and casual touches? You were created a whore; I haven't done anything to you that a hundred male vampires haven't already. Maybe more. Perhaps a thousand?"

Jazriel forced himself to stand straight, hauling together the shattered remains of his dignity. "My name is Jazriel. I was once sha'ref to the nobility. They did nothing to me without my full consent."

"Whatever," Garan sneered, dismissively, as he reached for the leather jacket his bodyguard held out to him. "You had it coming, Jaz. I couldn't take anymore. Throw him some cash, Toulon, he will expect payment. But not too much." Garan headed for the door, he knew he'd gone too far but his runaway mouth refused to stop. "It was hardly memorable. Though almost fun in a sort of necrophiliac way."

The dammed up flood of centuries of rejection, hurt and bitterness exploded into a roar of violence, Jazriel leapt forward with a furious howl, gripping Garan's throat, pinned him high up against the wall, his fangs grazing Garan's neck, drawing blood. Toulon rushed forward to intervene, but Garan shouted at him. "Wait outside, this is just vampire foreplay. Jaz has to prove the numerous legends of his bedroom skills are not wildly exaggerated."

Uncertain, the big man hesitated, shrugged, walked out, not realising his boss had acted quickly to save his life. Whatever the truth of what had happened in that bedroom, the Boss's attractive companion got everything he deserved! Though not of the same persuasion as his vampire employer, Toulon had watched from the sidelines; watched his boss being teased and provoked beyond reason for months. Jazriel had it coming. Big time.

Ignoring the stream of blood pouring from the fang wounds on his neck, Garan turned to face Jazriel's blazing eyes. "Calm down, my friend, there was no harm done. Yes, I helped myself to a freebie, but you are sha'ref, that's what you were put on this planet for."

"You were my friend." Jazriel stumbled to find the right words to express the weight of his hurt. It was too much, monumental. Crushing.

"Let me down, Jaz," Garan pleaded as the grip around his throat tightened. He could fight back, but Dark Kind did not harm each other. Why was Jazriel making such a big thing about this? It wasn't as if he hadn't had a long lifetime of male vampires using him just as hard. Garan raised his hand to caress Jazriel's face, to diffuse the anger but snatched it back, slashed away by Jazriel's raking fangs.

"Ow! That hurt!" For the first time, Garan looked fearful, this was going too far. He expected Jaz to be annoyed, but no more then if Garan had helped himself to the last of Jaz's vintage brandy. Not this outrage, this murderous fury.

"OK, I'm sorry. I am not one of your damned nobility. Then you would have taken the money with no complaints. At least we love each other, as friends, there was no harm done.

Jazriel threw the vampire to the ground with a snarl of contempt. "No harm? You have no idea how much harm, Garan."

Jazriel limped out of his apartment, oblivious to the threatening dawn. Garan thought about running after him, saw the first signs of lightening sky on the horizon and called Toulon back in.

"Go after the silly sod," Garan ordered, "Bring him back safely. It will be daybreak soon."

With no idea where he was going, Jazriel's tormented mind reeled, why was he still alive? What was the point of his existence? He had carried on living so long because he had made a solemn vow of honour centuries before, sealed in a mixture of purple and red blood. It would be the first vow he had ever broken.

Toulon caught up with the drug-weakened, unsteady vampire in the lobby. Before the human could speak, Jazriel grabbed him by the throat and lifted the big man off his feet. As a trusted aide of a friend, his life was sacrosanct, protected. Garan? Some friend! The bitterness rose in Jazriel's throat on a tide of poison, threatening to drown him. His body, his integrity should also have been sacrosanct, protected! The vampire smelled the fear-sweetened blood of his violently thrashing victim; it would give him strength, it would give him life.

Life? He'd had enough of life.

He broke the bodyguard's neck and threw the body down a lift-shaft. The Dark Kind could not cry but they could bay, and oblivious to an uncaring world, Jazriel threw back his head and howled, releasing long , too long suppressed grief and despair; the anguish of a broken and lonely Dark Kind soul.

Blundering out of the apartment, only vaguely aware that daylight was already coming, he reached the underground car park. Dawn was of no importance. He would be in another darkness before the sun rose.

Gabrielle finished the coffee and using her phone, checked in with her colleagues among Lady Eshan's team watching out for the vampires. On these guarding and surveillance assignments, she refused to deploy any of Reyes operatives. This was far too dangerous territory to be dealing with high-minded amateurs. Piet, the agent assigned to her that night was one of Eshan's most trusted men, a burly, sharp-eyed South African. In the long hours sitting about in the Audi, she discovered he shared her passion for blueberry cheesecake ice cream and the music of U2. Well, it passed the tedious hours! She would far rather make small talk with the craggy jawed Piet then engage with any Nemesis agents. If her grandmother had still been alive, she would have gone berserk, having reluctantly only agreed to Gabrielle being taken on by Reyes to do archaeology research. Dashing about in powerful, fast cars with heavily armed secret agents protecting vamps - even Khari's beloved friend Jazriel, would have horrified her. Gabrielle would not hide from Nemesis, the bastards had killed her mother and did God knows what to her father. She was determined to take the fight to them, not run away.

After a re-assuring discussion with Eshan's people, she relaxed and went back to her vigil. They told her there was no sign of any known Nemesis agents close to the Manhattan apartments. Mind you, there was no sign of Piet either. How long did it take to take a piss? She decided to check that Piet was all right and reached down for her phone - as the sound of an over-revved, powerful motorbike roared out into the street.

"Sorry Piet," Gabrielle muttered, frantically starting up the Audi, to drive in a flat-out pursuit of the bike, "I can't wait for you to zip up your flies!"

Kicking his beloved Ducati into roaring life, Jazriel drove into the fading night. It had to be the beautiful, swift, powerful machine that had become connected to his soul. Azrar's gift of love to him. He had no direction, no thoughts, channelling his whole being into speed, as much as the machine could take and more, forcing the fine-tuned engine faster and faster. In a corner of his mind, a trapped fragment of reason was aware of a silver car following, getting closer. He opened up the throttle to its fullest extent, leaving it behind in a cloud of exhaust.

Not for the first time Jazriel longed for the emotional release of human tears, instead jagged knives of Dark Kind pain wracked through him. His fingers gripped the handle bars tightly like a drowning man clings to floating wood, at least the familiar metal and rubber were solid, real.

As was the high wall his bike was fast approaching. Dark Kind life was precious, it could not be thrown away. But he had already been claimed by death, he had cheated his true destiny for too long. Time to return to death's embrace, colder and more lasting than Azrar's. There was no need to accelerate, he was already pushing the Ducati to its limit.

He closed his eyes, his mind filling with an image, a face from his past. "So sorry…"

Jazriel came to, snarling in pain, instantly drawing down his fangs, alert for danger. Zaard! Where the hell was he? His mind cleared. He was sprawled on the pavement, an inferno raging around him. Distorted lumps of burning metal lay scattered across the road. Stinking pools of petrol, some ignited, surrounded him. The Ducati! He tried to get up, but was too injured to move. Purple blood mixed with the spilt fuel and splashing rain in a widening lake around him. He was beyond pathetic. He couldn't even crash a motor bike into a brick wall properly! He'd killed the bike but not himself. How bloody useless was that?

He could hear sirens wailing in the distance but approaching fast. Shit, shit, shit! The police? They had followed him from the apartment but he had outrun them. Until now. And there was that damn silver sports car pulling up. Nemesis? Jazriel managed a feeble, defiant fang-bared snarl, whoever was in the car he was ready for them! He tried to move but a brutal stab of pain brought darkness to his vision. Unconsciousness sweeping in, he ceased to fight back. What did it matter? Let them come, let them do what they wanted.

Chapter Fourteen

Gabrielle parked the car as close as she dared to the blazing wreckage of the motorbike and hesitated, unsure what to do. Then an urgent compulsion to go to the stricken vampire overwhelmed her. Surrounded by burning debris he looked wounded, defeated, his head had dropped onto his knees as if he had given up, but at the sound of her approach his head snapped up with a fierce, threatening snarl, fangs drawn, ready to defend himself. Gabrielle was afraid but taking a terrible risk with her life, she dropped down to join him on the wet, filthy road.

"I must get you to my car. You are in grave danger."

She tried to haul Jazriel to his feet, but he was resisting, his will to live destroyed. "For fuck sake, move your bloody vampire backside! Now!"

Her anger and determination animated him and against his will, he allowed this unknown strident human to help him to her vehicle. She threw him on the back seat, chucking a thick blanket to him as protection against the rapidly strengthening light and reached into her collar to show him the dragon amulet around her neck. "I am Gabrielle. Khari's granddaughter. She loved you very much, Jazriel. She would want me to help you."

Gabrielle drove fast, gunning the car away from the debris and danger. Time was running out, she had to get this useless wreck of a vampire to safety. Madness really, she would be just as happy to leave him to perish in the sunlight; if it had not been respect for her grandmother's affection for this creature, would have done so.

In the cramped back seat of the car, Jazriel's addled mind reeled. The human female spoke his language! Wore the gold symbol of King Dezarn. This threw the vampire out completely, still wary, the razor-sharp curving fangs slowly, hesitantly disappeared back into the scabbard in his scull. "How did you find me?" his voice was a low, desolate growl.

Gabrielle gave a slight, humourless laugh. "You left a trail of destruction and mayhem a blind mole could follow!"

She rapidly explained how both her own organisation and Nemesis had staked out Jazriel's apartment block. "You made your last kill in the middle of Times Square in front of a crowd of horrified humans." Gabrielle fought hard to disguise her anger and disgust at this creature's casual disregard for human life. "You couldn't have been more indiscreet and reckless!"

She negotiated a busy junction. Aware that the New York dawn was strident with police car sirens. Drove on. "I followed you, roaring out into the street on that big bike of yours, riding like a madman with both Hain's minions and the police in hot pursuit. New York's streets are in chaos because of you."

Jazriel's memory was returning in disjointed flashes of recall. He remembered riding his bike, heading for a wall and the overdue appointment with the destiny he had already cheated... the death Azrar had put on temporary hold.

"You trashed the Ducati by riding into a wall at high speed, there was a huge explosion and impressive fireball but you were thrown clear." Gabrielle shook her head recalling her disbelief as she remembered the incredible series of events this long night. "It was uncanny, almost as if someone had grabbed you by the shoulders and yanked you backwards off the thing."

Jazriel shrugged, in his despair was indifferent to mysteries, he couldn't, didn't want to remember much about what should have been his last ride

"Anyway," Gabrielle continued, "the police are, no doubt, not far behind us. Nemesis too. We must get away from here. Now and fast."

Jazriel's head dropped even lower. What was the point of running? Without Azrar he was dead. Again. It wouldn't be suicide, just a return to what he had been before. Perhaps what always should have been. Maybe Death hated being denied and was punishing him. With life.

For the first time, Gabrielle felt a compelling and inexplicable urge to reach out to the broken creature, not out of pity, she only had that for his countless victims, but the compulsion to touch him was strong, overwhelming. Though frightened of him, she reached behind her and fumbling beneath the blanket, took the vampire's burnt and bruised hand as gently as she could. He did not push her away. A tingling sensation began to build up in the base of her scull, spreading through her nervous system, not painful but powerful and unsettling. Too unsettling to drive safely. She turned the car into an underground car park, found a darkened corner on the lowest floor and parked. It would be safe for a short time. Daylight would not be denied its triumph over the night, it would pour down from the entrance ramp once it rose and push away the murky, rain-sodden greyness of the strengthening dawn.

She pulled aside the blanket and looked into the pain-wracked, deep-shadowed eyes of the vampire and found she knew - knew everything that had brought him to such depths of despair. She experienced a sensation of time rushing past, of the long centuries passing in an instant. She witnessed Jazriel's languid, sheltered life in the lush green valleys beneath the Himalayas, an exhausting blur of beautiful and demanding bodies, all craving his erotic skills but never wanting him beyond the gratification he could give them. The endless giving, but never receiving pleasure.

Then salvation of sorts with his great love for Jendar Azrar filled her with overpowering waves of raw, alien emotion. So much love! Its strength could move mountains! It came at a high cost; she also felt Jazriel's searing hurt from the warlord's haughty domination, unable to think of him as anything beyond a commoner, worse, a sha'ref, something to be used, no more in status then a treasured sword or a favourite war-horse. More years rushed past and Gabrielle discovered Jazriel had fallen in love with a human once too. Extraordinary! Inevitably it had ended badly, in sacrifice and heartbreak. An emotional trauma that remained vivid and painful.

She experienced Jazriel's deep and abiding confusion over his feelings for the female Dark Kind Sivaya, wanting to love her but not being able to return her obsessive devotion. Discovered how angry Jazriel was with her for subjecting him to the torture of near-oblivion.

But then the sharing of even the pale shadow of those powerful emotions of another creature, one not human turned into something far more dark and sinister. Gabrielle wanted to snatch her hand away in horror as she relived Jazriel's pleasure in killing, the terror in his victim's eyes, their futile screams for mercy, but compulsion kept her hand clasped to his.

She forced herself to stay strong as she experienced his fear and loneliness, reliving those last moments as his life ebbed away in a gore-stained Berlin cellar; shared the emptiness of the nothing, his memory of self, fading into the silence, then forced to return into his own long dead corpse where he was trapped, unable to flee the cold slab of inert, dead flesh. She was battered by Jazriel's pain and revulsion as he discovered Garan's rape.

She snatched away her hand. Tears ran down her face, unnoticed and uncontrolled. Her body shook violently with the aftershock of such a roller coaster ride through another being's most personal feelings, memories and experiences. She had just scratched the surface of his tumultuous life, the centuries of joy and pain, of danger and the descent into dissolution, fear and anguish. She had the *Knowing*, she had entered a Dark Kind mind and it was a curse. A terrible curse. Should she tell him?

All Dark Kind thought of humans as animals, the male of the species as mere prey beasts. How could Jazriel allow a human female to know the secrets of his damaged soul? If he reacted badly he would not rip out her throat but even in his weakened state could - despite her dragon talisman - easily snap her neck with no hesitation, no remorse. Gabrielle was under no illusions. Jazriel was very dangerous, a suicidal, wounded, predatory creature at bay. One who was not helping her rescue him! Yet, he had twice fully trusted a human. Could she be the third?

Tentative, she reached to touch him again. "I am so sorry Jazriel…"

He pulled away, snarling savagely. "I don't need a bloody human's pity!"

He climbed out of the car, tried to stride away, but exhaustion and despair had weakened him; he stumbled, fell heavily to the ground, down onto the engine-oil puddles and filth of the car park. He tried to rise but gave up. Dropping his head to the ground with a low, keening animal-like whimper, his body rocked with misery as he waited for the inferno of the fast approaching sunrise to reach down from the street.

"OK, if that's the way you want it, stay there and fry. One less murdering bastard to plague us humans!" Gabrielle snapped, hurt at his ungratefulness, ready to leave the vampire to his fate. She'd done all she could for the stricken creature. Then she remembered Reyes's urgent entreaty, orders given for all in the team. "If you can't save them, don't let Nemesis get hold of a body. At any cost."

Gabrielle stepped from the car, calmly waiting for the sun to rise and vampire to die. Again, standard orders, a large can of petrol was in the boot ready to incinerate the remains. Could she do it? Stand by, watching, waiting. Do nothing while a living creature died slowly, agonisingly, as his eyes were seared out by daylight, succumbing to shock and blood loss? Then pour petrol over the warm body and watch it burn? She raised her hand high to catch the first rays and felt the soft warmth and faint light caress it. She would have her answer very soon.

Leaning against the car, something caught Gabrielle's eye, a shadowy presence standing close by. The form of a human, more cloud than substance. Khari? Was it her grandmother reaching out to help her? Gabrielle stood upright, staring intently. The shimmering form gained more clarity. A K'elphin like Reyes? No, this was - had been - definitely human. The vision grew clearer. A young man, dressed in old fashioned clothing with long, black hair, a jaw line beard, moustache and dark, expressive eyes. There was someone else, standing behind him, a woman, a woman also dressed in period costume, she too had compassion in her eyes. Gabrielle saw the man's eyes fill with tears as the apparition reached out his hand lovingly towards Jazriel. His lips murmured in supplication, "Do not give up on him. I never did, I never will. Help him, please!" Then he was gone. The woman remaining a brief second longer; kind, wise, concerned. "Help him, Gabrielle, for those of us who love him, for us, for your grandmother; help him."

Gabrielle felt the lingering distress, the love, did not dwell on this strangeness, too many strange things had been happening to her lately. These spirits, ghosts – whatever - of people from Jazriel's past were just more to be accepted. That was one conclusion. The other was she was going completely insane. Either way, their heartfelt, desperate pleas made her try again with the vampire. Perhaps she was being too harsh, too judgmental? From her grandmother, Gabrielle knew about Dark Kind honour and the deep bonds of love and friendship between them all. What Garan had done was heinous, could there be a more appalling betrayal?

She thought of how she would feel. She was a strong, bloody minded, no-nonsense woman, yet, how would she feel if a man had raped her? She looked down at the broken wretch kneeling on the filthy concrete that was Jazriel, dirty, dishevelled, dissolute, and totally unrecognisable as the stunningly handsome, debonair and vain charmer from her grandmother's memoirs. Khari had loved Jazriel. He had been so brave, so loyal, such a good friend. Would she have loved what he had become? Would she have helped him? And what of this man and woman from the past? They had shed tears for the vampire, pleaded across what could have been an ocean of time and space for Gabrielle to help him. Gabrielle was certain there was nothing evil about those spirit forms, in fact quite the opposite; the man clearly loved Jazriel and everything about the mysterious young woman was gentle, loving and wise. Was all that was good.

Her heart filled with complex mixed emotions; anger, disgust and pity merging into one nameless feeling. This creature was not a human, hard though she found it, Gabrielle could not blame him for what he was, for what he had now become.

The sirens were getting closer, too close. She had to get Jazriel back into her car, speed away from danger. Risking another jolt of his emotions invading hers, Gabrielle held out her hand to him. "You should really get out of that oil puddle, it will ruin that rather delectable Versace ensemble."

Jazriel raised an eyebrow, puzzled and, even in his miserable state bemused, by the human woman's courage and candour. And sense of humour. He noticed she had Khari's wondrous golden eyes, a good sign. He got up, slowly, stiffly and awkwardly as the bruises and broken bones began to make their presence felt, he smiled, a fleeting ghost of the dazzling, seductive and manipulative smile of old. But Jazriel's smile was genuine. He did not know why, but hope shone in the lustrous eyes of this human female. And he had always fallen an easy victim to hope.

He made an attempt to brush the oil and filth from his clothing with his left hand, his right shoulder was broken, but he gave up with a weary sigh of defeat. Jazriel reached into his ruined jacket with his good hand, winced as he realised there was nothing there. His pockets were empty. Another screw-up! He turned to the woman, one elegant eyebrow raised in hesitant query, "I don't suppose there's any chance of a cigarette?"

Part Three

SMOKE AND MIRRORS

In raiments of tears,
the fallen angel tumbled from the Light,
His heart burning to a cinder.
Falling to damnation.
But with such style, such grace.

© Aly James, An Irish Tale

Chapter One

Eshan stood at a discreet distance and watched the nurse administer to her patient. A one-way glass window protected him from seeing the vampire woman, a sight that would drive him into a terrified, enraged and murderous frenzy. But he knew she was there. His eyes seemed to burn through the glass with the searing acid power of his hatred.

The patient had been a handsome man once, athletic, tall with light brown hair and lustrous eyes in an unusual shade of dark gold. Now insanity had carved deep shadows beneath the once remarkable eyes, the glossy hair had turned grey and lank, missing in places where he had torn it out by the roots.

The nurse shrugged sadly and retreated, having given the man yet another new drug designed to alleviate his inner turmoil, an attempt to give him some respite from the spiteful and painful harpies crowding his fevered brain. Every attempt had led to disappointment for the dedicated team caring for the man. So far, the drugs had never worked.

The nurse rejoined the man's benefactor waiting in an anteroom and gave a brief progress report. It was not encouraging. Despite an entire clinic built to house the man in comfort and security, to give him 24 hr specialist care from the best doctors and psychiatrists in the world, Cameron Devane remained in torment.

What Eshan would not tell them was that his mind was cursed with the *Knowing* in a very intense and unrelenting form. Understanding the cause of his mental suffering would not help Cameron Devane, for what treatment could this clinic give to cure this human? In reality, nothing. Cameron had, somehow inherited an ability that was only passed down the female line for millennia. This was a wrongness, an aberration and one with dire consequences. An incurable deviation.

The *Knowing* had plagued him as a child, grown much stronger with adolescence. When he left Montana to seek answers, his encounter with Amela Railton had brought him some respite, a time of love and great joy. Her murder by Nemesis agents had pushed him into the abyss, into the tragedy of insanity.

His mother, Khari, had never known the fate of her son though she had gone to her eternal rest convinced he was alive. Eshan had kept it from her, to protect them both. For Cameron harboured a murderous loathing of the Dark Kind and also for Khari, hating her for the abiding friendship and love she had with vampires. He would have killed his own mother without remorse or hesitation. Was it not better to let Khari believe her golden boy was out in the world somewhere, happy, living his own life?

Chapter Two

A rural back road in Northern Bulgaria, 2010.

The man slumped heavily onto Diego's shoulder, first with a loud snort, then a deafening snore that reverberated around the lorry's cab. Diego took one hand off the steering wheel and gently pushed his foreman back across the bench seat, letting the man's head rest on the lorry's door. The foreman, Lev, deserved his sleep, it had been a tough week.

Diego turned his attention back to the difficult driving conditions, "Come on my valiant friends, you can do it!" His voice was a low growl as he urged on the tired old truck's worn and erratic windscreen wipers. Twisted out of shape and missing most of their rubber, the wipers struggled to clear the rain and mud thrown up onto the glass but it was a losing battle. Diego was forced to stop, leap out of the cab and cursing colourfully in many languages, wipe the filth from the screen yet again. The rutted country lanes, with their traps of deep pot-holes, fallen branches and occasionally straying livestock were a nightmare to navigate, but Diego would not stop, too determined to get his convoy out of Bulgaria by dawn.

He gritted his teeth and concentrated harder as if will power alone could push the lorry through the night towards the Romanian border. Behind him wound the rag taggle of trucks that transported his circus to their next venue, somewhere rural and remote and easily entertained. The journey through the storm-racked dark on these treacherous roads was even harder for the following drivers, they did not have Diego's special affinity with the night.

Some hours earlier the little circus had packed up, the troupe struggling with hot sticky air that had drained energy and left tempers short before getting underway from their last venue under the gaudy colours of a vivid sunset. The oppressive humidity had been a forewarning of problems to come. During the night, the journey became progressively worse and had now turned to a slow, tortuous slog as a heavy summer storm broke, spears of seemingly solid rain interspersed with short barrages of sharp hail turned the dusty dirt roads into torrential rivers of molten mud and exposed stones.

"Damn," Diego swore again as his truck lurched awkwardly into fast running water hiding an exceptionally deep water-filled pot-hole. He saw the cause of so much surface water, a section of the road ahead was damaged from a burst river bank with most of the hard standing washed away in the deluge. The ruined surface would be dangerous for the truck travelling directly behind his, the one carrying a precious and vulnerable cargo - the circus livestock. Driving into such a deep hole could jolt the animals badly, frightening them, perhaps enough to injure themselves seriously. As Diego slammed on the brakes, his foreman lurched forward, shocked awake.

Rubbing his eyes, he glanced across to the driver. "What's the matter, Boss?"

"This hellish weather is getting worse. We might be forced to make camp here."

The circus foreman shook his head in disbelief at their continued bad luck, they were uncomfortably close to their last venue, a small industrial town to the south. This had been a bad tour, poor attendance from morose crowds, sickness among the troupe and last week they had lost a star equine performer to a fatal bout of colic. It felt like a curse some village hag had put a hex on them, perhaps in retaliation for an imagined slight. Lev longed for the months of rest in their winter quarters but as it was only mid- June such heaven seemed far away, a distant dream. Instead they were bogged down in the middle of nowhere in a thunderstorm. As ever he looked to the Boss for guidance.

Diego lit a hurricane lamp and jumping lithely out of the cab, waved down the rest of the convey oblivious to the rivulets of rain streaming down his lean, sharp-boned features, darkening and flattening his shoulder-length mahogany hair.

"Come on, Lev, lets find a way round these deep craters," the Boss called to his foreman. "I have had more then enough of Bulgaria"

He handed the lamp to Lev and strode across the road to climb a short, steep bank to survey the surroundings. His sharp night vision took in a seemingly featureless landscape, flat scrubby fields lit vividly by flashes of lightning. He gave a low growl of frustration. A terrible choice for a camp site, there was a distinct risk of flooding and although there was no sign of the locals, security would be difficult in such an open area. Circus Yasuul faced a worsening situation, made more difficult if they got bogged down so near to the small industrial town close to Razgrad. Diego was angry with himself, he had chosen a damned bad time to get hungry.

The Boss came down off the bank and returned to the convoy, found the men of his troupe gathered around his truck in a deep and animated debate which turned to respectful silence at his approach.

"This is a filthy bastard of a place to get stuck in. Can we drive the beast truck through this?" Diego questioned. He had great faith in the courage and resourcefulness of his staff. Generations of the same family had served his circus and all newcomers were carefully vetted before joining the tight-knit team

His foreman shook his head ruefully. "If the heavier trucks move onto that ruined section of road, they'll be mired down, the flooding is getting worse by the minute."

Reaching into the cab of his lorry, Diego dragged out a battered old leather fedora, cramming it down hard on his head. "Get the horses off their truck and tack up Dourado, I'll ride them up to higher ground. Unload the old llama too, it should follow the horses. Thank your gods we couldn't afford elephants!"

"Are you sure about this, Boss? It will be dawn in four hours."

Diego nodded curtly, all too aware of the time. "I'll stop when the road improves or I find a farm to shelter in. Don't worry, I'll leave an hour to spare."

Within a few minutes, the horses were unloaded in a clatter of metal-shod hooves, wide-eyed and skittish from the storm. They lay their ears flat back and dropped their heads low in a display of equine bad humour, unhappy at being ejected from their dry, cosy horse box to face the appalling weather. As the wind picked up and howled around the convey like an angry banshee, their behaviour worsened, the horses whirled around and reared, lashing out at their handlers and each other. Only the placid old llama stood quietly at the side of the road, resigned to any adventure the humans threw at it.

In one easy movement, Diego leapt into the saddle and instantly took control of his high-spirited, palomino Portuguese stallion, its metallic golden coat already turned to sodden dark ochre from the rain. He took up the lead ropes of the other five horses, four flighty liberty stallions, all pure white Arabs and a broad-backed, spotted Knapstrupp vaulting horse. With the llama meekly following, he rode into the storm.

Lev watched his boss ride away and shook his head in mute admiration, it took one hell of a rider to control six terrified, highly strung equines and steer them safely through the darkness and a raging tempest, but he had not the slightest doubt the Boss could do it.

Diego pushed on through the hellish storm using all his strength, determination and superlative horsemanship to keep control. Taking courage from it's resolute rider, the Portuguese stallion remained steady and tractable beneath him. The nervous Arabs, held only by halters and long lengths of rope, shied and balked all the way, one reared and fought hard to gallop off, terrified, as lightning forked above their heads.

"Enough, Malik," scolded the horseman, his voice both firm and gentle. In a flash of eye-searing purple, a tree exploded on the horizon after a direct hit from the lightning. Only respect for the strong hand on the rope and the familiar soothing voice of the Boss kept the animals from bolting in panic. There was a final deep, booming thunderclap and at last the rain began to ease. With less then an hour before dawn, Diego could see no sign of the trucks. He was on his own.

Remembering a jumble of derelict farm buildings in a nearby valley, Diego circled back to find them. The whole farm was ill-kempt, malodorous but did have a spacious and solid barn. Ignoring the feeble warning growls from a lame, mangy old dog, Diego jumped off his horse and led them towards the oak planked building. All the equine bolshiness disappeared instantly at the sight of shelter and the alluring smell of hay, the animals meekly walked inside. The barn's inhabitants consisted of a few scraggy chickens long past laying age and two bony milk cows. There was plenty of room for the circus animals.

Diego bedded them down and dumped piles of hay in front of them. It was old and dried out but not mouldy, it would have to do. The farm had clearly once seen better days, the barn had been built well with solid planks that kept it warm and waterproof. There were no obvious gaps in the walls or holes in the roof. He could shelter safely here. Pulling the fedora low over his eyes, he waited for the inevitable visit from an angry farmer and his equally inevitable shotgun. He didn't have to wait long.

The man burst in, the cowering mutt by his side, gun already raised to shoulder height. He had thrown a filthy overcoat over his night shirt, his feet were bare and caked in mud and manure. He looked older then his years with a grey beard grown straggly and filthy from neglect. At the sight of the llama, he opened his mouth in surprise exposing his last remaining three black teeth.

"What the devil is that? And what is it doing in my barn?"

Diego kept the hat low over his eyes but raised his hands in a placatory gesture, "It is a harmless creature from distant Peru. Peace my friend, I wish you no harm. My circus is mired down by the mud back along on the road, I seek a few hours shelter for my horses and the llama, I will pay generously for any fodder used. Just a few hours rest and we will be on our way."

The farmer grunted and spat, giving the long necked beast another wary glance, it looked like a monstrous goat conceived by the devil. The horses were all fine beasts though, especially the sturdy spotted one, that looked well able to pull a plough with ease through the hardest earth. It would fetch a good price at the next market.

"The hay and shelter in return for that nag with those idiotic spots," the farmer demanded "Or you will be on your way."

Diego walked over to the Knapstrupp and stroked its placid, plain face. "And what would my beautiful ballerina use for her act without dear old Klaus here? She dances on his back as he canters around the ring. Such a pretty sight!" He sighed and shrugged as if regretful that he could not trade with the avaricious old man. "My money must be recompense enough, perhaps you should ask your wife what she would prefer."

The farmer spat again on the earth floor, "That bitch left me for a travelling brush salesman, took the only son with any brains with her. Left me with the hulking, idle idiot. But he's man enough to put you in the ground. The spotted horse or out. Now."

Diego sighed, he'd given the man a chance to be hospitable and to be paid well for the shelter. Now he would have to kill him. And the son.

Chapter Three

Remai sat on the top step to her parent's motor home, polishing the brass fittings of the llama's circus ring harness, she worked hard, buffing the metal till it lost its dull yellow colour and glittered instead like mirrors. Her eyes glanced up occasionally, across the clearing, beyond the circus encampment to the track through the forest. They had arrived in this pleasant area during the afternoon, the woods were thick enough to provide good shelter and firewood and a nearby stream of clean water tumbled through the woodland.

The sun had set three hours ago leaving the circus in a comfortably warm star-lit darkness. Everyone in the troupe commented on the contrast between this night and the tempest the night before as they busied themselves, fetching firewood, preparing an evening meal. But like thirteen year old Remai, they too, kept glancing uneasily down the track. Three members of the circus were still out on the road. Only their safe return could ease the tension.

Remai's mother, Shian, joined her on the step and gently took the brightly coloured leather harness from her hands. "Sweetheart, if you polish that metalwork any more, you will be able to see right through it, the buckles will be as thin and fragile as glass!"

Her mother gave her shoulders a loving squeeze. "You must not fret so, child. Your father will be back soon. Today's hot sun has already dried up the roads, it is just a short run from the border now."

Remai glanced up at her mother and gave a slight smile, one she did not feel inside. Her father, Lev, was the foreman of the circus, a responsible job, and one not without risks. If the Boss had got into trouble in Bulgaria, could her father be in danger too?

The throaty wheeze of an engine with exhaust explosions like bursts of gunfire broke the evening's anxious silence. A familiar tall, relaxed figure rode an ancient and ailing motorbike into the clearing, the

Boss, on Jerzy's old bike. The clearing erupted with cheers and screams of relief and delight. Everyone ran to greet him, including Remai and her mother. Diego switched off the engine and put the bike up on it's precariously rusted stand. He removed his battered fedora and used it to brush off his dust and mud caked clothes, knowing he would be enthusiastically embraced by all the women and children of his troupe. Diego glanced over to Remai and her mother Shian.

"Lev's here in Rumania, about half an hour behind me with Jerzy and the beast wagon. Everything is fine, all the animals are safe and well. Your llama could do with a good groom though, Emi."

Remai blushed at the Boss's affectionate use of a pet name for her, one from her childhood when she couldn't say her own name properly. She watched as he strode across the encampment to his own lorry, holding two young boys by their trouser belts, whirling the delighted children around, their arms outstretched as they pretended to be aeroplanes. Of course she had been worried that her father was late back, but she was also worried about the Boss. The lives of her family and friends in this little circus all depended on this enigmatic, rather melancholic being. And always had done.

Chapter Four

New York

In the brutally harsh and merciless light of a laboratory, a young man's body lay on a steel table. Hardly out of his teens, this was once a man who had dreams; had family; was loved. Well dressed, good looking, he had been someone. Now he had no name, no dignity in his untimely death, a specimen to be dispassionately examined in the minutest detail.

Two scientists stood back from their work, one was a geneticist, a pioneer in his field. The other, Oxley, was a top pathologist, who had once headed a New York police department crime lab. Both men now worked solely for Nemesis. Not as part of the main corporation, but in an unnamed subsidiary, working directly for Hain.

"Just confirms what I have said all along," the Svolenian geneticist, Widran, announced, putting down the latest report after glancing contemptuously through it. "Our deluded paymaster insists these creatures exist, but this supposed victim has told us nothing. The whole idea of vampires is preposterous!"

The pathologist shrugged. He too, as a man of science wanted proof. He was charged by Nemesis to minutely search this poor, unfortunate man's body for any trace of non-human DNA to give to Widran for his research. The corpse was supposed to be a victim of a vampire attack, stolen off the street where he fell in a well-orchestrated and clinically perfect manoeuvre by Nemesis operatives. It was the first untouched body to escape evidence contamination, the first not to end up lying in a police morgue. A healthy young man with no sign of disease but nearly completely desanguinated, the body had no horror film puncture marks, but a scalpel-neat incision into the jugular vein. There was no sign of blood loss on his clothing. Whoever had done this had been phenomenally neat. Too neat to be human."

On the contrary, Professor Widran. This body tells me a great deal." Oxley gently turned the head over to show the incision on the neck, quietly enjoying Widran's squeamish reaction. The Svolenian was a loathsome man, arrogant and contemptuous. He was happy to take Hain's money but bad-mouthed their employer at every opportunity. Oxley assumed he must be the best in his field for such open disloyalty to be tolerated.

"Whoever, whatever, killed this man was very quick, blood loss was rapid, he did not bleed slowly to death but perished when there was not enough blood reaching his heart. The incision is precise, it must have been from a very sharp instrument, possibly a scalpel."

"So not by fangs!" smirked Widran.

"A scalpel." The pathologist paused, deliberately for dramatic impact to wind up the Svolenian. "Or the edge of a razor- sharp fang."

"That is ridiculous! You cannot be serious Oxley!" Widran's snort of contempt irritated the pathologist who was determined to earn his high wage by keeping an open mind.

"One hundred per cent serious. This man was killed by something that moved very fast to overwhelm him, there is no sign of a struggle or any toxin or sedation in what little is left of his blood. Something that cut into his neck and drained him almost dry of blood without making any mess on his clothing or the ground surrounding the body.

Oxley paused, asked, "So, tell me Widran? What human killer could do that? And more importantly, why?"

Annoyed, Widran stormed out of the autopsy before the pathologist resumed his investigation, did any more cutting work on the body. He did not want Oxley to have the satisfaction of watching him vomit or faint. What a repulsive way to earn a living. He returned to the sanctuary of his own department, pristine and sanitary. An orderly place of quiet research and discovery. But there was nothing to work on; no vampire DNA; not a single hair or scrape of cells beneath the victim's nails. No saliva around the fatal wound.

When would Hain accept vampires did not exist? That his dream of discovering the secrets of immortality, of curing all mankind's diseases was just that. A dream.

Chapter Five

Chess Manor, The Chilterns, England

"I'm not a bloody psychologist, not a doctor or a damn skivvy! This is seriously unfair!"

Gabrielle's litany of complaint was fuelled by clearing up after Jazriel's latest explosion of fury. A stream of colourful curses which grew more profane as she scrubbed purple blood off the ancient wooden floor. Her knees hurt, her back ached and she was furious. Angry with the Cardinal for insisting she took on this assignment, nursemaiding the re-animated corpse of a suicidal, junkie, male whore vampire. Jazriel's words. Hers were more explicit!

The night before Jazriel had woken from a heavily sedated Rest, restless and distressed after a day spent enduring a succession of bad dreams. He had been desperate for a fix of anything, the enforced and unwanted cold turkey really hitting home, and then he caught sight of his reflection in a large gilt-framed antique mirror, the damage to his legendary beauty was shocking. For the first time he took in his appearance, gaunt and pale, his eyes dulled and dark shadowed. Jazriel had hit the mirror with his fist, over and over again, sending blood-stained shards and splinters of glass flying around the bedroom.

To her relief, he had meekly allowed Enver to take him away to treat the wounds, leaving her the wretched task of clearing up. But it was preferable to dealing with the vampire. Gabrielle was too furious to go anywhere near him.

The choice of Chess Manor as a refuge was proving disastrous. Jazriel had too many memories echoing from the oak-panelled walls, reminders of a time when he had been confident, controlled and respected. And loved. Every room resonated with memories of his devoted Sivaya, of his beloved human friend Khari. And it was from here he had embarked on the perilous mission to Nazi Germany that had killed him.

Gabrielle too, found the place a trial. She had trained here with the Spook Squad agents, preparing her for a more active role within the Reyes and Eshan alliance. And here, her brief but intense romance with its leader, the troubled telekinetic, Enver Thorne, had began and ended badly. Arriving back with the living wreckage of Jazriel could have been awkward for Gabrielle, but at least the pair of ex-lovers had managed to be civil. So far.

Muttering profanities, Gabrielle finished clearing up and returned to the locked and guarded suite where a now sedated Jazriel was again at Rest. The other agents of the Spook squad took turns at watching the vampire to give Gabrielle a break, though she insisted on taking the lion's share. They were eager to help, a mixture of concern and star-struck excitement. Jazriel was part of their history, a founder member of their unique squad. A war time hero. A legend. One who had returned not as a frail old man, but young and gorgeous, unchanged by the decades. Except the actuality was far from that romantic notion.

Gabrielle was not interested in their dreams being dashed by the reality of Jazriel's decline and increasingly likely demise by his own hand. The responsibility was too onerous. Too unwanted. As were the lingering echoes of Jazriel's emotions and experiences that had infected her mind, reappearing as graphically vivid dreams. Dreams where she was not the passive observer but re-living them through his eyes. Luckily, they were fading, becoming less frequent. Gabrielle prayed they would disappear forever - now would not be soon enough!

He howled, but still there was no sound. Just like that other place, that terrifying Nothing.

This was worse; he was tightly restrained, trapped by a leaden, frozen tomb. Sealed and suffocating. At least in the darkness, in the oblivion, he was free, floating in silence, his spirit, the knowledge of all he was, gradually dissipating to nothing.

'Jazriel!

His name! Someone was calling his name and he could hear him! A voice so wonderfully familiar. Jazriel fought to be free of the frozen tomb to reach the voice, but he could not move, could not make a sound, could not see...

Jazriel woke up howling, raking the air with his fangs. That nightmare again! Why was his mind tormenting him with these awful memories? Dragging him back to the moment he had regained awareness of life, his spirit awaking, trapped in his own long-dead body. Why?

He struggled to get off the bed, stumbling across the room on weak and shaking legs. He needed help, something to mask the horror, to blank the past out. But he was trapped in another prison, one designed to help him recover. Recover from what? He knew exactly what he was doing every time he opened a vein to let narcotics flood through his body. This enforced rehab was opening the sealed door to his old nightmares, ones he'd fought to keep at bay since his re-animation. It was time to stop fighting the inevitable. His return to life had been a mistake. One he could rectify. If only these human tormentors would leave him alone long enough!

A lurid day-glo sunset shone through the manor's Georgian windows, as Gabrielle hurried back to the vampire's rooms. He would be waking from Rest, she wanted to be at his side when his eyes opened. Possessive? She knew that's what the others thought of her. She called it being professional, detached, efficient. Well. Yes. And possessive.

Except his eyes did not open. Gabrielle pushed the young woman at the bedside away, frantically checking the vampire for life signs. Her hands used to the coldness of his skin, found a heart beat, slow but steady. But she could not get Jazriel to wake up.

"Has he taken anything? Don't lie, I must know the truth!" Gabrielle rounded on the young agent, she was a pretty girl, eager to please, one that Jaz could wrap around his elegant little finger with ease, even in his current dissolute state. The woman's eyes widened with indignation, this bitch from hell had gone too far!

"No way, Ms Railton. I have been at his side for hours, he's slept all through."

Gabrielle took the vampire's head in one hand and slapped him, hard. Twice. "Come on you fanged bastard, wake up!"

The other woman was outraged. "Do you know who this is, what he did for all of us in the war? Have you no respect?"

A male voice answered. "None whatsoever! She never has and never will."

Gabrielle spun around as Enver strolled into the room, a lazy half smile on his thin, quirky, nearly handsome features. Knowing they had once been an item, the agent flounced out of the room. How dare that stroppy madam insult and assault the exquisite and heroic Jazriel! Let Enver deal with her!

"So, Gaby, how is our unexpected guest?" Though used to Lady Eshan's company, he was understandably uneasy being so close to a blood- drinking vampire, even a comatose one.

Gabrielle was fuming, arms folded, pacing the floor with frustration. "How do you think?" She rounded on Enver, "Some idiot here at the Manor has let him get hold of something. All that effort, all the shit I've been through and it could be for nothing. Some silly tart has fallen for his wiles and this is the result!"

Enver was affronted, he was in charge of the squad. None of his highly trained people would have fallen for Jazriel's manipulative ways. Could they? There was nothing he could do when Gabrielle was in one of her moods. He'd learnt that the hard way. "I'll question my team. I too want answers." He announced, glad to have something to do, leaving Gabrielle to her vigil by the vampire's bedside.

As time passed, Gabrielle's anger turned to mounting anxiety. Why wouldn't the vampire wake up? He appeared to be in some sort of coma. There were no illicit drugs available at the Manor. The sedation dosage had to be the cause, it was all guess work, no one here knew anything about Dark Kind metabolism. But maybe it was nobody's fault.

Perhaps Jazriel himself had got to the medicine cabinet, upped the dose to a lethal level. She wouldn't put it past him. In a panic she had phoned Lady Eshan who had been reassuring and pragmatic. "Let him sleep it off, Gaby. He'll either wake up or die. There's nothing more you can do. You can only wait."

So Gabrielle remained in his suite, pacing the room, unable to settle to any distraction, no book or television show could keep her interest. Her entire focus was on the motionless, barely breathing form on the bed. At Rest, she caught a glimpse of his former legendary looks. Jazriel had once been stunning. Beautiful; on the outside. Gabrielle was not fooled. The beauty cloaked a ruthless and coldly calculating predator. The looks, the lazy charm were an illusion.

Enver returned with a tray of hot food. "Sleeping Beauty still in dreamland?"

Gabrielle nodded, refusing the meal with a weary smile of thanks.

"Fancy a quick bonk then?"

"Yeah, why not,"she replied with an indifferent shrug.

Expecting a caustic put down, Enver was taken aback by her unhesitant reply, delighted but surprised. "And what about your pretty but wasted boyfriend? What if he wakes up?"

"This dreadful creature is not, and never will be, anything to me but a damned nuisance. We are wasting time," she glowered, "let's get on with it."

Gabrielle led him into the main room of the suite, to the fireside rug and grabbing his belt, pulled him down on top of her. Her mind flashed back to another vivid dream-memory, a fading echo from Jazriel's past. Standing out high along the bowsprit of a tall ship, with nothing but the sea cleaving away from the bow beneath his feet. Watching, entranced, as moon-silvered dolphins rose and fell from the surf way below. Someone approached to join him on the precarious location, the narrow spar that soared ahead of the lifting and dipping ship. Gabrielle believed if she could feel just a tiny fraction of the vampire's overwhelming surge of love and desire, of the complete happiness that he had once had, to experience that intensity in her own life, then she would be the happiest woman ever born.

Would she ever feel the same about a man? Could any human love with such strength, such passion as Jazriel had - did? Thankfully, Enver's abilities were telekinesis, he would never know she was turned on by another being's memory! 'Mind you', thought Gabrielle as Enver entered her with the confidence of familiarity, 'even if I can't stand the guy, he is damn good at one thing!'

The impulsive moments of fevered desire over, Gabrielle and Enver lay on the rug, damp with sweat, sated and silent. Though it seemed they couldn't converse without having furious rows, their bodies got on with each other. Very well!

The door to the room opened and Jazriel staggered in, steps uncertain, hesitant, his turquoise eyes clouded. His voice slurred.

"Keep the noise down, you guys, there's a vampire trying to die in peace in here." He tossed a packet of cigarettes to Enver. "I bet she's a handful. You'll need these to recover."

Chapter Six

A rural road in Hungary

Wiping a streak of thick, foul smelling mud from her face, Sivaya glared at the humans. She had fallen heavily into a deep rut in the dirt track from sheer exhaustion, too tired to notice the obstacle despite her perfect night vision. For weeks her life had been flight, running from the cloying protection of Ha'ali Eshan and from the vengeance of grubby villagers whose men folk Sivaya had slain to survive. Perhaps it was going to end here. She was beyond caring. She lay, worn out, mud stained and sodden on some peasant farm track, fangs bared, ready to take on the small band of mounted pursuers.

They were on her now, surrounding her. Their horses snorted and shied in the swirling low mist, shod hooves scraping up sparks against stones. They calmed the animals, speaking not in some Magyar local dialect but an ancient tongue she had almost forgotten. Dholma! They must be gypsies, descendants of the once proud Asiatic race Dezarn had reigned over in antiquity. Most became implacable enemies of the Dark Kind, but the oldest, purest tribes had inherited the ancient respect. A dazzling beam from a modern torch caught her, a pathetic yet dangerous creature of the night at bay.

"Peace, lady - we mean you no harm. We have been searching the night to take you to safety, away from the vengeful mob hunting you."

One led a horse towards her and helped her, albeit nervously into the saddle. They rode hard and in silence, relying on her sharp vision to guide them swiftly through the night-clad countryside. The going was treacherous, the tracks a rutted nightmare, low branches swiped and clawed at them like demented tree spirits, but the gypsies pushed on hard, leaving as much distance as possible from Sivaya's last predation.

Just before dawn threatened to tear the night open with its harsh light, the gypsies reached their camp. It appeared to be a small travelling circus, a circle of gaudy motorised caravans and lorries. Sivaya accepted their offer of a darkened caravan with a nod of resignation. She had no idea what their plans were for her, she was too exhausted to care. She sank down into the down-filled quilts and went into a deep, dreamless Rest.

The chatter of human voices, the bustle of livestock and vehicles intruded into Sivaya's sanctuary of oblivion. She awoke, and became only too aware of the lurching, jolting movement of the vehicle, the stench of the diesel fumes. It was smelly and uncomfortable but it appeared to be a safe haven. With the brute force of the sun outside, she had no choice but to remain where she was.

The journey continued, the vehicle convoy pushing on hard through the day and next night, the speed suggesting they wanted to travel as much distance as possible. With only an hour left before dawn, it finally ground to a halt. There was a hesitant knock at Sivaya's door. A girl, no doubt a carefully planned first contact with the Dark Kind female. As if they knew all vampires only preyed on adult males?

"Lady. We have crossed the border. You are well beyond the reach of your enemies."

Sivaya gave a weary, humourless smile. She was certain the entire sentient world - Dark Kind and human alike were her enemies. For centuries she had lived as a hunted pariah, but always had the solace of her own people. Of Jazriel. Now, despite Eshan's claim to the contrary, she felt truly alone.

"Who are you people and why are you helping me? It is obvious you know what I am."

The girl though clearly afraid, spoke with great pride. "We are the last living Xenari, an ancient and pure bred nomadic Dholma tribe. We travel across Europe with our circus - the Yasuul Nair-rhed. We heard about your problems with those peasants and sent our men to find you to bring you to safety.

Sivaya was puzzled. Why would the plight of a Dark Kind female attract the interest of gypsy circus folk? Surely they would realise she would tear out throats before being subjected to any exposure or indignity in a travelling freak show? The name of the circus intrigued her too, there was something familiar about it.

"Where is your leader? I will speak to him."

The girl swallowed nervously, unwilling to disappoint their formidable guest. "Lady, he is not here. The Boss has gone to Spain to buy a new horse for the circus. But you have no cause for concern. You are safe with us. In the ancient days, our people were greatly loved by King Dezarn. To revere his memory we honour the Dark Kind."

Sivaya nodded. Her own memory of Dezarn was that he was the ultimate in high born fools. He had loved his human subjects so much they had crowded in their thousands into his capital city to cheer as they brutally severed his handsome, noble head from his body. As a commoner, she had no time for such suicidal heroics.

"When will your boss return?"

The girl paused before replying, anxious not to displease the female vampire in any way. Her own people insisted she was safe from the creature's fangs, but the dishevelled, filth spattered form before her was all gleaming, hard alien eyes and white, sharp -planed features.

"Diego is like the steppe wind, unpredictable and uncontrollable. We do not know when he will return. But he will come back to us. He always does."

The girl's broad Tartar features lit up at the mention of the Boss's name, the affection for him unmistakable. She had the near-black almond eyes and light golden skin of her ancient race, Sivaya had seen women like this for millennia. They had once been a proud race of nomad warriors who roamed large tracts of Eurasian tundra. Some had settled in the regions known as Dholma, Caradan and Altar under the reign of the great Vampire King Dezarn. The Xenari had turned their back on new thought, new religions and stayed resolutely loyal to the Dark Kind. It was a form of deliberate damnation, a self imposed pariahdom that inevitably brought persecution in its wake. While their Dholma cousins, the Isolanni stayed protected by Azrar in their remote mountain-ringed principality, what was left of the Xenari had become despised travellers, with no land and no future beyond their ceaseless wandering.

"Lady, you are welcome to stay with us as long as you wish. But there are conditions."

The young girl looked understandably more nervous, giving commands to a Dark Kind female was an onerous task for one so young. She took a deep breath to steady herself and continued, "You must not harm any of our men folk, they all wear the golden dragon talisman of King Dezarn. If you need nourishment, we will make the necessary arrangements. This is very important. We know how to make sure there are no repercussions for our people. Bring no danger to us and we will protect you. That is how it must be."

Sivaya considered a moment, then nodded assent. These humans, with their skewed, amoral loyalties offered her a much-needed refuge, a respite from a relentlessly hostile world. It was an extraordinary twist of fate; one minute she faced exhaustion and despair in a filthy mud rut, now she had shelter and protection and the chance to live, even for only a few days, openly as Dark Kind.

"It sounds as if you have had experience helping my kind?"

The Xenari girl's face remained impassive, her dark eyes unreadable. "We have, many times over the centuries. But there are hardly any of you left now."

"That can only be a good thing for you. Harbouring us brings danger to your people."

The girl gave no response. If there was any deep-seated resentment or hatred, she hid it masterfully.

"So what is your name and what is your role here?"

"I am Remai," she replied, her manner brightening, "I look after the llama, I can juggle, eat fire and do this..." The girl removed a floor length, heavy woollen man's greatcoat to reveal her reed-slender form, clad in a dark pink, sequin-spangled leotard, and lowered herself to the floor of the caravan. With the lightness of a boneless cat, she contorted herself into a series of extraordinary poses.

"I bet that goes down well with those hulking great peasant lads in your audience!"

Remai laughed heartily as she replaced her oversized coat.

"But not their sweethearts! Luckily the sight of our boss in action soon makes them forget any imagined slight. It is nearly time for your Rest. Do you need anything? You are our honoured guest."

Alone, Sivaya was grateful for the relatively safe haven, she allowed herself to sink into Rest once more, not realising the healing process for the many years of grief triggered madness had finally begun.

At first Sivaya hid away, wanting only to be alone in her caravan in darkness and silence. The discomfort and tedium of constant travelling on rutted rural roads, meant nothing to her. She did not know who drove her van or to what destination they were heading. She did not care. By day she remained lost in the oblivion of Rest, mercifully free of any tormenting dreams. But by night she was taunted by her mind's self-torture, a waking nightmare that would not stop. Her sense of hopeless, overwhelming loss of Jazriel in her life, in her arms, tore open cruel wounds in her heart like a jagged knife.

She had never truly mourned his death because her mind had refused to accept it. Now he had been resurrected she finally experienced the full crushing weight of Dark Kind grief. He was hers! Hers! Azrar had no right to him! Why should the Prince's astonishing feat of great power, his achievement in bringing Jazriel back from the dead dictate he had a right to claim her lover as his own? It was not fair, not after the centuries of physical and emotional abuse Sivaya was convinced the Prince had inflicted on Jazriel in the distant past. He was hers!

Like a demented, caged beast, Sivaya paced the caravan or sat on the edge of the narrow, hard bed, her arms wrapped tightly around herself as she rocked backwards and forwards in her self-made hell. A foetid brew of anger for Azrar and all those who had helped get Jazriel back to the Prince merged with the heartrending longing for her beloved.

Her whole being yearned to see his beautiful face again. To touch him, to make love. He had been an astounding lover, so inventive, skilful, giving everything he had to make her feel desired, beautiful. Selflessly, he had driven her delirious with pleasure every time. She once thought herself the most fortunate of commoner females, to snare one of the nobility's most prized and skilful sha'ref to be her companion in life, in bed. She had enjoyed such bliss, such ecstasy, she fooled herself into thinking it was enough. To forget Jazriel was not and never had been in love with her.

The long nights with the circus turned into weeks. Despite herself Sivaya gradually began to take some interest in the people protecting her, yet tactfully left her alone. On her own volition, Remai became her guide to the troupe and its nomadic existence on the edge of human society. Sivaya learned that not all the circus performers were Xenari; there was a Ukrainian high wire act, a band of jugglers from Mongolia and an East German family of knife throwers. That they all accepted the Xenari's tolerance of Dark Kind was extraordinary to the point of disbelief. Sivaya had been wary of these people and thought the presence of non-Xenari potentially dangerous to her. Remai did her best to assure her this was not the case.

As the weeks passed, Sivaya began to take occasional short walks at night when the camp was far from human villages. The circus folk left her alone, save for polite greeting. She watched, at first with disinterest, as the troupe practised their skills or repaired equipment. They travelled mainly by day and Sivaya would have had no idea where she was unless Remai told her. She rarely asked. Each forest glade looked similar to the last, each ramshackle village or meandering town, all were typical Eastern European. Sivaya had travelled these lands all her long life; once all were under the rule of the Vampire Kings. Now, with her people's proud history forgotten or suppressed, knowledge of her Kind was reduced to idiotic folk tales about graveyard haunting ghouls.

Screams and a commotion awoke her abruptly from Rest. Outside a storm cloud darkened twilight allowed her to venture early from her caravan to find the troupe frantic with fear. A small child had crawled beneath a local's abandoned lorry, jacked up by the gypsies to remove any usable parts. The old vehicle had fallen from its rusty stand, trapping the infant beneath. Any mechanical intervention would bring the whole lot down on the child. Emotions ran wild as the frantic men argued on the best solution, the women wailed in distress. Some did their best to comfort the distraught family of the trapped child.

There was no time for this fuss, the lorry could slip any second. Sivaya strode past them, got down beside the vehicle and wriggled her slender, lithe form beneath, placing the mercifully unharmed child beneath her, using her body as a shield. With the child covered, she ordered the men to work together to push the lorry over. There was a moment's shocked silence and brief hesitation then they agreed to her plan. As predicted, pieces of the rotten chassis crashed down; unflinching, Sivaya took the blows from the falling metal. With fangs bared she bore the pain from a great gash across her back, exposing the black bones of her spine. She was far stronger than any human and though severe, the wounds would heal. With the lorry lifted, she managed to pass the child to its mother before faintness from blood loss weakened her. Dimly, she was aware of strong human arms gently carrying her back to her van before unconsciousness overcame her.

Again it was Remai who tended her. In the weeks that followed, the Xenari girl kept her bandages clean, with no sign of disgust, brought Sivaya flasks of human blood to quicken the healing process and boost her strength. Sivaya was in no condition to query where it came from, just felt relief for the life-giving though foul elixir. In any other circumstance she would have rejected it as foul, as carrion. Dark Kind only drank from living victims. Instead, she repressed the urge to gag and gratefully swallowed the gift of life.

The thankful troupe filled her caravan with wild flowers, picked daily to honour her with their freshness. Sivaya mused on the bizarre amorality of these humans. They gave her shelter and gifts of flowers, yet someone must have died to provide her with sustenance. Had they killed a local peasant to provide her with blood? Perhaps, one day soon, out of curiosity, she would ask.

Chapter Seven

Diego drove carefully through the night, anxious not to disturb the precious cargo shuffling and stamping in the back of the lorry. He glanced across to the elderly but vigorous man sitting beside him in the cab, "Not long now, Hanto. You'll soon be sampling the delights of your wife's cooking."

The old gypsy laughed. Ruma's disastrous attempts at haute cuisine were a long running source of good-natured merriment among the Xenari. "Well, Boss, I'll happily skip the meal, but a good sleep in my own bed with the missus to keep me warm - now that *is* worth looking forward to!"

The old man had good reason to miss home comforts. Though a nomad well used to constant travel, the weeks of being cooped up travelling in a rattley old horsebox had grown increasingly wearisome. The Boss's concern over the welfare of a magnificent Spanish stallion he'd purchased in Seville meant a long, slow journey home. A star-dappled grey, the horse was destined to be the main turn in their travelling circus. Along with the Boss, Hanto travelled with another gypsy, a strapping taciturn giant of a man called Senec. They took turns to drive, the Boss covering the night shifts, but the journey had been delayed many times with long, tiresome detours around busy towns and cities, preferring the remote, more rural routes. They stopped frequently to unload and rest the horse, the Andalucian coping well with the rigours of his travel with the inborn courage and intelligence of his noble breed. It augured well for his new life on the road as the newest member of the circus.

On bright, moon-blessed nights, the Boss would take advantage of the silver light and exercise the horse. A magnificent sight. The rider, broad-shouldered yet slender and lithe was as one with the powerful stallion as it piaffed and pirouetted, reared and danced. The movements it displayed were natural, the actions of all stallions at play or posturing to rivals. The paces became a moon-silvered ballet under the Boss's masterful and sympathetic directions. Arrogante resembled a horse from a fairy tale, a dappled dark grey with luxuriant snowy white mane and tail. He was a natural show off, a star already in his own mind, with every movement exaggerated and extravagant. His exuberant flashiness delighted the gypsies. He was just what their little circus needed to delight their peasant audiences.

The travellers found their camp soon after sunset. The circus had camped in a grassy meadow intersected by a tumbling mountain stream. An ideal resting place. Far from any local settlements the circus families bustled about preparing for an enjoyable peaceful night. Sweet smelling wood smoke drifted in lazy spirals upwards in the warm night air. Tantalising wafts from cooking pots tempted reluctant children from their play in the surrounding woods.

At the sound of the throaty old truck the entire troupe ran out to greet them, hearty cheers rose above the clearing as their families exuberantly embraced Senec and Hanto like homecoming heroes. The Boss saw to unloading the stallion himself, not wanting to deny his people their longed-for reunion. His foreman, Lev, wandered over and filled him in on the circus happenings during the Boss's long absence. Including their guest.

With the new horse stabled, Diego prowled around the camp, taking time to personally greet each of his people, young and old alike. The majority, mostly the original gypsy tribe were relaxed with his close presence. The newer members such as the twin Mongolian contortionists and the Rumanian flyers, smiled a welcome but not without a shudder of fear.

Even after so many years Diego loved the tawdry glamour of his circus. Under a circle of oil lamps, a group of older women patiently repaired sections of the well-worn red and gold big top, damaged with jagged tears from recent violent hail storms. Others patched and painted the juggling clubs, platforms, sparkly boxes and other vital pieces of equipment.

Even at this time of rest and repair, muscles needed to be kept honed and pliable, skills sharpened and perfected. And around the camp's perimeter, armed men constantly patrolled, day and night. This was a long-term regular resting place for the circus, remote, sheltered and blessed with fresh water and abundant grazing but there was no such thing as complete safety. This was a wild, lawless region far from the seat of any government, gangs of murderous brigands roamed at will and for all their threat to the circus, they provided a useful source of nourishment for Diego.

The relationship with the villagers they entertained was always uneasy and often fraught with hidden dangers. The peasants welcomed the excitement and colour the circus brought to drab and drudgery-filled lives, but they also resented and hated the gypsies for their freedom. The men wrongly assumed the circus women were sexually available and eager for their heavy handed attention; inevitably their wives and sweethearts were jealous of the beauty and glamour of the women in their star-spangled leotards and fancy feathers. Many down-trodden housewives cast flirtatious eyes at the gypsy men as exotic and wild as their own men were dull and care-worn.

Over the years, Diego had encountered potential incidents of village girls accusing the circus men of rape, usually to cover up pregnancy following a taboo liaison with some village swain. Other accusations included theft, arson, murder and most alarming of all, witchcraft. Diego had perfected the skill of swiftly packing up the whole show and melting away into the night to a fine art. They needed this ability more times then he could recall.

He returned to the stable area to check that the new stallion had settled into the horse stalls. It has been a long journey for the animal but to his relief he was relaxed, tucking into generous wedges of sweet-smelling hay. Diego ran his hand down Arrogante's muscled, silver satin neck. "You have a hard task before you, my friend," he murmured, "my golden boy Dourado is the star of the show and will not take kindly to being upstaged."

As the stallion bowed his noble head to accept Diego's caress, the vampire became aware of an electric vibrancy and the scent of exotic flowers in the air. An exhilarating sensation that could only mean one thing - the unmistakable presence of another Dark Kind.

"I should have known," said a female voice. "I was right, the name of your little freak show is a corruption of our language. Do they realise you called it the Circus of the Damned?"

Diego turned to see the beautiful Dark Kind female with a glittering mane of thick golden hair and a hostile, wary coldness in her dark green eyes that was far beyond his species' normal predatory iciness.

"Of course! They find it amusing and accept it with pride and good humour," he replied evenly as he studied her intently. He had learnt to be a quick and accurate judge of character, both human and Dark Kind. Diego believed her wariness hid some secret but it was one of no interest to him. Not to one who was so burdened by secrets. She stepped forward and they kissed on the lips in the intimate Dark Kind manner of greeting.

"I understand from my foreman you have been with my troupe for some time. There is a lot to stay for. To live openly as Dark Kind is worth an Emperor's ransom in these difficult times."

Sivaya was disturbed and puzzled by the Xenari's vampire Boss. Everything about his build and manner suggested warrior caste, but surely all the warriors were dead? And had been for six hundred years. Only a commoner would ever consider enduring a life as the leader of a human circus, but this was no commoner. Inevitably, as a Dark Kind male, he was handsome but in the rugged, muscular way of the warrior caste. His sharply delineated features appeared carved from light brown granite; though he did not have the refinement of a noble born's natural elegance, he moved with an innate predatory grace. His shaggy mane of shoulder length hair was a dark glossy mahogany; his eyes were a unique colour for Dark Kind, dark chocolate, sparkling with unusual gold faceting. "My name is Diego. The Yasuul is my creation."

Sivaya raised a quizzical eyebrow. Everything about this vampire seemed out of kilter. "Diego? That is a human name. Who are you really? What are you?"

The circus boss shrugged and returned to settling the horses. Undaunted by his indifference, Sivaya boldly pushed herself in front of her benefactor. "There is no need for disguise with me. You are warrior caste, that is extraordinary! Amazing! All of us pitifully few survivors of our Kind thought the warriors were long dead. So what is your real name?"

The vampire picked up an empty bucket and strode towards the stream.

"My name is Diego and I am a circus boss who happened to be created Dark Kind. I have tired, thirsty animals to attend. There's another bucket over there, make yourself useful."

With the horses and llama content, the two Dark Kind went to the Boss's truck. Diego brought out two sturdy glasses and filled them with generous measures of an aromatic pale fino and slid one across the table to Sivaya as they sat in the living section. "I brought this liquid heaven back from Spain. Enjoy."

His mobile refuge, a wooden sided lorry was no different in size to those of his human crew, but while their nomadic homes were richly ornate and luxurious inside, his was spartan, functional and unremarkable. He had no favourite objects on display from his past, no indication of any accumulated wealth. There was no outward sign that a Dark Kind had spent centuries of his life with this ramshackle circus.

Sivaya slowly sipped her sherry, studying the intriguing but unsettling enigma across the table from her. "You cannot fool me, I know you are a Dark Kind warrior. Why do you live like this?"

Diego shrugged and looked down, clearly uncomfortable with her questioning. "I am alive and found a way to stay that way. That is all there is to it."

"Your people scavenge wrecked lorries for spare parts. You cannot be Dark Kind and not have wealth."

"Actually, I have nothing, but it wouldn't make any difference, I keep my circus obviously poor to show any would-be villains that we are not worth robbing. We have no magic or illusion acts because our audience are deeply superstitious and I have seen too many witch fires to risk another one. We blend in with each community we pass through and do our best not to offend anyone."

"And when you need to feed?" Sivaya persisted, both fascinated and shocked at the way the warrior lived.

"I am very careful. It is vital no suspicion can ever fall on my troupe."

"And you are content to carry on with this petty, shabby lifestyle?"

Diego raised an eyebrow in wry amusement. The first time she had seen him lighten his rather melancholic manner. It did not have the same devastating effect on her as Jazriel's amazing smile but it was good to see his attractive sharp- planed face light up, even if briefly.

"So much scorn from a vampire found lying filthy and rain-soaked in the mud."

"Touché," Sivaya replied, "I deserved that!" How many years had it been since she had found anything amusing? Far too damn long.

"Sometimes I wonder what it would be like to expand this circus," Diego murmured, looking into the golden liquid in his glass as he swirled it around with his strong, yet elegant fingers, "Go far away from these peasant backwaters forever. Bring in bigger, better acts to astound the world with amazing spectacle and magic."

Sivaya forced down a low growl of contempt. This was a disturbingly strange ambition for a Dark Kind warrior. It felt profoundly wrong. She reached for her wine glass as if to wash away the distaste, but tiredness made her misjudge, the goblet tipped over and rolled towards the edge of the table. A shiver of electric tension charged the air, the gold flecks in Diego's dark eyes flared with a strange iridescent light and the glass wobbled jerkily at first, then righted itself before sliding smoothly back to her hand.

Completely astonished, Sivaya sank into her chair, unsure of the evidence of her own eyes. Had she witnessed an act of magic? Not the sleight of hand or mirrored illusions of human entertainers but real, supernatural power?

He stood up abruptly, clearly unnerved. "My apologies Sivaya, but I have just travelled for many difficult and dangerous weeks to return to the Yasuul. I would like to Rest. Alone."

The following night as soon as the sun set, Diego awoke abruptly from Rest and sought solitude by riding out on his new Spanish stallion. He galloped hard, following the line of the rolling fields beyond their camp, urged the animal faster and faster in the quiet but demanding manner of the Dark Kind. Though the powerful, compact little stallion was bred for precision work rather then racing, it enjoyed the freedom and the speed as much as its rider.

Diego eventually reined in the horse near a pleasant, star lit glade and let it graze. He sat on a fallen tree trunk and reached under his shirt for a talisman on a sturdy gold chain; an intricately fashioned golden dragon, cut cleanly in half. One night a human wearing the other half of the talisman would encounter him. Hopefully it would never happen or at least be a time far in the distant future. It was not an event to look forward to but would be the start of chilling catastrophe, something to dread with every fibre of his being.

But now he faced the comparatively trivial and problematic task of dealing with Sivaya after his moment of weakness the night before. He berated himself for his lack of self-control. Letting Sivaya see even that tiny glimpse of his power was idiotic. Beyond idiotic. An act of lunacy.

On returning to the circus camp, Diego could not face any more of Sivaya's questioning. He hoped she would leave his circus; that night would not be too soon. It was nothing personal against the female Dark Kind, he had lived apart from his own for so long, by both design and choice. Sivaya's presence was uncomfortable to him and complicated his life of deliberate exile.

Ill at ease and distracted, he casually picked up a well-worn diabo, its glitzy sparkle remained in places amid the faded and chipped green paint. He tossed the wooden top high into the air and with no one in sight held out his hand and kept it aloft, spinning it frantically in the darkness. At the shuffling sound of an approaching human he let the top fall, and without looking up, caught it easily in one hand. Lev, smiled with relief at sight of the Boss. He had seen Diego's little flash of magic but kept a discreet silence on the subject. He knew the Boss kept them all safe by hiding his astounding abilities in this fearful, superstitious backwater.

"It's good to be back, my friend." Diego said with genuine warmth.

"It's good to have you back, Boss. Now we, the Yasuul, are complete again. The new horse looks good."

"It has to! We are all getting a bit frayed at the seams."

Diego threw the diabo to the man, whose juggler's reflexes did not fail him. Lev laughed and nodded in agreement. "None of us are getting any younger!" But that was not true. The Boss had not changed, not in his lifetime or that of his great grandfather before him. Their protector was forever young, handsome and vigorous. Which for Lev was a comforting certainty in this unpredictable nomadic life filled with hardship and danger. The Boss and his continuous strong leadership meant all was well with his world.

Chapter Eight

An unseasonable and drastic drop in temperature brought sharpness to the night air as the circus troupe working as one cheerful and busy entity, prepared to leave for a remote region of northern Amantzk. Winter was weeks away, there were many more venues to reach before the weather closed in, forcing the Yasuul to retreat to their secret over-wintering location.

Diego awoke from Rest, confused and angry. Unknown voices and images had invaded his dreams, insistent and demanding. As they had for three days in a row. Each dream shared one thing in common. Khubbuz. Why the name of this large but unimportant industrial town was repeated in his dreams was a mystery. One he could only solve by going there. He dressed quickly and left his lorry, preparing to help his people pack up the circus. He called Lev over for a private chat. "Change of plan, my old friend, we are missing out Pradarh and heading straight for Khubbuz, a town due West of here."

Uncharacteristically taciturn, Diego ignored the puzzled expression and many questions he knew his second in command wanted to ask and strode away to pitch in with the circus preparations.

Sivaya watched with incredulity as the warrior worked alongside the humans dismantling the circus ready to move onto their next engagement. She noticed how Diego shouldered the heaviest burdens, took the greatest risks, lithely and fearlessly climbing the ice-slippery, treacherous big top rigging to dismantle the tall metal structure. And all the while indulging in good-natured banter with the gypsies as he worked alongside them. Everyone pitching in together, that was the way of all circuses. From the youngest child able to help, to the fit old ones, everyone found some useful role as the troupe prepared to move on to another remote town, there to re-assemble the circus, perform, then move on again. What a bizarre and unnatural life choice for a Dark Kind warrior! Sivaya could not face another tedious journey along rutted country roads. Nor could she face another audience of malodorous, ignorant human peasants or factory workers, eager for some diversion from their mundane lives. How could the warrior possibly want to live this way? For centuries!

Sivaya was aware of his complete ease with his troupe and how much his humans adored him. Their steadfast loyalty a painful reminder of ancient times, when there was nothing untoward in humans serving a vampire master. But, Zaard! This lowly, impoverished existence was just not right, not seemly.

She'd had enough. Diego's reserved and melancholy mood was worsening with every night she spent here with the circus. Clearly he was uncomfortable with her presence, and in truth, she was unnerved at witnessing the descent of a once ferocious and noble warrior to living this tame and insignificant way of life. It was time to move on. But to where?

Sivaya had no plan, no thought of what she was going to do with the rest of her life. Without Jazriel, she had no purpose, no pleasure. She missed him so much, it was like a permanent wound, physically wanting him so badly it cut through her heart. And that would never change or lessen. She cursed her makers for the intensity of Dark Kind emotion, they must have been a cruel race with a twisted sense of humour.

Seeing Sivaya watching him from the shadows, Diego wandered over to his lorry, battered leather hat pulled down over his curious gold-flecked brown eyes. Unlike the humans also working on dismantling the big top metal frame, he wore no protective leather gloves. The unexpected cold must have made the metal rigging dangerous and unpleasant to work with, but the warrior was oblivious to any discomfort. Indeed, Sivaya was convinced he welcomed the drudgery of his life, the difficulties caused by foul weather, the constant exhausting travelling, as if he was enduring a punishment. But for what? He interrupted her thoughts, addressing her abruptly. "We are nearly ready to move on. Do you want to drive?"

"I want to leave."

Sivaya's simple statement evoked a sigh from the circus boss. A sigh of relief? If her instinct was right, this unnatural warrior wanted her out of his strange life. And without giving an explanation or clue to his true identity.

"We are playing a small industrial town next, it has good transport links." Diego stated. "Stay with us to Khubbuz. You can contact the Lady there if you need help."

Sivaya nodded assent. The thought of contacting Eshan again so soon after escaping from her care was galling, but Eshan was the key to Dark Kind survival in this century. It was her duty as a Ha'ali, a noble born administrator, Eshan had run the financial and intelligence network that supported the surviving Dark Kind with considerable success for many centuries. There was no one else to turn to for help.

Chapter Nine

The City of Khubbuz, Former Soviet Republic of Amantzk

Khubbuz was an unusually big venue for the Circus of the Damned. A drab industrial town on the edge of the steppes and growing, spawning hastily thrown up concrete slabs of new buildings. Plentiful work in new factories tempted peasants to abandon their villages for the mushrooming bleak high-rise concrete apartments. They traded their extended family life and sense of community for a life of certainty. The danger from bitter cold winters and the constant dread shadow of starvation from failed crops subsided. In its place they accepted soul-less servitude.

The circus camped on a bleak two acre building site, a rubbish-strewn wasteland, strafed by hard blown concrete dust, close to the nominal, featureless centre of the town. A daylight arrival meant Diego and Sivaya remaining in Rest while the others pitched camp, struggling to put up the big top against the force of a relentless wind. This was the last venue before the circus was forced to cease touring and head for their winter quarters. A bad summer season gave an extra importance to these performances, the Yasuul needed to make good money in this town to fend off hardship during the harsh months to come.

By nightfall, the depressing wasteland had been transformed with a transient illusion of magic and glamour. A noisily thumping, geriatric and unpredictable generator powered up a fairyland of twinkling lights. The small brass band enticed the crowds with jaunty show tunes, the music struggling to rise above the persistent whine of the dust-laden wind.

As the troupe prepared to perform the able-bodied retired ones manned the ticket booths or stocked up trays with sticky toffee apples, gaudy candy canes and small paper packets of vividly striped, boiled sweets.

Diego awoke and swiftly dressed in his usual inconspicuous work gear and more noticeable but necessary dark glasses. As he left the refuge of his darkened lorry, he surveyed the surroundings with grave misgivings. Slab -like concrete walls of the encircling high rises were a baleful, claustrophobic prison. He yearned for the safe familiarity of a jagged mountain range or deep, dark entangled forest. At least he no longer had the problem of Sivaya watching his every move with curiosity and suspicion. He certainly would not miss her judgemental scorn! She must have left without a word as soon as the last rays of the sun dropped below the flat horizon. He wished her well. But there was the night's performance to supervise. He dismissed Sivaya from his thoughts and went to join his troupe.

Diego patrolled every part of the camp in a well-worn ritual. No performer ever disturbed his intense concentration as he wandered across the fresh sweet smelling sawdust of the main ring checking and double-checking the fliers' rigging and the high wire support struts. When every performance began, Diego would always watch from the shadows, issuing commands when needed, scanning the crowds for any potential troublemakers.

The vampire occasionally took part himself when he sensed the crowds were placid and relaxed. He would ride in on one of the Iberian stallions to perform a brilliant haute ecole display. The audience on seeing his hidden eyes assumed the handsome young rider was blind. As he magically controlled the magnificent dancing horse with no obvious signals, they always applauded wildly - their admiration tinged with pity.

Diego had no intention of leaving the shadows tonight, not in this dour town on the edge of the steppes. A venue he would never have willingly chosen, yet the dream-fed compulsion to set up the circus here had been so strong, so compelling. Instead, he scanned the crowd, a densely packed sea of eager but pallid and worn faces. No doubt many were once weather tanned and ruddy from their long lost rural village life.

The show began. Such was the need for diversion in Khubbuz every performance had soon sold out. At first all was well, with every act well received. Diego always demanded, and got, excellence from his people. But as the circus neared the grand finale, the mood of the crowd turned restless and surly. Diego could sense a ripple of discontent and sent one of the sweet sellers to find out why.

She came back quickly, concerned. "Boss, they are expecting a magic show. Another circus played here two years ago with an illusion act. As it was an even smaller outfit then us, they want bigger and better wonders and spectacle."

Diego sighed as his forewarning of menace became justified. But he had been drawn here by premonition, the dreams of startling clarity with strident voices urging him to travel to this place, at this time.

Lev approached anxiously. "I can't believe I'm saying this old cliché, but the locals are getting ugly. If it gets much worse, we are in seriously deep shit."

"I know. I'm going in." muttered Diego.

"I'll get Arrogante tacked up while you get changed."

Diego shook his head tersely. To keep his people safe from the threatening and surly crowds, he was prepared to do anything. Even betray an ancient vow to his K'elphin protectors. "This could potentially be a volatile situation. I don't trust this crowd. A dancing silver horse will not be enough for this lot. I want a box of props; diabos, hoops, anything to hand. Darkened staging, lots of mysterious music and dry ice. I'll perform after Lina and her dogs."

Lev's grandfather had told him about the Boss's hidden abilities - seen glimpses for himself - and he knew enough never to mention them openly. Suddenly, he became very afraid, and not just of the surly audience.

Smoke wreathed, Diego entered the white sawdust ring. He wore his simple work clothes, a rough, brown cotton shirt and well-worn jeans, but minus his heavy donkey jacket, the only concession to showbiz. He stood, lit by a single white spotlight, a silent, motionless and mesmerising presence. His all-brown eyes caused many to shiver with unease, others muttered reassurance to each other; it was just a trick, a circus trick. The silent crowd held their breath in anticipation as he produced a gold diabo and a length of string. He ignored the low groans and angry grumbles of disappointment at the prospect of sitting through another juggling act.

Diego tossed the top high into the air with the sticks and string, then to gasps of astonishment, he threw away the sticks and stood back. It did not fall. The golden top remained in the air, spinning and whistling. He left it there a moment, then to the crowd's delight, tried to coax it back down. The top appeared to be alive, a teasing and coquettish thing, hovering above Diego's hand before flying back up again.

Then the hushed astonished silence was broken by a loud heckling voice from the crowd. "I've seen this done before. It's on a long wire."

Determined not to break the spell, Diego sent the diabo flying over the heads of the audience and let it down to hover over the heckler's lap before resting there briefly. The big top rang with rapturous, delighted applause as the man waved his hands in front and above him as he searched in vain for signs of wires. Diego stepped back into the spotlight and gave an elegant, solemn bow. The crowds bayed for more.

Lev ran in anxiously, on the pretence of helping with the props. *"Boss - that's enough. Finish it,"* he urged in the ancient gypsy language no one in the crowd would understand. *"You must quit now."*

Enraptured, the city dwellers were on their feet, stamping and clamouring for more magic.

"This is madness - Boss! They are going to tear the place apart, and us with it! You have always said magic acts were too risky to perform to superstitious peasants. Scratch the surface of any one these city dwellers and you'll find an ignorant peasant!"

Diego nodded agreement but sensed he must walk a thin line between leaving the crowd wanting more but content, or turning them into a baying, disappointed mob.

"I have to do just a little more, my friend, to buy us time."

Reluctantly Lev left the ring to find every member of the troupe gathered in the wings as word of the Boss's miraculous magic illusions spread. Their faces wreathed in excitement and wonder, they stood as mesmerised as the audience as the tall, serious figure in the ring paused, ready to produce another marvel.

"We have no time for this gawping," the foreman snapped anxiously to the others. "Break camp and start dispersing. Don't wait till the last performance, this is a bad place for us."

Diego held up one hand for silence and got it, an eerie stillness as if the crowd dared not even take a breath, as if the slightest noise would destroy the magic. He took a large, plain green ball from the props box and held it aloft. As he transferred it swiftly to the other hand, it became a vivid, glowing red. Again and again he threw the ball, each time it settled into his hand it was another beautiful colour. Then before the crowd grew comfortable with the spectacle, he made the ball disappear in a loud flash of golden sparks, which took on a life of their own. They floated above and around the audience, out of touching distance. Diego clapped his hands and the sparks became multi-coloured butterflies, fragile and iridescent. Many of the onlookers had tears in their eyes at such wonder, perhaps recalling the beauty of the countryside they had abandoned for a drudging life of certainty in the industrial city. A yearning for the colour that had drained from their lives on the day they abandoned their small farms and fresh, clean air.

Diego clapped his hands again and a butterfly landed on every hand to sighs of pleasure and astonishment. He clapped again and illusion became solid; a tiny filigree butterfly of finely worked silver.

"Good people of Khubbuz, my parting gift to you!" Diego stepped back into the shadows as the Big Top erupted with riotous applause, but once out of sight he collapsed heavily to the floor, completely drained of energy. Lev shouted for help to carry the exhausted vampire back to his lorry, distraught with anxiety - enough for him to risk the danger of angering a Dark Kind warrior.

"What the hell were you doing, Boss? A bit of sleight of hand, smoke and mirrors - that was all it needed to amuse them."

Diego could hardly speak, the ability to manipulate atoms of physical matter cost him dearly. "I can't do that sort of magic. I always drop the cards," he murmured with a weak, wry smile.

"Well, you've started something now! You've thrown open bloody Pandora's Box and all hell is breaking loose from it. And you will have to do more, each time they will expect bigger and better. They will seek us out demanding bloody silver butterflies, or gold ones! We'll never be able to disappear into the woods again."

Diego struggled to speak through the leaden blanket of exhaustion.

"That was my first and last performance. We break camp tonight, make a three a.m. dash for the border. Leave the Top behind. There's that spare in storage at our winter quarters. You can get the kids and livestock away now."

Lev shook his head in quiet despair. "I had the same thought, some are already breaking camp, but we'll never make it out of town. You've created a sensation, they'll be swarming over this place like a plague of rats. Hell, Boss, you look terrible."

"It's nothing, but I will need to feed soon."

"That's all we need," Lev sighed, heavily. "I'll see what I can arrange."

"No," Diego shook his head, insistent. "I don't want you to do anything now, its too risky. Leave me to Rest for a couple of hours. Get ready to move out as quickly and as unobtrusively as possible."

Lev returned to organise the secretive exodus, perturbed by the Boss's unusual behaviour. He had never deliberately put the tribe in peril before, the obsession with this foul town was disturbing, and his display of real magic an act of sheer, suicidal madness. Lev's wife Shian ran over, her beautiful eyes brimming with fearful tears. "The townsfolk are close to rioting, they are demanding to see more of the Boss's magic. They want more damned silver trinkets."

Inside his dark haven, Diego's mind spun in confusion and turmoil. Dark Kind were a simplistic species with no complex or contradictory emotions. They experienced anger, grief, love and joy, but not guilt or remorse. As a warrior, he knew about honour and duty. And obedience to command. His self-indulgent show of power had broken two vows of honour. In a few moments of madness he had abandoned his duty to protect his circus humans and his solemn oath to the K'elphin not to reveal his power till some non-specified time in the future. Exhaustion was a dangerous distraction, he needed to be outside, supervising the exodus, protecting the circus troupe.

Why the hell had he been drawn to this dreary, hostile city? The dreams, the voices, luring his people into danger?

The air in the lorry grew sweetly fragrant like a summer garden, brightening and shimmering with a golden light. Diego readied himself for a visit from his protectors - no doubt censorious and hostile. This time no beings arrived in person, there were only voices, silvery, gentle yet with authority.

"Creature. You have endured this exile for so long yet have resolutely kept faith with our plans for your future role. We will forgive you this night's unfortunate lapse. It proves to us that your abilities are great but you are not yet ready. Thankfully the time has not come to use them. We will keep faith in you by securing your escape."

"And what of my people? Is their safety part of your plan?"

"No - we can only get you away from here."

"Then I must stay."

Silence. Had the K'elphin abandoned him? Diego was beyond caring.

"Yet another test of your suitability passed! Wonderful! You never cease to confound our understandable and justified prejudice against your vile Kind. Our judgement is you truly deserve our continued protection. And of course all your humans will be safe."

Diego thought he heard their laughter, he was damned if he could find anything amusing in this situation.

"We are astounded at the changes in you. Not only are your powers developing at an extraordinary rate but these signs of compassion for humans shows you are evolving as a being. A remarkable and unexpected development."

Diego snarled, a low, harsh, feral sound. He heard humans approaching his lorry. Sensing the sweet, intoxicating smell of fear-heightened human blood, he growled a challenge to his unseen visitors. "Pity? Compassion? How dare you accuse me of those weak human traits. I am a Dark Kind warrior. A vampire. I will show you how much pity I have for humans. I dare you to keep watching."

The shimmering light faded but Diego was certain they remained as he heard loud hammering on the door. The circus strong man, Gregor, stood outside, a squirming sack over his broad back. "The Mayor of the town wants us gone by tonight. He has sent troops to keep the townsfolk off and they will escort us out as soon as we are ready. I found this rat trying to assault my Lina. You need to feed, Boss. We need you at full strength."

He threw the bundle roughly into Diego's lorry and left without another word. Opening the sack Diego revealed a burly local, bound and gagged, a man thrashing in impotent fury. With his night vision Diego could see the man's close-set blue eyes were defiant but terrified; his boots set up a frantic desperate scrabble against the wooden floor as he kicked away to escape from the ferocious gilded eyes, coldly glittering in the darkness.

Diego called out defiantly in his own ancient language; "*Are you watching, K'elphin, so proud of your moral superiority and wisdom? I am not your tame creature, your flawed Dark Kind weapon. I dedicate this kill to you. This man, who may have a family depending on him to not starve, a man perhaps guilty of no more then a moment's alcohol-fuelled lust and lack of self control. Witness this human's death and bear it on your conscience.*"

Diego paused to give a fierce smile of anticipation of the kill, adding; "*It will not be on mine.*"

His long, curving fangs were fully drawn. He lit a dim oil lamp and unbound the man. At sight of the vampire, the man went beyond screaming, let out a high pitched keening whimper of terror, an incoherent stream of agonised sound, wordlessly pleading for mercy.

Diego lifted him, pinning his arms with one hand, hauling his head back roughly to expose the neck with the other. He held him high as if in offering to the unseen K'elphin, paused to fully savour the moment of anticipation before the wildly exciting, brief thrill of the kill. He sank a fang in deep and hard, tearing open the human's throat and drinking, shuddering with sheer pleasure as strength and life coursed through him. He could hear the cries of horrified outrage, sense the shock and revulsion from his K'elphin mentors as the thrashing victim lost the unequal battle for life.

Diego needed to re-assert some control over his destiny. He may serve their cause, indeed, it was the cause of all living things on Earth, but they could not change him. He was and always would be Dark Kind with a fierce warrior soul. Killing humans to live was not a tragic necessity of survival but his greatest pleasure. He revelled in his dark heritage, his ruthless vampire nature.

"Everything I do now and in the future is for the good of the Dark Kind - not for the benefit of humans or for you bloody K'elphin. Never forget that!"

Silence. Good. He had shocked them. *"So why was I lured here, against my judgement? Did you plant those dreams in my head?"* Diego was furious, the K'elphin elders were cowards, too feeble to face him in person, projecting their ethereal voices while his people had been jeopardised by the visit to Khubbuz. *"Was it some kind of test?"* he snarled, *"Answer me, you sodding bags of wind!"*

"Indeed, favoured one. A test. Whether you will admit it or not, you are an honourable being, you do care for humans, with a great passion. But you're powers are not ready. The world must pray the Enemy is also not ready."

Diego finished draining his victim and let the body drop to the lorry's floor, wiping the blood from his lips, he knew he was once again alone.

Guarded by the local militia, the Yasuul were able to retrieve their precious Big Top. Late in the night the circus left in a staggered convoy, accompanied by the troops who stayed with them till safely over the border. In the early hours, a freak, violent ice storm swept across Khubbuz, the high velocity winds wiping clean any trace of where the circus had passed. Before dawn, every filigree butterfly had disappeared. Dissolving like a dream.

Chapter Ten

Nemesis headquarters, London

"This is really weird, sir, take a look," Phil Geddoe strolled across the thickly carpeted floor and handed a news report to his boss. "Could be the break we are looking for."

Hain grunted, disinterested. Geddoe was his keenest and most able agent, but his obsession with the vampires had led various Nemesis teams to many false leads, chasing their tails around the world. An expensive and time wasting exercise in futility. And yet, when closing in on that creature Jazriel in New York, Geddoe's team couldn't even scrape a reckless junkie vampire off the road. The easiest capture and they had blown it, big time. Since then, Hain had replaced most of his team but retained his pet rabid sewer rat, Geddoe, despite his own part in the shambles in New York. A flawed tool, maybe, but the man still had his uses.

Looking at the report that so excited him, he wondered why. A shabby little gypsy circus troupe in some god-awful rural Russian backwater? A display of real magic? What the hell had that got to do with vampires? They were not supernatural beings, were as much flesh and blood as the humans they preyed on.

Hain brushed the offending report off his desk and onto the floor with a snort of disgust. "If this crap is all you can come up with Geddoe, maybe I should have let you go with the other incompetent losers."

Geddoe was immune to his boss's insults. He expected and endured them for he had brought such scorn on himself since he let that fanged pretty-boy slip through his net. Geddoe scooped the report off the floor and urged Hain to read on.

"Forget the magic nonsense and look at the description of the circus boss, if that's not a vamp, then fire me now. I will deserve it."

"You already do," muttered Hain angrily but humouring the man, read on. He put down the report, unwilling but unable to stop the rising excitement, the near-extinguished hope flaring up again. Could this finally be the one? The lead that gave him more then an elusive scrap of DNA but gave him an intact Dark Kind specimen?

Chapter Eleven

The Southern Amantzk countryside.

A skein of noisy migrating geese crossed the moon in their straggling yet structured formation, flying directly over the top of a modest country house. In the last hours of a quiet night only one room at the back was lit. With a blazing log-filled hearth and a scattering of softly glowing candles, it looked a perfect place for wealthy, trysting lovers.

Once the secret hideaway of a mind-bogglingly rich Russian industrialist before his untimely death in Moscow during one of the world-wide Outrages, the dacha lay in its own quiet, secluded, lightly wooded valley of silver birch and willow. Peaceful and obscure, the large, yet rustic and unimposing building hid the most astonishing sophisticated surveillance system devised by 21st century man. Far from being virtually uninhabited, a small army of operatives waited in sharp readiness for action in a subterranean complex around its perimeter. All to protect one ageless enemy of mankind, the vampire, Jazriel.

Not that they knew that. To them he was a wealthy, spoilt, pretty playboy drying out from a potentially lethal substance abuse problem. The attractive young woman who acted as his defender and guardian, was ferociously protective and openly affectionate to her charge, so possibly a lover too. Who gave a damn? They were being paid enough to guarantee a lifetime's security just for a few months of watching wild geese fly across the northern night sky.

Gabrielle lay stretched out on an over-stuffed leather sofa, a glass of fresh orange juice in one hand, a good book in the other. After a while, she put the novel down and let the fingers of one hand stray down to rifle gently through the silky blue-black strands of Jaz's hair. He sat on the floor beside her, cross-legged on a thick, black bearskin rug. He leant back to rest against Gabrielle's leg, his eyes shut, face lost in apparent rapture as he listened to his favourite music blasting at high volume on an ipod. He wore headphones, so she was spared the dramatic ebb and flow of Muse and The Editors at full concert strength. A mug of strong black coffee at his side, Jazriel had recoiled at her offer of what he called "vile insipid fruit rubbish." She knew he craved a large measure of mellow 1886 Armagnac J Nismes-Declou! With no alcohol in the dacha, he had to make do with a long drag on a cigarette. Gabrielle was strict but not cruel. Not all the time!

She stretched out again and sighed with pleasure. A simple night, reading, listening to music and just being together. She knew she shouldn't feel contented like this. Keeping Jazriel from self-destructing was a duty, an arduous and perilous assignment reluctantly assigned to her by an anxious Cardinal Reyes as a necessity. Gabrielle had a new variation of the *Knowing*, she, alone of all Dark Kind and human alike in this present time, had gained the broken creature's trust.

Aware of what was at stake it was an awesome responsibility for one young human woman. There had been too many bleak and precarious occasions when Jazriel's heart-tearing despair had threatened to pull her down too. She had made a connection with his soul and an echo of him remained within her, a shadowy, alien presence, unwanted yet with a strange and powerfully seductive power.

There had also been moments of peace and quiet companionship, moments like this night. It was nights like these that kept her going through the bad times. There was no shortage of those.

Gabrielle dropped her hand down to gently give his shoulder a light squeeze, knowing his music was too loud for him to hear her voice. Well, maybe not really too loud; she suspected it was a ploy he used to avoid conversation. He removed them and look up at her, one eyebrow raised in query.

"Ja-az…" she began, hoping their ease with each other was complete enough for her to start interrogating him, her curiosity about the past was eating her up. Perhaps, she thought with alarm, she was another Parrish in the making.

"That's me," he replied, absentmindedly sipping his coffee, then cringing with a grimace of distaste, instant! More torture! Gabrielle ignored it. She had momentous things on her mind, far beyond his loathing of cheap coffee. No, she corrected, make that cheap anything! Here, slouched at her feet was a being who had actually lived for thousands of years. Had first hand experience of momentous times, was a contemporary of so many extraordinary characters. Had breathed the same air as mighty emperors and kings. Witnessed exciting world events whose chronicles had been lost or destroyed.

"Jaz...."

"That's still me. What do you want?"

"I want to know everything. All the fantastic things you have seen, the famous people you've met throughout history."

Setting aside her book and drink, Gabrielle moved down to the floor to sit in front of him, holding his hands tightly. Her body was shaking with excitement, eyes shining with enthusiasm. "Jaz, don't you realise how intriguing it is for me, being here with you? Like every Christmas and birthday rolled into one. We are stuck in this dacha, forced together by circumstances beyond our control. Neither of us wants to be here, miles from anywhere."

She stood up and began to pace the floor, "I'm going stir crazy with boredom, I know you feel the same. But you could make it all worth while by bringing the past to life for me."

The vampire's eyes widened, alarmed. This human's zeal was like a driver-less lorry running downhill with no brakes. He didn't give a damn about history. He had drifted through the ages only concerned where his next prey was to be found, where he could find a good tailor and a half decent wine merchant. Human world leaders? Great events? Who gave a damn about all that? Apart from Prince Azrar, who as Jendar of Isolann had to.

"Sorry, princess. You've got the wrong vamp for all that."

He rose from the floor, seeking sanctuary from Gabrielle's fervent questioning. He did not want to think about the past. Ever again.

The endless pain of bitter-sweet memories, no way was he going to open the door to them! The past was a graveyard, he thought, his throat constricting with a spasm of grief.

"You are not getting away from me so easily, matey." Gabrielle snapped. "You lived all those centuries, you have so much knowledge of the past. Even ordinary, everyday life would teach me so much"

Jazriel affected an extravagant yawn, lit a cigarette and shrugged. "The address of the best tailor in Venice in 1789? The finest source of pure opium in Bucharest in 1840? Does that interest you?" He felt a glow of satisfaction at her expression of horror.

"Like the words on that ratty old t-shirt you insist on wearing in bed, in my opinion, history is bunk." He strolled away, pausing to add, "Well, human history is. And fucking boring."

Gabrielle waited till he left the room, before taking out her frustration on a cushion, punching and kicking it, imagining it to be his beautiful, infuriating face. An indolent dilettante, a barely literate, vain, playboy! Of all the few remaining Dark Kind in the world she had to be incarcerated with, it had to be bloody, useless Jazriel!

So it was back to watching his every move and waiting to be relieved of this onerous, tedious assignment. The missed opportunity for unbelievable first-hand knowledge rankled Gabrielle more then she expected. How could he go through the centuries so indifferent to the world beyond fashion and pleasure seeking? She chided herself; of course he could. This was Jazriel, hardly an intelligent observer of life's rich tapestry! The days turned to weeks, but the chaotic momentum of Jazriel's emotional journey continued. He could be good company, charming and relaxed one night; morose, growling, pacing the rooms like a caged panther the next. Or worse of all, withdrawn and silent, spending the long night hours sitting alone, head in hands. The unpredictability of his behaviour wore out Gabrielle's nerves till they were painfully frayed and over-stretched even in the hours of broken sleep. She never knew when the next melodramatic episode would kick off. Like the suicide note incident.

Gabrielle guessed he had charmed one of the security team to get the pen and paper for him. And write down what he dictated. Painstakingly and phonetically written in the vampire language, his first big mistake! He thought no one could read it, but it was the same secret language Khari had used to write her letters and journal to Gabrielle.

Thankfully, Gabrielle had the *Knowing*, had 'overheard' his intention. They had found Jazriel in the kitchen, frantically searching through the medicine cabinet he'd manage to break into. A can of petrol at his side, ready to consume his body in flames. Too weak, too confused to fight back, he was over-powered, heavily sedated and under lock and key with 24hr surveillance. Gabrielle insisted on doing most of the watching. On her first session she had entered the secure room and angrily taken his face in one hand to roughly turn it towards hers. "Sorry, fang boy. You are not dying on my watch! You can do what you want later."

But what of the future? How long would this vigil have to go on? She had no idea what had triggered off this latest attempt, she had thought all that nonsense was safely behind him. There was no doubt he was in low spirits, unable to indulge his cravings and was weak from hunger. Idiot! He could have as much artificial blood as he could drink! But even the suggestion of trying it sent him into a snarling fury. Human blood from a donor bank was dismissed as 'stinking carrion'.

Still seething, angry at his refusal to engage with her about the past, Gabrielle read the note again.

I know what must happen now. When I died in that Berlin cellar, it was meant to be my time. It was not a good end, long and agonising and alone. It took many hours, time enough to say goodbye to this world, to those who loved me. I was ready to move on. Instead I became a fading thought, a dissolving dream, no voice, no sound, no sensation just a silent unheard scream in the blackness. Terrified and alone. Forgetting my name, what I was, what I had been.

But the horror did not go away when Prince Azrar resurrected me, I returned fully aware but trapped in a stone-cold corpse. My own dead body. Unable to move or breathe.

Now I live on borrowed time, masking the fear with alcohol, narcotics and reckless living. This artificial life is wrong, I am an abomination, I am spitting in the face of fate itself. Death wants me back, I have cheated him far too long.

I have brought only darkness to all those who love me. Death's cold embrace calls for me, a lasting more faithful lover then any in life. He grows impatient. I will not keep him waiting...
Jazriel.

The vampire made it clear he did not want to be saved. So why was she here on this godawful assignment, far from home in a remote foreign land?

Why did she have to baby-sit a dangerous and traumatised detoxing vampire junkie? What medical skills did she possess? None. What psychological knowledge? Zero. She didn't even share Khari's respect for the things. She had confronted Lady Eshan and Cardinal Reyes, sparking a mighty row over this unwanted assignment.

"Jazriel has made a connection with you, Gaby," her boss had urged. "You are the only one he trusts. If there is any hope for this creature's redemption, then it is you."

Trust the saintly Reyes to play the emotional blackmail card! It was unfair and it worked. A wretched, drugged-up vampire who did not want to be cleaned up, did not want to live was paired with a human woman who couldn't care less. But that was then.

A friendship, prickly at times but growing had begun between them. The biggest danger, the one thing she knew could destroy their temporary exile together was for her to fall for Jazriel. That would be madness of course. Sheer insanity. It would not happen.

She had been privileged, or more correctly, cursed, to enter his tormented and drug-distorted mind, had touched his long-damaged soul. She had no delusions as to what he was. What he was capable of, and how he used his looks and beguiling charm to make himself desirable, all carefully constructed and well-practised survival tactics of an arch-manipulator.

And how clever he was in making a foolish woman feel special and beautiful - a princess! Especially one emotionally raw and on the rebound from her messy break up with Enver. Unfortunately for Jazriel, he was unable to manipulate her into loving him, she wasn't fooled by his wiles, not for one minute.

Chapter Twelve

Jazriel stepped out onto the dacha's wide wooden veranda, and leaning across a rail gazed without enthusiasm at the night-clad landscape, Zaard, it was so depressing! Miles and miles of nothing. Forests and fields and remote farms. Though a kinder landscape, it might as well be Isolann, it was empty of any diversion!

Jazriel had another cigarette but he was desperate for something more, something stronger. He was here to detox and recover but neither his body or spirit wanted to get clean. How dare these humans try to control and change him! He had so few ways to fight back. Reduced to petty rebellion like chain-smoking and adjusting his music to play loud, setting the ipod to its highest volume and always choosing music he knew Gabrielle did not like. He hoped it was enough of a deterrent to keep her out of his mind. The intrusion was unbearable, a violation. Couldn't he even call his thoughts his own now?

When he had tried to kill himself it was not a cry for help. He had meant it, wanted it. Even though he knew he would be breaking a precious vow. Now he was not so sure. He had put that idea on temporary hold, but he did not want Gabrielle prying, discovering his plans, his life was his own to dispose of as and when he saw fit!

Yet despite the intrusive *Knowing* Jazriel liked the human woman as a friend, one he could perhaps trust. She was of Khari's bloodline, and of the original Queen Khari's bloodline. The fourth of that line to befriend the Dark Kind. But Gabrielle was different, the first human to be able to walk through a vampire's mind, she hadn't admitted it openly to him, but he knew. How else could she have so swiftly gained such insight to his long, troubled life? Did she know about Garan's betrayal and violation? Had she witnessed his humiliation replayed in his mind? Jazriel growled, deeply distressed that anyone else - human or vampire would ever know about that night.

Gabrielle was his friend and his jailer. What else was this dacha in the middle of nowhere but a prison? The guards, the high tec surveillance designed to keep him safe from Nemesis also trapped him here. And Jazriel had enough of protective custody. If he chose to live, he must be free, must be independent again.

He desperately craved all the indulgences and pleasures of his past life. What the hell was a hedonistic, vain and urbanite vampire doing in deepest rural nowhere? He'd gone way too far in New York, he recognised that, but Jazriel was convinced he was back in control of his habit again. A miracle considering his human saviour was torturing him here; weeks of wearing hideous off-the-peg casual clothes, a tedious array of shop-bought jeans, t-shirts and jumpers chosen for him by some unknown human with no taste, probably one of those stern, humourless guards. And all the clothes were made in gruesome peasant materials, cotton and nylon! His body had only known the finest fabrics, bariola velvet, wild silk and whisper-soft cashmere. Jazriel shuddered again with dismay. This was no way for him to live.

And he was so damn hungry! He gagged at the thought of drinking that synthetic crap Eshan's scientists had invented. Artificial human blood - gross! It would keep him alive -just. But at what cost to his self-respect as Dark Kind? He didn't just kill because he had to, he enjoyed it. Dark Kind were ruthless predators, even a commoner sha'ref like himself.

Jazriel's human companion in the past, during that time of adventure, freedom and bliss, had accepted his nature without censure or question. But then, he too had been a predator. Jazriel knew Gabrielle had great difficulty accepting what really lay beneath the chiselled perfection of his features. She had to learn to live with it or leave. He had no intention of living a half-life like Eshan, or becoming Gabrielle's tame lap-dog!

The hours he spent, appearing to drift about, listening to music, drying out, in an attempt to conquer his substance abuse were in fact times of sharp observation, watching the movements of his bodyguards, assessing any weak points in their surveillance. Jazriel was preparing to escape. Not letting Gabrielle pick that from his mind had become a greater challenge then any high electrified fences and trigger-happy guards.

He threw the cigarette butt away. It was time to claim back control of his life, even if it meant losing it.

Which, he had already decided, was frankly no loss.

Chapter Thirteen

Frantic, Eshan called the young human woman on her mobile, responding to her voice with a greeting of genuine warmth and sincerity despite the urgency. Gabrielle had more then paid back the faith she'd placed in her to rescue and care for Jazriel, it had not been an easy burden for any human to bear.

This girl was so different from her grandmother. Khari hid her courage behind a gentle demeanour. a thornless, soft-petalled rose with a steel core to its stem. Gabrielle had thorns, sharp, barbed ones ready to take on her enemies face to face. Fearless and maybe a touch naïve but there was no doubting her valour. Eshan had known from their first meeting, she would not be content to dig in the earth for ancient artefacts anymore. Once Gabrielle knew about Nemesis and their part in her family's tragedy, she would want to fight back.

To prepare and protect her, Eshan had arranged for specialist training at the Spook Squad at Chess Manor. Gabrielle could now out-drive most professional stunt men, handle a wide range of firearms, was an expert in several martial arts and spoke seven languages fluently, including Dark Kind. Khari would have hated the transformation in Gabrielle. The necessary hardening. Hated the brief, torrid relationship she had with the misfit loner Enver Thorne. But these were difficult times, more lawless and uncertain since the start of the world-wide Imadeen Outrages. Protecting Gabrielle was best served by making her less vulnerable, more aware. Preparing her for what may yet come in her lifetime.

As quickly as she could, Eshan explained the situation about the missing Dark Kind, the special one. She used her discretion, not mentioning it was Sivaya who had tipped her off about his whereabouts, there was no point in adding to Jazriel's instability. All that mattered was the unknown Dark Kind's centuries old cover had been broken in Khubbuz and Nemesis was closing in. Fast.

"Two questions, Gabrielle," the female vampire inquired, "Is Jazriel well enough to travel? And how quickly can you get to Khubbuz?

Risking two precious allies by sending them on this crazy mission was insane, Eshan hated having to expose them to discovery but what was rational about any of this? The special one had to be protected, even at such a terrible price, the possible sacrifice of Jazriel and Gabrielle. But what were two lives compared to billions?

"Jaz is far from ready, Lady Eshan," Gabrielle replied truthfully, intrigued by the urgency in the vampire's voice. "He'll cut and run and be using again at the first opportunity." Gabrielle hesitated, she had not told the Lady about Jazriel's third suicide attempt. It was an admission of her failure to help. "Or worse."

"Maybe giving him a purpose, something important to do will help," Eshan replied wearily, knowing she had no choice. Hoping she was right.

Gabrielle found her charge prowling about in the dacha's grounds, his mood was uncharacteristically surly and volatile like a caged panther pacing it's cage. It was clear he didn't want her around. Hurt, she risked stepping into his mind, but backed away quickly in sudden understanding. He was dwelling on Garan's assault again. His mind seethed with an emotional cocktail of anger and hurt, brooding over the betrayal and debasement of his body and spirit. That would explain his need to be alone. It was nothing she had done, but unfortunately there was no time for discretion.

"Do you want to kick some serious Nemesis butt?" Gabrielle announced, sounding ridiculously bright and chirpy like some sort of gun-toting, vampire-loving girl scout. "Eshan has given us an urgent assignment. We have to reach a Dark Kind male in north Amantzk before Nemesis gets to him. We must leave now and travel bloody fast. Khubbuz was the last known sighting and he's gone to ground again. Where would he run to and how do we get there?"

Who the hell was in trouble? The vampire quizzed her but Gabrielle genuinely did not know. Intrigued and anxious for the safety of one of his brethren, Jazriel studied the map she had brought with her. He couldn't read well and the place names were just a blur of squiggly lines, but he recognised rivers and mountain ranges. The unknown vampire would head for the most inhospitable and difficult to approach region. Nemesis was a 21st century outfit, relying on cars and helicopters. He would head for a remote, heavily forested region only accessible on foot or horseback. Or a motorbike!

"We?" Jazriel was adamant. "I will do this alone. You will slow me down."

"Hey! Not so fast, hot shot. Do you think we can let you loose to get scooped up at the same time? Two vamps for the price on one?

"Nemesis won't get me."

"On the evidence of your past record, I beg to differ!" Gabrielle retorted. Since when did Jaz become the taciturn action hero? Gabrielle knew she sounded distrusting and cynical but she was convinced he wanted to travel alone to get back to his old life, to kill and score some coke and then slip free of all human control and interference.

"And what's to stop you buggering off back to the nearest big city lights slaughtering the locals and scoring some nose candy?" she accused outright. Gabrielle pulled his face sharply around towards hers, "Or finally succeed in topping yourself?"

"I must help one of my own kind in danger," Jazriel continued, emphatically shaking her off, his eyes darkening to a dangerous navy. How dare she question his word, his integrity! "Keep the fuck out of my mind, Gabrielle. Give me the dignity of privacy."

"And you were doing so well before," she retorted, her voice heavy with sarcasm. "Where exactly did I find you?"

Jazriel gave a low growl, "I knew what I was doing."

Gabrielle laughed, her voice strained and devoid of humour, "You wanted to sprawl bruised, broken and burnt on a filthy road? Yeah, right."

Jazriel sighed, such a sad, lost sound, it cut straight into Gabrielle's heart. "I wanted to be free."

There was a long uneasy silence. A tension between them that was so tangible, it was almost visible. Then Jazriel reached into his pocket and fetching his case, lit up a cigarette and dropping his head down, took a few long drags. He raised his head, one eyebrow raised quizzically, and with a fleeting smile, his apologetic naughty boy one, "I take it this is our first row as official partners in heroics. Taking on the bad guys, side by side."

"First of many, I suspect," returned Gabrielle with mock severity.

Chapter Fourteen

"Other girls get Bruce Willis or big Arnie to help them save the world. What do I get lumbered with? A ridiculous fashion victim! Hurry up, get your fake-Armani-clad ass down here, now! " Gabrielle muttered darkly, as they loaded a heavily customised 4x4 estate vehicle, fitted with a special area at the back to protect a Dark Kind from harmful sun rays.

"Some action hero," she grumbled, "one that can't do daylight or bad clothes."

Gabrielle had read in her grandmother's journal that Khari thought the vampire's vanity amusing, a charming conceit. Gabrielle thought it as insufferable nuisance! Even with his current 'heroin chic' appearance, he looked bloody gorgeous, she had to admit to herself. No awful clothing could ever distract from those looks. So why this idiotic hold up? "Jazriel!" she shouted up to his bedroom, "You are a prize pain in the backside!"

Jazriel loped slowly down the stairs and into the dacha's immaculate gold shingle courtyard. He ignored the woman's bad mood, helping her lift a cache of weapons into the back of the vehicle. OK, so he had caused a delay, it had been hard to choose what to wear on the expedition, every garment had been equally hideous. This unknown Dark Kind male out there in the darkness could be a new admirer for him. And he had to rescue him looking like an impoverished Amantzki student. A geeky one at that. How much more degradation must he endure?

Gabrielle lifted the last box of provisions and headed for the driving seat. Jazriel opened up the door on her side and firmly held out his hand to her. "I am driving."

"No way, I saw how you handled that Ducati!" Instantly Gabrielle winced as she saw the turquoise eyes darkening with anguish. Idiot woman! She cursed herself for lack of tact, Jazriel had loved that motorbike, so much so, it was the only thing he had trusted to take him out of this life.

"Sorry, Jaz." she murmured, contrite, climbing out of the driving seat.

"It's all right. I guess I had that coming."

'How hard was it to drive a high powered bike into a wall and kill yourself,' he brooded bitterly. Too hard for him to do properly! He forced himself to focus on the task ahead. There had to be a way to stop this self-indulgent fixation on the past. His face lit up with a well-practised reconciliatory smile. "But I can drive much better and faster at night then any human. Even a Lara Croft clone. You must rest, you will clock up enough driving hours after sunrise."

As they left the dacha compound, Gabrielle was appalled to discover Jazriel drove the car without headlights. Or sidelights for that matter – nothing! A terrifying experience at first, until she realised his vampire night vision was far sharper then a human struggling to navigate with only a narrow beam of light illuminating the puddle ahead. But though it was soon evident he was a fast, accurate and highly skilled driver, tearing through the night on badly kept, rural roads in complete darkness was unnerving.

"Get some rest, Gaby," urged the vampire, lighting a cigarette while casually taking a blind bend on two wheels.

"I'll pass on that, Jaz. When the Grim Reaper appears, looking for me, I want to see the bastard coming."

Gabrielle waited till they reached a relatively straight stretch of road. Time to get her mind off the hair-raising drive, perhaps talking about something distressing might make him slow down.

"Jaz," she asked in a quiet voice, "I know this will be difficult and painful for you, but I want to talk about the night we first met. It was full of weirdness.

"Anticipating dredging up memories he'd rather forget, Jazriel raised his cigarette and took a long, deep drag. There was no point trying to change the subject, Gabrielle was like a terrier with a rat once a notion came into her head. She often reminded him of his past lover, Sivaya, when the times were good between them. Sivaya had been a she-cat, feisty and headstrong. He had liked that.

"Do you remember the night?"

"Hardly like to forget it," replied Jazriel, his normally honeyed voice harshened with unease. He had no intention of discussing his disastrously inept attempt at suicide with any human. Or any Dark Kind for that matter!

"I know the night was crazy but two very odd things happened. I don't think you were thrown clear of the bike from impact, I could swear you were lifted clear off the back seconds before it crashed."

"By an invisible, strong, and very fast man?" Jazriel shrugged with complete dismissal. "Happens all the time!"

Gabrielle was not normally fanciful by nature. He wondered where the hell she was going with this conversation. He let go of the steering wheel to light another cigarette, swerving past a deer in the road, steering with his knee. Gabrielle gasped with fright, clinging onto her seat with fear-whitened knuckles.

"What's wrong? I missed Bambi didn't I?"

Gabrielle paused, waiting for her hammering heart to climb down from her throat to return to its rightful place and rhythm. Why was she worried about Nemesis? This maniac would finish her off long before she ran into any nasties out there. 'Yes, Lady Eshan,' she thought, 'I will go on a perilous, life-threatening mission accompanied only by a truckload of guns and ammo, and a suicidal vampire junkie. Easy on the eye? Yes. Sane? Definitely not.'

But then how rational was she to agree to the mission in the first place? With her composure as recovered as it was going to be, she pressed on. "There was something else. When you were lying in the road, a man appeared, like a ghost. I could hardly hear him speak but he was pleading with me to help you. He reached out his hand towards you with so much love in his eyes." Added with self doubt, "There might have been a woman too. Small, dark-haired, standing beside him."

Jazriel grew tense, his eyes darkened. "Humans?"

Gabrielle nodded and carefully described the male apparition. "And I know this sounds crazy, but I could swear I could smell the sea, I could hear it; the creak of a ship, the sound of the wind in rigging and sails. Stupid, but I'm damned sure it was all there."

She laughed, uneasily. "Maybe it was just my over-active imagination. It was a very strange night after all."

It was too much for Jazriel. He braked hard and pulled over to the side of the road. His head dropped into his hands, unable to weep, his whole body shuddering with emotion. He knew who it was. A friend, a real friend from the past. More then a friend, someone who had the ability to reach out across the centuries to find him, to help him. As he had once promised he would. *"I'll never leave you, mi amante, never."* Jazriel closed his eyes murmuring, his voice choking with emotion in the vampire language, "So sorry, so sorry, mi corazon, ashari seymahl, I have broken my vow to you, so sorry."

Gabrielle's vision meant that he was worth something, worth more than a tryst with a brick wall and an incinerating fireball. He had friends, human friends who had once loved him as much as he had loved them. Still loved, as Dark Kind, past and present blended into one. He would go on living. For them.

For him.

Chapter Fifteen

Gred, a small country town in Northern Amantzk

Lev watched from the ringside as the Boss went through his nightly routine whenever the circus was performing; the almost obsessive checking of guide wires and ground pegs, of trapeze ropes and safety nets.

Nothing escaped the vampire's sharp vision, his deep understanding of all the Big Top's mechanisms honed over many decades. Lev hoped his understanding of the human mind was as acute. The foreman waited till the Boss paused in his routine then crossed the fresh, clean sawdust in the main ring. Born into the circus life from a family travelling with the Xenari for forty years, Lev loved the clean, pine smell of the newly laid sawdust. To him it symbolised a constant renewal, each night fresh sawdust was laid down before the performance started, as if the circus was reborn fresh and alive.

Lev caught the Boss's eye, with no outsiders around the vampire had removed his dark glasses and worked openly as Dark Kind. Maybe a risky move but understandable. The foreman could not imagine living for centuries in constant hiding and fear of discovery.

"We were lucky in Khubbuz, please, don't do that again Boss!"

"I agree, my friend," Diego replied, his face grim with anxiety. Why had he been drawn to that damn town? It had only brought misery for his troupe, and it wasn't over yet. The nagging sense of time running out had not left him, as if something was closing in on him, following, getting closer. Had it been a test, a party trick engineered by his K'elphin mentors to gauge his readiness? Well, if their kind had a Hell, they could go rot there. Diego was done being their obedient puppet, he was a Dark Kind warrior, his first allegiance was with his species, beyond his duty to the troupe. Always had been!

The debacle had left the circus in disarray, demoralised and worse of all, seriously short of funds. After a disastrous year financially, Khubbuz was the much needed last boost of income the Yasuul needed to get through the lean winter months. Reluctantly and against all his instincts, Diego was forced by circumstance to allow the circus to play a few more venues. As remote as possible. Gred was high in the Illurian mountain range, the unimportant centre of a scattered, backward rural community. One whose inhabitants were ethnically different to those of Khubbuz, with a history of age-old mutual loathing, erupting into occasional murderous hostility. Perfect!

"It's not over yet, is it Boss?" murmured Lev, instinctively glancing to his lorry where his wife would be getting Remai ready for the night's performance. Diego shrugged, returning to tugging at the rigging, checking for any danger to his artists. In truth, he had no idea. "All we can do is be vigilant."

Chapter Sixteen

"How many did they kill?"

Eshan switched off her phone, ice cold with rage. It was all out war now. Nemesis had raided the private sanatorium where her people had cared for Cameron Devane, killing doctors and nurses in their ruthless attack. Zaard! The bastards had finally shown their true colours. Amela Railton's death could have been construed as an accident, there had never been proof that it was not, but there was nothing accidental about machine-gunning innocents. And they hated the Dark Kind for being ruthless murders? Hypocrites!

Nemesis was a new malevolent enemy under Hain. Faster to act, infinitely more ruthless; better equipped and with a frighteningly accurate intelligence network. Never before had Eshan felt at such a disadvantage. This kidnapping of Devane was deeply disturbing. Why had they taken him? How did they know he could sense the presence of Dark Kind? Realisation froze her blood further. Her hand went involuntarily to her throat, they wanted a human bloodhound to search out the unknown Dark Kind, the one who had revealed himself in Khubbuz. And with Cam Devane on a leash, they would succeed!

And what of Gabrielle? Eshan was determined she must not face more peril, there was no doubt Devane would kill his own daughter. What a tangled mess! This was like a grotesque game of chess where all was being risked to protect the king. Eshan already had a panicking Alejandro Reyes on the phone seemingly every few minutes, terrified that Gabrielle and Sivaya were being unnecessarily compromised. He seemed less concerned about Jazriel, as if he was expendable. Yet Reyes was adamant the unknown vampire must be kept safe. How else then could she achieve that aim? This was desperate race against time, against a well-informed, well-prepared and ruthless enemy. There was only one option. Eshan must act fast and decisively. The consequences of failure were too dire to dwell on.

Should she phone Jazriel in Amantzk? It was a huge risk, he was psychologically dependent on his narcotics, so much so Gabrielle was convinced he would cut and run at the first opportunity. But the old Jaz had always been trustworthy and honourable. Was that loyal, brave being there beneath the drug-induced wreckage? Eshan made her decision, Dialled.

Rome

Reyes brusquely ushered his operatives out of his office, locked the door. Once alone the burden of his unwanted duty crushed down on his soul with brutal force. He sank heavily to the floor, wept openly into his hands. Pleading unheard to his elders to be freed of his responsibilities, of living with the on-going, relentless nightmare, one that begun on a clear, perfect spring day on his home world, one that had followed him to this place of exile. This beautiful planet with its wonderful human inhabitants.

One human in particular. Gabrielle. Thrown into extreme danger at Eshan's orders with his reluctant agreement. "No, please not Gabrielle." He prayed to whomever, whatever was listening. He had lost one daughter to the Enemy. He could not bear to lose the woman he loved as another daughter to the vindictive scum of Nemesis. But what choice was there? Fate or sheer bad luck had meant Gabrielle was closest to the endangered special one. The blood drinker Reyes' people had hidden for centuries. The Earth's only chance of survival, its unlikely champion. He had to be protected, at all cost. But please, he pleaded again, not with Gabrielle's life, that would be too cruel a blow. Reyes had never felt so old, so utterly helpless.

At least Sivaya was also close by. Now her grief-driven madness had abated, the vampire woman was tough, resourceful and focused.

A successful survivor who did not take foolish chances. Unlike the other one, Reyes shuddered at having to think about Jazriel. The debauched creature's self-indulgent excesses spread far beyond narcotic abuse. He was addicted to killing, a fox running wild in a hen house. Prince Azrar had known, had kept him on a tight leash. As had the human. The pirate. Now nothing controlled him, he could break free at any opportunity to create more havoc, slaughter more innocents. A massacre triggered by little more then boredom. There was but one comfort for Reyes. In the great scheme of things, Jazriel did not matter, he was unimportant. His life was dispensable.

Chapter Seventeen

The countryside beyond Gred, Amantzk

"Why is that wretched thing here?"

Dave Dent, Geddoe's second-in-command grunted his disapproval. An ambitious man, one who Geddoe instinctively distrusted and watched like a hawk. He ignored the man's scorn and passed a bottle of water through a metal grill to their unwilling and silent guest. The front part of the armoured truck they travelled in was air-conditioned and comfortable but it had a caged-off section to the rear, where a man sat huddled on the floor, imprisoned.

"He's clearly deranged and hasn't spoken a coherent word since my arrival."

Geddoe ignored the strident and self-opinionated man, one who did not believe in vampires. Was he in for a rude awakening! Geddoe was certain the man in the back, 'rescued' from a private clinic, was in shock. Geddoe himself had brutally forced him from the security and comfort that had sheltered him for three decades. With the aid of masked and armed men, had been bundled roughly into a helicopter and was now incarcerated in this armoured truck. Enough to unsettle a sane man, and Cameron Devane was far from sane.

"This is our secret weapon, our winning hand," Geddoe explained through gritted teeth. The heavy-set Australian, Dent, didn't believe in vampires, how would he react to learning about Cameron Devane, the human blood hound? "He has the unique and unsettling ability to sense the presence of the Dark Kind, he can literally tune into their mind waves. Probably something to do with the electricity in their brains."

"I've never heard such nonsense," spluttered Dent vehemently, "More of Hain's demented pursuit of fairy tales!"

"I wouldn't be so bloody insulting," snapped Geddoe, though he himself also found their mutual employer repellent. Dent was another paid lackey. In his view, a not very bright one. "Hain is lining your bank balance well enough." Geddoe sneered, "A little respect would not go amiss."

Dent shrugged, indifferent to his commander's opinion, he was just another enforcer, a minion of Hain. A vicious sociopath dancing to Hain's every insane whim. Dent wanted to keep in with him but could not control his open contempt. Especially when confronted by the wretched and unnerving spectacle of a deranged man, restrained in the back of a lorry by leather straps.

"Is all the heavy-duty bondage necessary?"

Geddoe nodded curtly, nursing the bruises and bite marks he'd incurred moving Devane from the helicopter to the lorry. "Too right it is, but you can take them off if you doubt me."

Dent blanched, cringed away as Geddoe pulled back his sleeve, exposing a mass of livid purple and black bruises with the clear indentations of teeth marks.

"He's a maniac. But a damned useful one. If any of those fanged bastards are within five miles of this man, we will know." Geddoe leant across to speak to the driver, another one of Hain's elite team of private commandos. "Pull over, I need a piss and we all need a short break from this bloody tedious travelling."

The convoy of trucks and armoured cars drove onto the headland of an unfenced, arid field, leaving their prisoner whining wordlessly in the back of the truck. The team took turns to step into the bushes, smoked and made taciturn small talk, pretending to relax, that this was nothing more then a training exercise. Trying unsuccessfully to ignore the animal-like sounds of demented distress from the main truck.

Dent walked a few yards away, shaking his head. Had the world gone completely mad? First Hain, now his commander actually believed in these so-called Dark Kind, in vampires! He lifted his head to the sunshine, closing his eyes; let the warmth and light caress his face, opened his senses to the sounds of bird song, the smell of pine trees carried on the humid air. This was reality, not the fantasy world of blood-drinking monsters!

Dent heard a distant rumble of thunder, opened his eyes and watched as fast moving, lead-grey and ugly-yellow storm clouds gathered their forces on the horizon. His heart sank lower. His reality was turning into a horror film, a cheap, clichéd over-the-top drama where thunderstorms always accompanied every coming terror. His body reacted with a shiver of fear as the shackled man in the back of the lorry suddenly began to wail, a loud, incoherent animal sound, a low bellow at first, rising higher to a ululating scream. A primeval resonance that curdled the marrow of Dent's bones.

Geddoe ran over, excited, gesticulating wildly, his face animated, eyes shining. "Back in the lorries, all of you. Dent! Move it. Move it! We've got one!"

Chapter Eighteen

Nightfall

Sheet lightning strafed the night sky above the dusty concrete, disused factories and near-derelict residential blocks of a small Amantzki town, Gred. It had been the last reported location of the Yasuul. Sitting alone in the car, parked on the outskirts, drawing the attention of a pack of thin, mangy, semi-feral dogs, Jazriel's mind raced with indecision. He had a chance to break free of this humiliating control, to live his life exactly how he wanted.

There were two routes that Nemesis could have taken to intercept the Yasuul. He was ordered to follow one, Gabrielle the other. The Lady had assured him Gabrielle would be protected and Eshan never lied. All he had to do was ignore Eshan's command and go, so what was keeping him on this tedious mission? Nothing! The unknown Dark Kind had plenty of help eluding Nemesis's clutches, a whole tribe of loyal gypsies, perhaps some of Eshan's tough agents. And there was the formidable Gabrielle! What use was one unstable vampire? And as for the pretence of looking for a new admirer. Mierda! Forget that! He'd had a wake up call in New York, a stark reminder that Jazriel's heart would always belong to someone else. Always. This mission was over, he was not needed.

He slipped the phone back into the pocket of the revolting faded denim jacket he'd been forced to wear. Lady Eshan's timing was perfect, Gabrielle had wandered into a nearby parade of tired-looking shops in the town, looking for fresh food and some clues to whether the Nemesis team had already driven through Gred. Knowing their lack of subtlety and arrogance, it would have been a conspicuous convoy of expensive all-terrain vehicles. Not hard to miss.

He hated that she had gone alone, and hoped she was able to communicate with the locals. Gabrielle spoke Russian but this was a remote town, proud of its independence, its own language and was hostile to its neighbours, to the memories of Soviet rule. But they both knew he would have been a liability, his handsome, sharp-boned features might remind someone, a rash Khubbuzi visitor perhaps, of the circus magician.

The throaty sound of an old well-worn motorbike engine snapped him into action, a bike would be perfect to help him move quickly. And alone. He jumped out of the car, straight into the road, causing the rider to swerve and brake abruptly. The biker was justifiably livid. Raising his fists, he strode over to confront the young fool standing in the middle of the road. Jazriel considered killing him but reasoned it would take too long to hide the body, instead, he reached into his jacket and pulled out a wallet stuffed with an extravagant wadge of local currency. Within seconds, Jazriel was roaring off on a battered old Honda 750cc.

And one inhabitant of Gred walked away, considerably happier and richer, not knowing how close he had been to losing more then a motorbike.

The sodding little shit! Gabrielle cursed, furious. She kicked a tyre, cursed again, her arms tightening around the bundle of supplies. She knew Jazriel was unstable, desperate for a fix, but she never thought he'd abandon her in the middle of nowhere! Vampire or not she hoped for his sake, he never ran into her again, she'd wear his damn fangs as earrings!

Dumping the packages into the back she received a call from Eshan who seemed surprisingly calm. "But I'm stuck out here alone!" Gabrielle protested, ready to turn the car around and head for the nearest airport. The damn vamps could sort out their own bloody problems.

"You are not, Gabrielle," the vampire woman attempted to soothe her understandable anger and panic, "Jazriel's mission plan has been altered, that is all. Keep your phone on till the satellite can find you. I'll direct you to where a Dark Kind woman, Sivaya, is waiting for you."

Change of mission? Not a word of warning, not even a goodbye! OK, so the idiot's fangs were safe, Gabrielle seethed, but maybe not other treasured parts of his intimate anatomy!

Wanting to be well clear of this miserable town and its suspicious inhabitants, Gabrielle began to alter the car seat to suit her shorter height, when she found a scrap of paper fallen between the car's hand brake and the seat. She struggled to decipher the child-like mis-spelt spidery scrawl in the dim glow of the car's interior light. No one else could have written a brief message quite so badly. At least she knew it was genuine, a perfectly written note from Jazriel would have been a fake!

"gabrel eshn sed I am too tak th norf rode yu too tak th eest rode I wil b alryte yu wil hav gipsees too hlp yu
jazriel"

"Yeah, right" Gabrielle said screwing up the note and throwing it on the floor of the car. "And Eshan reckons he will meet up with me after the mission, back here, at Gred. Who's she kidding? Sorry Eshan, you're pet vamp junkie has buggered off. That's the last we'll see of him!"

Hating herself for already missing him, Gabrielle started the car. Had no choice but to drive on alone.

Chapter Nineteen

'When was it going to end?' Remai wept to herself, 'What had they done? Why were they being hounded and harried?' She had heard rumours, anxious whispers spreading rapidly through the troupe that the circus was being followed. But the Yasuul had already endured hard-pressed travelling to put distance from Gred, so who could be pursuing them and why?

Remai sat huddled and frightened at the back of the family lorry, while her parents took turns to drive. The flight from Khubbuz had been bad enough, the fearful, crazy scramble to get animals and equipment stowed. The exhausting headlong rush to get as many miles from the town as possible.

It had not been much better in Gred. The performances there to full houses had gone without incidence but there was a fearful, wary atmosphere when the shows were over and the troupe speedily dismantling the circus. An anxiety that had spread to the youngest children and the livestock, with fractious babies refusing to settle, the horses baulking at loading back into the lorries.

'When is it going to be safe?' thought Remai. After leaving Gred, the Yasuul had not stopped, driving further and further along atrocious roads, never staying long enough to rest beyond what was needed for the livestock. The Boss never put lives at risk, human or animal. All trusted him without question or doubt but this headlong escape from danger pushed his consideration for them to the limit. He had never demanded so much from them before.

Now even the weather was turning against them. The cold, dry wind that had followed them all the way from Khubbuz had dropped and an oppressive humidity claimed its place. Growing tension in the dank air all day and a steady build-up of heavy yellow-green clouds led to an inevitable storm rolling in across the mountains. Remai had watched nature's pyrotechnics in nervous awe earlier in the evening; there was no rain, no thunder only arcing sheets of eye-burning white lightning scorched across the sky, briefly illuminating the surrounding mountains.

Once the blinding flashes had ceased, the rain had began. Remai could not remember experiencing such dreadful torrential rain, even worse then the time in Bulgaria when the lorries had mired down and the Boss had to ride and lead the horses to safety. She would never forget that night when she had to trust her much-loved llama would follow the horses and not be lost in the storm. Tonight the llama had been hard to settle in the beast wagon, moaning in that strange mournful way of his species when nervous. Whatever was upsetting the humans had infected the animals too. Lina's dogs whined and howled, the Arab stallions stamped and fretted in their horse box. Only the Iberian horses stayed calm, but even their large, dark eyes showed wariness and unease, their ears flicking back and forth, alert for danger.

The lorry braked violently, Remai was thrown from the bed onto the floor, heard shouting and gunshots. Father! She scrambled to her feet and leapt out the back of the vehicle to a scene of mayhem.

An ambush! A number of vehicles had blocked the circus in completely across a narrow pass. Black-clad men in masks, all with guns, leapt from them and shouting abuse in some unknown language. Remai saw her father start to stride towards them, "No! No!" she screamed. "Stop, Papa!" Her mother grabbed at Lev's arm, pulled him back.

The attackers ran up to the circus lorries, shouting commands no-one understood. Hauling women and children from their vehicles, the attackers pushed them with their rifle butts, forcing them to walk in front as living shields. The Boss leapt down from the cab of his lorry, his battered old rifle raised at what appeared to be the leader.

"They are looking for me, my friends", Diego commanded, his voice a harsh wolf growl, "keep calm and you will be safe."

A thin-faced man swaggered forward, gestured with one hand. Instantly Diego was surrounded by armed men, aiming their weapons at his head.

"Drop the gun, or your gypo friends will pay with their lives."

Diego snarled with impotent fury, duty bound as a Dark Kind warrior to protect those under his care, he was compelled to fight to the death to defend them, but that would mean casualties among those he was sworn to protect. The answer to his dilemma was humiliation, those damned K'elphin would be proud of him as he turned his back on his warrior heritage to throw the rifle onto the ground, uttering a snarling vampire curse.

The man, satisfied Diego was secured, stepped forward and shone a bright torch into his face, enjoying the gasp of horror from the gypsies as their leader cringed back in pain, trying to shield his night-bred eyes from the brutal light. On seeing his reaction, Geddoe braved a closer inspection, roughly grabbing Diego's face with a Kevlar-gloved hand to turn it towards him, shining the torch directly into his captive's eyes.

Diego's Dark Kind instinct overruled his discretion, he snarled at the insulting assault and unwittingly baring his fangs, raked at the gloved hands.

Anticipating an attack, the human backed off with surprising speed.

"We've got one!" Geddoe crowed in exultation, "A vampire! We've got it! Get metal shackles on it now and shoot dead any bloody gypo who tries to stop us."

Diego fought hard with fists and fangs, his greater strength, agility and vampire ferocity may have succeeded but his attempt at freedom was halted abruptly by Geddoe. He had Remai by the throat, a pistol pressed into her forehead, hard enough to break the skin. White-faced with fear and pain, blood pouring from the wound, she pleaded with her beloved Boss to fight on. He could not. Remai was a girl child, her life sacrosanct. He would also inevitably trigger harm to the other humans who relied on him. Diego was made to defend, to protect.

Geddoe's gamble had paid off; the intelligence about Dark Kind honour was correct. This creature had looked after his human troupe for centuries, he would not let them come to any harm. Even at the expense of his own life.

Swaggering, Geddoe threw a triumphal glance towards his second in command, Dent, the moron who didn't believe in vampires. Bloody hell, he had one! The full force of his success flooded through him, every nerve end bristling with excitement. That's why he was the leader, why Dent was a minion, a useless wannabee. Geddoe turned his attention back to his snarling captive.

"My name is Geddoe; you are now the property of the Nemesis Corporation."

Before he could answer, Diego was kicked to the ground by five of the assailants. With Remai in danger, the Yasuul looked on, horrified and helpless as he was brutally beaten up, shackled and roughly thrown into a lorry. It drove away without waiting for the rest of the squad. The circus women began an eerie mourning, an ancient and visceral song of total despair at seeing their boss taken away. To his death.

Geddoe shouted and swore at them to stop, the sound a disturbing, unearthly racket. The women did not understand his words and grieved on, he fired several shots from his pistol into the ground close to them. The lament stopped. He'd had enough of these vampire-loving primitives. He walked briskly towards his armoured car, pushing the child in front of him again, holding the pistol to her forehead.

"A bit of extra insurance," he sneered at the circus troupe. "We'll leave her on the road unharmed once we've put some safe distance behind us."

He curtly addressed his men, "Shoot out all the tyres and fuel tanks. I want every vehicle immobilised." He opened the door to his car and the child saw her chance. She squirmed from his grip and bit down hard into his arm. Roaring with anger, he let go of her. Instantly Remai sprinted away, running for her father. Enraged, Geddoe lifted the pistol and without hesitation shot her in the back.

Stillness stretched into a long, silent scream, shattered by a disbelieving howl of agony from the child's parents, from the others. Unconcerned, callous, Geddoe got into his car. Behind him, gunshots raked tyres, ignited petrol tanks, exploding, drowning the screams of those humans and animals caught in the inferno. Geddoe did not look back. A few dead gypsies did not matter. It was not even collateral damage. His mission was to capture a vampire and bloody hellfire! He had one!

Chapter Twenty

Her teeth clenched tightly in concentration, Gabrielle followed a difficult route up through the winding mountain track. In her mind it was barely wide enough for a lightly laden and very thin donkey, but the deeply rutted tyre tracks clearly showed many lorries had travelled this route recently.

Once again she cursed Jaz for deserting her; she needed the idiot's sharp night vision to venture further along this route with no idea what waited in the darkness. It could be Nemesis. Or a lynch mob of Hammer horror film peasants doing a spot of vampire hunting. Precious little else to while away the winter nights out here!

"Bloody marvellous," she groaned as the heavens opened, driving rain and mud thrown up onto her windscreen obstructing her already limited vision. Even with careful driving, her vehicle lurched alarmingly across the ruts, rapidly filling with more water. She did not dare glance across to the edge of the track, the darkness at least hid the sheer drop awaiting her if she over-steered or took a corner badly. And what if she met a vehicle coming down? There was no way she was going to reverse down this mountain track to find a passing space! And she was never going to moan about British weather again, this rain was awful beyond words.

Common sense shouted for her to stop till the pounding cloudburst was over but this mission had already overstepped any boundary of reason. Instead, Gabrielle exhausted by the danger and the intense concentration, pressed on. Maybe it was a good thing to be alone after all, at least she was responsible for her own fate driving up this nightmarish, flooded track. Jaz would have reached for a cigarette or gazed lovingly at himself in a mirror and driven the lorry over the edge to plummet to fiery disaster into the ravine. Maybe someone was looking after her.

Whoever it was came up trumps, Gabrielle reached the top of the mountain road and braked, to take in the new terrain. Lit by flashes of vivid sheet lightning a winding valley stretched ahead, the road following the route of a swift-flowing river swollen by the rains. "Please, keep the avalanches and flash floods away," she prayed. Lit by her headlights was a stand of wind-bent, straggly, silver birch trees, the meeting place arranged by Eshan. Gabrielle drove to the spinney, parked and waited. And waited.

"Let me drive, we have little time!"

Gabrielle's heart burst out of her chest as a female voice sounded suddenly beside her. She whipped around to see a woman. Dark Kind. Sivaya. There was no mistaking her. Every word describing her in Khari's journal was true. The wild she-cat, Jazriel's ex lover. Unexpectedly Gabrielle quelled a wave of possessive jealousy as the vampire woman glared at her, raw hostility burning from her eyes. She was beautiful, with her gilded halo of waist-length hair, like a hard-edged kick-ass angel, one with fangs. Though she knew her throat was safe from their razor-sharp edges, Gabrielle was relieved there were no sign of them. It was small comfort, there were many other ways of disposing of an unwanted human.

Remembering her vampire etiquette, Gabrielle leapt out of the car and dropped to her knees, ignoring the mud, she briefly touched the sodden ground with her forehead before addressing Sivaya in her own language, "I wear the golden dragon of King Dezarn."

Sivaya had already noted the human female's golden eyes, this was the one Eshan had sent to help her, but Khari's granddaughter had arrived alone. Relief and sorrow merged into one confusing emotion. Sivaya had steeled herself for a fraught showdown with Jazriel and he was not here.

"Get off the ground, human. You will get filthy," Sivaya snapped, impatient and derisive. "I am a commoner. You do not need to bow to me."

"Pleased to meet you too, Sivaya," Gabrielle muttered through gritted teeth. Bloody vamps!

She got to her feet aware she was shaking badly as she took her place in the passenger seat. This was not a 'tame' Dark Kind like Eshan, or a weakened, damaged and needy one like Jaz, but a fierce and hostile creature with no time for any unknown humans.

Sivaya started up the engine and pulling away from the spinney, negotiated the descent of the mountain road.

"Where is Jazriel?" the female vampire demanded abruptly, suspicion darkening her eyes further. She looked beyond Gabrielle into the darkness, her anxiety and disappointment apparent to the human woman's new sensitivity to vampire emotions.

"I wish I knew. The idiot stole a motorbike. Left me a note. Apparently Eshan sent him to look for the Yasuul on a different route." Gabrielle had her own idea where he was, halfway to Prague and another downward spiral of self-destruction but she kept quiet. 'You want to go to Hell, Jaz?' she thought bitterly, 'well, enjoy the journey, I'm not going to pull you out of the flames a second time.'

"He wrote a note?" Sivaya raised a quizzical eyebrow, not surprised he had disappeared into the night. He was always reckless, so eager to prove his courage and valour. No one had ever disputed these, just his judgement. "Are you serious?"

"Well, sort of a note," Gabrielle admitted, suppressing a weary smile. In other circumstances Sivaya's astonishment would have been amusing, this creature was only too aware of Jazriel's lack of academic prowess. But this was no time for levity.

The two females had one thing in common. Being abandoned by Jazriel. Gabrielle had learnt from Khari's journal and from her own *Knowing* about how the grief-maddened Sivaya preserved her lover's body after his death, unwittingly trapping his spirit in a frightening hellish limbo. Azrar had re-united the perfectly preserved body with Jazriel's lost soul. The memory of the darkness, the near oblivion had badly scarred Jazriel, he never wanted to see Sivaya again.

In Gabrielle's human eyes that seemed an unnecessarily cruel and harsh punishment to one who adored him. Surely her only crime was to love Jaz so much that grasping at a forlorn hope of his revival, she could not bear to give his body to the flames?

Gabrielle had only known Jaz as a living being, a damaged mess but very much alive. She shuddered at the thought of the years his spirit had spent in bewildering nothingness, while his corpse had lain in some Berlin bomb ruins. But without Sivaya's intervention, he would not be here at all, so why was he so hostile to a woman he once claimed to have loved?

Curiosity urged Gabrielle to ask, common sense kept her mouth shut!

"Does he still spend hours in front of a mirror before going out?" Sivaya ventured. Why couldn't her kind be able to switch off their emotions? To go on loving Jazriel was a cruel, unchanging torture. Sivaya knew it was best to not talk about him, but this human knew him, had spent time with him and knowing Jaz's wiles, no doubt foolishly thought she was in love with him. A sha'ref survival trick, one Sivaya had often wondered about. Had she also fallen for it? Was that why she had sacrificed her sanity over a male who was not and never had been in love with her?

"It has been hard for him lately." Gabrielle replied, not hiding the edge of sarcasm from her voice. "We whisked him away from New York without his extensive wardrobe of designer clothes. He claims we've been torturing him, brutally forcing him to wear ghastly rags. Inflicting the full horror of shop-bought clothes on him."

Sivaya's face softened for a brief second before recovering her composure. "What exactly happened in New York?"

Gabrielle was uncomfortable, nervous at what to say. Did this ferocious creature really want to know about the misery and degradation her ex-lover had deliberately put himself through? His long drawn out suicide attempt?

"I did my best to keep him off it, you know," Sivaya stated, the bitterness rising through the layers of self-control. "All that human-made crap. He will never stop over-indulging. It will kill him one day."

"So, to prevent it, what will make Jaz happy?" Gabrielle snapped, surprised with herself at her own reaction. Maybe she wasn't so ready to write him off after all? This could be a chance to gain some insight into his psyche, something deeper, beyond what she had learnt during the brief journeys into his confused, grieving mind.

Sivaya did not answer. Concentrated on the road ahead. This was Dark Kind business. Jazriel had been created with a flawed design, a sexual plaything that yearned for a higher destiny. A Dark Kind sha'ref who needed to be unconditionally loved as an equal. She had tried to be his special love, to be all he dreamed off, far better then that arrogant Prince Azrar and far more suitable then the other one in his past! Her gorge rose at the thought of it! The human one whose name she could not bear to utter, even in her mind. A human! Her mind reeled with the insanity, Jazriel had loved a human! Sivaya's relationship with him had been a one sided affair. Jazriel had been in love, but not with her. Never with her.

Not that they didn't have several superficially happy centuries together. Carefree and exciting but never satisfying enough for Jazriel. He craved sensation, intensity, danger. And most impossible of all, he craved passion. Hence these crazy adventures with humans, trying to find a place in the world, one different to the one he was created for. And these escapades always ended badly. How could they not? Jazriel was out of his depth dealing with the continuous lies and treacheries of humans. Beautiful, brave but not very bright. Would he ever learn?

The two women continued their journey in a terse silence until vehicle lights in the distance caught their attention. By rights it should be the Yasuul. But equally, it could be a Nemesis team. There was no time for caution.

Gabrielle tucked a pistol into her belt, another in the inner pocket of her jacket as Sivaya drove on, accelerating, risking even greater speed along the rock-strewn, flood damaged road.

Chapter Twenty-one

Gabrielle swore as shockwaves from explosions down in the valley rocked the car. This was bad, very bad. Sivaya growled, her fangs lowered, as she put her foot down hard, forcing the car beyond its capabilities. As it weaved and swerved precariously through the darkness, Gabrielle gripping hard, she could see that even at this suicidal speed, the action was still a couple of difficult miles away, the Yasuul and its Dark Kind boss was in serious trouble. They may be too late.

Ten, fifteen minutes later, Sivaya hit the brakes hard. A man stood in the road, aiming a rifle at the car. She hauled at the steering wheel, trying to swing the vehicle around him but there were others now, surrounding it, all with rifles. Gabrielle was furious at her own blundering. 'That's right Gaby,' she berated herself, 'just let the crazy vamp woman drive you straight into danger. Forget everything Enver and the Spook squad team taught you.'

As Sivaya switched off the car's engine, Gaby quickly tried to assess the men surrounding her. Nemesis? Their rifles were a motley collection of ancient museum relics; most of the stern faces glaring at her were of Asiatic origin. The Yasuul. A wiry, middle-aged man stepped forward, speaking in an unknown language. It was clear he knew Sivaya. He bowed his head in deference to her.

The vampire woman was distraught, furious, pounded the steering wheel with her fists. "Nemesis! The bastards ambushed the circus. There have been deaths." She paused, growling in distress. "They have taken Diego."

"I am so sorry," Gabrielle manage to utter, feeling helpless in the face of this bad news. This no longer felt like a wild, exciting adventure. Innocents were suffering.

"Get out," snapped Sivaya, "His humans have failed Diego. This is Dark Kind business."

Gabrielle started to protest, but stopped at a gypsy's approach, his face was carved from misery, his body tense with anger. He pulled the car door open and gestured for her to get out. One murderous, armed man and a vicious vampire against one ex-archaeologist…no contest. She jumped out of the car.

"What do you want, Lev?" Sivaya snarled, "What were you doing when they took Diego? Juggling?"

"Drive on, Lady," he muttered, climbing into the car beside her, his voice and manner set in stone, defiantly unafraid of the vampire's fangs. He was living in hell, nothing more could frighten him. He gestured for Gabrielle to get into the back which she did with bad grace, what was it with all this ordering around? Who did they think she was? An archaeologist?

As they arrived at the line of circus lorries, Gabrielle felt ashamed of her childish pique, her heart hammering in shock as they drove through a war zone. She turned her head away at the blanket covered shapes on the ground, all with distraught, weeping families beside them. The screams of disbelief and anguish from the bereaved gypsies cutting sharply into Gabrielle's soul. Was it possible to hate Hain and his Nemesis drones any more then she did? Hate was a corrosive emotion, it destroyed all it touched. But what else could she feel at the sight of those pathetic, shrouded and forever-still bundles lying on the muddy roadside. Choking grief rose in her throat, there had been bloodied shrouded bundles at Whitethorn

"I have medical supplies" Gabrielle managed to mutter feebly to Lev, feeling helpless in the midst of the horror. The man nodded bleakly, pointing to a hastily thrown up tent, now a makeshift hospital.

Sivaya growled with impatience, her hands tightened on the steering wheel, she had no patience for this human time-wasting. "I am going now. Leave or stay, I am not waiting a second more."

"Not without me," Lev roared back, his voice breaking with emotion. "I will have revenge for my wife and daughter. I must rescue my Boss from danger."

He pointed to two blood-stained shrouded forms beside the hospital tent. One distressingly small.

"Your family?" whispered Gabrielle, her heart wrenching with sorrow for the man. Lev nodded curtly, his broad hand roughly wiping away tears. "You will take me with you."

Gabrielle got out of the vehicle, walked to the back and removed a new automatic rifle from the boot; taking it to Lev, she pressed the modern weapon into his hands. "Sivaya is right, we must move now if we are to catch them."

Lev nodded, grateful for the young foreign woman's determination. Sivaya dropped her head, lowered her eyes to hide their troubled darkening, she was fond of Remai, remembering the courageous welcome the young girl had given her. Recovering her fierce poise, Sivaya declared, "Nemesis will still be travelling in their convoy of vehicles, it's too difficult a terrain around here for helicopters to land. They will be heading for the flat farmlands beyond this valley. There is very little time."

She had neither the time nor inclination for small talk with this latest manifestation of golden-eyed human. Turning to Gabrielle she demanded, "Eshan said you would be well armed."

Gabrielle threw open the boot of her car to display a small but effective portable arsenal. Sivaya nodded her approval. "We leave now but Lev - I'll drive."

What was it with these creatures and driving? Gabrielle mused dourly, sitting in the back seat and double checking her seat belt was tight and secure, gesturing to Lev that he did the same. Did the vampires get some sort of satisfaction proving they could out-perform mere humans? Or some sick pleasure in frightening the bejaysus out of them?

Gabrielle braced herself for another hair-raising high speed journey in total darkness, distracting herself from Sivaya's driving by thinking up all the things she would do to Jaz's elegant, perfect anatomy, if she ever caught up with him!

Chapter Twenty-Two

They drove in tense silence through the night, closing the gap with their enemies with every hard-pushed, difficult muddy mile. Nemesis had taken Diego in a convoy of heavy trucks, Sivaya was driving a powerful and well-equipped 4x4. but it was still an exhausting tortuous journey. The gypsy sat slumped, too traumatised to speak, lost in his own thoughts, staring bleakly out of the windows.

"This is crazy," Gabrielle protested. "Why haven't we found them? They must be mired down with all this mud and slurry on the road surely?"

She turned to the hard-edged Dark Kind beauty, "Maybe they turned off somewhere, we could have missed them."

Sivaya's response was a muted growl of disdain, the human could not see the road as well as a Dark Kind, there was a clear track to follow from the slow moving convoy. It had not turned off.

"We have not lost them." Was her curt reply before continuing on in silence.

As they began to descend into another broad valley, opening out into flatter terrain, Sivaya could see a farm complex some two miles further down. A perfect location for a helicopter to land. It must be there! As they grew nearer, a few lights were visible from within the farmhouse. A convoy of trucks was parked in a protective circle in the overgrown and neglected farmyard. Nemesis! Sivaya approached slowly, cutting the engine and coasting most of the way downhill before parking well out of ear shot of the farm. For the only time that night, Gabrielle was relieved the vampires drove without headlights, it gave them a distinct advantage by remaining undetected for longer.

They got out of the car and looked down at the deceptively peaceful farmhouse, counting three large lorries and five armoured cars in the courtyard. There was no sign of any Nemesis agents, but they would be there, watching every approach with night-vision equipment mounted on their weapons.

Gabrielle fixed Sivaya with a steady gaze, a show of courage, one she hoped would gain the vampire's confidence. "This situation stinks. There are only three of us. God knows how many of them. I think you should take Lev and scout around the back. The road is where they will expect an attack. Kick off with a loud, noisy diversion and I'll go in and get Diego."

Gabrielle ignored the sharp growl of derision from the vampire woman but continued on, aware she sounded like a gauche, nervous child trying to play a grown up game. "I know how much you Dark Kind love each other, how you would do anything to protect Diego. But I give my word, I will get him away from those creeps. And if it is too late, I will do the right thing."

"Touching words," Sivaya hissed back. "I seemed to remember your grandmother promising me to look after Jaz in Berlin. And look how that ended!"

Gabrielle grabbed an automatic pistol from a bag at her feet. Hitched a belt of hand grenades across her shoulder. Gestured to the man to take more weapons from the back of the estate. Said curtly. "I am not my grandmother."

She began to walk towards the farmhouse but Sivaya blocked her way, a darkening cloud shrouding her forest-green eyes. "Exactly how much covert combat training have you had, human?" Sivaya snarled scornfully, "A few week? A few months?"

"Enough.

"It would never be enough. I have Dark Kind strength, speed, ferocity and night vision. And experience. You have an Uzi and a naïve, over-inflated self-belief."

Gabrielle opened her mouth to protest. Closed it again. Only her sense of commitment to the mission and her blind fury at the death of innocents had spurred her on to take the lead. Sivaya was right. It made more sense for her to go with Lev. She stood a better chance of living through the night with him. Gabrielle nodded in terse assent. She gestured to the gypsy, "OK, its pay back time for you and me! Let's go."

Chapter Twenty-Three

Geddoe and his minions left Diego alone in a dusty cellar, as the Nemesis agents dealt with some disturbance upstairs. The vampire used the precious time to concentrate, weighing up his options for escape. He could hear a frantically over- revved engine and terse shouting above in the farmhouse courtyard. Geddoe and his cohorts were tense to the point of near panic and with good reason! Knowing the fanatical loyalty of his people, the Yasuul must be closing in fast. Geddoe could also anticipate trouble from any local police or militia possibly alerted by the gunfire from the raid on the circus. Any investigation now would immediately rob Geddoe of his prize specimen.

The pandemonium up in the yard had been sparked off by the caged human, another Nemesis captive. Close proximity to the vampire circus boss had sent the man into hysteria with high pitched screaming, crying out wordlessly like a maimed animal caught in a gin-trap. The sound was disturbing the Nemesis crew. Diego could hear the heated arguments as they insisted Geddoe remove the tracker from the farmhouse. His screams could alert any locals and it was unsettling their concentration. This wait for the Nemesis helicopters to arrive to whisk them out of Amantzk was becoming too long and too unbearably tense. Their human sniffer dog had done his job, helped them track and capture a living vampire. There was no reason for the man to stay. Geddoe apparently gave in, the vampire could hear cheers of relief.

Diego had two choices. He could use his special abilities or wait till they unshackled him and then let rip with an orgy of violence. Time was running out, soon thin daggers of daylight would pierce gaps in the cellar's rotten wooden roof. There was little chance of his captors waiting here for another sundown. Geddoe and his thuggish crony, Dent, would know how much more dangerous he was in darkness. Diego held his breath, paused the drumming of his heart beat and listened, sharply alert for any clues. It was imperative to find out when the helicopters were arriving, his move must be made before then.

Could his skills help him escape? Engineer some bizarre distraction? His protectors, the K'elphin, at tiresomely frequent intervals, warned him to keep his abilities hidden, to be patient and wait instructions for when to use them openly. They could evaporate up their own ethereal backsides! He was no use to them dead! But any manifestation of his power depleted him, what was the point of creating havoc if unable to escape through exhaustion?

All thoughts of escape were put on hold as Geddoe and Dent opened the door and came in. Their expressions both fearful and fascinated. Dent, in particular could not take his eyes of the vampire, like a mantra repeating over and over in his mind, 'Bloody hell, they do exist!'

"Not long now, creature," remarked Geddoe's side kick uneasily, clearly unnerved by the close presence of the blood drinker. A creature from peasant folklore, a thing to be dismissed as a ridiculous ignorant legend. Until now. The legends were based in truth, he shivered at the stark reality, trying not to get too close to the vampire shackled before him. Why hadn't Geddoe, his arrogant fool of a leader planned this better? A refrigerated transport would have solved the problem, the added danger of keeping this creature alive. Without such a vital vehicle, it had to be kept alive, a corpse would deteriorate quickly, be useless to research.

"You have a whole new world of pain to look forward to," Dent taunted, finding his courage. "You will pay for every torn throat, every grieving widow, every distraught child left fatherless."

Diego fixed the human with a fierce, relentless and fearless stare, growled, his voice more animal then the human he closely resembled. He continued his defiant stance, amused at the terror rising in the human at being so close, and being openly challenged by a monstrous being from his darkest nightmares. "Are you going to start torturing wild animals next? Tigers? Wolves? How about virus and bacteria. Or the weather? That kills people too. And as for your own kind?" Diego gave a slight, humourless smile, "Just where would you start?"

Geddoe's indignant voice interrupted. "You are an intelligent, sentient being. You have a choice."

Diego gave a slight dismissive shrug. "You need to do your homework... Dark Kind have no choice. We need male human blood and only human blood to survive. Kill me by all means. It is your right as a species to protect and defend yourself, but spare me the sanctimonious claptrap. I kill without remorse because I am not human. You are my prey - nothing more then a clever little ape."

"And you are no more then a captured, defeated specimen waiting experimentation and eventual dissection." Geddoe retorted, "So much for the so called superiority of your kind."

The vampire's composure was unnerving. Was it because it thought it's situation held no danger? That escape or rescue was imminent?

Dent suppressed another shudder of growing unease. What was his commander playing at? Ready or not, Geddoe must order the removal of the creature now. "We must make a run for the border in the lorries. We can't afford to wait for the helicopters." His voice betrayed his fear and panic.

Sowing seeds of doubt and confusion in their minds, Diego taunted his captors. "Of course, the rest of your scientific team are expecting something to work on - a body in good condition. If you expose me to the morning, I will be incinerated by the sun. You will have nothing. A pile of useless ash."

"Nonsense!" Geddoe barked to hide the uncertainty he felt inside. His small eyes blinked with a nervous twitch, betraying his unease.

"The sun will burn out your eyes - that is all. We will protect them. We must discover the secret of your night vision." Geddoe announced confidently, his boss had taught Geddoe all he knew about vampire metabolism. The creature was lying to save its miserable life.

Diego shrugged again. "Then you have an explanation to why there are no records of any Dark Kind bodies found anywhere in the world, at any time in history?"

"You are lying."

"I am going to die soon anyway, you are the only one with something to lose. So, go on. Take me away now, it will soon be dawn before you leave Amantzk. Risk taking me into the sunlight."

Unlike the unimaginative Dent, Geddoe realised there was no question of making a run for the border in the trucks. They would wait for the helicopter rescue in the shelter of the farmhouse. This was a good defensive position; they had enough men and fire power to see off a few enraged gypsies, should they stupidly follow...

"We have not planned this moment to be robbed of our prize, by interfering gypsies from its pet freak show, or the risk of exposing it to sunlight." Geddoe stood too close to Dent, glaring into his face, intimidating him. "I am in command. Unlike you, I am not afraid of a gang of contortionists and clowns. We will not leave here tonight except as planned by helicopter."

Humiliated by his leader's scorn, intimidated by the defiant monster, Dent walked over to the shackled vampire and with all his strength, struck him across the face breaking the skin above his cheek with his array of sharp-edged biker rings. Unflinching from the blow, the vampire's handsome face broke into a courageous smile of defiance as a thin trickle of purple blood followed the line of his sharp-boned features. Dent struck the shackled vampire again with greater force, dragging the rings deep into and across the already open wound. This time he got a reaction, the creature roared with fang-bared fury.

Geddoe exploded with rage. "What the fuck are you doing?"

He pulled Dent off the shackled vampire, throwing him across the room. "Hain is paying us for an undamaged specimen! Idiot!"

Nursing a bruised arm, Dent's eyes narrowed with spite, no one humiliated him like that. No one! "Just having some fun with the blood sucker! Before it's taken away to the men in white coats."

"Get back up to the yard," Geddoe thundered. "You've just volunteered to get the tracker away. He has served his purpose here. For now."

Dent got to his feet, dusted himself down, pulling together any last shred of self-respect. The prospect of a long journey with a howling lunatic was an insult, a sign of Geddoe's contempt for him, but, he mused, if he had control of the tracker, he could capture his own vampire... and all the financial reward and status within Nemesis that would bring. As he climbed in beside the driver of the truck, Dent fantasised about becoming head of Nemesis; live, captive vampires would need feeding. Geddoe might serve some useful purpose after all!

Chapter Twenty-Four

'Ouch!' Gabrielle thought, gritting her teeth to stop herself crying out as she stubbed her toe on a large rock, immediately regretting parting company from the female vampire. As the two humans cautiously crept towards the farmhouse, the night grew even darker as unseen above them, over-laden rain clouds lumbered across the valley.

They found a small spinney of tired, straggly silver birch and scrub. Not ideal cover but it was the only one within reach. Selecting a log they rolled it to the front of the spinney, this was all they had to protect them from Nemesis bullets. The sour taste of anxiety in Gabrielle's mouth grew ever more bitter. She had chosen this perilous life, this vigilante role. Never had breaking her back, up to her knees in mud, sifting through earth for ancient artefacts seem more appealing!

As she prepared to lie down on the sodden earth to hide herself behind the log, the clouds gave up their struggle, releasing their burden, apparently directly above her. The rain fell straight down, in well spaced out, large pendulous drops at first before organising itself into a full-on torrential downpour. Accompanied by the obligatory thunder and lightning. Gabrielle felt hexed. Her life had become a horror film. The last warm sunny time she remembered was when she had unearthed the Cornishman in the cliff. Storms and heavy rain seemed to follow her from that day onwards, as if his vengeful ghost was punishing her for disturbing his eternal rest. Or for stealing his dragon amulet!

There was nothing she could do but lie on the cold, muddy ground, behind a rather small log, soaked through to the skin in the company of a traumatised, murderously vengeful gypsy man. Waiting for a deadly exchange of fire with ruthless, child-killing maniacs. "What did I want to do when I left school?" she mused to herself dourly as the strength of the cloudburst forced her to close her eyes, "not bloody this!"

And where was that reckless idiot Jaz? Could he not have got his sorry not in-Armani-clad backside over here in time to help by now? Doesn't do sunlight, doesn't do shoddy clothes or cheap wine, she doubted if he did rain storms either, play havoc with his perfectly cut hair! All thoughts of Jazriel and what she would do to him if they ever met up again were pushed aside as activity increased from the farmhouse. A handful of men, one Gabrielle identified from intelligence reports as Geddoe's lieutenant, Dent had hurried to a truck and left the courtyard at high speed through the worsening storm. Even above the deluge, she could hear unearthly screaming - Dark Kind? No, it was a human scream coming from within the departing truck. What in Hell was in the back?

Reluctantly, she pushed aside her curiosity, the truck's departure was good news. She murmured through clenched teeth to Lev,

"Phew! A few less Nemesis tossers to deal with." He did not reply, she suspected he would settle for nothing less then every Nemesis agent dead. And, thought Gabrielle, why not?

There was a brief, unpleasant lull, broken only by the rumbling thunder and driving rain that Gabrielle was convinced augured the start of something bad, something very bad for the captured vampire

"You have no choice, girl," she announced to herself, 'this being must not be harmed.' Though his identity was still unknown, one day, her children or grandchildren's lives might depend on this Dark Kind to be there for them. Not that she would have any descendants if this went badly for her! In her mind, she focused all her anger again at Jazriel, to drive out her dread of what was to come. "Lock and load, Gaby!"

Chapter Twenty-Five

Geddoe's game plan had worked with almost clock-work precision. He sighed contentedly at the rumble of the departing truck as Dent took the madman away. Two nuisances out of his life.

There was a near-miss glitch when the bravest of the Nemesis operatives, hearing the roars of fury, tentatively returned to check the vampire. Furious, Geddoe had barked an order. "Leave me alone with the creature. Now!"

The others had looked at each other, uncertain. This was a deviation from their orders. Why was their commander taking a pointless risk?

"Come on. You are a bunch of old women. There's only one and the bastard's well shackled. Go upstairs and get some hard-earned down time, try to rustle up coffee. There's a heavy storm overhead, no one will attack while that's going on."

Nor could the helicopters come. The men continued to look doubtful, especially at the nonsensical remark about the storm, they doubted it would delay the determined and badly wronged Yasuul. Geddoe had seen the hesitation, the doubt in their eyes and swiftly changed tack. "Need I remind you, home and a big fat pay cheque is waiting. But only if you obey my orders. Without question."

At last he was alone, completely alone. Geddoe carefully studied the manacled creature. So handsome, so full of life. It was almost a pity to destroy something that had lived so long. Had to be done though.

"I apologise for the brutality. Totally unnecessary. Dent was a moronic thug."

Diego fixed him with the full power of his inhuman all-brown eyes, fangs fully bared. A low warning snarl in his throat rose to a threatening growl of feral menace. The man stepped back sharply, startled at the raw ferocity of their inhuman prisoner. Geddoe appeared to be struggling to control a potent inner compulsion. He paced the floor in increasing agitation as if a power struggle was going on, a battle within his own mind. He halted, eyes closed, fists tightly clenched, then he relaxed, opened his eyes and approached his prisoner. One side of Geddoe's inner conflict had won the battle.

"What would it take to make me like you?" Geddoe asked, his voice an urgent, sibilant whisper, unsure whether his men could hear upstairs through the gaps in the rotten wood flooring. "A bite? Would that be enough?"

Diego's black eyes narrowed. Was this man mocking him? Or did he really believe all the old folk tale nonsense? He remained silent. Watchful.

Geddoe's whole manner changed, he paced the floor again, excited, the words tumbling out in a dam-burst of repressed thought. "I have worked so hard, climbing the corporate ladder, playing ridiculous power games with snot-nosed little shits in smart suits. I've planned and waited so long, endured endless bloody insults and humiliation from that pig, Hain. All for this moment."

The man's eyes glittered with a feverish animation; "Now is my chance. My only chance. Make me like you, I'll be your slave, I'll do anything you want. Just make me an immortal being."

Diego was certain now, this man genuinely thought a bite from a vampire could make him immortal! Such stupidity. Such an opportunity!

Diego wished he had Jazriel's gift of silken seduction, of charming humans to do his will. But he was a warrior, made to fight and kill in battle. He tried his best to sound convincing. "Of course. A brave man like you would make a fine addition to our brethren of darkness. Are you ready to renounce the light forever?"

Geddoe dropped to his knees in front of the vampire. In a moment of perfect irony, lightning forked with retina blasting brilliance above the farmhouse, instantly a momentous crash of loud thunder completed the horror film special effects. "I have always been ready. Master."

Geddoe heard the click of bone on bone, the sound of descending fangs. He glanced up, shaking, waiting for the painful benediction that would transform him to immortality. Puzzled, he frowned. The sound had come from behind him...

Chapter Twenty-Six

Geddoe whimpering with fear, watched from a filthy corner of the cellar. Cowering, nursing a broken arm, he tried to make himself appear small, unthreatening, anything to stay alive. The female vampire had hauled him from the ground and thrown him across the room with a contemptuous toss of one hand. Her speed and power brought him back to a chilling reality. These things were frightening, deadly. Where had she come from? How did she get past the team guarding the farmhouse? Two vampires! There had been no warning from Nemesis intelligence about a second one. But the madman had known! Alerting them from his lorry in the farm yard, warning them with his hideous screams of terror, and Geddoe and his men had ignored Devane's danger signal! A fatal error of judgement.

Like a blood-drinking Adam and Eve, he watched them kiss in a prolonged, passionate, intimate greeting. Geddoe's mind raced with the exciting possibilities. He could still emerge the victor in all this. If they would not let them join their Kind, he could capture them both, a breeding pair! His journey to Nemesis directorship assured. The two creatures were at a disadvantage, trapped in a cellar, his men controlling the farmhouse.

"Do you want him?" Sivaya asked in the Dark Kind language, as she released Diego from his shackles, her hand gently caressing his torn and bleeding face. Briefly, quickly, she answered his questions about the troupe. He closed his eyes in the sharp intensity of grief and fury then kissed her hand, shook his head. *"Bind and gag him. That bastard destroyed Lev's family. By Yasuul tradition, it is his right to take revenge."*

Sivaya nodded a terse, reluctant agreement, it was a waste of blood when Diego needed to feed. She would have also taken great pleasure in killing Remai's murderer.

"It will not be so easy to escape, dragging a prisoner."

Diego kissed Sivaya again, lightly on the forehead. "One vampire warrior with a beautiful Dark Kind tigress at his side? Easy!"

As the wall of rain began to ease up, Gabrielle's discomfort grew; she was cold, soaking wet and filthy, a cramp seized up the calf muscles in her right leg, yet she couldn't move to ease the sharp pain. Nor knew how to ask Lev in Russian to reach over and give her leg a therapeutic rub. Her command of the language was good but not that good!

Gabrielle had to do something! The odds were crazy, one woman and one circus performer and somewhere in the darkness one female vampire versus many armed, possibly highly trained men. Gabrielle had two advantages, surprise and their almost protected spot on a slight incline above the farmhouse. But Nemesis most certainly had night vision equipment. Time to load the odds more in her favour. Gabrielle took a high risk gamble, aimed her Uzi at what she was certain was an empty truck, sent a missile into the gas tank. Cheering at the satisfying whoomp, then an inferno of flying metal and exploding fuel. And more importantly, obscuring, choking smoke.

The lights went off in the farmhouse. Men poured out firing blindly in their direction, one bullet thudded into the tree-trunk, inches from Gabrielle's face, hitting her with sharp, hot splinters. "Shit!" Her heart raced, "Shit, shit! Shit!" She muttered between clenched teeth, the vampire was right, she did not have enough training. She took aim with the Uzi and returned fire.

The kick back knocked her but there was no time to nurse her bruised shoulder, forcing her hands to stop shaking, Gabrielle hastily re-aimed, she could already hear the shouts of fury from the Nemesis agents. They were too vulnerable in one spot now Nemesis were under attack. Their advantage was over, survival paramount.

"That was for my mum and dad," she growled, then flattened to the ground as a shock wave blasted from a bigger and more violent explosion, the truck must have contained spare ammunition. "Good," a shaken Gabrielle managed to gasp, "less to fire back at us!"

She re-aimed her automatic rifle as more heavily armed figures broke from the farmhouse. She heard their voices, the scuffle of their

354

boots on cobbles, but could not see any moving shapes; everything was obscured by the acrid, black billowing smoke from the wrecked lorries! Damn! The dramatic attack had given her enemies an advantage. Could the two of them keep the Nemesis men pinned down long enough for help to arrive? In any form, local police or militia would do! And where was Sivaya?

"Good girl," growled Sivaya, at the sound of the explosion in the courtyard. "Perfect timing!" Gabrielle had given them the diversion they needed. Sivaya strode over to the cowering Geddoe, who forgot his long-held plans to become a vampire, to live forever; forgot everything but his fear, and released it in one long, terrified scream. With a snarl of disgust, Sivaya knocked out the human, and dragging his limp body across the cellar floor, stood beside Diego. Readied to fight their way to freedom.

A high-pitched, hideous wail from the farmhouse cellar told Geddoe's troops all they needed, why had the fool insisted on being alone with the vampire? That sound could have only one origin. Somehow the vampire had broken free of its shackles and torn out their leader's throat. Continuing to use the foul-stinking, oily smoke from the blazing truck as a cover, one group ran to a vehicle and sped away. This was not their war, never had been! Taking on blood drinking creatures of the night, murderous gypsies, and now an army was not in their contracts! Geddoe's fanatic elite remained to fight on, the night lit up with innocent looking traces of light, the traces of automatic rifle fire straking the darkness with unfocused and deadly venom.

With Lev drawing fire away from her position, Gabrielle risked peering over the log to see one of the armoured vehicles speeding away from the farmhouse in the opposite direction of her hillside position. Shit! Now what was she to do? Was Diego in the cellar? Or in one of the trucks? Did she rush back to her car and pursue them? Why did she have to be teamed up with an understandably morose man and unreliable nocturnal beings?

Looking through the night vision of her rifle, she caught movement, forms running swiftly away from the farmhouse. One was unmistakably the lithe form of Sivaya! She had done it!

Gabrielle's cheer of celebration was drowned by the sound of a motorbike rapidly approaching along the track behind them. It raised her hopes for an ill-judged milli-second. Stupid bitch! It wouldn't be Jaz. He was hardly the type to be riding to the rescue like the clichéd cavalry in a film. She turned, her rifle raised to see a man from the circus approach on a battered old motorbike. His eyes were reddened, his mouth set in a grim determined line. The man dismounted and keeping low, crept straight past Gabrielle to embrace the circus foreman. Lev broke away from the reunion and crouching low, approached her.

"The men from the Yasuul are here, coming from the south on horseback. This is our battle. We will finish this. It is time for you to go home."

He gestured to her weapon, holding his hand for her to pass it over. When she refused, he politely but firmly took it off her. Gabrielle folded her arms, the bloody cheek of the man! Of course her heart was saddened, the poor man had lost his wife and his only child, but she had risked her own life to rescue his vampire boss. Only to be dismissed like a skivvy! And that was her gun! Well, Lady Eshan's.

"Bloody hell! Not even a thank you?" Gabrielle demanded, snatching back her rifle. "Nemesis lackeys are determined sons of bitches. You had better stay here, stay down low, pick them off in the darkness."

For a moment Lev considered using force to deal with this foreign vixen. But reason returned, overwhelming grief had clouded his judgement. It was true, this young woman with the face of a saint and the mouth of a harridan had taken great chances to help them.

"Forgive my manners, this has been a tragic and frightening time for my people. For myself." Lev bowed his head and turned to creep back to his comrade.

"Oi! Lev! Other Gypsy! " Gabrielle shouted, "You'll be needing this!" She threw over the gun with an impudent smile. "You only had to ask nicely!"

The men bowed their heads in gratitude, too traumatised by the night to smile back in return.

"And this," said Gabrielle pulling off the grenade belt and draping the strap across Lev's back. "If you do manage to rescue Diego, they will be back for him. It won't stop. Next time you must strike first. Hard."

Gabrielle switched into English, "I won't be there to save your sorry gypo backsides next time."

"The Boss and I will look after the gypo backsides, just take care of yours."

Gabrielle left the circus foreman, to scurry down the hill, leaving him on his quest for bloody vengeance. She shook her head, finding herself amused, even in this perilous situation. "The wotsit spoke English all along!"

She had no intention of being a good little girl and obeying the Yasuul's foreman, cheeky git! She took no orders from him! Reaching her car and unlocking the estate's spacious boot, she re-armed herself from a secret compartment beneath the floor and went back down to the battle zone, seeking Sivaya.

The thunderstorm fireworks moved swiftly away across the valley, the rain ceased, leaving hot mist rising from the earth. It mixed with the stench of cordite and stinking, oily smoke from the blazing lorries, creating a bilious miasma. The clearing sky brought no helpful moon-light, Gabrielle struggled and stumbled, colourfully cussing Jaz again, needing his night vision. Hell, she was sounding boring. He was gone, buggered off forever. "Get over it woman!" she muttered, furious with herself for giving the fanged idiot another moment's thought.

Several heavy falls over tree roots and rocks later, Gabrielle reached the direction Sivaya was last seen heading. With an ear-deafening roar, to the right of her, the battle recommenced. She was torn, it felt cowardly leaving the Yasuul to fight on alone, but Sivaya might need her help. The tenuous bond of sisterhood won her inner conflict and she pressed on, desperate to catch a gleam of gold or flash of forest-green fire, some sign of the vampire woman in the darkness.

Inevitably Sivaya found her first.

"So, they didn't teach you how to move unseen and quietly through the darkness then?"

Gabrielle bristled defensively as the vampire silently appeared beside her. Enver and the team had done their best to change a swotty archaeologist into a tough commando in such a short time. Bloody vampire arrogance again!

Sivaya had clearly been in close quarter combat, Gabrielle could see a dark, wet, stain drenching her clothes, the stench of the gore was mixed with cordite, like the surrounding mist.

"I have succeeded. Diego is safe with his people and co-ordinating the battle with what's left of the Nemesis team. He is warrior caste, he will prevail over his enemy."

"We must go back to them," Gabrielle declared urgently, "two extra combatants could be vital. Make all the difference."

"I will go to join them. The battle is nearly over, the Yasuul are winning. You must go home now, Gabrielle," the vampire woman said, "Diego values his seclusion from the world. You are an outsider."

Gabrielle was livid, what was it with these people? Another one wanting to dismiss her! "No way, lady! I want to see this through to the end, to meet this mysterious Diego. Lady Eshan would want me to make sure he is unharmed."

Sivaya fixed her with her intense dark green eyes. "You are different from the other one. I like you."

Gabrielle shrugged, angry at this dismissal. "I'll take that as a compliment, shall I?"

"Your work here is done, Gabrielle. But your assignment is far from over, you have been entrusted to care for Jazriel. You must do what I cannot, care for him, keep him safe."

Sivaya walked away but stopped, hesitated and turned back. "But do not love him, human. *Never* love him."

The vampire woman strode into the foul miasma, a warrior wraith disappearing with eerie speed and silence. Gabrielle weighed up her options. Staying alive was highest on the list. And she knew when she wasn't wanted. Sivaya was right, there was nothing more she could do here. Her job – no - more accurately, her millstone, was to baby-sit that damn vampire junkie. Yeah right. Fat chance of finding him again!

She began to return to her car but paused as her head spun, her legs weakened, unable to bear her weight. Gabrielle sank to the ground shaking with the aftershock of the traumatic night. Her mind filled with stark images, of those pathetic shrouded bundles on the road, deafening explosions, the screams of unseen wounded men. Her hand reached up and touched her forehead. Felt wetness and pain. At first puzzled, she remembered the splinters of wood thrown up from a bullet's near miss. A minor injury but Gabrielle shivered, her blood froze as realisation sunk in at just how close she had been to having her brain shot out. She wanted to be sick but her stomach was too tense, too cramped to oblige. Some fearless, highly trained commando!

She sat on the wet ground for a few minutes, recovering her composure then made it back to the car on unsteady legs. Driving slow and carefully to a nearby vantage point, she watched with grim satisfaction as twenty minutes later, the Yasuul rode and drove past her. Not smiling in triumph, no celebrating. They were returning to their broken, grieving circus family as survivors not victors. There was no sign of either Sivaya or the mysterious Diego.

Lev, on the old motorbike, seeing Gabrielle sitting there, pulled over briefly and nodded to her in silent and respectful gratitude. She could tell from his face the two Dark Kind were safe. Her mission here was truly over.

Chapter Twenty-Seven

Cold and drenched from the torrential rain, Jazriel eased back on the old Honda's throttle, another stretch of empty road lay ahead. Mile after mile of fucking empty road. What was it that bastard Garan had once called him in a spiteful taunt - a vampire boy scout? He'd be mocking again. So what if the plan to bugger off back to a life of freedom and over indulgence had been put on hold. Temporarily. That small but strident streak of honour had gnawed at him long enough to decide to finish the mission, to make sure the unknown Dark Kind was safe. And yes, make sure that harridan Gaby was safe too. Maybe Garan was right about him, he was a vampire boy scout at heart.

So where was this circus? Or more pertinently, where was the sodding Nemesis convoy? Had Eshan sent him on some sort of wild goose chase, thinking he was too useless to pitch against the enemy? That noble-born female vamp always looked down on him, never forgetting he was made sha'ref. Maybe that's why he was still here, the real reason, that ridiculous compulsion to prove to the world he could do more with his life then fu.. What was that noise?

Jazriel rounded a tight corner in the road and skidded to a halt. Driving rain had turned the roads to a fast moving river of treacherous liquid mud, streams of freezing water ran down his face and into his eyes. His bare hands were numb with cold as he struggled to control the bike with the rain-slippery throttle. The sudden and violent storm made the road dangerous to travel at speed, but Jazriel had pressed on, recklessly fast, trusting his riding skill and reflexes. Again, there was that noise. The rumble of a hard-pressed big engine and dim yellow headlights vainly trying to illuminate the road ahead through the sheets of rain. An oncoming truck. Good. Time to play.

Whether the truck contained Nemesis agents or harmless peasants heading for a tavern, he didn't care, he was hungry.

He switched on the motorbike's headlights and gave the machine a reassuring pat on the petrol tank. "Don't worry little Honda, I am not going to treat you like my Italian beauty. Just trust me and obey my commands."

He faced the oncoming truck head on and gave the bike full throttle, aiming for the centre of the steel radiator grill. The back wheels spun and slipped badly at first in the fast-flowing mud and floodwater; Jazriel battled and won control over the Honda and set it straight again. It was not his first game of chicken played against humans, a lethal boredom-beater he had always won. But there was always a first time to lose! Did he care? Not particularly.

He heard the truck's angry horn blaring, saw the flashing warning from it's headlights but kept his course, unwavering, aiming for the centre of the heavy vehicle. Fighting hard to stay in control, he did not slow down or swerve, just let the inevitable collision take its course.

The startled and panicking truck driver braked violently and through instinctive reflex hauled his steering wheel to the right, giving Jazriel a split second to flick the bike left. The heavy truck could not cope with tight manoeuvring at its already reckless speed on the submerged road, with the roar of a dying dinosaur, it lurched over onto two wheels, crashing onto it's side, skidding for many yards before halting, its wheels spinning in its death throes.

Jazriel waited in the darkness, straddling his bike, attempting to light a victory cigarette and cursing the torrent for spoiling his moment of triumph. Wondered if there were any survivors worth preying on, as several dazed and groaning humans began to crawl from the wreckage. Those less injured, though confused and disorientated, began to help evacuate the truck, too shocked to remember the madman on a motorbike.

He gave up on his cigarette before dismounting and wandering over, dispatched two badly wounded men before the others realised what was happening and made an attempt to stop him. Knocking their raised guns from their hands, Jazriel disposed of two more guards, breaking their necks with practised ease and insouciance. The other, a giant of a man, he knocked out. He'd keep for later. Jazriel needed to feed. His concentration was shattered by the sound of high pitched screaming coming from the stricken truck. His fangs bared with trepidation at what lay behind the armoured doors. He shuddered at the nerve-shredding sound of frenzy and terror. A badly injured human? He'd heard enough of those over the centuries to be familiar with the sound. Dark Kind did not usually feel much fear but this, this thing, whatever it was, was different.

It was no good, his curiosity aroused he had to know what lay behind those doors. Jazriel attempted to open them, but they were sealed shut; snarling with frustration, he searched through the clothing of the dead bodyguards and found nothing to help him. Zaard! Bloody human technology at its most infuriating. Brute strength might do it, but his drug abuse and recent months of starvation had seriously weakened him. Furious, frustrated, Jazriel hauled the big man from the ground and dipped his head into a deep water-filled rut in the road. The man came too with a roar of fury.

"What is in that truck?" Jazriel snarled, fangs bared, ready to strike.

His captive, Dent, shook with abject terror, gibbering for mercy. Vampires did exist! They did! That lucky bastard, Geddoe, had his prize, his glory, while he was about to die. "Please don't hurt me, I'll tell you all you want to know, I will help you. Anything! Just let me live. I have a wife, three children..."

"Do I look like I care?" replied Jazriel, already bored with his prey's pleading. He tightened his grip on Dent's throat. "Answer me, what is in that truck?"

Dent gasped for air, pointing at his throat for release. He couldn't speak, wanted to scream. The vampire relented, and eased his hold on his neck.

"I don't know who he is. My commander, Geddoe, called him a tracker. He can sense the presence of vampires. We used him as a human bloodhound." Dent decided not to mention capturing the circus boss, he was in enough serious shit already. The vampire's eyes narrowed briefly as he took in the information. Dent survived long enough to catch a glimpse of flashing silver fangs striking downwards.

'That was good,' Jazriel mused, dropping the body, wiping the last drops of blood from his mouth. 'So good. Hot, fresh blood at last.'

How dare Eshan insult his fierce heritage by trying to force him to survive on that hideous artificial carrion! Energy surged through his body; he found a box of car repair tools in the cab of the truck and with a tyre iron levered the back door.

As it swung open, he heard a piercing shriek of raw terror from the unlit interior. Jazriel could see a human male cowering at the back of the truck, screaming in a weird high-pitched ululation. The figure, a tall middle-aged man began to babble, incoherently at first, then Jazriel realised he could make out some of the words. The man spoke in rapid English, denouncing vampires as devils, Satan's spawn, cursing all Jazriel's kind to burn in hell, to suffer an eternity of agony. Jazriel had enough hardship already that night without listening to the nonsensical ranting. So this was Nemesis's secret weapon? A madman.

The man's incoherent terror at seeing the vampire at the door of the truck surpassed any he had encountered, his was without colour, as if he'd been drained of blood already and yet lived. His boots scrabbled frantically, throwing his whole weight against the back wall trying to force his way through solid metal and heavy mesh to escape. Jazriel paused, unwilling to enter the confines of the steel compartment. A cage? No chance! Instead, he lit a cigarette and waited, maybe by not overtly threatening him, the man's terror-filled gibbering may lessen?

At least the Nemesis agents had left him unarmed, a wise move in Jazriel's opinion.

"I am not going to haul you out of there, so why not make it easy on yourself and come out." Jazriel announced, already bored with waiting.

The sound of the vampire's silken voice re-energised the man's distress and the gibbering returned to the high-pitched ululating scream.

"Fuck this," muttered Jazriel in cold fury, his sensitive hearing assaulted by the screams. Checking no alert and moving humans were within scenting distance, he leapt up into the truck and grabbing the man by the throat, hauled him out, despite his wild flailing and kicking. And to the vampire's great disgust, spitting. His eyes narrowing with disdain, Jazriel held him up, gripping him firmly by the neck.

Interesting. Jazriel's head tilted to one side as he studied his victim. Golden eyes, just like Khari and Gabrielle's. But Khari's eyes had once shone with life, their gilded hue sparkling with gentleness and understanding and Gaby's were lit with an inner light, brimming with sassy courage and uncompromising candour. These were a flat, dull yellow and totally insane.

The human found his voice, a well educated American accent, a man who could once have had a normal life, a family perhaps. One who never dreamt he would end his days a mentally unbalanced prisoner, pulled by the throat by a vampire from a steel cage.

"I'm toxic. You evil bastard. Demon! You can't drink my blood!" he screeched, trying to gouge at Jazriel's eyes with his overlong, dirty, yellow fingernails. Clawing at a chance to live.

"I can shut you up," Jazriel returned in a low menacing growl. "Permanently." The vampire turned the man's head to show him the mayhem he had created among the man's protectors, or jailers, whatever. The sight of dead men, four with their necks at unnatural angles, the other with a ripped-out throat sent the man into a paroxysm of panic. Kicking and flailing his arms again with renewed wild energy, he began a wordless terrified wailing, soiling himself in his distress. Jazriel threw him to the ground with a howl of disgusted loathing. Humans and their stinking animal bodily functions were so gross!

On the ground, away from Jazriel's grip, the man curled into a foetal position, head down, rocking himself, seeking comfort from his own arms gripping his knees. He had been safe from these demonic creatures in the care home, but not safe from constant ordeal. The pollution of every nearby human's thoughts entering the open portal of his mind, left torn and exposed after the shock of his lover's murder. A portal he could not close, even in sleep.

He turned his anger on the glossily handsome creature before him, the pain-driven awareness of the vampire's proximity, an extra bitter twist, an added cruelty to the curse of his inherited *Knowing*.

"Evil murdering bastard. You and all your foul, accursed kind are doomed!"

Jazriel faked a yawn of disinterest. How many times had he heard such threats over the centuries! Doomed maybe, but it was the 21st century now and the Dark Kind were still here. Living among their prey in the shadows now, but their fangs remained sharp, the need for human blood as urgent as it had ever been.

"What is your name, human?" Jazriel demanded suddenly. The man's eyes had intrigued him.

"Does it matter? I am just food to you." He spat again at Jazriel "Get it over with."

"I wouldn't soil my fangs on a filthy lunatic! I only hunt worthy prey."

A flash of animal cunning shifted across the man's eyes as a brief flicker of sanity returned. Was this creature going to let him live? "I am Cameron Devane."

Startled, Jazriel snapped, "Related to Khari Devane?"

Madness overtook the man again, he began to rant. "That vampire-loving bitch! My mother! I am toxic. Infected with her *Knowing.* Voices invading my head! Not one moment of peace. No silence!"

He looked away from the vampire, whimpering; "It never stops. The crowding, demanding voices. It never stops. I wanted to die, but they wouldn't let me, incarcerating me in a clinic. For my own good! Years and years of pointless treatment. Nothing worked. Hah! The only kindness would be to free me from this endless torment. To let me end my life."

His head dropped, all fight draining from his body. No human should be born cursed, a childhood blighted by being different, too aware, too open, too sensitive to other people's emotions. He had fled, seeking answers, finding them after losing the only good thing in his life, Amela Railton. Answers that had stolen his sanity, stolen his life. Exposing him to the nightmare reality of vampires and his mother's open love for them. The only men who slept easily at night were those who did not know the Dark Kind existed.

Thoughts of Amela gave him the last dregs of fading courage to look up at the vampire again. Gaze directly into its lustrous turquoise eyes and defy it.

"You cannot drink my blood, you cannot have my power!"

"You can keep it, mate. You are far too old and ugly and I cannot stand that stench," Jazriel replied with an elegant shrug of complete disinterest. "Won't stop me from putting you out of your misery though."

Shivering and weeping with fear, the man curled back into the tight ball and began to rock back and forward, whimpering again.

"Hain gave me back a reason to live, a purpose, a sacred mission. To use my curse as a weapon, to seek out the infestation of vampires. To destroy them all."

He glared up at Jazriel, becoming aware in a brief window of clarity that he had dashed any hope of mercy, condemning himself with those rash words. His body shook, he began to wail like a snared beast, a wordless cry from the depths of his tortured soul.

Jaz had enough, this was getting tedious. He stepped forward, ready to snap the madman's neck and get going. The bright lights of the nearest big city were calling out to him and so were all the illicit pleasures to be found there. He had months of Gabrielle's enforced cold turkey to wreck!

Devane became intermittently coherent again. "I have sinned against humanity, I have spread my bitch-mother's evil toxin down to another accursed generation. Hain told me I have a daughter…golden eyes - another cursed child."

Jazriel stopped. This pathetic, deranged creature sobbing and grovelling in the mud beneath him was beautiful Gabrielle's father?

"Let me live, vampire. I must make amends, seek redemption. I failed to rid the world of that abomination, my witch mother Khari, I must destroy my cursed, evil-infected daughter. The malignancy I brought into this world."

"Kill your own daughter?" Jazriel was horrified, was there any depth humans wouldn't sink to?

"Yes! Yes! Yes! I must purge the world of this wickedness. One I unwittingly spawned. I will kill her without hesitation! For the good of all humanity, she must die!" Devane looked up at the tall monster before him, extraordinarily handsome despite the drawn fangs. Why did pure evil come in such beautiful forms? His own mother had been lovely too. As, according to Hain, was his daughter.

Calming down. Devane's voice grew quiet and wheedling. "You must help me." Devane pleaded, then perhaps realising the folly of angering a vampire, changed his demeanour again, his eyes grew cunning, his voice changed to a more assertive tone, "For the sake of your own people, you have no choice but to help me. She was born like me, a threat to your kind. Help me protect your brethren. Help me kill the witch."

Appalled, Jazriel stepped away. He had no intention on touching this soiled lunatic again. A danger to Gaby. Her long lost father was a murderous crazy man, one who wanted to kill her. Blinded by human pity and compassion, she would try to help him and Devane would either kill her or break her heart. Perhaps the burden of caring for this hate-filled wretch would crush the feisty spirit that defined her. Jazriel decided this must not happen.

"I will not help you. I am going to kill you."

Jazriel approached closer, dropped into a crouch so he could look the man in the eyes. "But first, I want you to know that Khari Devane was my friend. My princess. I loved her, would do anything to protect her. Now I work with your daughter, Gabrielle. And though she drives me to distraction, I care for her too."

Jazriel was convinced the man was already dead inside from a broken heart and spirit as his words sunk in, that picking up one of the guard's hand guns and calmly shooting him between the eyes was a formality. He loaded all the bodies into the truck and ignited the petrol tank.

As a vampire, he had no concept of Gabrielle's possible feelings for a father she had never met. Would she ever discover Jazriel had killed him? Of course she would, the feisty madam could read his mind! He had risked Gaby hating him forever, perhaps even killing him out of vengeance for the murder of her father. He shrugged, indifferent to the consequences. It was all hyp... hyper... whatever the damn word was... he would never see her again.

He returned to the ancient Honda, catching a glimpse of himself in the wing mirror. At least he looked a little better. The blood feast had invigorated him, his victim's black leather jacket an improvement on that old denim rag Gaby had forced him to wear. He checked his appearance again. OK, he shrugged, only a slight improvement!

He gave the surrounding countryside a weary glance. What a dump! Mile after mile of goat-infested nothing. No sign of a town with a bar open anywhere. Sod alcohol. He would willingly trade his soul for a line of pure coke.

"How about it, one of you demons that humans are always on about! One damaged but stunningly beautiful vampire soul in exchange for a few ounces of white powder...a bargain."

No takers. Even the damned did not want him.

Chapter Twenty-Eight

The road to Gred

Exhausted, Gabrielle drove back to Gred. She'd seen a decentish hotel there where she could clean up, rest. And when was the last time she had eaten? She had time to kill, to gather her thoughts before flying back to her apartment in Rome. She had won a battle but the war was gathering momentum. And this was just a brief skirmish with the irritating distraction that was Nemesis! They were minnows in a world threatened by sharks. Bloody big sharks. Nemesis was wasting precious time and resources. As was the bloody Imadeen! Blasting away at the world with continued malign fervour. Why didn't they all use their intelligence, their determination, their fanaticism to unite against a common foe? The leaders of both organisations had been warned by Reyes what was to come, but the future of all life on this planet meant nothing to them, the Imadeen unprepared to lift a finger to help unless everyone embraced Tahjr. Nemesis could see no future profit in co-operation.

It was shadow play to them, the crazed ranting of alien mystics. Gabrielle negotiated another deep, rainwater-filled rut in the road. Short-sighted idiots! Thankfully, the real war had not started. She held onto the steering wheel with one shaking hand, the other instinctively reaching for the dragon amulet around her neck, it must never start!

Her life had become a confused blur of action, danger and raw emotion. It was too much. Once in Gred, she would book into an anonymous hotel and switch her mobile phone off. It wasn't as if Jaz would try to reach her! She needed to rest, to figure out what exactly had happened during this wild night of storms and bloodshed. Think what to do next. Sivaya had disappeared without a word of thanks or farewell. Just her strange statement about loving Jazriel. Was it to protect Gabrielle from heartbreak or just a warning shot of the vampire's

369

jealousy? Gabrielle had not expected any pleasantries, not from the formidable, human-hating Sivaya.

At least, Gabrielle was certain that Diego would be safely back in the fold of his circus, probably already many miles away. He must have been a remarkable being to have created so much loyalty and loving devotion and sacrifice from his human troupe. Gabrielle wished she had the chance to meet him. Perhaps, one night in the future.

At the top of a hill, she pulled over and made brief contact with Eshan and Reyes, their concern for her touching, genuine. As was their anger over the whereabouts of Jazriel. Gabrielle had been more philosophical. What did they expect? Of course the fanged wreck of a vampire junkie had reverted to type, buggered off at the first opportunity. She had warned them he was not ready, the enforced rehab far from complete. Let his well-being worry someone else, she had done enough! So what that she could touch his damaged soul? She was better off a million miles away from that nightmarish mind.

In an effort to reclaim some normality, she decided to find a hotel with a hot bath, a comfortable bed and sleep for as long as possible. This was the real world again and she liked it. Before continuing down the hill, she reached into her bag for a tissue, felt a leaden weight brush her fingers. Real life! That was a joke! With a loaded gun in her handbag, her eyes trained to discreetly watch every passer by for danger, that was the reality of her life from now on.

Chapter Twenty-Nine

In the distance, Jazriel could hear gunfire, explosions, the sky lit from what appeared to be burning fires. Mierda! He was right, bloody Eshan had deliberately sent him away from the action, expecting him to screw up. That stopping Nemesis's tracker, a threat to all Dark Kind, was vitally important too, did not occur to him. Jazriel was too wrapped up in wounded pride, yet another blow to his fragile self-esteem. No doubt Gabrielle was doing her job brilliantly, he thought bitterly, probably taking on Nemesis single handed. Bloody Action Woman in action.

He walked down to the river bank, seeking fresh clean water to wash off the blood and filth. The deluge had finally stopped, the wind had dropped to let the star-strewn sky appear through the last fleeing clouds but the river bank was sodden and treacherous. One slip and he would be swept away. Would it matter? However his death happened, he would end up the same, as nothing.

He found a shingle inlet, a pool of water, sedate and calm, protected by a semi-circle of rocks and washed the blood from his face and hair, paused, his reflection in the glassy, green, river water showed his beauty had returned but his eyes were dulled, the colour flat and lifeless. He scrambled back up onto the bank, lit a cigarette; thanks to Gaby's strict regime his mind was clear, able to think, to plan. What a curse! He had spent so much time, so much energy, so much money blocking out all thought. He did not welcome this cruel clarity. Sobriety? It stank as high as this debris-clogged river!

The water's swirl caught and held his attention. Its unceasing, hypnotic movement, its raw untamed power. When not swollen with flood water it would be lazily meandering, and ancient. Fed from the melting snow from distant mountains, it was at the half way point to its final destination - the ocean. Jazriel shivered. He had spent centuries shunning all sight of the sea, the loss of joy, of the freedom it represented. This place was a symbolic half way point for him too. Between the two overwhelming loves of his life, Azrar in the snow-bound North, and on the wild oceans…He could almost feel the sad disapproval at what he had become, almost feel the rough, yet so gentle touch of a pirate's callused hands on his face.

"It's all right for you, my friend. You were human. You have an immortal soul and the promise of adventures in worlds beyond this." A keening, fearful sound escaped from his throat. "I know what will happen to me! I've been there!"

Jazriel dropped his head at the hopelessness of his fate. "You see, seymahl, I know what it is like to break apart in silent darkness, to fade away to nothing. I don't give a damn about your disapproval, I need something to block out the hurt, the reality."

Something caught his eye in the water, something glinting brightly, something beautiful. A flash of bright blue. He crouched down and stretched out, further and further but it was out of reach. Probably just some rubbish dumped by damned humans. Careless bastards, polluting his world! Jazriel pulled back, the object forgotten, already swept far downstream.

Zaard! As he moved away his foot slid on the slippery bank and he plummeted into the swirling flood, lost to the fast flowing current. He went down. The starlit darkness replaced by stinking, green water. Carried along, as helpless as the flotsam around him, fellow travellers in the relentless flood. The vampire fought back, after all the danger he had faced head on, this death was ridiculous, drowning like a sewer rat!

He struggled to swim to the bank, his body strong from the recent kill but the water claimed him, wanted him, another thing to add to it's fast-flowing accumulation of jostling debris. The river was too powerful, an overwhelming force of nature far older then he. Exhausted and demoralised, he gave up, let the water carry him onwards, filling his mouth, his lungs. His head went under, his body grew heavier, detaching from his mind.

The river battled against every stroke but he would not give in, would not give it the satisfaction of claiming a vampire life. Even one as flawed as his. Jazriel reached up and caught something, a branch? A strong-gripped hand? And he was on the bank, his body heaving, vomiting up filthy river water and slurry. He rolled onto his back, fangs bared, glaring defiantly at the stars in their silent progress across the universe. "OK, you win. You are so damned determined not to give up on me. But I live on my terms, do you hear? For once in my bloody life, on *my* terms!"

He struggled to get to his feet but exhaustion chained him to the earth. "I will not be dictated to, lectured or patronised. I will drink what I want, smoke and shoot up what I want. I will be in control, not the damned substances."

He hauled himself to his knees, vomited again, disgusted at this so human trait.

"I want to live!" Jazriel howled to the indifferent stars. "Only by living can love still touch me. So, bring it on! Death? I'm not sodding afraid of you. You had your chance tonight, you won't get another!"

He managed to climb to his feet, to stumble through the darkness, retracing his route along the river bank to find the Honda. He had no idea where he would go. What he was going to do. It was hard to admit to himself that this mission with the formidable Gabrielle had given him a taste of the old satisfaction; he did enjoy working with humans, having a purpose. For once it had not ended badly. Freedom, he realised, had many faces, he had no idea which one he would seek next. But it would be *his* choice and his alone.

He was soaked to the skin, and stinking of mud and slime, his whole appearance was humiliating and disgusting - but who was to see him out here in the middle of nowhere? Revving the Honda so the engine whined and protested, he topped the brow of a hill, braked and sat, legs straddled across the brave little bike, gazing over the night-shadowed landscape spread below as wide and as open as the ocean. The lights of Gred illuminated the low clouds to the north; he shook his head, go there? Get a bollocking from that blonde harridan? Forget it! How Gabrielle would laugh at him, mock his wet and squalid appearance! No way was he going back there!

He needed new clothes - a new Ducati, a new life. *His* life, *his* way. He could go anywhere, anywhere he chose. Back to Paris or the

New World... not New York, but America was a big place, so he had heard. Or east, he could go to the Orient where the best narcotics came from. A new place to play, he realized as a slow smile spread over his face. Ah yes, that idea appealed!

He reached into a sodden pocket of his jacket, fumbled in another - Zaard! Where were his cigarettes? His papers? His credit cards? He searched again, more frantic. Nothing. Absolutely bloody, fucking, nothing!

Great.

Epilogue

Refreshed from a long soak in a bath, and a nearly edible hot meal, Gabrielle sat outside her hotel nursing a bottle of vodka. Realised, suddenly, surprised, that she was not alone. Across the street, in the darkness of an unlit shop window she saw the reflection of a battered old motorbike. Hearing the soft creak of leather, she steeled herself for a show down. Sipped her drink. Smelt a tell-tale waft of cinnamon, honey and tobacco, And something else, something rank! Stagnant river water?

"Brilliant job of sneaking up, you prick!" Gabrielle taunted, taking yet another long swig of vodka. It burned the back of her throat but the brutally raw spirit did not numb her rising anger.

Jazriel wandered over, began his apologetic naughty boy smile then, though better of it and sat beside her at the table. She handed him the bottle without turning her head to face him. Reaching into her jacket, pulled out a battered pack of cigarettes and threw them at him. Hard.

"Moron."

"But a devastatingly handsome moron," he added, retrieving the battered packet from the ground and lighting up the least crumpled cigarette. "You have to give me that!"

He paused, savouring his first drag, lazily blew smoke into a perfect ring.

"We going to save the world then?" he asked.

Not ready to turn and face him Gabrielle shrugged. With a scowl, she reclaimed the bottle and finished the last dregs of the vodka, relishing the harsh yet comforting warmth as the liquid slid down her throat. Carefully, precisely, she set the empty bottle back on the table.

"Yeah. Why not."

Author's Notes

Blood Lament is a work of complete fantasy, I have taken outrageous liberties with history and geography to create a world where my Dark Kind can live and thrive. There are no real events or characters. Well, no real human characters!

I am currently working on the next two books in the series; Blood Alliance and a prequel, Blood Legend - and I plan more adventures with Azrar and the other Dark Kind. Jazriel's growing army of fans will be delighted to know that he will remain an unredeemable, unrepentant but beautiful bad boy!

The occasional reference to pirates in Blood Lament is intentional. Acclaimed author Helen Hollick is writing an exciting series of novels chronicling the exploits of Captain Jesamiah Acorne and his pirate ship, the Sea Witch. They are robust, adult adventures with an intriguing supernatural sub plot. I am delighted to be working with her on a planned fourth book in the Sea Witch Chronicles - 'On the Account' - which will feature my beloved, deeply flawed, Jazriel as a lead character co-star, and will narrate the adventures he occasionally recalls here. A pirate and a vampire, both, formidable predators who ask only for their freedom! Publication is planned for 2008, but my website and www.helenhollick.net will carry up to date information. As with my own, Helen's books are available from all good book outlets, including online.

You are invited to visit my website: www.bloodtears.co.uk or e-mail raven.dane@bloodtears.co.uk

All feedback, even negative, is most welcome.

Raven Dane
2007